Two action-packed novels
of the American West!

SIGNET BRAND DOUBLE WESTERN:

TROUBLE
IN
TOMBSTONE

&

BRAND OF
A MAN

SIGNET Brand Westerns You'll Enjoy

Trouble
in
Tombstone

by *Tom J. Hopkins*

&

Brand of a Man

by *Thomas Thompson*

A SIGNET BOOK

NEW AMERICAN LIBRARY

TIMES MIRROR

Trouble in Tombstone

COPYRIGHT, 1951, BY TOM J. HOPKINS
COPYRIGHT © RENEWED 1979, BY TOM J. HOPKINS

Brand of a Man

COPYRIGHT © 1958 BY THOMAS THOMPSON

Published by arrangement with Doubleday and Company, Inc. *Trouble in Tombstone* and *Brand of a Man* also appeared in paperback as separate volumes published by The New American Library.

SIGNET TRADEMARK REG. U.S. PAT. OFF. AND FOREIGN COUNTRIES
REGISTERED TRADEMARK—MARCA REGISTRADA
HECHO EN CHICAGO, U.S.A.

SIGNET, SIGNET CLASSICS, MENTOR, PLUME AND MERIDIAN BOOKS
are published by The New American Library, Inc.,
1633 Broadway, New York, New York 10019

FIRST PRINTING (DOUBLE WESTERN EDITION), JANUARY, 1980

1 2 3 4 5 6 7 8 9

PRINTED IN THE UNITED STATES OF AMERICA

Trouble
in
Tombstone

For present-day Tombstone, with thanks for a friendly visit and apologies for the few liberties I have taken with the time element in your very colorful past.

T.J.H.

1

SAM CHALMERS drove the fast-stepping team of bays with a steady hand on the lines. He sat back easily against the cushions and was well shaded for a time by the top of the buggy. Behind him on the roadless plains of west Texas a rising, widening spread of fine dust went into the sky, to be seen for many miles. If anyone had chanced to be in that wild country to see it. Chalmers was not smiling, but he was comfortably warm inside with the thought of a good job almost completed.

With that thought Chalmers let his right hand feel the flat packet of papers buttoned and pinned inside his vest. He drove the fast team with almost uncanny skill across the open, trackless country and it was strange for a man dressed as he was dressed not only to be in wild and dangerous country, but to handle a pair of horses across broken land as he was doing. He felt again for the packet of papers and shoved his hand after that down into his pants pocket. No more five-dollar gold pieces, he thought automatically. He would get some more when he met the men.

The topped buggy was swinging west now and the sun slanted in under the top and hit Chalmers' eyes. He pulled the narrow-brimmed derby hat forward on his forehead and suddenly his snapping black eyes twinkled with a thought that amused him. He looked down at himself: a well-tailored dark gray suit, white shirt, black tie, polished low shoes, and socks. He chuckled once. The socks and the hard black derby hat did the trick, he thought.

He kept the team stepping fast across the flats and down and up again out of swales. He whistled softly. He would be meeting the boys soon, for now he saw the two dead cottonwood trees and the low ruined walls of an old adobe ranch house. Deserted, ruined. Comanches had done that. Two miles more and he crested a low rise and went on down into a hollow a mile wide. In the center of the wide hollow he saw about forty head of horses and six mules in a rope corral, smoke from a small fire and nine men lounging about it. There were no cattle to be seen, just a roundup wagon and a hoodlum behind it.

Chalmers thought, That will be the boys. He showed no surprise at finding them there three months after he had named

7

the day and the hour. Just two hours before sunset, he had said, October 1, 1879. Why should he be surprised at finding his trail crew? Hell, he'd told them to *be* there.

As Chalmers came up and stopped his snorting team the nine men stood up, some with their hands on their pistol butts, while a few reached alertly for their rifles. He pushed back his derby hat from over his eyes and they recognized him at once. There was an indented line from the hatbrim on his forehead and thin trickles of sweat rolled down past it and over his nose. He wiped it off without speaking and looked at his men.

For a time they studied his clothes in speechless surprise and dismay. Then Jack Baldwin put their emotions into words. "Well I'll be damned. He's even wearing socks!"

At the foreman's words Jeepers Jones rose and glowered. "Take them socks off, Sam. Take them damned dude clothes off, too. Take 'em off or we all quit, here and now. Hear me, Sam Chalmers? You ain't decent that way."

"No, I won't take 'em off." Chalmers spoke for the first time. His voice was even, steady, but slightly high-pitched. "No, not yet. I've got one more man to see before I burn these things. Or maybe I won't burn 'em. I can use 'em when I see Newman." His black eyes twinkled again. "Newman and his notes. One more man to see and then we go on to see Newman!"

The hard-bitten and rough Texas range men shook their heads. They didn't like the notion of being seen with him when he was dressed that way and Chalmers knew it. They were tough, hard men to handle, but he had to hold them in order. He couldn't give them an inch.

"I mean what I say," he snapped at them as he got out of the topped buggy with a quick leap. As the team started nervously when he jumped, Baldwin caught one bridle and held them. "I always mean what I say, you boys know that. Don't be damned fools now." Chalmers turned to the two Negroes, Harley and Brett. "Give me fifty dollars in gold pieces, fives, like I had before."

The Negroes were burly, tall men with wide and heavy shoulders. They never wore hats and their skin was as black as Chalmers' derby. Their eyes, black with strange red glints in them from their trace of Seminole blood, were almost menacing as they looked at Chalmers now.

For a moment it seemed the Negroes were going to say no, deny Chalmers his own gold pieces. Then they turned slowly to the front of the big wagon. Bolted and fastened down with heavy iron bands, under the seat, was a strongbox. As Brett opened it with a big key, Harley stood near him, his big hands touching his pistols. When the Chalmers money was concerned, the Negroes trusted no one, not even Chalmers himself.

Brett counted out ten five-dollar gold pieces and closed and locked the box. He walked to Chalmers and handed him the money, not speaking. His eyes glinted in the low sun and there was much of danger and menace in his big black face. He said evenly, "That does it, boss?"

"That does it," repeated Chalmers. "Fifty dollars will pick up a thousand from a ranchman about twenty miles west of here. Then we go on, to New Mexico, and we meet Bigelow Newman. I wonder how he is going to like us?"

And there was nothing humorous in Sam Chalmers' voice when he asked the question.

They broke camp at dawn and Sam Chalmers gave them curt orders about where to meet him at noon. He stood with one foot on the hub of the left wheel, reins in hand, while two men held the nervous, restive team. He jingled the gold pieces in his pocket and nodded once, then swung into the seat. He set himself, nodded again, and the two men stepped aside. In two quick jumps the team was on the dead run, Chalmers steadying them with his strong hands.

As they watched him go Brindle Nelson asked, "I wonder why he loads himself down with those fives, instead of taking double eagles?"

"That's easy," retorted Wes Adams. "Four fives jingle a hell of a lot louder than one twenty."

And that was why Chalmers did it. For when the rancher he called on about nine-thirty that morning showed some hesitation at his offer of fifty dollars for a thousand-dollar, unsecured note signed by Bigelow Newman, Chalmers jingled the ten fives in his hand. And the rancher fell for it. He took the money, assigned the note to Samuel Chalmers, Jr., and grinned a little.

"I guess you know what you're doing, Chalmers?" he asked. "There's a lot of those notes around and not a man among us has got the nerve to try to make Newman pay up."

"Yes. I'm not going to ask him for any money," he said evenly, and he made no further explanation. He had exactly forty thousand dollars in notes, signed by Bigelow Newman. But he did not mention that either. He climbed into his buggy and gathered the reins tight in his left hand. He nodded, ready to drive on, and then did not.

Three people rode around the corner of the ranch house, a man and two women. And as Sam Chalmers' eyes stared at one of the two women he thought: Hair as pretty and light as a palomino's mane. And the girl under the hair was plump, pretty, and very pleasing to a man's eyes and thoughts.

"Mr. and Mrs. Wiswold, and their daughter Jean," said the rancher. "This is Sam Chalmers."

"How do you do?" said Chalmers. The girl smiled at him and he felt suddenly cold. He said, almost roughly, "I've got to go now. Good-by."

He spun the team and buggy in a wide circle and drove off swiftly. And as he went he looked back once. They were staring after him, he saw, and his face seemed to stiffen suddenly. Probably telling each other what a fool he was to buy up those outlawed notes of Newman's. Half of the west Texas folks knew about it. Newman, cattle drover, had given the notes to cover a big trail herd he had taken to Dodge City. And there he had gambled away the money needed to take up those notes. Not a man among the tricked ranchers dared tackle Newman, thought Chalmers.

Those folks back there, his thoughts rambled on, are saying I'm a fool. That Newman will kill me if I show up and try to force him to pay on these outlawed notes. Well, maybe. Maybe he will. We'll see about that.

Yet there was one thing Sam Chalmers was certain about: he was a fool to drive off, to leave Texas behind him. For he knew he was going to see Jean Wiswold in his dreams for a long time to come. And almost certainly leaving Texas meant he never would see her in anything but his dreams.

He swore once and turned his mind on the business ahead. A hard and tricky gamble that might mean almost any end to come. He went over his plans again, to take his mind off Jean, the girl with the lovely light hair. Over them, slowly, methodically, carefully working out each detail even to how he would dress and act and talk—to Newman. And if talk didn't do it—his eyes raised now and he saw his men waiting for him—well, pistols would.

2

IT WAS almost inevitable that a man of Bigelow Newman's size should be nicknamed either "Big" or "Bull," and Newman, with a broad grin on his face, answered to either name. For he was a big man, physically and mentally, and his voice was deep and powerful. His wavy red hair was long and well trimmed under his white sombrero, and his snapping blue eyes danced with life and zest. And few men other than Newman himself knew what went on in the big man's brain, until he wanted them to know. For he had the masking face of a born actor and could cover any emotions with whatever expression he felt most suitable to the moment.

Now, staring down about seven inches to meet the eyes of the mild-mannered city man with the soft and quiet voice, Newman covered his amusement with what he considered proper dignity to the moment.

"So you want to go into the cattle business?" he said quietly. But even speaking quietly, Newman's voice was a deep rumble that carried to a half-dozen grinning cow hands a dozen yards behind him at the chuck wagon. "It's a tough business. Do you know anything about it?"

Sam Chalmers had stepped down from the buggy and idly wiped his forehead with a white handkerchief, after pushing back his derby hat. His grin was boyish and friendly as he tried to give the impression of being a very modest man. "Well, not a great deal. But I know there is money in it, and I've hired some good men to help me. Will you sell me that herd? I understand you want to sell out and move on. It's a good time to do it, isn't it?"

Newman nodded wisely, his expression giving due worth to his pronouncement. "It's a good time to either buy or sell cattle," he said. "Personally, I'm selling. I've sold my two ranches up north, and this is my last bunch. There are some English buyers in El Paso, and they are paying well for cattle and for good range. I suppose you've heard, Mr., er, what did you say the name was?"

"Chalmers," was the quiet answer.

Grumbling and bellowing cattle were moving past in a long line and the dust clouds sifted back from them. Chalmers looked toward the cattle and smiled. "Nice cattle," he said, and thought he heard a cowboy snort in derision. But his expression did not change.

"Yes, they are nice stuff, Mr. Chalmers." Newman made a faint signal to his men to move away. He watched them mount and ride off, grinning among themselves, and hoped that the young stranger did not notice and take offense. "What I started to say was, I suppose you know the English and Scotch investors are buying up everything that's for sale. It's a fine time for a young and upcoming man to get into ranching. It's becoming big business when even European money comes out West!"

"So I've heard, Mr. Newman," answered Chalmers. "How much do you want for this herd?"

"I wouldn't be selling out if my other interests didn't demand my attention," said Newman somewhat pompously. "I've made some investments around Tombstone, in the mines, and I planned to sell the herd to those men in El Paso before I leave."

"Yes. But you haven't told me how much you want for it?" Chalmers' voice was so soft it was almost pleading.

"It's a mixed herd of fairly good stuff, Mr. Chalmers. It will tally about twenty-five hundred head. And I can get fifteen dollars a head for a herd like this one."

"All right," said Chalmers, "I'll take it. I have forty thousand dollars to invest in the cattle, and if it runs a little over your estimated tally, I can handle it."

"It's a deal," said Newman promptly. He shoved out his big hand to shake hands with the young man and was a little surprised at the hard grip he received. "Now, where are your men?"

"Down the road about four miles," was the answer. Chalmers eyed the last bunch of cattle swinging past with the two dusty riders at the drag. One of them yelled and lashed at a lagging cow with his picket rope end. The cow bawled and jogged on faster and as the dust rose slightly Chalmers could see through it to the distant green line of the Rio Grande. On the far side, he knew, was Fort Selden. Southward lay Dona Ana, Las Cruces, Mesilla, and other little villages until El Paso and the Mexican border were reached. He turned back to Newman and spoke rather helplessly.

"Just what is the procedure now?"

Newman laughed. "Well, we'll swing on ahead of the herd and pick up your men. Then our men, together, will line out the herd and put them between my foreman and me on one side and you and your foreman on the other. We'll tally the herd—that's counting them, you know—and pay up on the basis of an averaged count. Right?"

"Right!" agreed Chalmers briskly. He stepped back and turned to climb into the buggy again. Newman's eyes danced with quick inward amusement. He had a brief instant of wondering if Chalmers could ride a horse and then he decided it was none of his business. He had made a good deal, a very good deal, for his cattle and needed the money. What Chalmers could do, or did, was not his business after he got paid for the herd.

Chalmers spun his team and drove rapidly past the herd, keeping a good quarter mile from them. Newman rode with him, on an easy lope, without trying to talk. When they were well past the herd with the two point men lounging easily in their saddles, Chalmers began to swing in front of the herd and cut over toward the river bottom. Newman thought, He can handle this team, all right, and rode with him.

Twenty minutes later they passed Chalmers' men at their camp in a willow thicket on a small feeder of the Rio Grande. Chalmers signaled briskly and waved. Then he drove on to the crest of a low roll of land and stopped there. He looked back and saw his men were already mounted and coming toward him, all riding slowly, and he nodded to himself. It would not be long now, he thought, but his expression did not change. He glanced toward Newman and smiled.

"So you're going to Tombstone?" he said. "Isn't that a new mining discovery someplace in Nevada?"

Newman laughed. "No, in southern Arizona, right in the heart of the Apache country. That's how it got its name; they told Ed Schieffelin that he wouldn't find a mine, but only his tombstone. But he fooled them. The Apaches killed a lot of prospectors and cattlemen, but not Ed Schieffelin. He's going to be a millionaire from his mines. It's going to be a great camp with a great future, and I'm buying into it. That's the only reason you're getting those cattle, Mr. Chalmers."

Chalmers shivered. "Heavens, Mr. Newman, it must be awfully dangerous going way out there into the Apache country!"

Newman laughed. "It is," he said. "But here come your men and there come the cows." He shifted and glanced around quickly. "I guess this is as good a place as any to put them through for a tally. Put your foreman here with you, line the other men out slanting away from you. I'll tally on the far side with my foreman."

Newman waved his big hand, spun his horse, and galloped off. Chalmers watched him go, and a slow smile came over his face. He turned his team and waited for the men to come up. And as they gathered around him he snapped out, "Wipe those damned grins off your faces. Baldwin, you and Harley tally. Brett, you keep near. The rest of you line out and be ready to

13

take over the herd. And ready for anything else that turns up. Hear me?"

"We ain't deaf," said Galloway rubbing his long upper lip which seemed to have crowded his pug nose up between his cold blue eyes. He was as Irish as the country his name came from, but there was no trace of brogue in his voice. "When does the shooting start, boss?"

"When they start it and not before, get that?"

"He'll start it, all right," said Curly Horton. "Any man that could put over what Newman put over on those Texas ranchers ain't going to let you get away with it, not without a little jag of shooting as dessert."

"All right, then we shoot," retorted Chalmers. "But not until they start it."

Joe Webster grumbled, "Hell, we gotta wait until they draw and shoot?"

"No. But let them make the first move."

Chalmers clucked to his team and sent them into a swift trot. He wheeled them in a wide sweep and ended up at the camp in the willow thicket. As he stepped down near the chuck wagon and the hoodlum, a grinning Mexican boy came out of the willows to take the team. He was almost the same size and height as Chalmers, though darker of skin.

"Okay, boss, okay?" said Chico Gonzalez, still grinning. But he pronounced the word as though it started with an *h*: hokay.

He held the team and watched Chalmers skinning out of his city clothes with a speed that showed a great desire to get rid of them.

"Okay and *bueno!*" answered Chalmers, grinning. "Tie the team to the hoodlum for a minute while you get into these clothes, Chico. Fast, now, *pronto!*"

Chalmers dropped his clothes on the ground and, clad only in his underwear and socks, jumped for the back of the hoodlum wagon. He pulled an old and battered carpet bag from it and jerked it open. With one move he had dumped its contents on the ground and was grabbing for an old hickory shirt. Two minutes later he was dressed, booted, spurred, and had his head well tucked into a battered sombrero of straw. Around his waist he had belted two guns in low-hanging, well-oiled holsters that dropped from a single wide belt. And the belt had a double row of cartridges on.

There was a hard expression on Chalmers' face now as he looked at Chico Gonzalez. "You know what to do?"

"*Sí, sí.*" Chico was almost skinning himself as he shed his

14

old clothes and grabbed for Chalmers' handsome suit. He laughed, chuckled, laughed again. *"Dios,* boss—can I wear these after the fun is over? Can I show those pretty ones, the cold ones, in Las Cruces, what I look like when I am dressed?"

"You can have the damned things for good," almost snorted Chalmers. "Where in hell is my horse?"

"In the willows, waiting." Chico was beaming and turning as he dressed. He squatted and pulled on the low shoes. "I saddled that new roan for you. He is the best of them all, I think."

Chalmers agreed when he looked at the roan. A big rangy horse, with powerful shoulders and a broad chest. He swung into his old and worn saddle and eased himself, grinning. It was good to ride again after the five weeks of pretending to be a city man. He looked back at the rope corral where about seventy horses were held now, with the six mules. They had added to their string at a horse ranch a week back, and picked up Chico as a wrangler. He had a feeling the young Mexican would do to ride the river with, and he wondered if he would be willing to leave Texas and New Mexico for a new and more dangerous range. He hoped so, for the wrangler knew horses, Chalmers thought as he galloped up toward the herd now passing the two groups of tally men.

The cattle were a mixed lot, all right, but worth what he was paying for them. Chalmers laughed shortly. He'd add some good bulls and come out all right. And he was coming out of the deal with capital enough to spread when the time came. There was no thought in his mind of failure now. Nor had there been at any time since he had started to put through this deal against Newman. He would put the deal through and Newman had it coming to him for his trickery.

Chalmers stopped now about midway in the line of his men. And there, rolling a smoke, he waited. It was getting hot but a wind was blowing the dust now, kicked up by the hoofs of the bawling, fretful cattle. Beyond, there was a meadow in a big bend of the Rio Grande and Chalmers thought, The herd will be in that meadow, no matter what happens around here.

He had smoked four cigarettes before the last of the drag had passed him. And the two riders rode slowly along, their bandannas pulled up over their noses. The wind was quickening and shoved the dust away fast now. Chalmers raised his right hand as the last man passed him and went on toward the tally point. He waited for Jeepers Jones and Brindle Nelson to join him, and none of them spoke. They rode with him until

15

Galloway was picked up. Then Horton, Adams, and Webster. And still none of them spoke.

The herd moved on and the last cow, the drag riders behind it, went past the tally men. The dust was shifting and blowing now and the air cleared rapidly.

"I thought so," said Chalmers, pointing, and he nodded. "I wonder if he's tumbled, or been warned about me?"

Newman had eleven men in his outfit, and now they all gathered near him. Not a man had followed the last of the herd as it drifted on, picking up a little speed now, toward the green meadow and the smell of water. Chalmers rode on toward his tally men, Baldwin and Harley, the big Negro, and he kept his head down so his face was shaded. A hundred yards away was the buggy and what appeared to be Chalmers sitting in it dressed in his city clothes with his derby hat on. And Brett hovered like a hawk nearby.

"What do you make it?" called Newman as he rode, alone, across the two hundred feet of hoof-cut ground toward Baldwin and Harley.

"Twenty-six hundred and thirty, even."

"I make twenty-six thirty-three," said Newman, "but I guess we won't fight about three head." He laughed. But he looked big and tough in his saddle as he straightened a little. "Now." His voice was a little hard as it boomed out. "You Chalmers riders go on with the herd. It's yours from here on. I'll ride over and get the money from your boss."

"You ain't giving us any orders, mister," said Baldwin flatly. "And don't bother to ride over to that buggy. That's our wrangler in it. Here's the man you talk to!"

Newman's mouth opened and shut, once. He stared briefly at the buggy, at Baldwin, and then his eyes shifted. They fell on and stayed on a hard-eyed, nerveless man whose expression told him nothing. A man who resembled the fellow in the city clothes in face only, and scarcely there. Newman's eyes ran up and down Sam Chalmers in his rough range clothes and double-holstered guns. He looked at the riders, not bunched as his men were, but spread out. Then his bull voice rose angrily.

"There's a trick here! What the hell does it mean?" And Newman let his hand drop to his gun. "Pay up, man, or you won't get a bill of sale to those cattle!"

"Don't get excited, Mr. Newman," said Chalmers in his low, even voice. "I'm going to pay you for the herd. I said I would, didn't I?"

Chalmers rode up within four feet of Newman and there he stopped. His black eyes never winked as he reached into his shirt pocket for a flat packet. With his left hand he reached across toward Newman, holding that thick flat packet toward the other man. Newman reached out for the packet and as he thumbed through the dozen or more notes his face grew darker and darker as the hot blood boiled into it. His hands shook a little and then the notes crumpled in his tight grip.

"Those are your notes, Newman," said Chalmers quietly. "Just forty thousand dollars' worth of them. They more than cover the cost of the herd, but I won't bother you for change. Just endorse over to me the bill of sale that John Chisum gave you when you bought the cattle two years ago. That's all I need to prove ownership. Just add, for value received. For it is good value, isn't it? They're your notes, Mr. Newman. You said you would take them up someday. Well, this is the day!"

The last four words come out, not softly and quietly, but with the stinging lash of a bull whip hitting bare flesh.

3

NEWMAN did not speak. His eyes were half closed and his angry expression seemed to fade into a cold look of hate he plainly thought would be intimidating. Still wordless, he handed the packet of his notes back to Chalmers and then, slowly, backed his horse away. When ten feet from Chalmers and without taking his eyes from the younger man's face, he stopped the horse.

Then Newman spoke and his voice was a rumbling growl that carried to both his men and the Chalmers riders. "You poor damned fool." He held his reins in his left hand and he slowly, unhurriedly, let his right hand move down until he touched, gripped, the butt of a pistol holstered to the right side of his saddle horn. Then his voice rumbled again. "You've got two choices, Chalmers. You can take your men and ride away without those cattle, or you can fight and die right here. Take your choice, damn you. And I hope you ride away. I'd hate to have to kill you. You look like a kid running a whizzer on somebody. You thought you could outsmart me, Bigelow Newman—you fool. Ride, before I draw and kill you."

Chalmers kept his snapping black eyes locked on Newman

17

and his voice rose a little so it would carry to the Newman riders. He spoke evenly and without tension, and his hands did not touch his twin guns.

"Wait a minute, Mr. Newman. And you men over there, don't crowd this fighting. It's dangerous. Men get killed doing that. Mr. Newman, those are your notes and you said you would take them up. The men you gave them to took them in good faith and believed you. You killed the first man who tried to collect one of those notes for the trail-herd money you gambled away. Nobody else dared to even ask for their money after that. You had them bluffed. Well, I don't bluff. My daddy taught me that. He taught me something else, too."

His pause, without any effort to be dramatic, was just that. It left his hearers almost breathless. Then Chalmers went on. "He was a wise and experienced gun fighter. A peace officer. A fine man. He said never to touch your gun unless you were going to draw it. Never to draw it unless you were going to shoot. And never to shoot except to kill. It's good advice, Mr. Newman. And, damn you, take your hand off your gun before I kill you!"

Newman's hand jerked away from the gun almost before he thought. He swore angrily, clenching his fists. "You can't bluff me!"

"I'm not bluffing." Chalmers rode toward Newman and held out the notes to him. "Take up your notes, man, make yourself decent again. Don't have it known that you wouldn't do it. Take up your notes and, as far as I'm concerned, this deal is ended."

So they sat their horses for a long moment. No one spoke, not even a whisper among the riders scattered out and ready. A horse shifted position and a low, almost frightened voice steadied him. The Chalmers riders were calm, steady; but the Newman men stirred a little and glanced about them. One man wet his lips.

For the Newman riders were puzzled. And being puzzled, they were either curious or uncertain and disturbed. And several were downright frightened. For Bull Newman was being held motionless by the steady stare of two snapping black eyes. And Bull Newman was their fighting boss, a man they had believed could whip anyone.

The thing held. Chalmers' left hand was reaching out with the packet of notes in it. Newman kept his hands clenched, his lips locked with the upper one half over the lower. He was thinking it out and it took many angles and turns. They were

18

his notes and he owed the money. He knew he had never seen this young man before and he wondered how he had got himself into the thing. And with that wonder came the quick desire to stall it for a moment. He swallowed, for he found it difficult to speak.

"How did you happen to cut yourself into this, Chalmers?"

"I didn't have enough money to buy a herd," answered Chalmers. "I went around and bought up your notes with what I had. I gambled you would take them up, Mr. Newman, and I know you will. Here."

Chalmers moved the notes an inch forward and Newman took them. Chalmers settled back in his saddle and said, "I think you're smart, Mr. Newman. Now give me the bill of sale."

Almost automatically Newman shoved the notes into his pocket and pulled out a soiled bill of sale he had been given two years before, from John Chisum. He wrote slowly, signed his name, handed the paper over to Chalmers, and sat there, his expression brooding and showing his bewilderment. He looked at Chalmers as the latter opened the bill of sale and glanced at it, and Newman wondered how it had happened. He wanted to curse the younger man, to draw and kill him. But he knew he dared not. And suddenly he knew what to do.

"Hell, Chalmers, I was trying to feel you out." He laughed. "No hard feeling. I was selling my herds to pay off those notes, really. The men who sold them to you cheap are the fools, not me. They lost by it. Me, I'm squared with the world now. I don't owe any man anything!"

"Good," answered Chalmers. "Now, if you and your men will just ride back north, and keep going, I'll take my men down to pick up our herd." His lips moved faintly in what might have been called a smile. "Good-by, Mr. Newman."

Sam Chalmers sat his horse and waited. Newman stared at him a moment, then his lips parted and he spoke very softly so no one else could hear: "Don't think this is ended." Then Newman turned and rode away.

They watched him pick up his men, say something to them, and then watched still as Newman and his riders headed north. Chalmers sat and smoked, his face quiet and almost without expression. No one would have thought that he had gambled almost all of his capital, trusting to his cold nerve to bluff a man as well known as Bull Newman. He had a thousand dollars left in the strongbox. It had to take him a long ways. When he got there he would be able to write a certain banker in El

Paso and say that he had done it. And the banker had promised to back him with money as needed to expand his holdings in the new land.

Chalmers laughed suddenly, sharply. He saw the Newman crowd go over a low hill more than a mile away. He turned to his men and said, "Newman told me he was selling out to go to Tombstone. Tombstone." He chuckled dryly. "That's funny, isn't it? Funny as hell. Tombstone. I wonder what Bull Newman will say, or *try to do*, when he finds I'm there?"

They rode down in silence and circled the herd once. Brett, Harley, and Chico went back for the horses and the wagons. Chalmers stepped down and stood beside his horse after circling the herd. His expression was soft, half smiling. A fair to middling bunch of cattle. Mixed, from yearlings to old mossyhorns and plenty of bulls. Not good bulls, mostly, but the money from the banker would take care of that. Cattlemen already were talking about breeding up the scrubby range stuff. There was some talk about various breeds from the old country. Durhams were too big and heavy for the rough country. But Devon and Hereford bulls bred to range stuff, or to Durham cows, would bring up the grade to a good level.

"Jeepers," he said shortly. "You and Brindle take the herd. Let 'em feed up the rest of the day. We're moving on tomorrow, and the way is west to the San Pedro Valley." He smiled as he watched Jeepers and Brindle ride out to a slow circling of the herd. And slowly, the smile faded.

Chalmers smiled when the names and places he had seen the year before passed through his mind: soon the Rio Mimbres would be crossed, then Silver City, then on to either Bear Creek or the Gila. Then swing across through the Peloncillo Mountains, San Simon, Apache Pass. Fort Bowie and probably he'd talk to the commanding officer at that post and see about beef contracts for the men and the Indians on the new reservations. He'd lead the drive into Sulphur Springs Valley and maybe winter there before going on to the San Pedro and the spot he had picked out there.

Then he shook his head. No, somebody might get there first! The smile faded and a strange, haunting sense of hurry came to him as he saw in his mind that great stretch of the San Pedro Valley, lush with grass that rose belly-deep on the horse he had ridden through it. Miles and miles and miles of it! The Huachucas on one side, the Mule and the Dragoon mountains scattered along the other, the Whetstones to the north and still the wide sweep of the San Pedro going on and on!

20

Cattle country. Hell, he couldn't let anybody get there first! It was his. He stiffened, almost ready to shout orders to send the cattle on. But he calmed himself. He would be the first real cattleman in there. He would make it his. They couldn't get there first or stop him if they did. He had no one in mind, just "they"; anybody. No, they could not break his dreams and visions. He knew just what he was going to do.

He was going to run a bunch of twenty-six hundred head of cattle and a thousand dollars into an empire!

4

AND day by day through the next two months the places that had been only names to the Chalmers riders were picked up in the dust of the herd. Picked up, real and vivid and sometimes shot with danger and hints of death. And then passed as the grumbling, bellowing, and fretful cattle drove on from valley to valley, through pass after pass, to camp near stream, river, or water hole. On as time was measured by the dull pound of split hoofs, the clink and rattle of horses. Threats of Indians. Storms that sent the cattle bellowing and spreading and meant a day of hard riding to gather them again. But on, toward the wide lush valley of the San Pedro River. Day after day of hard work and danger.

And it was at Fort Bowie that Chalmers, after talking with Major McGonagle, who was in command, learned the news that he dreaded yet somehow had realized was coming to him. There was a herd ahead of him. His face tightened a little and he spoke crisply. "I'll bid lower than any man dare bid, Major, to get beef contracts."

The major nodded with a grin twisting his lips under the thick black mustache. "It's open bidding," he said. And then he waited for Chalmers to question him about the herd ahead of him. But no questions came.

They moved on at dawn the next morning as the faint thin sounds of reveille spread through the adobe-walled post and the two troops of cavalry came to life. The herd bellowed and showed fight, fussed and then slowly lined out for the day's drive. Chalmers rode well in front, his rifle slanted across his thighs and his big straw sombrero slanted back from his head. Baldwin was behind him and to either side rode Galloway and

21

Horton. And farther back along the sides of the long line of protesting cattle rode Jones and Brindle Nelson. Back of them, taking the drag, rode Wes Adams and Joe Webster. Harley drove the team of mules that dragged the heavy chuck wagon, with the strongbox bolted in under the seat. The hooligan creaked and banged and rattled, and back of it rode Brett, hatless as always, rifle ready, sideways in the saddle. Brett's strange red-shot eyes were never still, never fixed, always roaming and shifting and scanning. Chico drove the horse herd behind Brett.

They passed Helen's Dome and saw the great outline of the mountain that was to be called Cochise Head. Far to the west in the thin haze of early morning lay the Three Sisters Butte and not far from it the sulphur springs that gave the great valley its name. And distantly they saw the rugged outlines of the Dragoons, where the dreaded Apache Cochise had his stronghold and hiding place. And as Chalmers rode on a slanting line south and somewhat west, wild and ugly stories kept coming into the minds of the riders. Cochise was not fighting now, but Geronimo was, and the much less known Victorio; less known and infinitely more dangerous and the real leader of the Apaches. Stories they didn't like.

They camped that night with a sense of danger brooding over them and did not know why. And before dawn they were on the move again. South and west lay the Mule Mountains and the low, rolling ridges that separated them from the Dragoons. Miner's Pass was in there, near the Dragoons, but Chalmers was heading south of that for a long canyon that went between rolling ridges and would, if followed, take him and his men and the cattle out into the great sweep of the San Pedro Valley. And then toward noon Chalmers saw something ahead of him.

There was no dust. It was just a blur of something. He signaled without turning his head and then he rode on at a gallop. He went down into a low swale and when he came out at the crest of it he had his rifle almost at his shoulder. He lowered it. The range was too long. He saw cattle, horses, and as he pulled his own horse to a stop he listened. And like breaking small sticks, he heard the sound of rifle fire.

Now he looked back and waited for a time until the first of his cattle and his men came over the hill a half mile away. He signaled with great sweeps of his arm and saw the two point men swing toward each other and then deftly, easily, turn the herd and start the cattle milling.

22

For weeks past those men had had orders for a moment like this, and now they moved rapidly. Some of the men stayed with the herd and the others came toward Chalmers on the run. As they swept up to him and stopped, he pointed.

"That cattle outfit that got ahead of us—in trouble. Come on."

He spurred his horse and the others rode with him. No one even thought it might be strange to be riding to help an outfit that had moved in ahead of them and might even be ready to fight for the very range they wanted. They were cattlemen, weren't they? And in trouble. Men may fight each other, but not when a common enemy threatens them.

The group raced on through the scattering clumps of greasewood and sage. Chalmers centered them, with his wide straw sombrero pulled low over his black eyes, his face set and hard. Adams, Webster, Galloway, and Horton rode on either side of him, the first two on his left, the others to the right. Galloway shot a quick glance from his blue eyes to Chalmers' face and a crooked grin pulled his long upper lip to one side. He looked across at Horton, jerked his head slightly, and nodded.

Horton knew what he meant and he grinned acknowledgment: a fighting man, that boss of theirs. They had seen it before, heard stories of him before they had signed on. Otherwise they probably would not have followed him into what was then the most dangerous county in the entire West. Horton touched his pistol, his cartridge belt, and then levered a cartridge into the barrel of his rifle. He was ready.

They swept on rapidly and as they rose out of a hollow they could see five riders swinging into a compact group and riding away. Riding fast, too. What they left behind was a small cattle outfit of perhaps four or five hundred head. The stock was scattered and drifting, the saddle horses had bolted and now were a quarter mile away, feeding, and the wagon, which seemed to be a cross between a covered wagon with family goods in it and a roundup mess wagon, was half tilted over. Two of the four-horse team were down, and the front near wheel was in a gopher hole.

"Damn them, they won't stay and fight!" Chalmers spoke angrily as he urged his horse on. "Damned cowards. Look, one man down and just those two that look like boys to fight. And when they see us, the buzzards run!"

He raced up to the wagon and threw his right hand up in a quick gesture, like a cavalryman halting his command. He

23

called sharply, "Boys!" And then he stopped short, his mouth partly open.

They were not boys. They were women, rather plumply built women, in men's work clothes and with big felt sombreros pulled low over their eyes. One was young, the other old enough to be her mother. And the young one had a plump little figure, was pretty, and the hair that looped out from under her old hat was the color of a finely bred palomino's mane.

"Those men!" The older woman's voice now broke shrilly as she went on, "Murderers, thieves! They've shot my husband. Oh, we were warned what this country was like: no one safe from robbers and murderers!"

Chalmers watched her as she wheeled and ran to the fallen man. The man was rolling over and moaning. He had been shot in the shoulder on the right side and it looked high enough to be fairly safe and an easily healed wound. Chalmers looked at him briefly and his mind clicked a thought: They don't recognize me in these clothes.

He looked at Jean Wiswold, the girl he had met back in Texas when he had bought the last lot of Newman's notes, and he gave no hint of his thoughts as he spoke crisply and gave curt orders to his men. No hint that he had dreamed of a situation something like this, riding in to save her and her family, and laughed at himself when he had dreamed. Hell, not even a chance to fight for her. The thing was over before he got there!

"That won't be a bad wound to work on," said Chalmers. "But we've got to teach those rustlers a lesson. Got to make them understand that cattle are coming into this country and coming to stay." He swung his left hand in a quick gesture. "There's a hide-out for outlaws up in those mountains. I heard about it last year when I was out. They raid stages, ore trains from Mexico—anything that offers a chance to rob and kill. Well, a lesson is coming to them."

He looked at Horton and said, "Go back to the herd and tell Baldwin and Brett to ride with you. Slant toward that big rock at the base of the mountains. We'll ride to it from here, following those fellows. And we'll run them right up into the hide-out. Maybe . . ." He pulled his straw sombrero down a little and shielded his eyes briefly. He looked up from under the brim and his eyes were snapping with life. "Maybe they'll really fight up there!"

Horton nodded, spun his horse, and raced off toward the

24

herd. Chalmers thought quickly and gathered his reins in his hand. "Ma'am," he said to Mrs. Wiswold, "we're riding now, but don't worry. My men at my herd will watch you and see nobody attacks while we're gone. Have your daughter build a fire but don't light it. Get a lot of greasewood piled by the fire. It makes a heavy black smoke when it burns. If you need help, touch off that fire and stack the greasewood on it. Good-by."

Without looking at Jean, who was studying his face curiously, intently, Chalmers nodded to his men. He clipped his heels in and his horse broke into a jerky trot that in five steps turned into a slow gallop. No hurry now, a long way to go. He studied the rising mountains. Maybe fifteen miles across the flatland and into the canyon, as he remembered the stories he had heard. Galeyville, he thought they called the place, and you could find anywhere from six men to sixty-five or seventy, they had told him. Hard men. Killers who thought nothing of murder. Drunken fools who sat around between crimes and bragged of what they had done to get the money they threw out on bars and whisky-sodden table tops.

"Teach 'em a lesson," Chalmers clipped his words short. He did not care whether his men heard him or not. "Teach them to let cattle and cattle outfits alone. Shoot 'em or hang 'em. But teach 'em a lesson. The Bloody County, they called this place. It needs draining and drying of that blood. Teach 'em a lesson if we have to make the damned county a lot bloodier in doing it."

And they rode on, across greasewood and sage flats, around mesquite thickets, and in and out of swales and gullies. In an hour they had covered six miles and picked up Baldwin and Brett. Chalmers nodded and rode on without speaking. Why talk? They knew what they were there for, didn't they?

They walked the horses, trotted, galloped, and all the time they watched cold-eyed for trouble. They were in the foothills and could be ambushed from any ridge now. A thin stream edged out of a small feeder canyon and died in the sand near a scrubby canyon oak. Above it they could see wild walnut trees, a couple of cottonwoods, and some heavy-trunked mesquite. Also some rocks.

"Scatter!" said Chalmers, and he edged around in the saddle to throw a bullet up at the rocks. "I had a hunch," he added to no one in particular, a moment later.

For a man yelled, two rifles cracked and boomed out in echoes among the rocks. Two more and then another chimed in. As Chalmers explained it later, he had figured the five men

25

who had raided the Wiswold herd were dry, and their horses equally so. And that bunch of rocks and trees up the side canyon was the first hint of a watering place. Also, knowing outlaws and fighting tactics, it was a good place to lay an ambush and catch them between fires if the bunch above at the outlaw hide-out jumped them. And his hunch had been a good one.

Chalmers emptied his rifle steadily at the rocks and then raced off toward some clumped mesquite. He was reloading as he rode. He had pushed the wide-brimmed straw sombrero back on his forehead so that it half dangled by the chin strap. Now he turned his horse and fired steadily again, feeling out the cracks and edges of the big rocks where smoke puffs showed men were lying and shooting.

His men had scattered and were firing steadily. The rattle and crash of shots echoed in the rocks and from the walls of the two canyons. Someone cursed them heartily in a short break in the firing, shouting down from the rocks above. Brett, the big Negro, rode back and forth like an Indian begging for a fight. He was hatless as always and his heavy-lidded eyes sought targets. It was he who laid a fine shot down at the cursing man, and they all saw the lunging body come out between two rocks. Brett kept riding, daring them to show themselves and shoot at him.

Adams was off his horse and behind a rock, lying down. Horton rode past him now, shouting at him mockingly, and found his own shelter among some scrub brush. Galloway and Webster were thirty yards above Chalmers, working on and shooting as they went. Brett and Baldwin were near the center, almost in line with the men in the rocks, and drew the heaviest fire.

Chalmers thought fast. If he ordered those two out of their dangerous spot they would pretend not to hear him and keep right on fighting there. He grinned briefly and then shouted and waved as he would to a well-trained dog. "Baldwin! Brett! Go 'way round 'em, boys!" And as they looked, he signaled again, waving his hand toward the crest of the ridge on the low side of the feeder canyon.

As they broke their horses into a gallop down the canyon bullets whistled sharply about them and splashed from rocks. The firing quickened as they rode, for the outlaws knew what was coming. But their shooting failed to block them or turn them, and in a moment Baldwin and Brett had disappeared.

But Chalmers knew where they were and what they were doing. On the far side of the ridge. Riding up it, keeping hid-

26

den, ready to pop up and outflank the outlaws in the rocks. The outlaws knew it too. There was a sudden flurry of shooting and then that died. A moment later four mounted men raced out from behind the clustered rocks, riding low in the saddle and racing for the crest of the ridge they were on.

Chalmers and his riders opened up in a blistering hail of lead, throwing it steadily, wickedly, after the fleeing riders. The range was long and uphill, and only chance would help them. Two men went over the ridge. A third, close behind them, disappeared. The fourth man, his horse lunging up the slope, suddenly reeled in the saddle. He lurched sideways. He caught himself, steadied—and then reeled backward out of the saddle. As he hit the ground his horse disappeared over the ridge.

Baldwin and Brett showed suddenly on their ridge and waved their hats. They raced on to the crest, horses lunging and crashing along. There Chalmers saw them halt briefly. They raised their rifles and fired a half-dozen shots, then stopped. And they made no effort to ride on.

Chalmers raised his voice in a high, carrying shout. "What's up?"

The answer drifted back almost casually from Baldwin. "They separated and are breaking out across a big flat. They're heading out into the valley again, along the foothills."

Thoughts came rapidly to Chalmers; the remnants of the five were getting away, separately, and not heading for the hide-out in the hills. All right, they could play it that way. He grinned coldly as a thought came.

"Bring those two down with you," he called to Baldwin and Brett. "I want to send a message by them!"

His other riders were coming in now, and he swept them briefly with his glance. "Tie that up for Webster," he said to Horton. "Does it hurt much, Joe?"

"No, just through the meaty part of my arm." Webster snorted. "And not much meat there for it to get."

He rolled up the sleeve of his woolen shirt and Horton looked at the blue-rimmed hole and the thin red line draining down through the hair of Webster's arm. "Hell, blood's red, ain't it?" And then he made a pad from his handkerchief, took Webster's bandanna, and tied the pad on with it. He nodded cheerfully at Webster and said, "Well, that means you'll get prunes for dessert tonight, Joe, instead of just prunes."

They sat around and smoked now, eyes wary and often trained up the canyon. But no sign of trouble came from there. Baldwin and Brett were working their way down the slope into the canyon, bringing the two dead outlaws with them. Soon they were within a hundred feet and Brett called out, "These buzzards are dead, boss. You can't send a message by a dead man."

"Maybe you'd like to take it up to them?" asked Chalmers. "Right on up the canyon. I'd like to go, but I don't think we got time. A message will do and those two dead men can carry it for us."

He was writing now on the top page of his notebook with a stubby pencil. He finished the message and looked briefly at the two dead outlaws. He shook his head. "If that's a sample, it's no wonder this is called the Bloody County." For they were, in death, hard and mean-looking fellows beyond question.

"We'll leave them here with this note pinned on one of them. Their friends will find them and, I hope, take warning. I wrote on it just that: 'Take Warning! Let the cattle and the cattle outfits alone!' And I signed my name and my Boxed S.C. brand to it."

He pinned the note to one of the men, then all mounted and rode off down the canyon toward the flatland.

In the flatland Chalmers went on with Joe Webster toward the Wiswold outfit and sent the others north and west toward his own herd. He told them to bring the herd on into the bottoms, about two miles from the Wiswold herd, and hold it there until he came to them. Then he rode on silent for a time. When he spoke it was to ask, "How you feeling, Joe?"

"All right," was the gruff answer. The arm was beginning to ache, but Webster would not admit it.

"I figured this was the shortest ride for you, fellow," said Chalmers. "I don't think Wiswold will be able to move on for a few days. I figure we'd best camp near them, and see nobody starts anything with them again."

Webster looked at him curiously. "Wiswold? I didn't hear them name themselves."

"Met them back in Texas when I bought up the last notes. Just met them. They don't remember me, so don't say anything about it, Joe."

Webster opened his mouth to ask why, but thought better of it. Anyhow, a few days of rest wouldn't hurt his arm any, and he was glad to hear of the plan.

They found Wiswold was resting easily, sleeping, when they reached the wagon. Mrs. Wiswold and Jean had brief but plainly sincere thanks for their efforts and said them quickly.

Jean smiled at Chalmers and his heart jumped as though someone had hit him. He stared at her, smiled back, and fought for control. No wonder he had dreamed about her and cursed himself for a fool for leaving her behind him in Texas!

He covered his leaping emotions with calm words. "Your husband shouldn't travel for a while at least," he said to Mrs. Wiswold. "And we're not in a hurry. We'll make our camp about a hundred yards away, hold both herds separately in the bottoms, and wait till your husband can travel in the wagon. Right?"

They both thanked him heartily and assured him they would feel much safer that way. Joe Webster was lying down, flat on his back beside his horse. And Jean saw his bandaged arm. She knelt beside him and inspected the bandage. "I can do better than that for you," she said gently. "We'll change that tonight." She smiled at him and the very sight of it brought a wave of jealousy over Chalmers. He knew he was a fool and he fought the feeling. But it still made him jealous and angry to see Webster get the attentions of Jean Wiswold.

They loafed about for three days, growing more and more friendly, all of them. Wiswold said a couple of days more would see him fit to move on in the wagon. It was nearing sundown and they were building fires for supper. The Wiswolds were eating Brett's cooking now, it being simpler that way. Or so Chalmers had said. He listened, his head on one side.

Wiswold stared at him and started to speak, but Chalmers signaled him to silence with a curt, chopping wave of his hand. He listened, then rose almost stiffly.

"Horses coming on the run."

They circled out a little from the women, Wiswold, and the wagons, and waited. Jones and Galloway came in on the gallop and slid their horses to a stop. They had been riding herd on the two bunches of cattle down in the bottoms, with orders as always to be alert. Now Jones spoke briefly.

"About twenty men, riding toward us. They came from the direction of Tombstone and Miner's Pass. We didn't wait to see who they were," he grinned briefly. "I figured we'd learn soon enough."

Chalmers made quick motions with his hands, sending them all out and around the wagons. "Get your rifles from the wagons and your saddles," he commanded. "And be ready for trouble."

In five minutes the twenty men rode into sight and kept right on coming. They closed in to about four hundred yards, a compact, rough-looking bunch of well-armed men. And then Chalmers stepped out, waved his hat, and yelled to them.

"Don't come any closer! What do you want?"

5

THE group of oncoming men pulled up sharply at the yell and one of them turned to speak to the others. There was a quick shifting of those men after he spoke and they opened out into a less compact mass. Then the man who had spoken to the others turned to face Chalmers. He studied him and his men and their positions for a brief time. Then his voice rose.

"My men will stay here," he called. "I'm riding in to talk to you."

And the crispness of his words was an implied threat.

Chalmers watched the man ride in slowly with neither hurry nor hesitation in his manner. He saw a burly, heavy-set fellow with a round and swarthy face. Curly black hair showed under his pushed-back sombrero and his blue flannel shirt, despite the cold December wind, was open at his hairy throat and chest. An alert man, heavily armed with two pistols, a knife, and a rifle in a saddle boot. But he grinned now and dimples showed in his face.

"I'm Bill Brocius," said the newcomer, grinning until dimples showed in his round cheeks. "They call me Curly Bill." And he laughed outright as though expecting a startled reaction. He then pulled up his horse in front of Chalmers and waited.

Chalmers stared at him coldly. "Brocius, now? Well, I heard of you in Texas and they called you Bill Graham then."

Curly Bill blinked, a little taken aback, but he laughed again. "Texas man, eh? Well, I might've figured that from your hat, fella. What's the name?"

"Chalmers. Sam Chalmers. These are my men," and he named them rapidly. "And those folks there are the Wiswolds. They were jumped a few days back by some raiders. We shot 'em off. We killed two men in that canyon up there and I left a warning on their bodies. Lay off the cattle and the cattlemen, Curly Bill. Or you'll be damned sorry."

Curly Bill looked at Chalmers and laughed again. "You got an army with you?" he asked bluntly. And when he did not

30

get an answer to his question, he shifted his stare. "Did you say the name was Wiswold?"

"That's right," said Chalmers, still doing the talking. His eyes were cold and sharp and his face had a somehow mean and tough expression on it. "Wiswold. They're taking up range somewhere in the San Pedro Valley, near enough to me, I think, for me to do their fighting for them."

He laid it down flatly and coldly in the open for Curly Bill to see and hear. And the laughing outlaw leader, who sometimes even dared to raid the horse herds at the cavalry posts, accepted it. His dimples deepened and he said, "A fighting man. You talk like your daddy did. I knew him—once—in Texas."

Then Curly Bill shifted his eyes coldly away. He looked at the Wiswolds for a short time, then touched the brim of his sombrero. He looked back at Chalmers and smiled. He glanced over his shoulder at his men, seemed to brood for a short moment. Then he chuckled.

"*Bueno,* Chalmers. Sleep easy tonight. We got other things on our minds right now. But we'll meet again. So long, Chalmers. Ladies." He swung a glance their way and touched his hat. And then, fearlessly, he turned his back on Chalmers and the rest and rode back to his men.

Chalmers and the others were ready. It might be a trick, to lull their watchfulness and then wheel and open fire. But nothing happened. Curly Bill, notorious outlaw and killer that he was, took his men away in a close bunch, heading for their Galeyville hide-out.

"That doesn't make sense. Got us cornered and outnumbered, and he rides away." Chalmers puzzled for a moment, then shrugged it off.

"Maybe you threw the hooks into him, Sam," said Baldwin, smiling. "It won't be the first time you've made big and bad men back off like a scared cow."

"I'm not so sure," said Chalmers. "Curly Bill is no man to back off without more reason than my words. He's a devil. A murderous devil with a grin, who kills just for the fun of killing. I could tell you stories about that fellow that would curl your hair till it looked like his. But one will do; an ore train coming out of Mexico with thirty-five guards. Curly Bill and his outfit jumped them and killed every man. That's the kind he is. Now why did he ride off? Could it be the women?"

He waited, but there was no answer from his men. He sent Horton and Adams out to watch the cattle, and stood frowning and staring after the notorious outlaw and his men. He watched them disappear, reappear, and then disappear for good. And somehow the thing made him suspicious. But of what he could not say.

They broke camp three days later and started on a long slant across the valley toward the rolling land between the outposts of the Dragoon and the Mule mountains. Webster's arm was almost healed, but Wiswold was weak and shaky. He rode in the Wiswold wagon, taking it easy, and smiling up at his wife from time to time. She drove the wagon, and glanced sometimes at Jean and Sam Chalmers riding together. She thought, smiling: I know, even if they don't seem to. And she was pleased. Sam Chalmers was all a woman could ask for in a son-in-law. She wondered how soon he would gather courage to ask Jean to marry him.

They camped on big meadows that night and Wiswold wondered why they saw no cattle. But Chalmers did not. He knew that small cattlemen had no chance against Curly Bill and the other outlaws. Only the famed Colonel Hooker, so far, had been strong enough to fight both Apaches and outlaws. But Sam Chalmers had laid down the gauntlet. He stood and stared at the sunset through the wide sweep of land and in the dim distance thought he could see the rugged lines of the Huachuca Mountains. His range lay in there; he couldn't see it but he would fight for it!

They moved on at dawn, drove through some low, rolling hills that had clumps of mesquite and stunted willows in the shallow gullies. The pass widened and became many miles of rolling, rising, dipping hills, all covered with graze for cattle. The Mule Mountains were a dark mass to the left, and distantly to the north on their right rose the ragged, slanting line of the Dragoons, breaking off into several isolated ridges. The hills beyond which lay Tombstone rose almost in a line with the far-distant Whetstone Mountains. And the cattle bellowed and grumbled.

They watered that night at some springs and went on the next dawn. There was a growing sense of excitement and hurry building in Chalmers' mind. This was the moment that he was reaching for, had been reaching for during the past years. And he had someone to share it with. He looked at Jean and his sparkling black eyes drew her gaze, held it until she blushed suddenly. He spoke.

"Come on. I want to show you something!"

He spurred his horse into a run and she followed him, laughing in strange excitement. He rode at a gallop for ten minutes

32

away from the winding line of the herds. Then he pulled up on the crest of a low ridge, yet it was the highest spot before the valley was reached. His voice, usually calm, broke a little as he said simply:

"There it is."

It was a great sweep of valley that they stared across, lush with belly-deep graze and the winding line of the San Pedro River, bordered with cottonwoods, reaching through it. The Huachuca Mountains rose on the west side of the valley, with deep and well-watered canyons reaching down the face of them. Great slopes of dark green were the conifers, and in several places seen now in the clean crisp air were lighter patches that were aspen thickets. But it was the land that held them. The valley.

A cattleman's paradise, watered through the whole year by the ever-flowing San Pedro River. Cottonwoods for heavy shade, mesquite thickets for shielding cattle from the noonday heat in summer. An endless thing, it seemed that the valley reached on into the north and the south without a break, mile after mile, watered by feeder canyons and streams and the San Pedro.

"Look, Jean," said Sam Chalmers at last. "Coronado, the Spaniards, the Jesuits, Indians of a dozen tribes, followed that river. Mexico is down there, with a half million cattle grazing and running wild. Waiting to be bought cheap and brought up here to fatten, and sold at a high price to the Indian reservations, the cavalry posts, and when the railroad reaches us, to the Eastern markets. That's what I'm going to do, Jean. Take up my range right down there where you see that great clump of green trees. I'll build my house there and I'll run my cattle far and wide. I'll kill the rustlers who dare to touch them! I'll ride into Mexico and bring out herds to fatten. I'll sell them and buy more herds, and I'll turn this bunch I have with me into a cattle empire!"

He fought to get his eyes away from his dream and he looked at her. Her eyes were gleaming and they came now to meet his, and a smile broke over her pretty, plump face. She waited, but not for long.

"Jean, that's my dream, and I want you to share it with me. Marry me. I'll run the ranch and you run the house. I love you, Jean, I've loved you since I saw you at that ranch back in Texas. Remember?"

She nodded. "I—remember."

"You'll marry me, Jean—just as soon as we can get the cattle

33

spread out over that valley?" His voice was pleading, yet somehow commanding at the same time, the voice of a man who knew what he wanted and was thoroughly sure of his ability to get it.

She stiffened a little as that feeling came over her. A nervous, high-strung girl, like a restive horse who fought the curb, Chalmers sensed at once. He had spoken too sharply. And he knew it. But he had to win her.

"I—can't," she said quietly. And as she put it into words her courage came and her voice grew stronger. "My father needs me, and will for some time. He is an old man, he can't work cattle now, and won't perhaps be able to for months. I can't leave him."

"You'll be wearing yourself out doing the work that one of my thirty-dollar-a-month cowhands can do for him! Marry me, now—let me put one of my men over your herd, until your father is well enough to work again. Brindle Nelson is a good steady man——"

She broke in almost coldly. "Can Brindle Nelson give my father that love and affection that I can give him?"

It stopped him, left him speechless for a moment. And she weakened. "Sam dear, I do love you. But give me time to get used to all this, including being married to a man I've known scarcely a week! Do you always have to do things on the run, Sam? Get what you want at once?" She laughed a little to take the sting from her words. Then her hand reached out to his arm. "Sam, give me time to think as well as time for my father to get well. And give me something to think about and dream over. Sam, kiss me, now."

He kissed her and held her in his arms for a long time, her head resting against his thick shoulder. The horses stirred and forced them to separate at last. She smiled at him, catching her breath, and then spoke in a low voice.

"Sam, I think you're going to win again." She drew a deep breath, staring at him and studying him as though she had never seen him before. "Do you always win?"

He laughed softly. "So you will marry me right away?"

"No. Not till my father is well." Her determination came again. "He needs me now, in this new and somewhat terrible land. But when he doesn't ..." She smiled swiftly, sobered, and spoke again. "Come to me then. Now take me back to my father, Sam."

They turned the cattle loose that night three miles from the river bottom and watched them break and move on in ragged

34

clumps, bellowing at the thought of water. It had been a long drive that day, but the smell of water and green things kept them moving. Chalmers and his men only kept a line of riders between the two herds now, sending the Wiswold Circle W stuff to the north.

For that was what Wiswold said he wanted. He was going to take up his land closer to Tombstone, about four miles below Charleston, on the same side of the river as the mill town. He had his reasons for it, he said, but he did not name them. And Chalmers asked no questions.

They said good-by at dawn of the next day, and Chalmers told the Wiswolds he would see them in a couple of weeks or so. For he thought it would take him that long, perhaps longer, to get his herd broken up and scattered over the range. And there was more to do than that, also. Mexicans must be found and hired, to start making the adobe bricks for his house. Mesquite to be cut for firewood, and corral posts. He had to look around in the neighboring canyons also. He wanted to know the land, every foot of it. His range. The start of his cattle empire.

And he waved good-by to them with a curious sense of eagerness to have them go. Woman stuff could come later, he thought almost grimly. She wanted it that way. All right. He was starting his ranch this day!

Chalmers almost yelled aloud as he sent his men into the bunched cattle and split them as they ranged the big meadows. "Spread 'em out, push 'em around—then let them go and find their own ranges." So he ordered them and he rode with them as they worked for three hours. And then, tired and hot despite the crisp air, they rode after Chico and the horse herd, the big wagon and the hoodlum behind it which Brett and Harley had taken on.

They had found the spot, all right. Just where he had seen it the trip before, and without trouble. A roll of land that reached down a gentle slope to the river. No cutbanks here. Just the sweep of soil, the grass, water, and trees. An adobe would rise soon on that crest, just where a man could look out and see things. A well must be dug, for a fellow had to have water in his home in case of Indian attacks. And a cottonwood or two could be planted for summer's shade on the south side. Just a slip an inch through and a foot long would make a tree! Crazy, wasn't it? But cottonwoods grew fast if well watered. The only care a man must take was in choosing the tree from which to cut the slip. A male tree. For the female trees bore the cotton that drifted in spring like a snowstorm!

He laughed softly now, seeing the adobe rise in his mind's eye, seeing himself riding home after a long journey into Mexico, with his men and cattle stringing out behind him. And Jean would be waiting in the doorway—right there, under the cottonwood!

In a week he had two Mexican families camping down by the stream, north of the house. They were making bricks, for they had found some good red clay nearby. Sixteen-inch bricks with some twenty-four inches for corners and angles. No straw was to be had and the Mexicans cut the prickly pear lobes and mashed them into the mud, for the strength the fibers could give, and one of the old men insisted that the juice they pounded out into the mud made the bricks stronger and tougher.

In another week the bricks were made. They were turned, then set on edge for further drying. And then the lines were drawn with a crooked stick, in the dirt. Chalmers laughed. The Mexicans argued and did as they pleased, no matter how he swore at them. And finally he gave up.

Baldwin laughed at him and Chalmers grinned ruefully.

"After all," he told his *segundo*, still grinning, "they only agreed to build me an adobe ranch house. They didn't say anything about it being what I wanted!"

While the bricks finished drying, the Mexicans had ridden up into the big canyon cutting into the Mule Mountains, with axes and rude saws. They came back two days later with enough timber on their pack mules and burros to make door and window frames, and one door. One door only, the rest, they insisted, if *el señor* wanted all those openings, could be closed with blankets.

And that was the lazy, slipshod, but quite successful way the ranch house was built.

It was more than four weeks after saying good-by to Jean and her family that Chalmers started north to find them. He rode a good black horse, and Brett and Harley drove the big wagon, empty now. For they had to go to either Charleston or Tombstone for supplies. Chalmers rode with them and then grew more and more restless at the slowness of the wagon. When at last he saw four cows with the Circle W on their flanks he gave up.

"Hell, I'll ride ahead. I'll find you later." And he spurred off.

Brett grinned thinly. "Funny, ain't it? He was ragged crazy

to get to the valley before anybody else did. He was ready to bust out and fight any outfit that tried to get ahead of him. But when he found the outfit ahead of him he sure slows down. He camps for a week with 'em, so he does. Harley, d'you figure the girl's got something to do with it all?"

"Look at him go!" was Harley's answer, and they grinned at each other.

Chalmers rode on rapidly. He was as eager as a boy. His eyes roamed and roved and sought sign of riders. A pretty, plump girl with light hair, mostly. But he saw no one until he reached a meadow in a sweep of the river about four miles from the mill town of Charleston. There he saw some men working on an adobe house. Two well-shaped horses, fast and with ornate harness, were hooked to a light buggy. But there was no sign of Jean or her family.

Chalmers rode up and stopped and called to one of the workmen, "Is this the Wiswold layout?"

"That's right," said someone, stepping into the doorway. A big man, grinning, and with a heavy, bull voice that boomed out again. "How are you, Chalmers? Did you get that herd through safely?"

And at Chalmers' blank expression, Bigelow Newman roared with laughter.

6

IT WAS a cold moment for Sam Chalmers and it was not only from the shock of seeing and hearing Newman. It was finding the man there at the not yet completed adobe ranch house where Jean was to live. Or was she? Did the presence of Newman explain her reluctance to marry him? The thought shocked him almost to the point of being stunned.

Newman's big laugh rose again as he seemed to savor every moment of the scene. He stepped out of the half-finished house and lounged against the still doorless frame. He rolled a smoke, smiling now as his fingers deftly twisted the cigarette into being and lighted it.

"Welcome to the Tombstone country," said Newman, puffing a cloud of smoke out before he spoke and letting the rest curl almost lazily around his lips as he talked. "Or have you been welcomed already?"

Chalmers held his answer for a long moment as he thought over the remark and what he suspected was some meaning behind it. Thoughts were coupling in his mind: the Wiswolds at the ranch back in west Texas where he had bought the Newman notes. They had not mentioned knowing Bigelow Newman, and did that silence mean something? He had an oddly flurried moment of feeling that he was a man alone. And then he fought that odd feeling away.

Newman was dressed in a tailored suit, with fine gray trousers, a wide-open frock coat, and a flowered silk vest. He wore fine linen, white as snow, and a big white sombrero. But under that wide frock coat was a broad leather belt that held many cartridges, and a big leather holster hung low and filled with a Colt pistol. Somehow there was a difference now from the man Chalmers had met in New Mexico. Something that puzzled and almost worried the younger cattleman. He spoke flatly and bluntly.

"What are you doing here, Newman?"

"I told you I was coming to Tombstone," said Newman. Then his quick smile broke again. "Oh, you mean here, at this ranch. I'm here with my wife." He turned and called, "Dear, will you come out a moment, please? It's Sam Chalmers!"

Chalmers felt sick as he waited: Dear. My wife. Dear. My wife. It tolled like a funeral bell in his mind. It just couldn't be. Fate could not trick him and cajole him, and then fling him down that hard. He waited. The sickness rolled within him and he fought a tortured expression away from his face. He forced a smile that was hardly pleasant as he heard a sound from within the house, and then the girl stepped into the doorway. She was plump, pretty, and her hair was—red. Strangely, frighteningly, like Jean. But not Jean. Or—and murderous rage flared—was he being fooled?

Emotion surged and Chalmers gulped. He stammered, "I—I——" and then he stopped. He was staring fixedly, and to keep from reaching for his gun to kill Newman, he reached for his sombrero. He took it off and switched it from his right to his left hand. And then he smiled suddenly.

It was not Jean. It simply could not be Jean, and that was all that mattered at the moment.

As though he read the other man's mind, Newman grinned with mockery still plain in his expression. "My wife, Mr. Chalmers," he said.

"How do you do, Mr. Chalmers?" said the smiling girl who

38

was so much like Jean and yet not her. "My sister has told me a lot about you."

Chalmers swallowed and smiled. He was fighting down the surge of cold and murderous rage, fighting other and harder emotions. Harder to keep hidden; his wild feeling of delight that he still had a chance to win Jean.

Newman chuckled at his speechlessness. "I guess you still don't get this straight, Chalmers," he said. "This is my wife and Jean's sister. You didn't hear about her on the trip because her family didn't approve of her turning actress and had lost track of her." He seemed to have read Chalmers' mind again. "And they didn't know me, or know that we met here a couple of months back and were married. I'm going to manage a new theater here. You rather upset my plans for mining, you know. But there's no hard feeling about it. Especially now that I hear that we may become brothers-in-law."

"Uhm, yes, I hope so," said Chalmers quietly. He put the big straw sombrero back on his head and stared straight at Newman for a moment. He smiled. And in the very brief interval between the stare and the smile Chalmers had learned something. Newman hated him and would never lose a chance to do him harm. There was no question in his mind about it.

And as though Newman with equal ease read his mind, the big man's bluff and friendly smile changed oddly. It became cold and mocking and somehow daring. Daring Chalmers to start something. Almost defying him, yet wordlessly. Newman's hand moved in a quick and careless gesture. It swept aside his wide frock coat on the right side and showed the gun holstered at his waist. Yet he did not touch the pistol, simply exposed it and let the coat swing back into place.

"Well, it's great country, Chalmers," said Newman with a sweep of his hand. "A man can grow in this land, make money in any number of ways. Cattle, mining, stage and freight lines. Stores, merchandising. And amusements for tired men. Bars and gambling and the theater. That's going to be my field now, amusing tired men." He put his arm about his wife and she snuggled against him. "We have a great little actress here, Chalmers! She'll draw the crowds to the new theater!"

"I'm sure of it," agreed Chalmers, smiling, but his eyes and his thoughts were going to Jean. He looked about quickly and saw no sign of any of the Wiswolds. "I, ah, are the Wiswolds about somewhere, Newman?"

"They've gone to Charleston for some supplies. It's about as far as Wiswold can drive in his condition. He's not gaining very rapidly, I'm afraid."

"I'll move on then," answered Chalmers. He waved toward his wagon which was passing. "I'm after supplies also."

"You can get them in Charleston or in Tombstone," Newman answered, his arm still about his wife. "We can go with you to Charleston, for we want to see the family. Talk on the way, too. I want you to get to know my wife, Chalmers—you may be related soon!" And Newman laughed.

Chalmers smiled but his thoughts were stirring in bitter turmoil. Related? He wondered dully as he turned his horse and waited for them to get into the buggy behind the smooth-looking team. What chance did he have to win Jean now, with Newman already a member of the family? No question, Newman hated him and was vengeful about the past. He would harm Chalmers at any opportunity and meant him to know it. Yet both men smiled and talked as they moved on, Chalmers' horse trotting easily beside the light buggy. Chalmers' comments were only occasional, for Newman carried the talk in his big, rather pompous way.

"Al Schieffelin is building a huge adobe hall for traveling shows and entertainments," Newman said as the team spun along the open land toward a thickening group of cottonwoods in a bend of the river. "The Masons are planning to use the second floor. But our owner's plans are different." He patted his wife's knee and she smiled at him. "He's going to build a theater with a bar in front, gambling, dancing, all the things rough and hard-working men ask for. A balcony, boxes where liquor can be served too. And we'll keep a steady talent on the stage, like the English music halls. Something going on all the time. Songs, dances, jugglers, musicians, plays. And there my wife will shine, sir!"

"Uhm, sounds interesting," agreed Chalmers, his mind roaming far ahead to where he could see a column of smoke rising from Richard Gird's big reduction mill. There, he knew, the rough and tough town of Charleston was already growing.

Newman talked on, expanding in his big way on their plans about the theater as though he owned it. The sketches and the design already were laid out. He laughed as he described the boxes with their slatted sides seemingly hung on the side walls in the designer's sketches. "Like bird cages hanging there. In fact, with men and beautiful women leaning over the rails to watch my wife and the others in their acts, I think they will

40

look even more like bird cages. So that's to be the name, the Bird Cage Theater. Like it, Chalmers?"

"Yes, fine, fine," agreed Chalmers. He shifted a little in the saddle now, and then quickly swung his horse in closer to the buggy, for Newman had been edging away from him in the open land. "Fine, good idea. You have lots of ideas, don't you, Newman?"

As Newman flashed a quick glance at him, Chalmers jerked his head slightly toward a mesquite thicket that bordered their way about a hundred yards off, now. He spoke flatly.

"Did I see somebody riding in that thicket, Newman, speaking of ideas? It would be a good place for an ambush wouldn't it!"

"Yes, if a man wanted to arrange one," said Newman casually. He looked at the thicket, raised his right hand, which held the whip, and straightened his sombrero.

Newman began to talk of Tombstone, growing rapidly; of its hopes and wild desires and almost terrifying tragedies. Men killed for little or no reason, wild drinking and gambling, the inflow of the wildest and most villainous group of rustlers, outlaws, train robbers, and badmen that the West could produce. Of Johnny Behan, the deputy, who reported to the sheriff in Tucson, and the hope that they would have their own county soon. Of Marshal White and his troubles in trying to keep the peace, or even a semblance of it, in the sprawling, wildly growing place of tents and shacks and hovels of boards, tin, and canvas.

But Chalmers was not listening. He knew much of the growing enmity between the deputy sheriff's offices and the town officials and all the trouble it made for all men. His mind was active and clear and his eyes scanning. He knew some man had been riding in and out of that mesquite thicket and that it was a fine place for an ambush. Knew also that Newman could easily have seen him coming and sent a man out of the back of the adobe house, to cut him down at the first chance. Was that raising of his right hand with the whip in it a signal of some sort? To shoot or not to shoot?

Chalmers thought that he would know soon, for they were almost past the mesquite thicket. He had kept his saddler in a line between Newman and the thicket all the time. First by crowding up, now by dropping back. And any man who shot at him, Chalmers, would risk killing either Newman or his wife. Chalmers grinned swiftly and rode on.

No shots came. They swept in and out of two low-walled

41

washes, too shallow to be called barrancas, one of which had a small stream feeding down. Cottonwoods thickened now, and far to the right on the rising slope of a hill Chalmers saw a huddle of mine buildings and two shaft-head frames. Farther up, near the crest of the ridge, were more workings, and what appeared to be a small town growing midway between the two groups of mines.

They were a quarter mile now from the huddle of adobe buildings, tents, and rude shacks that was Charleston. Brett and Harley were trotting the team of mules ahead of the unladen wagon and people could be seen in the wide space, about which buildings were scattered, that was called the main street of the town. Nearest to them and shaded by a huge cottonwood was a big adobe building where a half-dozen horses and three wagons were tied. That was the general store, as Chalmers learned a few moments later. Across from it were two smaller buildings about thirty feet apart—saloons by the signs on them.

As they came closer two men ran out of one saloon, spun, and began trotting backward with drawn guns. But they did not shoot. A third man came almost diving out the front door of the saloon, half regained his feet, then plunged forward on his face. He slid about two feet in the dust and lay still. Smoke puffed lightly in the doorway of the saloon the three men had come from, and then a dull sound came.

Harley and Brett pulled up their team and waited. Chalmers stiffened a little in the saddle. He saw a man step out of the saloon doorway and stand with his feet flat, his body balanced. The two men backing away fired at him three times before he answered their shots. Then the man in the doorway fired once, twice. One of the men shooting at him went down and the other swayed a little. The man in the saloon door raised his pistol for another shot, but a harsh voice called to him, "Save it, Ringo, you've killed me."

And then the second man spun and fell on his face.

John Ringo stood for a moment, holding his gun. He was smiling thinly as he reloaded his pistol. They told many stories of Ringo, but none was wilder or worse than the truth. He looked about coldly now, his eyes scanning swiftly the street and the buildings. Now he stepped out a little. His voice rose.

"My gun's hot an' so am I." He held it almost loosely in his hand. Something moved across the street and behind the store. He snapped a quick shot that way and a hot voice called a

42

curse back at him. Ringo laughed. His eyes shifted, shifted again. They seemed to be caught by the big freight wagon with its six mules and the two huge Negroes in it. He half raised the pistol and then lowered it. He stepped out a little farther into the street and then took a dozen steps toward the freight wagon.

"Get down from that wagon and pray, you black apes," said John Ringo flatly, angrily.

Brett and Harley looked at him and then at each other. Brett nodded and started to get down from the wagon on the far side, Harley following him on the near side.

"Those are my men," said Chalmers simply.

"And that's John Ringo," said Newman, smiling oddly. "Seems to be on the warpath, as usual. Trouble," he added sententiously, "seems to happen around him and anyplace in this crazy country."

"I've heard of John Ringo," answered Chalmers. "He's a friend of Curly Bill Brocius, isn't he?" He sent a sharp glance at Newman. "I'm riding in to take a hand, Newman. Can I trust you to protect my back?"

Newman did not answer. But Chalmers had not waited. He was riding forward now, at a trot. He pushed his big straw sombrero back on his forehead and called out sharply, "Ringo!"

He rode on and stopped about fifty feet from John Ringo and spoke again. "Ringo. That praying, now. My men don't pray for the living, only for the dead."

Ringo stopped and stared at Chalmers, his gun hanging almost limply in his hand. He waited. He saw Chalmers stop his horse and get down on the side away from him. And still he waited.

Chalmers did not draw or touch his pistols. He let his right and left hands hang loose and relaxed against his sides as he started walking forward. He did not walk rapidly, simply paced on with his cold black eyes fixed on John Ringo's mean and cruel face. Ringo was a killer of unquestioned courage and Chalmers knew it. He also knew something else: the power of those hard, snapping black eyes that he fixed so unwinkingly on John Ringo. He spoke once as he walked.

"Brett, Harley," he said. "This may be a trap set for us because we killed those rustlers in Sulphur Springs Valley. Be careful, and watch for any man who tries to get into this from ambush."

43

Then Chalmers stopped. He was ten feet from Ringo. "Is ten feet about right, John Ringo? Would you like to try it? Would you like my men to pray for you—dead?"

7

THE wide space about the buildings in Charleston seemed to build up with strange tension that stiffened men who appeared in doors and windows. Curiosity drew them at first, for John Ringo was known as a cold and courageous killer with a record that reached into the higher brackets of the famed or notorious gunmen. They said he wanted to die and was looking for someone faster and more deadly that himself, to save himself the trouble of committing suicide. His nature was mean and his habitual expression was saturnine, wrapped in the gloom of a man whose thoughts were bitter and somber. When he grinned, as he occasionally did when drinking, his face did not lighten, a haunting menace simply flashed over its lean features.

Now, standing in the open space between the buildings, Ringo and the newcomer to the dangerous country that was growing up around Tombstone faced each other in stiff silence. Ringo had his gun in his hand and Sam Chalmers let his hands swing idly and loosely at his sides. He waited, having said his piece, for the other man to start things. And John Ringo, cold and nervy, waited. He did not shift his keen stare from Chalmers' black eyes.

Chalmers let a thought flicker across his mind: He's waiting for something—a signal from someone? And with it a second, cold thought: Newman is back of me. Then he held his mind and his stare on Ringo's face and he too waited. He heard someone call something from a house about a hundred yards or more away, toward the river from where he stood, but he knew Brett or Harley would be watching and alert. And he set and held his mind on John Ringo. He waited a moment longer, then spoke suddenly and sharply.

"Don't be fooled because my two men got down from the wagon when you told them to. They're fighting men, Ringo, and they got down to fight, not to pray. I've seen them do some fine shooting. Maybe you've heard of them, Ringo. They're from Texas, like you and a lot of us in the place. Brett and Harley. They took our family name of Chalmers. They fought

44

with my father when he led some men into the Big Bend country and cleaned out Twister Macarthy and his breeds in that four-day fight about ten years ago. Remember, Ringo?"

Ringo nodded, his thin lips a little pursed. "Don't be in a hurry, Chalmers," he said quietly. "I'm just sort of looking you over. Curly Bill is my best friend and I've heard about you and the message you left up that canyon on you way in. I'm just looking you over and wondering."

"Wondering if I'm big enough to make good on my warning to leave my cattle and my men alone? Well, I am," retorted Chalmers. His voice did not rise but its somewhat high-pitched tones carried it far. "I'm laying it down again in front of you toughs and killers. Let my men, my cattle, alone. Let everything alone that has my mark on it. And don't think I can't back it up. I'm bringing another herd out in two weeks, Ringo. There'll be ten men with that herd and every damned one of them is a fighting Texan. That gives me twenty men. Twenty fighting men. And I'll hire more if it isn't enough to make you outlaws let me and my stuff alone!"

Ringo said flatly, "I'm still wondering about you. I just don't believe any man is as hard as they tell about you."

"There's a way to find out," said Chalmers. "Maybe I'm too far away for you? I'll move up a little," and he moved one step closer to the other man.

The silence was so great that the distant splashing of a horse crossing the river came to them. A shod hoof clicked sharply on a rock, and then the same sound came again. Some men in the background, to Chalmers' right, said, "It looks like Curly Bill. This should be a cleanup fight here and now!"

Brett's voice rose, but calmly. "It is Curly Bill, boss. Shall I cut him down now?"

"No. Wait."

Someone coughed and a woman who had moved out on the flat ground in front of the store door was pulled back quickly into the building. A horse stamped a hoof and then Curly Bill's voice rose as he stopped his horse near the saloon.

"John. I want to talk to you."

Ringo said flatly, as though in disgust, "This will keep for a little while, Chalmers," and then he holstered his gun and walked away without looking back, a tall, lean, hard man who seemed gravely disappointed at the break in his plans.

"He's been drinking for three days and he walks as straight as an Apache war arrow," said a smelter man, nodding his head. "He's going to take a lot of killing."

45

Chalmers stood still in the street, hands hanging at his side. He watched and waited, almost idly, as four men came from the store with blankets and rolled the three bodies in them. Others stepped out to help and no one seemed at all disturbed over the killings. Already the people of Tombstone and its surrounding towns had become hardened to daily killings. Men drank and fought and some died and were buried. The bother was to locate and notify the relatives if possible.

Brett spoke softly for only Chalmers to hear, but he ignored it. He had seen the two women and the stooped and limping man come out of the store. One of the women waved to him. The plump young woman with the pale hair. But he ignored her and her waving hand that signaled him to come to her. It was in his mind that the thing had to be settled now. Danger meant nothing. He never had feared death because somehow he was certain that he could not be killed. He didn't know why. Perhaps it was what the old woman, part Negro and part Seminole, had told him. Perhaps all those fool brews and charms and prayers meant something. Brett and Harley, her sons, thought so. But he was not born to be killed, he was certain of that little point. Lots could happen to him. Lots would happen to him. But not killing.

Chalmers said sharply, "Come on, boys," and he started walking toward the saloon door.

Curly Bill's horse was there, ground-tied by the dropped split reins. But Curly Bill and Ringo had disappeared. No faces were visible at the single window or the door as Chalmers walked up to the adobe building. Nor was a voice to be heard from inside. Chalmers did not pause at the open door. Harley was back of him and Brett slanted to one side and stopped at the window. Chalmers strode in and Harley followed him like a great black shadow, and almost as silent. As the people in the street saw them disappear a curious, sighing sound went about among them. Wanting to see and yet not daring to go closer, they waited for the outburst of shooting they were certain would come.

Chalmers had squinted a dozen steps before he entered the dark room and now his eyes were set and ready for the gloom. He saw a rude bar of unpainted wood at one side, three rough tables, each with four chairs, and two chairs against the rear wall. Other than the dozen bottles of whisky and the glasses on the small back bar, that was all the room held except the men and a fat, frowzy woman behind the bar.

Curly Bill grinned, John Ringo grunted, and the woman

46

almost whined, "Buy a drink, gents, and don't fight in here."
Two young fellows, standing at the back end of the bar, moved
a little, but steadied at a sharp word from Chalmers.

"Stand, you two." And then Chalmers surveyed them all
coldly. "Well, do we fight?"

Curly Bill laughed without speaking. John Ringo said, "I'd
say yes, Bill. I'm spoiling for it. I'd say yes, let's fight now."

"No," retorted Curly Bill, as though planning a poker party
for that night. "Not now. Later. Let's feel him out and see how
tough he really is. And anyhow, John, the word has come
from Tucson that Wyatt Earp and his brothers are coming to
Tombstone. Doc Holliday may be with them. You never did
like Wyatt and Doc. Let's wait for them."

Ringo said sourly, "Oh hell," and turned to the bar. "Give
me some whisky."

Chalmers said flatly, "I've laid down my word and I'll say
no more on that subject, Curly Bill. What happens between us
from here on is up to you. Let me alone and I'll let you alone.
I'm interested in raising cattle, not in killing men."

And Chalmers turned and walked out of the saloon. Harley
waited for him to pass and then followed him. Brett stayed by
the window till both men were outside and then he walked just
in back of them toward the wagon and the saddle horse where
Chalmers had left it. Chalmers caught up his reins and said,
"Get in the wagon and stay there. Pull over by the store."

As the six mules threw their weight into the collars, Chalmers swung into the saddle. And while he was in mid-air two
pistols barked sharply from the corner of the saloon. Chalmers
lurched a little as his horse jumped. He hit the saddle and his
gun was out even as he did so. He was spinning his mount, his
gun held high, his eyes on the two young fellows who had been
in the saloon. They were standing about four feet apart and
shooting fast.

Chalmers steadied his horse and his gun came down. He
fired, fired again, and again. One of the men was down and the
other turned and ran at top speed to disappear behind the
saloon. Chalmers yelled once, "Boys, watch that saloon!" And
then he spurred his horse after the man who had disappeared.

As Chalmers raced around the corner of the saloon he heard
a shot and saw a flash from a clump of mesquite about forty
feet away. He fired at the smoke, fired again. A man ran out,
staggering a little, and headed for the front of the saloon.

Chalmers reholstered his right-hand gun and drew the left,
shifting it to his right hand. He spurred forward again, calmly

47

certain that the two Negroes were covering the front of the saloon. He rode out into the wide-open space about the buildings, drew up his horse, and fired once. The running man plunged down on his face. Chalmers rode on grimly, eyes sweeping about for more trouble. He stopped by the young fellow and stared down.

A sigh came from the man on the ground and he rolled his head a little to look up at Chalmers. His hand twitched as though to reach for the gun butt about six inches from it. Chalmers flipped his pistol up a little and the man stopped moving his hand. He was young, hardly more than twenty years old, but his expression was mean and hard.

"Go ahead, kill me, you bastard," he said.

"I brought my birth records with me in the family Bible to prove you're a liar," said Chalmers. "And being where you are proves you're a fool. No, I won't kill unless you show fight. But when you do, I'll kill you or any other fool who wants to start something." His voice rose a little. "Brett, Harley, if this man makes a move, kill him."

Then Chalmers holstered his gun and rode on to the store steps. Jean Wiswold, as well as her father and mother, were staring at him strangely. Now Newman and his wife came over, walking from where they had tied their buggy team. People were moving about. A dog went out and sniffed at the man in the dust and two men walked toward him. They picked him up and carried him toward a tent about a hundred feet away. And no one spoke for the moment.

Chalmers felt suddenly and cruelly on the defensive. He could see by the Wiswolds' expression just what they thought of his actions and what interpretation they put on them. It seemed unfair, uncalled for, why couldn't they understand that he had to do it? He was going to live in this country, to develop his ranch and his holdings in it. He had to teach the outlaws a lesson, and that at once. To teach them he meant what he said and to leave no doubts in their warped brains of his willingness and his ability to make good on his words. He loved Jean, and yet somehow he could not explain it to her, especially with so many people about.

He spoke almost curtly. "I stopped by your new house to see you. My men and I are up here to buy supplies."

"Yes, I see you," said Jean stiffly.

Her mother said, "Jean," and then stopped.

A curious smile twitched at Newman's lips, but he straightened them at once. He said gently, "Jean, it was forced on him. Don't you see that? He had to do it."

Jean said sharply, "He didn't have to go into the saloon, did he? That's what started it."

"Oh, no!" Newman laughed gently. "It started before that, and it isn't ended either."

Chalmers spoke bluntly. "Is that a warning, Newman?"

Newman looked at him for a moment and then asked, "Do you need any more warning than you've had?"

Chalmers shook his head. He stepped down from his horse and said quietly, "Jean, can I talk to you for a moment? Alone?"

She shook her head. "My father is tired. This is his first trip out since he was wounded. We want to take him home. He's too weak for all this excitement." She and her mother took her father's arms and walked with him to their wagon. Then she seemed to relent a little. "Don't stop here for more trouble, Mr. Chalmers. Go to Tombstone and do your buying there."

Chalmers sat his horse, and watched them get into the wagon and drive off. He was silent, cold. Newman spoke. "That's good advice, Chalmers. Try Tombstone for your supplies. Curly Bill and his men like this place."

Newman then took his wife's arm and walked with her to their buggy. He helped her in and then untied the team and climbed in beside her. He gathered the reins and drove off after the Wiswolds. He looked back once and then swore softly. "Clytie, look at that fool!"

Chalmers was in the saddle, his face cold and hard. He was riding now. But he was not riding out of Charleston. He was riding up and down the street between the two saloons and the big store building. He trotted his horse. He walked it. He galloped it, and then he trotted it and walked it again. He made a hundred-yard ride to the north, turned his horse, and made a hundred-yard ride to the south. Once, in sheer rage that left him cold, his voice rose in a wild, high-pitched yip-yipping, the old Rebel yell. The two Negroes sat on the high seat of the wagon and waited with mocking grins. They had seen this happen before. Once before. And they waited for the finish.

"Curly Bill! John Ringo!" Chalmers' voice rose again. "Come out and fight!"

And still the Negroes waited with their mocking grins as they watched Chalmers ride back and forth. In the street and around the buildings no one in sight moved. What was happening in the saloon, Chalmers had no way of knowing.

49

8

SAM CHALMERS rode two more trips back and forth, and then pulled up his horse squarely in front of the saloon where Curly Bill and John Ringo waited inside. His face was cold, set into stiff lines that made it hawklike and cruel, vengeful. He dropped the reins as his horse stopped, facing the saloon door, and his hands relaxed at his sides, hanging with only a slight crook at the elbows. His snapping black eyes were set and unwinking as he stared fixedly at the door.

Nothing happened. There was neither sight nor sound of the men in the saloon. The Chinese at the restaurant beyond the big store came out with a dishpan of water and threw it at a dog. The water splashed and the dog yelped and ran. The Chinese grinned and walked back into the kitchen. He seemed completely uninterested in what was taking place in the street.

Now Chalmers took his reins in his left hand and rode thirty feet to the right, and back again. He stopped once more, and then snorted a disgusted oath. As though in complete derision and disgust, he spun the horse and rode very slowly across to the store, his back turned all the time to the saloon. And he was not shot at.

As Chalmers got down from his horse in front of the store and close to his men and the wagon, the store seemed almost emptied of people. Only Pete Laskey and Trinidad Chavez, the two owners, were in sight. They both stood near the front of the store, and Pete grunted a curse as he watched Chalmers and the two big Negroes heading for the door. He said gruffly, "Now *we* get it."

Chalmers came in and stopped six feet inside the door. Brett and Harley stood to either side of him and waited in grim silence. Chalmers glanced about swiftly and then stared at the two storekeepers.

"They tell me this town is run by Curly Bill and his bunch," Chalmers said flatly. "That's all right with me. They can run it."

"What do you want?" demanded Trinidad. He was a thickly built Mexican with a small head over a bull neck. A friendly enough man but he knew only too well where his interests lay

50

and they were not with a man who talked tough to the outlaws. "Whatever it is, we ain't got it right now."

Chalmers laughed at him, and suddenly broke into very good Spanish, his words tumbling rhythmically over each other and all finely accented, a smooth-flowing burst of talk that left Chavez shrugging his shoulders helplessly. He turned to Pete Laskey and said plaintively, "Pete?"

"He talked too fast for me," explained Laskey. "You heard him, answer him."

"We still ain't got it," Trinidad Chavez answered Chalmers.

"That's a lie and you can't either lie to or bluff me. There's bacon there on the shelf, there's sugar in sacks at the end of the counter. I see a dozen sacks of flour in the back room, and any fool can see the salt too. I bet I can walk back there and find prunes and other dried fruit too. And hell, if those aren't cans of stuff right there, I'll eat the cans and throw the contents in your face."

"Tough, ain't you," retorted Pete Laskey.

"Maybe, and if you want to really find out, just refuse to put this list of stuff in my wagon. Here's the list." He handed Laskey a long list written on a page from his notebook, and then went on. "My men and I are putting the mules up at the stables. We're getting saddlers for the boys to ride and we're going on to Tombstone. We'll be back in the morning, and we'll expect to find the wagon loaded. So long."

As Chalmers and the two Negroes turned to go out, Chavez spoke. "Curly Bill ain't going to like this."

Chalmers stopped, looked back, and grinned fleetingly. Then he walked out with his men following him.

As they stepped out into the sunlight two men were just riding up the slanting road to the summit of the cutbank on the far side of the river. One look was enough. They were Curly Bill and John Ringo. They rode on and then disappeared where the Tombstone road dived into a steep-sided gully that rose toward the higher land.

Chalmers stood for a moment, staring about him. Life had somehow returned to normal in the little town, and no one paid much attention to him. There was one woman to be seen and she was a Mexican. A few boys, Mexicans also, and a half-dozen men loafing about. Across the river the smoke from the mill and smelter rose thinly, shifting in the wind.

"Unhook the mules and take them to the stable," he ordered, "I'll meet you there," and Chalmers was swinging into the saddle as he spoke.

51

He rode about two hundred feet to the adobe-walled stables and feed corrals and saw a small sign saying, STAGE OFFICE. He swung down from his horse and stood holding the reins as he stared about. Two hostlers were grooming a six-horse team, making ready for the Tucson stage to come in and change horses. A man sat on a broken-backed chair by the wide front door and spat twice at a beetle. The shiny black beetle stood on its head and remained that way. The man laughed and said, "Funny how they always do that, ain't it? Like humans, they most always do things the same way. Mules is different. Nobody ever figured out how a mule would act, except to be as ornery as he could. What you want, mister?"

"Feed for six mules and the rent of two saddlers with saddles."

"The feed's easy but the saddles ain't. No got." The liveryman spat. "C'n give you a buggy and two good trotting horses. No saddlers, though." He looked at Chalmers speculatively. "You ain't so big, mister, but you must be hell on wheels. I guess men is like buckers, the size don't count. Anybody that can ride up and down in front of Curly Bill and John Ringo is tough meat." He grinned. "Y'understand, though, I ain't taking sides. I just run this feed corral and livery barn."

Chalmers stood for a time, his black eyes steady and hard on the liveryman. He was shifting his thoughts swiftly and wondering about Tombstone and the two men who had ridden that way. Wondering if he should follow them and again force the issue in front of even more people. The word would be passed but it seemed to Chalmers that the more people who saw him throw the hooks into the outlaws, the better. He was going to have to make good on his words and he knew it. The harder he hit them at first the better his chances would be in the end. So his decision was made and stood.

"Hook up the team," he ordered briefly. "My men will use the buggy, I'll ride this black. He's good for a few miles more."

"He looks it," agreed the liveryman.

Ten minutes later Chalmers led the way across the ford, noting the big freight wagons with bodies piled high with bridge timbers. More piles of bridge timbers were stacked on the ground and men already were lining up the stringers for the bridge to be thrown across at that point. The road went through some narrow flats where mesquite crowded out almost all other growth. It slanted up the thirty-foot cutbank and straightened out across a wide-rising bench that was slashed with gullies and dry washes.

The road showed briefly ahead of them, then slanted into a gully and followed it for a time. It passed some adobe huts huddled together on a low ridge where men stared idly at them. Ahead, twice, they saw the dim dust cloud that probably was Curly Bill and John Ringo. Chalmers rode the ridge whenever the road dived into a gully, and kept a wary stare swinging about the country. He thought that dust cloud was Curly Bill and John Ringo but he was not certain. And ambush was easy in that broken country.

The mine workings were ugly blotches on the hill high above Tombstone, and dotted here and there across the flats and ridges were raw spots where tents or adobe huts, a headframe, and a small dump showed where men dug and gambled with nature.

Chalmers thought: The damned fools, to come into this country and dig for silver, gambling with their lives for it. And then he grinned briefly at his own inconsistency. For who was gambling more than he?

In two hours they had covered the eight miles up the slope to Tombstone and came out on the flat where the first of the buildings were rising. Some huts, frame and canvas, showed first. Then a half-finished adobe with a tarpaulin thrown over it to make a roof. Four rocks made a fireplace in front of that one, and not far beyond was the start of a frame house. As they rode past it the man dropped his hammer and grabbed for his rifle. His face was mean as he called to them.

"You can't steal this lumber!" and he watched them pass before he laid down his rifle and picked up his tools again. Lumber was more than gold or silver at that time in the wild growth of the camp.

Now they could see the larger buildings rising on either side of Allen Street, Tough Nut Street, and the raw, newly brushed-out roads that were to bear the names of Fremont, Safford, and the numbered cross streets. The road crossed a low gully where some goats fed and some mean shacks of tin and canvas had been built. A woman came out of one and called to the Negroes suggestively, but they did not look or speak, simply drove on after Chalmers.

Chalmers led them across to Allen Street where a trail came up the ridge from Contention and Fairbanks and pulled up there. As the team drawing the buggy came up and stopped, a sharp clicking sound pulled them all around to face down the trail toward a greasewood thicket. They waited, briefly, and then knew that the click was not of a cocked rifle, but a shod hoof hitting a rock.

Two riders came into sight around the thicket and up out of Walnut Gulch. Two tall and lean men, one of them so thin he was cadaverous. They were riding good horses, among the best Chalmers had seen out there, he thought. The two riders stopped and stared at Chalmers and his men for a moment, then came on at a slow but steady walk. Both men were light-complexioned with pale eyes gleaming under their dark, wide-brimmed hats. One, the heavier one, wore a tawny mustache that drooped below his jutting, heavy jaw. He was florid, healthy-looking, and hard as nails as he rode past them, his cold blue eyes swiveling on them as he went. The other, ema-ciated and pale, had ash-blond hair that drooped under his hat. His cold gray eyes swiveled with his companion's. Under his well-made coat as it swung in the wind Chalmers could see a short-barreled shotgun swinging from a shoulder thong. And both riders had pistols belted under their dusty frock coats.

"Just getting in," said Chalmers as he watched the two men ride up Allen Street. He shifted in his saddle and looked at Brett. "You and Harley saw them both in Dodge, didn't you? That man with the shotgun is Doc Holliday, and the other Wyatt Earp?"

"That's them, boss," said Brett, his teeth flashing in a wide grin. "They rides together now, folks say. Funny, a peace officer having a badman for a best friend."

"Maybe Wyatt Earp ain't a peace officer any more," said Harley.

"He had a star on, I could see it under his coat when he rode past. A small star, a gold one." Chalmers puzzled for a mo-ment. "Deputy United States marshal, I'd guess. I wonder who started that, anyhow, Wyatt riding in with Doc Holliday and wearing a star? It's crazy."

He frowned, grinned, said, "Hell, it's all crazy. Let's go on up this street and see what's going to happen."

As he rode he thought of the two men. Wyatt Earp, cold, calculating, nerveless gunman. A man who sometimes avoided fights, but never through lack of courage. A man up to now always on the side of the law, and wearing a badge. Yet he had Doc Holliday with him, the cold killer who had been trained as a dentist and had turned outlaw and gambler and gunman extraordinary. The man who laughed and said he didn't mind having tuberculosis because it made him lean and hence harder to hit with a bullet. That man, with Wyatt Earp, the lawman.

54

Chalmers shook his head again. It looked to him as if Tombstone was going to be a hell-roaring mess of trouble for almost anyone who even looked at the raw, ugly little town that kept growing day by day as men, women, material, and supplies kept piling into the place. Even as they went up Allen Street a dozen new buildings were being started, and fifteen huge freighters were being unloaded at stores, saloons, and building jobs.

Chalmers rode beside the buggy and they passed four frame houses on their right, then came to the O.K. barns, on Allen Street, with the corral yard back on Fremont. They stopped about twenty feet from the barn-door and waited, cool and alert now.

Wyatt Earp and Doc Holliday sat their horses calmly, almost lazily. Doc grinned wolfishly as he dusted his coat sleeve and then left his hand hanging by his wide-open coat. The short-barreled shotgun showed plain. Wyatt Earp's face was expressionless as he combed his fingers through his mustache. Neither man spoke.

They faced three men, Marshal White, Deputy Sheriff Behan, who officiated for the Tucson sheriff's office, and a smiling, rather innocent-looking young fellow who was wearing a peace officer's star for the first time in his life: Billy Breakenridge.

"We don't want any trouble with you men," said Marshal White evenly. "Just don't make any trouble, Wyatt. I'm asking you that."

"I'm asking more than that," said Johnny Behan officiously. "I'm asking you two to give me your guns while you're in town, or leave!"

"Is that an order?" said Wyatt Earp evenly.

"It most surely is!" Behan spoke sharply now. "I mean it."

"It wouldn't be, now," said Earp quietly, "because I saw you leave Curly Bill and John Ringo, up there by the Oriental Saloon? You wouldn't be setting us up for them, would you?"

"Marshal White and I are trying to keep things in order here. Trying to prevent the shootings and killings that go on. It's a hard job. Don't make it harder, Earp. Obey the rule we've put in. Give up your guns."

Doc Holliday spoke sourly. "Oh hell, Wyatt, tell him to come and take 'em."

"All right, I will," agreed Wyatt Earp in an even voice. "If you want my guns, Johnny Behan, come and take them."

9

A THIN little smile sneaked across Sam Chalmers' face as he stared at the scene. He had placed snap judgment on the men before him in scant seconds and the verdict already was in. He knew beyond question just what was going to happen in a few seconds and he was not going to do anything to change it, for the moment at least.

He knew Johnny Behan was a fair enough peace officer, as far as politics and getting along with people were concerned. But when it came to a showdown fight, where in three or four seconds at the most a man had to kill or be killed, Chalmers did not think Behan could "cut the mustard." He looked at Billy Breakenridge and saw a smiling, friendly, and rather dapper young fellow and thought he would bear watching. Fred White, the first town marshal of Tombstone, was a fighting man to be reckoned with and proved it the way he stood and waited without moving.

Johnny Behan backed up one step and said, "Well," and Billy Breakenridge shrugged his shoulders. The thing was off and Breakenridge knew it. It was then that Sam Chalmers came into the picture, by speaking crisply and sharply.

"If you're collecting guns, Behan," said Chalmers, "there's three more of us right here for you to work on at the same time."

Doc Holliday flashed a wide grin at Chalmers and then turned his cold eyes back to Behan. Wyatt Earp chuckled once but did not look around. And Behan stuttered slightly as he started to speak: "I, well, you," and he stopped.

Then he tried it again. "I'll expect you men to be at my office in an hour's time," he said. "You've got to leave your guns with me. And if I can find Curly Bill and Ringo, I'll disarm them too."

"How about the rest of the town?" asked Chalmers, waving his hand toward a half-dozen men who were standing across the street. All of them were armed.

"It's only the troublemakers we're disarming," said Behan stiffly. "Come on, Billy," and he turned and walked away.

Fred White shrugged and grinned. "So, he leaves me facing you five men. And you know what I'm going to do, Wyatt. I'm asking you and the others not to make trouble in town. If you do, I'll have to take a hand."

He nodded, wheeled crisply, and walked up the street toward the corner where the Oriental and Crystal Palace saloons stood. And he did not hurry.

"I'd class him as a good man and a fighter," said Sam Chalmers quietly. He stepped down from his horse and met Earp's stare with an even glance. "My name is Sam Chalmers. I'm a cattleman and I been laying down the law to Curly Bill and John Ringo. I followed 'em up here from Charleston, to throw it in their teeth again. I know who you gentlemen are, and I heard the outlaws mention your names." He spoke crisply and shortly as he told what had happened in Charleston. "Now, gentlemen, my thought is that we can put up our horses and take a walk, together. Five of us. Two on each sidewalk, and one in the middle of the street." Chalmers grinned thinly. "I'll match you, Wyatt Earp, to see who walks alone in the middle of the street."

For a time the noted peace officer did not answer. His cold blue-gray eyes were fixed on Chalmers and it was impossible to tell what he was thinking. He looked at Doc Holliday then, and nodded. Holliday nodded. Earp put his hand in his pocket and took out a silver dollar.

"Heads," said Chalmers.

The coin spun and flashed in the low rays of the afternoon sun that was dropping toward the ragged crests of the Huachucas across the valley. It hit Earp's broad palm and stayed there.

"Let's put up the horses, Chalmers, it looks like you walk the middle of the street—this time." He smiled. "Man, you'll do to ride the river with."

Without speaking now, they led their saddlers into the barn and Brett drove the livery team in after them. Two silent hostlers came up and listened wordlessly to Chalmers' brief instructions about the horses.

"Walk them to cool them off, rub them down, and then grain them. Some hay too. We'll want our stuff early in the morning. These two gentlemen will give their own orders."

"What you said fits us," said Doc Holliday. "Except we ain't leaving early. We're here to stay."

The hostlers grunted and took the horses. Then Chalmers led the way to the door. All five of them were easing and loosening their guns in the holsters. Now they spread out in the wide doorway. Across the street the half-dozen loungers broke up suddenly. One of them looked up toward the Oriental Saloon and yelled.

"Hey, hey!" the man yelled. "Look out, boys, they're coming!"

Earp and Holliday laughed softly. Chalmers smiled rather thinly, and the two Negroes walked out with the others into the street without changing expression. Earp and Holliday walked straight across the street to the right-hand side, Chalmers paused briefly in the center to give them time to reach the sidewalk. On the left walk Brett and Harley waited, calm and cool. And the sun was low and dropping fast as they started up the street looking for Curly Bill and his men.

Not one of the five walking men, alert and wary, held a question in his mind about Curly Bill and his men. If trouble started there would be more than the outlaw leader and John Ringo alone involved. Curly Bill had gathered about him the toughest bunch of outlawed killers the West had ever known, men said. And if he was ready for a showdown it would be a fight. A fight to go down in the annals of a fighting country.

Like a great broom the five men walked slowly and steadily up the street. Before them men moved back: miners, craftsmen, teamsters, clerks, gamblers, bartenders off duty, and women of many kinds. Back, hurriedly now as the five grim and stern-faced men approached. The street and the sidewalks ahead of them cleared. At each open store or saloon quick glances were sent in to locate Curly Bill, John Ringo, or any man who showed signs of wanting a fight.

Earp and Holliday on one side. Brett and Harley on the other. Sam Chalmers in the middle of the street, a fair target for any man. So they walked slowly to the corner of Fourth Street. Across it with wary sidelong glances, up toward Fifth; clumping at times on the new wooden walks, passing under the freshly built awnings over them, Chalmers alone kicking dust in the street.

They neared Fifth Street now and a voice yelled a warning. They walked on grimly and slowly.

At the corner they heard the bang of a door and Chalmers crouched as he swung to the left, looking down Fifth Street. Two men were running. A third came out of the alley behind the Crystal Palace Saloon and snapped two quick shots at Chalmers. And the crash of his shots seemed blended with a roll like thunder.

Brett and Harley leaped around the corner of the Crystal Palace onto Fifth, facing north, and their pistols were in their

58

hands as they came. Doc Holliday had his shotgun swinging in his hand as he ran to get clear of Chalmers, and Wyatt Earp threw four shots whistling past Chalmers' head. Then he too ran forward, half crouching as he came.

There were eight men scattering down the wide dusty place that was called Fifth Street. And a ninth man held a bunch of saddle horses at the corner of Fremont. It was too long a range now for pistols and Chalmers ran with the others, reloading as his booted feet clumped swiftly on. Now they were at the alley and the nine men were mounted, swinging their horses about and scattering.

The positions of the five men still were the same: Brett and Harley to the left, Holliday and Earp to the right, and Chalmers in the center. And so they stood now, flat-footed and shooting a deadly roll of shots at the nine riders, a banging and crashing of shots that echoed and rolled over half of Tombstone.

But it was over in ten short seconds. Harley said, "Damn them," and walked after them, thumbing shells into his gun and hoping for another shot. But the nine riders were leaving, fast, heading east out over the ridge and down into the big canyon that would lead them toward their main hide-out from trouble in the Chiricahua Mountains. And two of them were being held in their saddles by their friends as they left.

So the five stood for a short time, watching the Curly Bill men ride off into the growing dusk. Then, turning, they gathered slowly around Chalmers. They grinned at each other briefly and Chalmers said, "I'm buying."

Wyatt Earp nodded. "I think the Curly Bill crowd have a favorite saloon. What say we have our drinks in there?"

"Suits me," agreed Chalmers. "If we're shoveling it into their teeth, we might as well give 'em a whole damned mouthful."

So, coldly, quietly, the five men walked into the Oriental Saloon.

It was a dark and shadowy place with only two of the five big kerosene lamps lighted. There were five men at one end of the bar, six at the other, and Chalmers led the way to the center, squarely between the two groups.

"Whisky," he said flatly to one of the two bartenders. Like an echo the four others repeated the word. They tossed off their drinks, drank a second more slowly, and then—grinning coldly at the bartenders and the two groups at the end of the bar—Chalmers, Doc Holliday, Earp, Brett, and Harley walked out into a silent street.

Chalmers and his two men left Tombstone at dawn and reached Charleston an hour and a half later. They noted their heavy wagon beside the store—loaded. And they sent sly smiles at each other as they rode on to the livery stable. They had breakfast at the restaurant known as the Chinaman's and then went back to the stables. The two Negroes got the three spans of mules and harnessed them, led them to the wagon and hooked them in. Chalmers had ridden up to the store and called out Trinidad Chavez. He made no reference to the trouble of the day before, simply paid his bill and rode away after telling Brett and Harley to head for the ranch.

He rode slowly toward the Wiswold ranch, his mind turning over all that he had learned in Tombstone the night before. And it was plenty. The town was going to take a lot of taming, and he wondered if Behan and White were men enough to handle it. He doubted it. Earp was, if he got the backing he needed. But Behan had the backing of the politicians in Tucson, and Earp had nothing but his gun, his nerve, and the small gold star he wore.

It looked as if a rough session was coming, thought Chalmers as he rode through the flats, automatically keeping away from possible ambush from the mesquite and willow thickets. They were splitting Pima County and forming Cochise County with Tombstone as its county seat. And Johnny Behan, strong politically in Tucson and the territorial capitol at Prescott, was certain to be appointed sheriff until an election could be held. And somehow Chalmers did not think Behan was man enough to handle the job properly.

He had made a friend in Wyatt Earp, he was certain. Nothing had been said, but they had eaten together, and said a friendly farewell. Doc Holliday had even shaken hands with the two big, silent Negroes. Which was something for a Texan to do. Chalmers thought briefly, I can take care of my end of it. If they break out and rustle my cattle or horses, they'll learn that soon enough. And he thought on, making plans, dreaming of the empire of lush grama grass bottoms and rolling hills and high mountains.

He laughed, dreamed of Jean, and came up to her in the flats a half mile from the house where she was driving a small bunch of cattle toward a meadow in the bottoms.

"Milk stuff!" He chuckled as he rode up to her. "You're starting a dairy!"

She smiled at him. "Of course. There are women in these towns, and women have children and children drink milk. If

60

Dad doesn't get well it will be something we women can handle alone." Her voice, despite her smile, sounded tired and forlorn.

"Look, Jean," he broke out impetuously. "Marry me. Forget all this hard work. I can take care of you all. Your father can help me at the ranch——"

He saw her back stiffen as she turned away, driving the cows on toward the small river-bottom meadow. And he cursed himself for a fool again. He couldn't drive her and he had learned it before. Why couldn't he remember?

"My father brought up all of us to fend for ourselves," she said evenly. "You can't expect us to accept things we don't earn."

"I know, I know," he kept at her, riding up beside her and smiling now. "You will marry me, promise me that. When your father is better and can handle his own work."

"I——" Jean put out her hand pleadingly, and as he caught it he thought for a moment she was going to lean over and kiss him. When she swayed back he pulled lightly at her browned hand. She set her lips and jerked it away, yet in a moment the set expression faded and she smiled again. "Did you go to Tombstone, as I asked?"

"Yes," he said briefly, then could not let even a half lie exist between them. "But I bought my supplies at Charleston. They didn't want to sell me for fear of Curly Bill and his outlaws, but I insisted. And I rode on up to Tombstone afterwards." He told her briefly what had happened, knowing she would hear in the end.

Her expression was set as she turned in the saddle to face him. The cows were spreading now over the meadow. But neither looked at them, at the wide shallow sweep of river or the lovely blue of the sky. They were fighting a battle then, between two strong wills, and one of them in a nervous, highstrung girl.

"You didn't do as I asked," she said accusingly. "I asked you not to force trouble, and you wouldn't listen. How much can you really care for me if you won't even do a small thing for me? Now, before we are married. What will it be later—if we do marry?"

"But this is a fight. I can't let those men get the jump on me. I've got to teach them I mean business and that they must let me alone. It is the only way I can protect my cattle."

"I see," she said quietly. She didn't say it, but the impression was plain. She thought he valued his cattle above her love.

And he told her that, but she shook her head. "No, Mr.

Chalmers, I didn't say that." She turned now and rode toward the ranch house. He went along almost helplessly.

In an hour he was riding alone again, after the wagon. It was as though he had tossed feathers at a brick wall. And somehow he blamed Newman for it. The man had most certainly, probably by lying, put him in a bad light with the Wiswolds. He had talked briefly with Earp and Holliday about Bigelow Newman and they admitted to having known the man at Dodge, the trail's end. But nothing more.

He passed the slow-rolling wagon with a wave and rode on. There was much on his mind, many things and many tortuous angles to be worked over. He raised his head and shook it with an odd, almost animallike gesture. He was on his own range now and ahead, miles away in the dim southern reaches, was Mexico. Plenty of wild cattle to be bought down there, the grama grass would fatten them and he'd meet the beef contracts he was sure he could get.

The Southern Pacific was building toward Tucson and on to meet the westward-growing lines. A town would be formed and grow somewhere around the river where the railroad crossed it. Cattle could be shipped east and west. Dreams grew and expanded and rose sky-high, so that Chalmers almost shouted his joy as he rode up to the new, fortlike ranch house. If the outlaws had just learned their lesson and would let him and his stock alone!

But that too was a dream, for a week later Chico Gonzalez came in, reeling in the saddle with a bloody shirt. He coughed, slid out of the saddle into Chalmers' arms, and whispered, "*Dios, patrón,* they were too much for me," and then he fainted.

10

SAM CHALMERS eased the young, slightly built Mexican boy to the ground and knelt beside him. He examined the high shoulder wound quickly, his lips set and in stern lines, his eyes warm and kindly. He nodded once, felt Chico's pulse, and then came to life.

"Baldwin, get his feet; gently, damn you. Put him in my room. Tell a couple of those Mexican girls to watch him and I'll murder them if they don't take the best care of him. I'll bind that wound myself, and he's going to be all right. Hear me? He's going to be all right!"

They were carrying Chico, very gently, into the big corner room where Sam Chalmers slept and had his most cherished things. Two of the Mexican women, wives of the youngest among the half-dozen Mexican hands Chalmers had put to work, came in with hot water and clean cloth for bandages. In five minutes Chalmers had Chico well bandaged, lying in *el patrón's* bed, and with a half-dozen sympathetic dark brown faces peering in doors and windows.

Chalmers nodded to them with a quick smile that faded as he looked down at Chico's face. He said it again, grimly, as though it were an order to Destiny: "He's going to be all right."

It was characteristic that Chalmers' first thoughts had been for Chico. But now his mind was cleared. He grabbed his new Winchester rifle that he had been testing for the first time only the day before. He caught up two boxes of shells for it, two more for his pistols, and strode out into the hundred-foot-square patio of his ranch house. There was no one in sight.

He cursed them softly and headed for the wide gate, open now and facing the river bottoms. He called once, "Baldwin, damn you!" And strode on through the gate, swearing vengeance on his men for not being there when he needed them. He yelled again, "Baldwin!" And then he stopped in his tracks, set his rifle butt against the ground, and stared.

"What in hell is this, an army?" he demanded, but a pleased grin twitched briefly at his set lips.

Jack Baldwin was there and in a flat line away from him, each sitting his horse with a blanket roll and a sack of provisions behind his saddle, were the rest: Jeepers Jones, Brindle Nelson, Galloway, Curly Horton, Adams, Webster, Harley, Brett, Arsenio, Jayme, Ramiro, Felipe, Luis, Fermin, the last-named hurrying up to the line, his expression worried as he fought to drag a clean shirt over his head with his hat still on and lead Chalmers' horse at the same time.

"Somebody's got to stay——" Chalmers' words broke off.

A sleek black head had popped out of the window of Chalmers' room and an excited voice called, "*Patrón,* Chico, he is awake!"

Chalmers ran to the window and the sleek head popped out of sight. He stuck his head in and stared at the lean dark face on his own pillow. "How many, Chico, and where?"

A weak voice answered, "Five men. I had left the horse herd

—like you said—and gone toward—Mimbres—" and Chico's head rolled as his eyes closed.

But it was enough; beyond a willow thicket five miles away was a meadow where a bunch of calves, unbranded, were pastured with the cows and two new bulls. Chico had had orders early that morning to check on them. In a way, placing that herd of cattle with the unbranded calves had been a trap. Something to draw any of Curly Bill's rustlers, or any other deft-fingered artists with a running iron and a tendency to work other people's cattle. But the trap had backfired and Chico had suffered.

That stung Chalmers and made him harder than ever about rustlers and renegades. He had never dreamed they would be daring enough to work in daylight, or he would not have ordered Chico there alone. Sending him there had been only for a check, to see if the stock was safe, and if not which direction they had been driven in. And now Chico was in bed with a bad wound and his cattle had been raided.

Chalmers spoke crisply, yet with an instinctive regard for the feelings of his men. "Somebody's got to stay and take care of things here. That's damned important. Arsenio, Felipe, Jayme; you stay here with Webster and Horton. You boys all are levelheaded and careful. I can trust you. Watch this place, the women, and most of all—watch Chico! Take care of him and my things, men. I depend on you. Don't expect us back until you see us."

The men he had named dropped out of line, a little disgusted at missing the fight, but considerably pleased at Chalmers' open expression of his trust in them. Chalmers hit the saddle now with a slapping sound and spun his horse. Without a word he rode off at a trot, his wide-brimmed straw sombrero pushed far back on his forehead.

Chalmers rode with a hard mind and grim thoughts. So the outlaws wanted a showdown, did they? They would get it. His thoughts grew harder as he rode through the twenty-foot stream of water in the river bottom, his horse trotting fetlock-deep at the ford. The men splashed behind him, none speaking. They cut across the flats and into a gully that led west and up out of the bottoms.

In a quarter mile they swung up onto the wide sweep of valley that went west to the ragged, green-black line of the Huachucas. They passed a spring where a dozen small-leaved willows tossed their thin branches in a quickening wind. A thin stream trickled from the spring and fought its way about sixty feet out into the sand before giving up. A quarter mile from them now they saw the horse herd, bunched and grazing in small groups. Heads came up as they went past and the most nervous of the horses snorted and trotted away a few hundred yards.

They rode down into dry gullies that in the summer storms fed torrents of water into the San Pedro, and out across three miles of flats where the grama was belly-deep on much of the land. Some mesquite thickets were crowding the grass on a raw patch and then a ragged line of the growth spread before them, cutting off from their view what lay beyond.

They wove their way through the prickly, ragged growth, rounded a thicket of nopal, and there came onto the forty-acre spread of lush grass where the herd had been. They pulled up. Two calves were bawling forlornly from a gully to one side, and that was all.

"Spread out and see what sign you find," said Chalmers, his voice a little thin and high.

He went straight across the forty-acre patch, eyes on the ground and riding slowly. There were cattle signs, droppings, stretches of tracks cut deep into the soil and pushing the growth down, and cropped grama where they had fed. But no horse sign.

At the end of twenty minutes Brett's voice rose in a shrill, Indianlike yell. They closed in on him and he pointed down. "They came out here," he said, pointing to a sandy stretch at the bottom of a low swale. "Five horses and most of the cattle."

Nobody said anything. Chalmers sat his horse and stared due west to a raw sweep of land that led into a great canyon in the Huachucas. To the left and southward, the Huachucas ended and the rolling land that led into Mexico began. But around that way were trails and roads to Tubac and Tucson and northward, or south toward Guaymas. Or cattle could be driven along the foothills to the pass between the Huachucas and the Whetstones, the latter mountains a pale line to the north and west.

Chalmers rolled a smoke, lighted it, and then got down from his horse, puffing lightly as he walked to the nearest of the undisturbed tracks. He stared briefly, paced on, staring, bent and watchful. Now he straightened up and spoke around the cigarette, setting it dancing with his words.

"Harley, Baldwin, you two are the best trackers. Take a look here."

They got down and walked to him, careful to avoid stepping

on any sign. They stared, walked forward, eyes intent and scanning. Now Harley stopped and stared more intently at a set of hoofprints.

Harley straightened up then and glanced at Chalmers.

"You make it?" demanded Chalmers.

"Two riders went on with the herd sometime last night," said the big Negro. "There was three others and their tracks ain't four hours old. I figure the three stayed behind to take a few shots at whoever they saw."

"And they hit Chico. They'll pay for this," said Chalmers. He tossed his cigarette down on the sand, and with the caution of an outdoor man ground it deep to prevent fire. He walked back crisply and swung into the saddle, his men following him.

Now they rode at a jogging trot. It was nearly noon but they made no stop for food. The cattle had probably twelve hours start on them, the three riders about four hours. And the way was due west up the slow-rising swell of land that reached toward the Huachucas.

An hour and a half later they were riding through scattered oaks at the mouth of a wide canyon. To the north a great ragged pile of rocks rose, and sweeping back into the mountains, the canyon pitched upward like a great steep slide dotted and shot with conifers. On the crest of the high ridge was a bright green patch where aspen grew in moist land. Chalmers had seen it from a distance and often thought he would ride up there and see it. A good place for deer, he had thought. And now he was a few thousand feet below it and no time to ride up. For the trail was plain to see even for a man in the saddle and it swung north along the oak-studded foothills.

The Huachucas angled west and the hills were rolling before them like blankets in the wind as they rode on. They ate crackers, cheese, jerky, about three o'clock, not stopping for the meal. They smoked and drank lightly from their canteens and kept moving until they came to a creek feeding down a small canyon where there was lush green grass.

It was still three hours to sunset, but shadows crept down toward them from the high ridges. Chalmers gave the word to dismount, unsaddle, and graze the horses. Each man took care of his mount, wiping its sweated back with bunches of green grass, drying it well, and then picketing it in what to his own judgment seemed the best grass.

Their saddles were in a ring twenty yards across and each man lounged there, smoking, dozing, eyes opening to stare. And the ring meant no one could approach from any direction

66

without a man being faced that way to watch and see movement. Chalmers gave them three hours of rest and grazing for the horses, and then they rode on.

The sun had dropped and it was getting cold. They pulled blanket coats and canvas jackets about them, buttoning them tight about their throats—with their guns belted outside. The three vaqueros drew blankets over their shoulders like Indians and trotted along without protest. It was going to be a bitter night's ride, but they were certain the finish would be good— and warm.

Later they passed a long mile to the west of the camp that was to grow into Fort Huachuca, and heard the thin tones of the bugle spreading far across the land as taps was blown.

Four miles beyond the post Chalmers drew up his horse and waited for the men to cluster about him. "Even with some resting, this is about as far as that herd could be driven without a night's rest. So they're around here someplace. Spread out. Ride carefully, keep your eyes and your ears open. Locate that herd," he said flatly. And he paused briefly.

"Then come back here. We meet here in two hours. And I expect one of you to tell me where that herd is!" He stared bleakly at them in the darkness and went on. "Don't get seen or heard. Don't do any shooting. Just find that herd, come back here, and tell me where it is."

They met again near midnight in the dismal light of a half-moon. Nobody had found the herd. Chalmers grunted. He swore softly, and then spoke.

"Got to be here someplace. Maybe we've overridden their trail. Try it again, cut back toward the mountains. And be careful. We don't want them warned."

There was something very ominous and dire in his last words.

They scattered and met again about two in the morning, and that time Ramiro, a grinning vaquero of about thirty years in the saddle, came back with the news they wanted.

"In a canyon two miles back. The men are camped at the mouth of it. I know the place. It is a box canyon and we will have to kill those men to get to the cattle."

"Kill them?" said Chalmers. "What in hell else did you think we came for?"

Ramiro led the way now, after they had rested their horses for a short time. Two miles back he led them down into a low roll of land not a mile from where they had first passed. He spoke softly, telling Chalmers it was another mile to the first

67

scattering of oaks, then a quarter mile to the narrows where the rustlers were camped.

"Take us to the oaks and we'll tie our horses there." Then he changed his mind suddenly. An attack on foot would mean they could not chase any who fled mounted. "We'll wait there until an hour before dawn," he said grimly. "Then we ride in and give them what they gave Chico, with trimmings!"

11

AT THE first scattering of canyon oaks they drew up and spread out, each man picking a tree to lurk behind. They dismounted, eased latigos but left their saddles on and partly cinched. No smoking, no talking. Just the long dragging wait, silence broken when a man broke hardtack or crackers or gulped water from a canteen. Horses at times grew restless and pawed the ground, to be soothed by their owners.

It was the bitter, hard, usually dreaded wait before action, the time when even brave men could not control their thoughts. Bitterness would crowd in and hard memories or stinging ones would follow it. Men would see the death of others in their minds; bodies huddled in dusty creek beds, streets, or face down in the sawdust of a saloon floor. Oddly limp. Dead. Or perhaps hanging from a corral gate, or a tree; swinging, twisting, swinging. The rustler's ending. And even a brave man would wonder, then: Was it all worthwhile?

Yet it had to be done. A man can't sit back and take the easy path. Perhaps that was the way to get there the quickest —but what did you have when you got there if you dropped your self-respect on the way?

Sam Chalmers pulled his thoughts out of the mire of death that lay ahead of him and thought of Jean. He had seen her three times after that hard moment of good-by after the Charleston affair. She had not even mentioned that again, nor had she mentioned her sister or Newman. She had been sweet to him, smiling softly when he caught her eyes, and he was sure she loved him. But Henry Wiswold still was far from a well man and Chalmers knew restraint when he was forced into it. He had to wait. And in the meantime Newman was in the family and could put what construction he pleased on the cattle-buying episode back there in New Mexico.

Chalmers' lips were a thin line as he thought of it. But not a smile. It was too far back in the past now for smiling at his trick. It had worked. It had turned a small stake into a big one, the start of his dreamed-of cattle empire. He had not tricked anyone but a man who would not make good on his own notes. And he had not tricked that man either. He had forced him to make good on his notes, that was all. And even now, knowing what it might mean to his chances with Jean Wiswold, Chalmers felt he would do the same thing again under the given circumstances.

He stirred restlessly. It was a long wait. But it was almost over. He heard a cow bawling up the canyon, and another answering it. Somewhere below them a mule brayed sourly and unhappily. Silence followed that until a big owl rushed past on whirring wings and ten seconds later a thump sounded. It was followed by the frenzied scream of a dying rabbit, strangely like a frightened woman's scream. Then silence again.

Chalmers stood up and snapped his fingers once. Every head came up instantly, and without words all tightened the latigos on their saddles and mounted.

"Spread out and ride in," Chalmers said softly as they grouped about him. "Then do your own fighting."

He rode in the center and his men spread out to the right and the left. He rode past oaks and around big spreading sycamores and as the first hint of gray came into the sky he drew both pistols, took his reins in his teeth, and looked to the right and the left. He raised his right hand and then touched heels to his horse. Trotting, galloping then, they drove on.

Ahead in a quickening moment they saw the dim glow of some coals as a man crouched and kicked them to life with his boot heel. The crouching man had sticks in his hand to throw on the coals and then the blasting lead hit him. He rolled over, screamed once, and kicked himself clear of the fire.

The camp came to life in a splash of lancing flames from rifles and pistols. Someone was cursing slowly, angrily, another screamed his hate and fired rapidly. A horse bawled excitedly and then raced off alone.

Chalmers felt the wicked, deadly bucking of his two guns as he came in closer and closer. First one, then the other fired with what aim he could take in the dim light. He heard the dull hammering of other guns, heard sometimes the whistle of lead, or the thud as bullets hit trees or rocks. A crashing, crescendo whine came at times: one of the vaqueros called a crazed oath in Spanish and reeled out of his saddle.

Jeepers Jones was down, flat on his stomach but still shooting. His horse had rolled under him and died with a broken neck from a stumble over an unseen log. Beyond him Jones could see Brindle Nelson riding in closer, his carbine at his shoulder and sending shot after shot at dim figures ducking and running from tree to rock as they backed off from the steady approach of Chalmers and his men.

Galloway's horse suddenly began to pitch in a frenzy of pain from a bullet wound. It pitched, drove forward in great lunging bucks, and carried Galloway helplessly into closer contact with the rustlers. He rammed his rifle into the boot and whipped up a heavy old Remington pistol that he loved like a woman. Its banging roar sounded twice and then his horse fell with him. He rolled, twisted around, and found shelter behind the horse's dead body. And the old Remington began to pound again.

Only two men were shooting at Chalmers and his riders now. And then, in the slowly growing light, a man broke out of the trees mounted on a swiftly running horse. Low in the saddle, riding like an Indian on the attack, he came straight for Chalmers. Not shooting at first, the rustler came on, urging his horse to greater efforts. It leaped rocks, small brush, and then, when about forty feet from Chalmers, the rider fired once and again. Chalmers shot once, spinning as the horse and man passed him, and fired again.

Swearing softly, Chalmers spun his saddler and leaned forward for a race after the fleeing rustler. Not one of them was going to get away alive, if he could prevent it. He spurred his horse, and then suddenly drew the reins taut, sending it into a gravel-throwing slide. For the rustler's horse had plunged forward, dying on its feet. The rider was catapulted against a tree and lay there, limp and motionless.

Chalmers hit the ground and dropped his reins. He ran to the limp rider and stared briefly. It looked as if the fellow was alive, and he wheeled to grab the rope from the man's saddle. A dozen quick twists and he had the unconscious rustler looped and tied to a tree by his own lariat. Chalmers tested the knots and the tightness of the loops, and then ran back to his own horse.

More light was growing now as Chalmers rode back into the fight. He passed Jones, who was running and swearing softly at being left behind. Then Ramiro, curled on the ground, holding a shattered leg and showing his teeth in a long grimace of pain as Chalmers went by. He passed Wes Adams, on his face and motionless, and grim curses rolled from Chalmers' lips in a soft flow. Somebody was going to pay, and hard, for the death of a good man.

By the time Chalmers was through the narrows the fighting was over. A last flat crack had sounded, and then silence. Somewhere deep in the canyon some cattle bellowed. And that was all. Chalmers gathered his men and looked over the dead rustlers. Four of them, hard fellows they seemed even in death. His lips were a thin line as he gave orders.

"Put their bodies on horses and bring them with you. I think we've got a live one down among the trees. Bring a horse for Jeepers Jones. Then—Brindle, what the hell?"

Brindle Nelson had started to slide slowly out of his saddle. He hit the ground in a heap and rolled over on his back. He spoke, slowly. "Sorry, boss, but I took one in the ribs." And then he fainted.

Chalmers dropped to the ground and tore open Nelson's shirt. It was a nasty-looking wound but not necessarily a fatal one.

"Get him bandaged and make him as comfortable as you can. Fix up Ramiro's leg, too, then come down to where I've got that fellow tied up."

Chalmers rode back then. Jones had found the man at the tree and was staring at him coldly. He was alive and fully conscious by the time Chalmers got there. He was a young fellow, about nineteen, clean-looking and trim. His reddish hair and pale eyes gave him a very boyish look, and his lips, which trembled slightly, were parted in what seemed to be plain fear. He shifted his eyes and saw the men coming down with five led horses, four of which held bodies tied across the saddles. He licked his lips and turned to Chalmers, automatically selecting him as the leader.

"What are you going to do to me?" he asked.

"Hang you to that tree," was the blunt answer.

"You—can't do that," the young fellow almost shouted.

"I can and I will," was the grim retort. "I gave you outlaws fair warning. You wouldn't take it. You shot one of my riders, you stole my cattle, and you've wounded two of my men and killed another. D'you think I'm going to let you fools get away with this?"

"I, I," and quick tears broke into the fellow's eyes. He blinked, rapidly. "Damn you, damn you." He choked. "It's a rotten way to die."

Suddenly rage flared. He struggled against his bonds, shout-

71

ing, "Give me a gun, damn you! Let me die like a man. Don't hang me!"

Chalmers made no answer. He simply reached into his pocket and drew out a notebook and pencil. "If you want to write anybody, I'll loosen your right hand."

The young rustler's head sagged suddenly. His voice broke a little as he said, "All right," and then it stiffened. "I'm not blabbing, I'm not crying, I just can't see any sense to this, Chalmers. You're tough and hard and you're taking an eye for an eye. But what good does it do, anyhow? Hanging me, I mean? I'm nobody. Just a damned fool who thought I could get some easy money and then go somewhere and start a small outfit of my own. A horse outfit. I love horses and I want to raise them. That's why I did it. So what good does it do to hang me and then let the big fellows go their way? Hang them!"

"I'll get to them sometime, don't worry about that." Chalmers had freed the young rustler's right hand. "Here, write your note and I'll mail it for you—but I'm going to read it, I warn you. So don't lie in it. Don't say we hung you for nothing."

"Someday"—the young rustler looked up at Chalmers bitterly—"someday somebody will break you, Chalmers. Your toughness can't win always. Somebody will take something away from you. Something you can't get back! They'll find your weak spot and make you suffer for it!"

Chalmers leaned forward, his fists clenched. "D'you mean Newman? Is he the big man, the higher-up, that you want me to get? Is he the one who's going to hurt me by finding my weak spot?"

The young rustler did not answer.

"Damn you, answer me!" Chalmers shouted, holding his balled fists as though about to hammer at the rustler's lowered face.

Slowly the young rustler raised his face and looked squarely into Chalmers' eyes. "You go to hell," he said roughly, and then he lowered his eyes and began to write.

Chalmers stepped back and stood there, his hands on his hips. He watched the young fellow writing slowly and even from where he was he could read the heading of the note, "Dear Ma: I'm going on a trip . . ."

Nobody said anything as the young fellow filled two pages with scrawled words. There were tears rolling down his cheeks as he finished.

Chalmers' face was set into taut lines that seemed etched

72

into the flesh. A young fellow, trying to get a start, rustling cattle, now he was going to hang him and other folks would suffer for it. Chalmers thought grimly that there wasn't a hell of a lot of difference in people and their desires. It was mostly how they went about making their dreams come true. His mind went back to his own stunt of buying the Newman notes. He had gambled and won: he might well have lost and have been killed by Newman and his men for his trouble.

Chalmers reached down and took the note, and then read it slowly to himself. It read:

DEAR MA:

I'm going on a trip into the mountains to try to make a stake. If I make it, I'll get that horse outfit started before long. If I don't make it, I won't get back, for the Apaches are thick in this country. And if I don't get back, here's my love for all of you. Tell Dad I'm not mad any longer about that whipping that made me run away. I deserved it. He's a fine man and I'm proud to be his son. I hope I'll get back, but if I don't, good-by to all of you. And I love you, Ma.

PETE

Chalmers looked down swiftly at the young fellow, hoping to catch a sly upward glance that would tell him the rustler was working on his sympathies. But the young fellow's head was lowered, his shoulders heaving a little.

Chalmers drew a deep breath. This was something he hated, but he had made his plans and he was going through with them. He had to teach the outlaws and the rustlers that anything belonging to Sam Chalmers was untouchable, and he spoke harshly now.

"This tree will do."

"You want me to get your rope, boss?" asked Jeepers.

"No. This is my job."

Chalmers got his rope from his saddle and walked to the young rustler, who still half lay against the tree trunk where he was bound. Chalmers stood there, his expression stiff and hard as he looped the end of the rope and began the thirteen wraps about it to make the hangman's knot. He was not going to use the honda end of his rope, for he wanted the thing to be as merciful as possible. And the hangman's knot, placed properly under the left ear, with sufficient drop would snap the neck.

Chalmers finished the knot and looped the noose about the

73

young rustler's neck. The young fellow was beyond struggling or speech now. His head rolled as though on a socket, though his pale eyes were open and pleading.

"Tie his hands and feet and untie the rope around the tree. That's good. Bring the highest horse, and we'll stand him in the saddle. I want that drop to end it, sharp!"

Galloway and Jones changed the bonds of the rustler while Fermin and Luis, the two vaqueros who were unwounded, brought a tall horse from among the clustered saddlers. Chalmers threw the honda end of the rope over a branch of the tree and caught it as it came down. He said flatly, "Now, put him on the horse, standing. If he can't stand I'll tighten the rope."

As they started to lift the rustler to the back of the horse a voice came through the trees from about a hundred yards away. It was crisp, commanding, and it called, "Hold it, there!"

12

CHALMERS and his men lowered the young rustler to the ground and he rolled away on his face. Chalmers stooped and turned him face up, then straightened.

Jeepers Jones flashed a quick look at Chalmers and then winked at Jack Baldwin. Both had the same thought: Chalmers was pleased. Then he turned and watched the file of men coming through the trees; a smiling young lieutenant, a gray-haired sergeant, and two corporals with thirty troopers trailing him. The lieutenant stopped his men with a quick toss of his gauntleted hand. He smiled, quickly.

"At your service, Mr. Chalmers, what's the trouble?"

"We've had a fight with a bunch of cattle rustlers. This man here is the only one left alive and we're hanging him, as a lesson to the others."

"Sorry, sir." The young lieutenant was polite but firm. "We have our orders from headquarters about these things. Colonel Wayne sent this detail out when the sound of shooting carried to the post. He said to break up the fight, whatever it was, and to bring you all into the post. D'you mind?"

"I'd planned to go there with my wounded men," said Chalmers. "And then take the dead into Charleston. The post is on my way." He started to add something about the wounded men, and did not. He turned instead to Jack Baldwin. "Gather the cattle up there and bring them along, Jack."

He looked questioningly at the young lieutenant and the officer nodded. Chalmers said, "I don't know about my wounded riding," and stopped.

"We'll leave a corporal and four men with them, and order an ambulance out from the post to bring them in," said the lieutenant.

"Thank you," said Chalmers, rather stiffly. He looked at the young rustler and then stopped to take off his rope, crisply pulling through on the hangman's noose and then coiling the rope. He did not speak aloud, but his mental thought was a relieved Thank God, yet he was grimly determined not to show the softness.

In ten minutes they were on their way to the post with the recovered herd bellowing and grumbling behind them. And an hour after their arrival at the post they were on their way to Charleston with the four dead rustlers. But the young prisoner was in the post guardhouse.

About an hour's ride from the post Chalmers drew up. "Jack; you, Brett, Harley, come with me. You others take the cattle back and put them on that same meadow. We'll be in sometime tonight."

He waved to the others, rode on with his three men and the four dead rustlers on their horses. He slanted across the rolling land toward the river, a green line in the distance. They reached Charleston about noon and drew up their horses in front of the store, under the eyes of most of the town loafers. A bartender came into the doorway of the saloon where Curly Bill and his men had been and he stood staring at the four dead men, his fat lips pursed into a soundless whistle.

Chavez and Laskey came to the door and started to turn back when they saw who it was. But Chalmers called to them. "Come out here, I want somebody to identify these men, and see they're buried properly."

Chavez growled something under his breath but came out with Laskey. The two men stared, shrugged; "I've seen them around," was all Chalmers could get from either one. And not a man in the town would admit to knowing who they were or if they had any relatives.

Chalmers grinned and there was nothing pleasant in it. "All right," he said. "Now, I want some men to bury these fellows. And I want crosses put on their graves. I'll pay for it all, of

75

course. Put on the crosses, UNKNOWN. KILLED RUSTLING SAM CHALMERS' CATTLE."

Two beery-looking men stepped forward and one said, "What's the pay for the job?"

"Five dollars to each of you, and another five for whoever makes the crosses and paints them."

"It's a deal," said one of the men. He gathered the lead ropes of the four horses that carried the dead rustlers and grinned up at Chalmers. "Brother, you're hard, mean, and a damned good advertiser. Do you think this is goin' to work?"

"I hope so," said Chalmers, and he spoke as though he meant it. "Who's going to make those crosses?"

A Mexican stepped out of the gathering crowd and touched his wide sombrero. "Me, senor, I am Segundo, and I do things like that."

Chalmers drew some gold pieces out of his pocket and tossed one to the Mexican, two more to the gravediggers. Then he said, "Let's eat," and he turned his horse toward the Chinaman's.

Before going in, each man loosened the cinch and eased the saddle. Chalmers ordered his meal the others took "the same." They waited in silence, ate in silence, and then Chalmers paid the bill. Outside, Chalmers stood by his horse for a long moment, carrying on his chain of thoughts. He was staring across the street at the Curly Bill hangout and then his eyes shifted to the ridge where the mines and the town of Tombstone lay. A curious light flickered, glowed, died in his eyes. He spoke softly: "I wonder, now?"

Many things had moved in and out of his mind while he had ridden that morning. Connections with things in the past, guesses at the future, and a man. A man who was determined enough to make even Curly Bill and John Ringo take orders at least some of the time.

Now there was a drumming sound as a fast-stepping team came over the newly built bridge on the Tombstone road. Chalmers and the others shifted their stares to watch the top of the cutbank where the road came up. In a moment they saw a light buggy drawn by a familiar team, with Newman and his wife in it. It swung past the town and headed south toward the Wiswold ranch.

"We'll let the horses rest for three hours, and grain them. We'll rest ourselves. Then we'll go home." Chalmers looked around quickly, saw no one was near, and asked, "Jack. How would you like to go to Tombstone with me sometime—and let me punch you right square in the nose?"

"What in hell do you mean?"

"I'll explain later," was all the answer he got.

It was three in the afternoon when they neared the Wiswold ranch and Newman's buggy was there, the team unhooked and tied under a tree with some meadow hay thrown down for them. Chalmers led the way toward the ranch house and grinned once at Baldwin. "Let me do the talking," he said softly. "And then see if you can guess why I'm going to punch you in the nose, in Tombstone."

Jack Baldwin swore softly and stared first at Chalmers and then at Brett and Harley. The two big Negroes shrugged expressively. They could not guess any more than Baldwin could.

Sam Chalmers had been doing a lot of thinking about Newman and his wife, the bright young actress known as Clytie Collins, and named for her mother. Somehow things were beginning to tie in. And it hurt him. He was convinced that Henry Wiswold was a fine man, and certainly his wife Clytie was an admirable woman who could play her part very well in the rough life of the frontier. But they could be fooled, anybody could.

He worked back mentally through the few weeks that he had known the Wiswolds, checking over the little they had told him of themselves and their past. Texas ranch folks heading west for new lands about summed it up. They had not known Newman prior to meeting him in Tombstone when they had learned of his recent marriage to their daughter Clytie. Newman probably had fooled them about himself, just as he had fooled a lot of other people.

By the time they reached the newly finished adobe ranch house Chalmers had found his pattern and was willing to stand or fall on it. But he had no intention of falling, then or later. He was tired, fagged almost to exhaustion, as were his men and his horses. But no one could have guessed it from his manner or movements as he stepped down from his horse and called, "Hello, the house!"

Jean heard him first and ran out almost into his arms. "You're safe!" she cried out, and then flushed prettily. "I—we heard you had ridden after rustlers."

Chalmers caught her hand and held it for a moment, smiling at her and not speaking. By that time Henry Wiswold and his wife were in the doorway, coming out, followed by Newman and Clytie. Henry Wiswold was a tired-looking man, but he was gaining strength more rapidly now, and his smile was hearty. When greetings had been passed they were called into the big main room of the house, all of them. But the two Negroes excused themselves and made their manners, saying they must take care of the horses.

No one spoke as Chalmers rapidly outlined what had happened, his voice a little thin and high with his smoldering rage at the wounding of his men and Wes Adams' death. And he finished with, "But I think I've taught them a lesson. And if I haven't, I've got men coming who will. Harry Wayne and his men. The trail driver. He's going to stay here with that crew of ten fighting men as long as I need him and them. They'll gun-whip any fools, Indian, white, or Mexican, who fool with my stuff. I'll teach that bunch of wild men that fooling with me means get out or get killed. I mean that."

And Sam Chalmers was staring straight into Newman's mocking eyes as he said it. Newman did not answer him, but Jean took it up swiftly.

"Killing," she said slowly, "always killing. Does it have to be that way?"

"Mad dogs. You've got to kill them. There's no cure for mad dogs." Chalmers spoke bleakly, half afraid of what it might mean to his chances of marrying Jean, but still blunt and determined.

"Six men dead. Two in the canyon fight, four in the Huachucas. Six men, to prove your point!"

"Six men, among the fifty or more killed already in this hell-camp and its surrounding country. Six mad dogs the world is better off without."

"You could take them in for the law to deal with," suggested Mrs. Wiswold slowly, and her keen eyes shifted from Chalmers to Newman. "There is a law, isn't there, even here?"

"Of a sort," said Chalmers stiffly, and he closed his lips, making it plain he was through on that topic. He turned to Wiswold and asked bluntly. "How many cattle have you lost, Henry?"

"Not one that I know of," said Wiswold. "I guess I'm too small for them to bother with. And I'm glad of it. I'm in no shape to fight now. I'll be riding and taking over the range work in another month or so, but I don't want to fight unless I have to."

"Nobody else does, that's human," snapped Chalmers. "But I'm not so sure you're being a small outfit is any reason for your not losing stuff." His eyes shifted to Newman. "Lots of other small outfits are raided, aren't they, Newman? Isn't Colonel Henry Hooker with his army riders and gunmen the only other man you know who hasn't lost stock?"

Newman answered crisply. "That's right as far as I know," and then he grinned again at Chalmers. He seemed to be enjoying his moment, as though he knew Chalmers' thoughts. As though he knew Chalmers was putting it all together: Curly Bill's refusal to make trouble in the Sulphur Springs Valley meeting when he had learned Wiswold's name, as the most pointed fact. And the other things he was certain Chalmers must have learned on his several trips to Tombstone recently.

"It is a rough country, an outlaw's paradise," Newman went on. "I've had to hire men to guard the lumber we're getting in for the new theater. Hard men, killers. Sime Canby for one. He's going to tend bar when we get the theater built. And my dealers will be Faro Johnson and that tough brother of his, Harry-Joe. They all three are sitting around my site and the lumber piles with guns in their laps, ready for trouble. If I have any trouble with any man," Newman smiled at Chalmers, "I plan to use those men as my bodyguards."

"You expecting trouble with anyone?" said Chalmers, easing in his stiff, handmade chair.

"No," came the flat answer. And then, bewilderingly, Newman took a quick slant away from the topic. "Have you heard we're going to have a church? A young minister has come in and is holding services right now. But he wants a new church, wants a fine brick building at least, he says. His name is Endicott Peabody. He's a fine fellow too. Why don't you and Jean have him marry you, Chalmers?"

Jean flushed swiftly, "Why, Bigelow ... !" and then she stopped.

Sam Chalmers felt a dull flush grow and spread over his tanned face. A blaze of rage almost carried him out of his chair at the thought of Newman breaking into things like that. He drew a deep breath and tried to smile but he was sure it was a miserable failure. The man was smooth, he was going to have it that Jean would marry Chalmers and so block off any revenge on Chalmers' part if he learned the truth about him. And he would always hold the point over Chalmers, or aimed at him like a gun: he had helped him win his bride.

Chalmers smiled now and there was a full hint of menace in his eyes alone as he looked at Newman and spoke. "Perhaps you'd better let Jean decide for herself, Newman. I've tried forcing the issue and it doesn't work. She's a strong-willed

79

little mustang," and he smiled at her. "Or rather a thorough-bred that just won't be forced into driving in double harness. So I just keep hanging around and hoping."

"Jean dear," her mother started to speak, but the girl had jumped to her feet.

"Give me a moment, alone," she almost whispered, and then hurried to the point of running out the front door.

Mrs. Wiswold and Henry got up, then, on the plea they must start supper. "You and your men will stay, I'm sure. Spend the night here and rest. Jack, you talk your boss into that, will you?"

"I don't reckon he's going to need much talking, ma'am," grinned Jack Baldwin. And he rolled a smoke with a slow grin twisting his hard face as he watched Chalmers now. "We're all downright tired."

Chalmers turned to Newman and ignored Clytie, Jean's sister. His voice was just a little harsh as he spoke in a low voice. "Newman, I don't welcome interference in any of my affairs—not even to win Jean. Please understand that, will you?" It was more of a command than a question.

Newman smiled politely. "I hope you won't let it interfere with our friendship, Sam? I'd hate to have trouble with my brother-in-law."

"I can give you my word, Newman," said Chalmers flatly. "Being your brother-in-law won't change things between us, not a damned bit."

And then Chalmers turned and walked out the front door. Half an hour later he was back with his arm around Jean's plump shoulders. Both were smiling, but Newman noted one thing—Chalmers' arm was around Jean's shoulders, but she was not leaning against him. She was stiff and rigidly erect, though smiling. Newman thought briefly: Hard to handle, a troublemaker for a stubborn man like Chalmers, they'll fight like hell! And he smiled.

"When?" demanded Clytie. "Oh, Jean dear, when?" She was as eager as a child over her sister's coming marriage and she almost danced her way to her. "When? What color of flowers are you going to have, and will you wear Grandma's old wedding gown, the one Mother was married in also? I've only one regret about marrying Bigelow—I didn't have time to send for that gown."

Jean laughed, drew out of Chalmers' arm, and caught her sister in a great hug. "Two months. Just two months, to let me get used to the idea of having this bear of a man around, and

80

let Dad get really well. Then, yes, I'll wear mother's and Grandma's old gown. With roses, pink roses, and maybe some Cecile Brunners mixed in, I saw them growing on that house the mine superintendent built last fall. The yellow ones, not the pink. Pink and yellow roses."

"Two months," Sam Chalmers almost groaned.

"It's not long—in a lifetime," Jean threw at him over her shoulder. And she ran from her sister into the kitchen to throw herself into her mother's arms. There, hugged and held tight against her mother, she suddenly began to cry. "I'm afraid," she whispered. "I love him, but I'm afraid."

Newman clapped a broad hand on Chalmers' shoulder and shook him lightly. "Fine, fine! Two months. We'll have our new theater built by then. You can be married by the Rev. Endicott Peabody, and we'll throw a party to christen the new theater as the Bird Cage, and to celebrate your wedding at the same time. A party that Tombstone will remember for a long, long time!"

13

SAM CHALMERS buried those two months in work. He tried to forget that Wes Adams had been buried at the army post, that the young rustler had been allowed to escape from the Tombstone jail by some strange quirk that never was explained. His wounded men got well, and worked hard with the others. Harry Wayne, lean, grizzled and rough-looking, brought in three thousand head of mixed range stuff, and looked the place over with quick, pleased grins. He and his men went to Tombstone after their long hard journey and put on a wild drinking and brawling show that waked up even the jaded spirits of the hard men who lived in the place. Wayne and his men made it known they were there to work for Sam Chalmers and for one reason alone—war.

War if anybody wanted it, and to the death.

But nobody did, it seemed. Chalmers did not lose even one calf to free-meat hunters in those two months. Near the end of them he went south with Jack Baldwin and eight riders. They came back with two thousand head of scrubby Mexican outlaw stuff bought at five pesos a head. About a dollar and a quarter, gold, at that time. Mean stuff with murderous dispositions, a man dared not dismount anywhere near them or they would charge instantly. A rider was safe, though, unless a wild one went on the prod for some fool reason. Then it took an alert man and an agile horse to evade the deadly, murderous horns that reached out ahead of lunging rushes, to gut either or both.

The steers would fatten, though, the calves grow, and the lean, half-mad cows would breed to good bulls and bring more beef stuff into the world to fatten on the lush grama grass. Chalmers sold a thousand head to the different posts in the surrounding territory, for army use, and for the Indian reservations. He paid off part of his loan to the Texas banker, and promptly borrowed more for another trip to Mexico! This time he sent Wayne and the ten Texas fighting men, for there were rumors of bandit raids in retaliation for some of Curly Bill's numerous forays and murders across the border. And it was too close to his wedding for Sam Chalmers to make the trip. It had been Wayne's idea; it was getting too tiresome sitting around waiting for trouble. And if he could find it across the border and bring back some feeder stuff at the same time—why not?

Tombstone was a roaring hell-town by now. Thousands of men and women and children roamed the streets and the surrounding country, where not much more than a year past it had been dangerous ground for the lone prospector who had found the hill of silver instead of his tombstone. Houses, business blocks of frame, brick, and adobe, some one-story, some two, had blocked out the town with startling rapidity. Wagons and pack teams still hammered into the place with supplies. Stages departed now for all the big and little towns and camps in the various localities where men, cattlemen or miners, thought they saw fortune to be had for the asking. And death strutted the streets by day or night. No man knew when his time might come, for little reason or none at all. Even the innocent bystanders got killed by mistake and buried in the ever-spreading rows on the crest of the knob known as Boot Hill.

There in Boot Hill, if the dead could see, a man might lie in peace and stare across the sweep of Walnut Canyon, over the mesquite flats and across the wide swales and gullies to the old stronghold of the dreaded Cochise, the Dragoon Mountains. And the haunting rocky ridge where the great ragged cleft rocks made the Sheep's Head.

At times sheriff's posses raced out in pursuit of stage robbers and bandits, usually without result. It grew so bad in those short days that the smelters cast their silver in ingots weighing over two hundred pounds, too much for a man to carry away on horseback. Outlaws by the dozens came in, strutted around spending the money in saloons and gambling houses that were never closed. And when they had spent their money they simply rode out into the open country and disappeared for a time.

It would be then that the word would come in, perhaps carried by a bloody man riding bareback on a stage team horse. "Benson stage robbed. Shotgun guard and two passengers killed. Where the hell is Johnny Behan, the sheriff?" An hour, perhaps two hours or more, later a grim-faced posse would hammer out of town watched by half-amused people standing under the awnings of the store buildings on Allen Street. Hell, they never caught anybody anyhow—why make the ride?

Then the amused watchers would turn and go into the Alhambra, the Oriental, the Crystal Palace, for a drink. Or into the Grand Hotel, or Nellie Cashman's, or the half-dozen other places where townsmen and visitors lived. It was a rough, wild, and busy place that midday when Sam Chalmers drove up the wide stretch of Allen Street in a fine-topped Brewster buggy he had ordered especially from Tucson. He had bought from Colonel Henry Hooker a team of the best trotters in that part of Arizona, and the harness was trimmed with silver. There was a fringe on the buggy top, lemon-yellow to match the wheels, and there was a red snapper on the whip which Chalmers held in his right hand, slanting across the rising and falling rumps of the team. He turned into the livery barn where he had first met Wyatt Earp and Doc Holliday, and his four men came in with him, riding the best horses the ranch could afford.

"Take good care of this team," ordered Chalmers. "And wash the buggy. Not a spot on it, mind, when I order it up tomorrow, for Mr. and Mrs. Sam Chalmers!"

He grinned and tossed the hostler a five-dollar gold piece. He took his big carpetbag and snapped open his thick gold hunting-case watch. "You got three hours to the wedding time," he said, and snapped the case shut again. "Stay as sober as you can. Jack, I'll see you later," and he winked broadly at Jack Baldwin.

Baldwin rubbed his jaw and winked back. He, Brindle Nelson, Galloway, and Joe Webster had been chosen to come with the boss man for his wedding. Steady men, and older than the others, to be trusted as were all his men. They watched Chalmers walk across Allen Street and turned toward Tough Nut. He was heading for Nellie Cashman's new two-story hotel, and walking proudly. They grinned.

"Strutting like a Mexican gamecock, and why not?" was their verdict, and then they headed for a drink.

Nellie Cashman was a beautiful woman and, if her eyes and proud mouth were signs, far superior to the running of a rough, brawling mining camp hotel. But run it she did, and in a way to make her words respected and her commands obeyed.

"Room is waiting, Sam," Nellie said in her sweet voice. "The front corner, to the right. You can look straight out toward your ranch, and Mexico, from there. But draw that east-window curtain if you want to sleep late."

Chalmers chuckled and walked on up the stairs. He went into the big room with its nicely curtained windows, and stood there smiling. He drew a deep breath. Sam Chalmers and his bride were going to occupy that room. It jarred him, somehow, and left him breathing heavily and blushing like a boy stealing his first kiss. He put his bag down, stared once at his image in the big plate-glass mirror set over the walnut chest of drawers, and nodded.

He was dressed to kill. That was the word for it. A new, finely tailored frock coat, gray pants over well-polished half boots, a black silk tie, and a white shirt of finest linen. But the hat did it. No longer was he wearing that battered, high-crowned straw sombrero that had made him known as Sam Chalmers. He was wearing a new Stetson, pure white, with a high crown and a wide brim. And he was proud of it. He had one thought, a bleak one as he stood there staring at himself in the mirror: My gun shows. I'll have to take it off in church.

Then he walked out and down the stairs, out into the street.

Chalmers walked to the corner of Allen Street and looked back. A team drawing a light farm wagon had just pulled up in front of Nellie Cashman's. Henry Wiswold was driving and as the team drew up, Clytie Wiswold helped her daughter Jean from the wagon. Henry tied the team and lifted out three handbags. Then he turned and followed the women into the hotel.

Chalmers blushed again, like a boy. He walked around the town nervously, in and out of the saloons, hotels, gambling places. He refused a dozen drinks and accepted fifty congratulatory remarks, shyly. He saw men he knew and liked, Colonel Hooker, Jeff Milton, Gage, Safford, Vail, Slaughter, old Pete Kitchen—cattlemen and mining men whose names were to go down in history with his own. He saw other men he knew and did not like. Curly Bill, John Ringo, Zwing Hunt, Bill Grounds, Billy Claiborne, Buckskin Frank Leslie, Frank Stilwell, the Clantons and the McLowery crowd. The men who were giving the newly formed Cochise County its hard name, the Bloody County. The county that held more wanted men, more killers, more toughs, than any county the West had known.

And Sam Chalmers walked on, nervously. He walked out Fourth Street past the Safford Street corner and down a slope to a little flat. He sat there alone on a rock. He stared out toward the Dragoons and the Sheep's Head and he grinned foolishly.

It was three-thirty when Sam Chalmers stood before the Rev. Endicott Peabody, waiting for his bride. Jack Baldwin lurched once, standing beside him, and got a swift jab in the ribs that many saw. But who was going to fret about a man who lurched from drink, in Tombstone? Not the crowd that packed St. Paul's Church and waited as they stared.

The small organ rolled and pealed and the voices of two women rose in a song that was to ring in Sam Chalmers' ears for a long time. And then he saw Jean. A smiling, demure face lowered under a great veil that reached to the ground and rested on the long train of her grandmother's wedding gown. Her father walked with her, proudly, as he led her forward to stand close to Sam Chalmers.

The Rev. Endicott Peabody had a fine voice and the rolling words reached even outside into the street. "Do you, Samuel?" and "Do you, Jean?" and the ring was found safely after a little fumbling and more words flowed until the last few rolled heavily. "Until death do you part," and so they were married.

There was much laughter and shouting and rolling of carriages toward the new Bird Cage Theater then. The whole town seemed to be celebrating. Bigelow Newman ran out into the street and fired a pistol, six evenly spaced shots. It was a signal for the mine whistles to start a roaring blast from each metal throat. Up the street a hastily organized "Miners' Band" started a wild racket that they called an "Irishman's Wedding March," horns blew, drums banged and rolled. The carriage with Sam Chalmers and his bride rolled up the street, turned into Allen Street, and men shouted and fired series of pistol shots into the air. Somebody let go with a huge ten-gauge English duck gun, and a dozen horses bolted in the block-long parade behind Chalmers and his bride.

So they reached the new Bird Cage Theater in an uproar

that was not to calm down for several hours more. Drinks and music and then a great wedding supper kept them all busy until at least eight that night, and then, as dessert was finished and the crowd broke up into groups, the music started on the balcony for dancing.

Sam Chalmers, alone with his bride, circled the floor once to the wild shouting and handclapping of the several hundred people jammed in the place, and then general dancing started. Chalmers led Jean back to her mother and whispered, "Take her away now, Mother Wiswold. I'll follow you in an hour, or less."

Jean flushed heavily and almost ran with her mother to a rear door, unnoticed by most.

Chalmers walked restlessly about, laughing and joking with friends and acquaintances. He killed half an hour, glanced at his watch, and swore softly. He killed another fifteen minutes by going up front to the bar and watching the fun there, but refusing drink after drink. And then Jack Baldwin, lurching and laughing foolishly, made his way to Chalmers' side. In his hand he had a big water tumbler full of whisky.

"Come on, Sam, drink this. You're going to need it, fella!" And swaying a little, Jack Baldwin shoved the glass at Chalmers.

"Stop it, you drunken fool," Chalmers snapped out angrily, his hands clenching at his side.

"Come on, Sam, drink it!" Baldwin brought all eyes on him now. "Drink it, or by God I'll pour it down your throat!"

He made a sudden rush at Chalmers and threw the full tumbler of whisky at his face. Chalmers cursed him, stepped forward, and hit a sudden one-two of punches that sent Jack Baldwin back against the bar, and then in a heap on the floor. He lay there briefly, shaking his head. Then, slowly, his hand went fumbling for his gun.

Chalmers made a quick jump for him and knocked the gun away, two men closed in, and there was a short flurry of blows. Then Chalmers backed off. He was conscious of a curious numb feeling around his right eye but had no recollection of having been hit. He stared grimly at Baldwin and his voice was thick and rough as he said, "You drunken swine."

Baldwin staggered and fought against the two men holding him. "Damn you, damn you," he flared out. "I'm sick of your high and mighty ways. I've stood it as long as I will. Give me my time, Chalmers; get yourself another boy!"

White-lipped, Chalmers pulled a wallet out of his pocket

and peeled off three bills. He shoved his hand deep into his pants pocket and pulled out two double eagles. "There's your pay," he said angrily. "And don't let me see your drunken face again."

"To hell with you," said Jack Baldwin drunkenly. "You got eyes, you'll see me again!"

Chalmers brushed through the crowd angrily and turned down Sixth to Tough Nut and on down to the hotel. The flesh around his right eye felt oddly tight, but the crowd gathered in front of the hotel took his mind from that and the reek of whisky on his wedding suit. The Miners' Band was there, and a hundred men and women were crowded about. Yells greeted him, cheers, whistles, shouts, and the band began to play. As he stormed through the crowd he knew what it meant —a charivari, corrupted into shivaree, was starting. And when would it end? The rough wit and humors of that wild Western crowd could easily carry it on all night, he thought with wry bitterness. He strode through the lobby to meet mingled grins and startled gazes.

At the door of the room on the corner he paused and knocked once, sharply. "It's me—Sam."

A shy voice answered, "Come in, dear," and he walked into the room, shutting and locking the door behind him. Jean stood against the far wall, looking almost frightened. Suddenly her eyes widened in a stare and her lips parted. "Oh, Sam! Coming to me on our wedding night, like that!"

He stared at her amazedly, then shifted to look at himself in the mirror. His right eye had turned an ugly black and was swelling fast from a blow someone had thrown at him in the struggle with Baldwin. And he reeked with whisky, already staining his fine white linen shirt and frock coat.

He laughed shortly and said, "But, dear, it was——" and he took a quick step toward his bride, holding out his arms. She crowded back against the wall and her lips formed frightened words, "Go away, go away."

14

SAM CHALMERS dropped his eager arms and stepped back three paces. He drew a deep breath and fought his eagerness, striving for the calm control that he knew he must have now.

Outside the wild uproar of the shivaree grew more and more frenzied as the tumult and the crowd increased. Pots and pans banged and crashed, pistol shots rattled and roared against the walls that echoed them far and wide. The bandsmen, half drunk or wholly so, made a crazy racket that was almost ear-splitting. And Sam Chalmers stared at his frightened, angry bride and tried to be calm. He spoke at last, smiling and calm.

"I'm sorry, dear; I didn't realize. I had some trouble with Jack Baldwin, and in the row somebody hit me in the eye."

"But you're drunk, reeking with it!"

"No, I'm not. That was part of the row. Jack tried to force a drink on me and it spilled. Jean darling. Can't you understand?"

She shivered a little, put her hands to her ears, and moaned, "That noise is driving me mad. Will they never stop?"

He sighed a little. "It's part of the game, Jean. It's supposed to be funny. They'll keep it up as long as their strength holds out, or until I go down and buy them all some wine. I knew it was coming. I've arranged for it. There are two cases of champagne in the lobby and four cases of whisky. I'll go down and tell them about the stuff, move it out into the street, and then they'll go away soon."

"And you'll drink with them, and you'll fight again on your wedding night. Sam Chalmers, is there no limit to your brawling and killing? No limit to this madness that holds you, to subject everybody to your will and your wishes?"

"Jean, Jean." He shook his head sadly as the noise and tumult continued outside. "You're tired, nervous, keyed up so high that you need rest more than anything else. Calm down, darling; sit down, take it easy. I'll go down and talk to them. Perhaps I can get them to go, or at least be quiet."

His words were soothing, gentle, as he would talk to a frightened child or animal. He realized what was wrong with Jean, now. Nerves, pure nerves from the strain of the wedding and suddenly finding herself there alone with him. Shy, modest, and thoroughly upset by the many things that had happened, she was blaming him for it all. And he thought, quietly, I'm man enough to take it.

He smiled at her gently. Words were such futile and useless things at times. A man used them to express his thoughts when he could put them into words, and felt so damned helpless when they failed him. And they failed Chalmers now as he stared at his bride and saw her eyes widen again and her palms flatten against the wall where she stood. She seemed to be striving to force that wall to give way back of her, and so allow her to get farther away from him.

"Jean," he started to say, and then stopped. Strangely, almost frighteningly, the noise in the street died to grim silence.

They stood for a moment staring at each other; she wide-eyed and frightened, he worried at the sudden break in the wild shivaree. He wondered what had happened, and then he tried to calm them both with a quick thought spoken aloud.

"They've tired already, see, Jean?"

She said, "Yes," forlornly, he thought. And then words floated up to them both.

"Chalmers! Chalmers!" the shout came from the street below their windows.

"It's a trick," he said thickly. "They're trying to fool me."

"Chalmers, Chalmers!" The cry came again and closer, "Chalmers," it dimmed as a running man crashed through the hotel doors into the lobby. "Chalmers, Chalmers!" The words rose in sound now, as booted feet pounded up the stairs and along the hall, to a bellow at the door. "CHALMERS!"

It was Brindle Nelson's voice, shouting loudly in his excitement. He pounded on the door and almost hit Chalmers in the face with his fist as the latter jerked the door open. Nelson gasped for breath from his run and his shouting.

"Speak, damn you," said Chalmers. "And if this is part of the shivaree, I'll beat you half to death!"

"No, no," gasped Nelson; then, getting his breath, he went on more evenly. "A vaquero just rode in. Wounded. Said he was one of the Eliases' hands, who had come north with Wayne and the herd he bought. They were jumped by a big crowd, badly outnumbered. They've holed up in a canyon of the Mule Mountains, down near that new copper camp. Come on, boss! We got a horse saddled for you! The boys at the ranch have gone on ahead of us. Come on!"

Chalmers swore once, sharply. He spun in his tracks to a small table and grabbed his gun belt. "I——" And then he stopped. His expression froze. "Brindle, can't you boys handle this—it's my wedding night?"

"Go, go!" Jean ran at him, pushing and shoving. Forcing him toward the door, almost panting in her anger. "Go, save your cattle. That's all you think about anyhow. Your cattle. You'll kill and kill and kill, to protect your cattle. You'll drink and fight on your wedding night, and you'll ride away to save your stock. To make money, to get power. Is there no limit to what you will do, Sam Chalmers?"

89

She pushed and shoved and he tried to plead with her. People were coming into the hall and others were staring out of their doors. And in the end she had forced him into the hall, slammed the door behind him. He heard the lock drive home with a dull click.

He drew in a deep breath and spoke softly. "This is a hell of a wedding night." Then, belting on his gun as he walked rapidly toward the stairs, he went on grimly. "That's right, damn you. Stare. But the first man who laughs at me gets killed!"

He forced his way down the stairs, roughly, past some men who were coming up. He strode through the lobby, eyes straight ahead. In the crowded street outside he saw four saddled horses, one a rented horse and a saddle from the stables. Webster and Galloway were sitting their horses waiting, and Chalmers almost asked, "Where the hell is Jack Baldwin?" and then he remembered. He swung into the saddle and Nelson hit leather a scant second behind him. Then, spurring, all four men forced their horses through the silent crowd.

Chalmers made a straight line for his ranch, cutting well away from the road to Charleston, slanting across the foothills below the Brunckow claims, and hitting the flat land five miles south of Charleston. He spurred his horse then and galloped for two miles, his men crowded about him and as silent as he was. And suddenly a jarring memory came. As he had walked out of the door he remembered, now—Newman, grinning mockingly at him.

"By the holy, it's a trick, part of the shivaree!"

"But, boss," Nelson pleaded, "that Mex was shot up. He had blood all over his shirt and leather jacket. It took a couple of men to drag him off to the doc's office."

"A trick, a rotten, foul trick!" Chalmers groaned. "But I can't take a chance now. Maybe it isn't, maybe they *have* Wayne and the boys cornered. Come on, damn you, what are you stopping for?"

It was three in the morning when they rode up to the silent, dark ranch house. A yell brought sleepy faces and puzzled words. Nothing was wrong. No one had brought word of a fight in the Mule Mountains. They stared sleepily at their raging boss and shrugged, waved hands, went back to their beds and blankets.

Chalmers turned his horse for the ride back to Tombstone. He could hardly speak. A trick, part of the shivaree, and he had fallen for it so easily, so heavily. He could see Newman again, grinning mockingly at him as he strode out of the hotel.

His wedding night. Jean upstairs, crying and beating the pillows with her fists as her jangled nerves tore her to pieces mentally. And he cursed Bigelow Newman, heavily, slowly, as he rode back toward Tombstone.

It was broad daylight when Chalmers, alone, came to the door of the hotel. He walked in, went upstairs, and waited a moment. Then, hesitatingly, he knocked on the door. There was no answer and he knocked a little louder. Still no answer. He tried the knob and the door opened. He forced a smile but it was wasted. There was no one in the room to see it. Only his carpetbag, flung on the floor as he had left it. He looked about for a message and there was none.

Chalmers picked up his bag and walked heavily down the stairs. Perhaps there was a message at the desk, he thought. Nellie Cashman stood there now, shaking her pretty head. She spoke gently, sympathetically.

"It was a dirty trick, Sam."

"Yes," he said, and walked on out. He knew now there was no message for him. Jean had gone, presumably home with her family.

Chalmers rode the tired horse to the barns and got his fine buggy with the fast-stepping team. It was clean, washed, the high varnish gleaming. He knew people looked after him as he drove down the street, and laughed. But he knew also that none, or very few, would dare laugh where he could see them.

He stopped at the Chinaman's in Charleston and got breakfast. He drove on slowly to the Wiswold house and when he reached it he saw the light wagon in place at the barn. Wiswold was rubbing down a horse, and he looked up. He lowered his head as he saw Chalmers and jerked a thumb toward the house. It was plain that Henry Wiswold did not want any part of what was coming. And that seemed ominous.

As Chalmers stopped his team at the front of the ranch house Jean came to the door and stood there. Her back was stiff and her face seemed frozen into hard lines. She spoke jerkily, but rapidly, as though from an already prepared text.

"It's no use, Sam," she said. "You might just as well drive on to Benson alone and take the train for Washington. Go ahead, get your big beef contracts from the government. Raise your cattle to fill those contracts, make your fortune—and kill anybody who gets in your way. Drive them out of the way or kill them. Drive or kill. But you can't do that to me, Sam Chalmers. I won't stand for it. You've got to change, to soften, before I'll have anything more to do with you."

He tried to plead and protest, but it was useless. Jean stood stiff and firm and would not weaken. "Go alone," she said again. "Cattle, money, fighting; that's all you are interested in. I should have known that a man who would trick a fine gentleman the way you tricked Bigelow Newman would never make a good husband. A man who would drink and fight and chase away after another fight on his wedding night."

Chalmers spoke tiredly. "So, Newman told you. Did he tell you that my going away last night was a trick, part of the shivaree?"

She wheeled and went into the house, shutting the door.

Chalmers stood for a time, then climbed back into the buggy. He sat there, brooding and waiting and hoping. He smoked three cigarettes, one after the other, and waited for ten more long, lingering, sad minutes. She did not come out, nor was there any hint she might. At last the cold, almost numbing thought came: it was over, ended.

So Sam Chalmers kicked off the brake and drove away, turning the team and heading for Benson, to take the planned honeymoon trip alone.

15

IT WAS one of those clear and crisp days that southern Arizona can produce for the joy of mankind. The mountains were sharp and clear and the distant ones only faintly softened by the blue haze. High scudding white clouds shifted along in a sky so blue it hurt a man's eyes just to look at it and dream. And grim hard thoughts could not change the beauty of it all. Cattle country, to hell with the mining and all that mining brought with it, thought Sam Chalmers.

He let the team trot swiftly along with thin lines of dust boiling up behind the fast-turning, bright yellow wheels. He tapped once on the near horse with the bright red snapper of his whip, to chase off a big horsefly that threatened trouble with its beelike sting. And the off horse switched his tail, once.

The team swung into Charleston and Chalmers was turning them toward the Fairbanks and Benson road when he saw the other buggy. It too was clean and bright and the team a fast-stepping pair. There were two people in the buggy, with the top down, and they were Newman and his ugly, blotch-faced bartender and gunman, Sime Canby.

Sam Chalmers swung his team squarely across the road and waited for them to reach him.

Newman recognized war signs when he saw them and pulled up his team about twenty feet from Chalmers, swinging them so both he and Canby had clear shots at the other man. Then, wordless, he waited.

Chalmers held the team with his left hand and had put the whip in its socket the moment he recognized Newman. Now he sat quietly, his eyes locked on the other man for a long moment. Then he spoke. His voice was flat-sounding and brittle, slightly high-pitched and somehow very ominous.

"Newman, when I started to hang that young rustler over in the Huachucas, he told me some things. He said *he* didn't count. That there was a man higher up, above Curly Bill and the outlaws like him. He was right, there's always a man higher up. And I'm going to get that man someday, like the rustler told me to do. The man higher up who sends outlaws and killers out to do their dirty jobs. The man who sends young fellows on the wrong trail, to get killed or hung. He told me something else. That I was too hard, too confident of myself, or words like that. That someday somebody would find a way to hit me where it would hurt. And that's happened. I was hit where it hurt yesterday, last night, and today. And I think I know who framed the thing, and why. The same man who is the higher-up in the outlaw stuff here in the county. I'm going to get that man—either *now* or *later!*"

And having said that, Chalmers sat motionless, his right hand ready to go for his gun. It seemed there was nothing left ahead of him now but to kill Newman. And so he waited. There were two of them to get, and he knew it: Newman and Canby. But that made no difference in Chalmers' mind or intentions.

Newman studied the thing out from its several angles and did not hurry. He was a game man and a brave fighter and he had known what he was going into when he set himself up against Sam Chalmers. He faced it now and he wondered if killing Chalmers at that moment would satisfy him.

There was more to it than just killing him. There was the chance to hurt him, and hurt him badly, not once but several times. And then he could be killed after he had been hit and hurt to the extreme of suffering.

And Newman was sure he knew how to do it.

He smiled now and said quietly, "Sam, I'm sorry to see you

93

take a joke so hard. After all, it's the sort of rough horseplay you run into in a rough country."

"That's not all I'm talking about."

"It's all I'm talking about."

"So you won't fight?" Chalmers spoke thinly. And then he began to swear. He drew on each and every word in English and border Mexican that he knew, could guess at, or invent. And the inventions were good, crisp, tough-sounding, and mean. Galling, like the bite of ragged spurs rolling on a mare's flanks and making her squeal with pain. So he talked and labeled Newman for several long minutes. Newman sat and took it. Only Sime Canby stirred restlessly under the cursing, yet he made no move to interrupt the hot, even flow of words.

When it was over Newman smiled, though it was a thin and plainly forced smile. He said evenly, "Are you through?"

"If you won't fight, yes. But there's a last warning, Newman. I'm going East. When I come back if I find that any of my property, my cattle, or any of my men have been touched by outlaws and rustlers—it means war. I'll put on more gunmen and I'll start out to kill each and every man who had anything to do with it in any way. Get that, Newman, and get it straight. Now I'm driving on. Swing out a little to let me pass."

He turned the team back into the road and waited while Newman gave him half the road to pass. And then he drove on.

Newman and Canby turned and watched Chalmers go. Neither spoke for a time and then Canby said roughly, "I can take him. I can take him any time you want me to."

"He's dangerous, don't be too confident."

"Hell, Newman, nobody is really dangerous when their back is turned, is they?" Canby spat into the dust.

Benson was a raw ragged little place, mostly tents, and half-frame and tin houses, a few adobe stores, and some adobe hovels in the river bottoms. Larger homes were being built, and some Indians were farming a piece of land in the bend of the river, peaceful-looking and far from the murderous fighters they had been a few years back. The railroad was a raw line across the country, and in the dim eastern distance a column of black smoke showed where the westbound train was coming from its connections at El Paso.

And for the first time since starting, Chalmers wondered how he was going to get his rig back to the ranch. He stopped at the livery corrals, with a small barn in front of it, and gave curt orders about taking care of the team. Then, "Is there anybody here who might be going back to Charleston or Tombstone in the morning?" he asked the liveryman.

"Wyatt Earp's here. He said he was meeting his brothers, some coming in on the westbound, and Virgil and Morgan on the eastbound from Tucson at midnight."

"I'll see him," said Chalmers.

Wyatt Earp was in a grim mood when Chalmers found him with Doc Holliday in a tent saloon. He readily agreed to take the team and buggy back to Tombstone and see that some of the Chalmers men picked it up. It would save him getting two more horses or sending Virgil and Morgan in on the morning stage. And having settled that, he talked.

"Things are due to bust loose somehow," he said grimly. "That's why I sent for my brothers. The Clantons and the McLowery crowd are ganging up with Curly Bill and his outfit. And I'm in the middle. I can't get anywhere with Johnny Behan, and from what's happened, I don't want to. I'm standing alone, with only Marshal White to help me. I got him over to my side, but how long the outlaw crowd will let him live is something else."

He swallowed his drink glumly. "Hell, they've even gone the limit of trying to prove Doc Holliday, here, held up the Benson stage last week!"

Doc Holliday laughed. "I'm broke. I couldn't even buy a round of drinks today—so what did I do with the money if I robbed the stage?"

"I'm trying not to take sides," said Chalmers evenly. "But I'm against the outlaws. I'm neutral," he smiled suddenly. "Just neutral—I don't give a damn *who* whips the outlaws!"

They laughed and had another round of drinks, then stepped outside into the dusk that was dropping around the land. Chalmers said, softly for no one else to hear, "Watch Newman in this. I had a runaround with him in Charleston just before coming here today. I laid it down for him and he wouldn't fight. That means he's got big plans. He's not a coward."

"I am watching him," said Earp meaningly. "And last night I saw him buying drinks for Jack Baldwin."

Chalmers nodded. "I might have expected that." Then, "Are you fellows eating?"

"Not now. We'll wait for the train to come in."

So he left them.

It was five weeks before he saw them again, and then it was a meeting where all the signs pointed to sudden death for most

95

of them. It was at the O.K. corral, on Fremont Street across from the courthouse.

Chalmers had come in on the stage that day, fresh from his Eastern trip. In his pocket were beef contracts that in the next three years would mean a fortune to him. He had made arrangements, also, in Chicago and Kansas City, for huge shipments of beef by railroad. He was going to be a rich man, and he knew it. A letter at Benson had told him that no one had so much as dared touch one calf of his great herds now roaming the San Pedro Valley.

Yet he was not happy. He was tired, worn, and anything but in a good humor. He had got off the stage an hour before and gone straight to the O.K. barn to make arrangements to be driven to the home ranch. And almost at once he had felt the tension. A tension that grew steadily as he walked up the street to the restaurant and ate, then down and around the corner of Fourth, making his way to the old courthouse. By then and without being told, Chalmers knew trouble was building somewhere, somehow.

He paused briefly by the low, one-story hotel at the corner across from Schieffelin Hall and glanced about. Up Fremont Street he saw small groups of people staring down. And not at him. Beyond, on the down slant of Fourth Street, he saw others including some small boys. They too were staring and not at him. And he looked down Fourth toward the courthouse. Several groups of men were dotted here and there on the street and on the steps of the building. And some stood at windows, talking in low voices or staring about.

Then, "Sam Chalmers," a voice said from back of him.

There was so much tension about him that Chalmers wheeled and swept back his coat at the words. But he did not touch his gun. He did not recognize the man, but he seemed to be a gambler, more than a miner type. He spoke again. "Wyatt Earp is down there across from the courthouse. He said he wanted to see you before you left town."

"All right, and thanks," said Chalmers briefly, turning away. He was going to the courthouse to register some deeds, and it was not out of his way. Later, he was to add that small fact— what the man had said—to some others. But at the moment he walked on. He kept on the left side of Fremont Street, passed Fly's Photographic Studio, and came to the open space of the corral yard. Across it on the west side was the assay office, and young Fred Beaudezart was standing, staring out at some men in the corral yard. He had not been in Tombstone long, and he was greatly excited at what he was sure was going to occur before his eyes, and soon.

The O.K. corral and barn fronted on Allen Street, but reached clear through the block to Fremont. There were freight wagons and light farm wagons parked in the open space on Fremont Street and some horses stood by small piles of hay. It was here, in the O.K. corral, that some Western history was about to be written.

Later Sam Chalmers heard what had gone on before his arrival. Marshal White had been killed by Curly Bill in a tangle that involved Wyatt Earp also. And Marshal White said, before he died, that Curly Bill had not fired with intent to kill. That in the struggle the gun had been fired accidentally. And that death had brought about the appointment of Virgil Earp as town marshal. Naturally Virgil had Wyatt and his other brothers on his side in all things. And against him were Johnny Behan and the entire county crowd.

By his own testimony later, Johnny Behan, as sheriff, had failed to make any effort to stop what was now coming. In fact it was said by many that he had warned the Clanton-McLowery crowd that a fight was imminent with the Earps, and to be ready. So they had selected the O.K. corral for the battle. In defiance of the town law, they had armed themselves and now were waiting for the Earps to approach them. And that was the scene that Sam Chalmers walked into.

Trouble had been building for weeks between the Clanton-McLowery crowd and the Earps. There were versions from both sides that differed widely. But no one ever differed much in their opinion of what happened in the fleeting seconds of shooting that followed the appearance of Wyatt, Virgil, and Morgan Earp, with Doc Holliday and his hidden shotgun by their side. They faced, and grimly, Billy and Ike Clanton, brothers, Tom and Frank McLowery, also brothers, and young Billy Claiborne. Five against four and all heavily armed.

As Chalmers moved forward to speak to Earp from about twenty feet away he heard Virgil's voice rise in a harsh command.

"You men are under arrest," Virgil ordered. "Throw up your hands and drop your guns."

With his words, the thing exploded.

Frank McLowery, the best gunman in the crowd, drew instantly. So did Billy Clanton. There was a sudden explosion of gunfire from all of them, the Earps and the cowboy crowd as they were called. And in the midst of it Sam Chalmers felt his hat jerk. And the pull was from one side, not the front. And that meant somebody up the street near the Fly studio was shooting at him.

He wheeled swiftly, ducking as he did so, and pulled his gun. There were three people in front of the studio, all staring intently at the shooting in the corral. All but one man. A lean, dark-looking man with a long-barreled pistol, who fired and kept his left arm across his face as though to conceal it. The man shot again, evenly, and Chalmers half turned. That shot hit his left arm not six inches from his heart. He fired once, again.

And he knew at once he had missed. The dark man jumped into the studio and disappeared. Later, Chalmers learned, his attacker had gone crashing out a back window, taking the glass with him.

Chalmers heard a woman scream in back of him but did not turn.

Frank McLowery and Billy Clanton had opened their fight on Wyatt Earp, for he was the man they hated most. But Earp was hard to kill; he let three shots go through his clothes as he took steady aim and drove a bullet full into Frank's belly. Frank McLowery doubled up and staggered away, helpless and out of the fight for a time.

Billy Clanton fired again and missed and took a ball in his left arm which barely creased it. Things were happening right and left then, with Wyatt driving Tom McLowery out from behind a saddle horse, by shooting the horse. McLowery tried vainly to get the rifle from the saddle boot and missed it in his excitement as the horse raced away. He wheeled, drawing his pistol and driving a shot at Morgan Earp, and Morgan went backward with a bad neck and body wound.

Morgan staggered back against Wyatt and the latter moved him on gently. "Get behind me, Morg," he said, "while I get the son who shot you."

Ike Clanton, whose nerves had broken under the smash of the ghastly fighting, now ran into Wyatt as he tried to get away. "Don't kill me," he screamed, "I'm not fighting." And he grabbed at Wyatt's gun arm.

"Fight or get out!" Wyatt roared at him, shaking off the clutching hand. And that move gave Tom McLowery a chance to kill Wyatt Earp with his thoughts diverted.

Tom McLowery raised his pistol. But the chances of fate sent a bolting horse between him and Wyatt Earp. In that scant moment Doc Holliday saw what was happening and fired both barrels of his shotgun into Tom McLowery. The cowboy dropped his gun and ran, and Doc Holliday cursed heartily, thinking he had missed.

Chalmers watched, gun in hand, alert for any chance ambusher. He saw young Billy Clanton hit, hit again, and driven backward by the impact of bullets from the wounded Morgan and his brother Virgil. Morgan staggered around and fell, as did Billy Clanton. Frank McLowery, instead of dying as he should have from the belly shot, was staggering near by and trying to get back into the fight.

Shots came from a window in Fly's studio, where Billy Claiborne and Ike Clanton had disappeared. Both Morgan and Doc Holliday fired at the window but drew no answering shots. But as they turned away to shoot at others in the fight, two quick shots came. One touched Chalmers' hat, and the other whistled past his ear.

He dropped in a low crouch and emptied his gun at the window in Fly's studio. He heard the dull crash of the remaining glass. And then feet pounded behind him, and close. He half rolled around in time to hear an agonized cry of "Sam, Sam!" and he looked up to see Jean almost in his arms. Her face was wide-eyed, frightened, and her voice still agonized as she cried out, "Sam! Sam! They've killed you!"

"No, no!" He caught Jean and got his body in front of her to protect her. He saw Newman running up and heard the man shout, "Lie down, they're still shooting!" and he thought bleakly, This is some of your work, Newman. But he said nothing.

A hard voice called, "Got you now, damn you." It was near him and Chalmers jerked around, still trying to protect Jean. He saw Frank McLowery fight to stay erect with his gun on Doc Holliday.

"Think so?" said Doc Holliday, laughing and turning sideways to offer as little target as possible. Morgan Earp, on the ground, saw his friend's death coming, and he pulled on his remaining strength to raise his pistol and fire. All three shots roared at once. Morgan dropped down weakly, Doc Holliday cursed and winced as McLowery's shot creased his back. But Frank McLowery dropped to the ground with two fresh wounds, one in his head and one in his heart.

So the grim battle was over, with three peace officers wounded and only Wyatt Earp untouched; and three dead in the Clanton-McLowery crowd.

99

The whole street stirred then, it seemed, for people came out of stores and offices and buildings all about, and from behind whatever hiding place they had found for the battle that had lasted less than a minute. But Sam Chalmers was paying no attention now. His arm did not hurt, nothing mattered. He held Jean locked in his right arm and close to him, her lips raised to his, and nothing else mattered. She was his wife now, body and soul.

16

LIFE began again for Jean and Sam Chalmers there in the dusty, bloodstained street of Tombstone. Men were standing about staring at the dead and picking up and caring for the wounded. Voices rose, calmed, shouted words back and forth sounded, men talked rapidly and excitedly as they explained to newcomers just what they had seen and heard, and some even stood and acted out the shooting and killings. But Jean and Sam Chalmers saw only each other, for a time at least.

Newman left them standing there in the middle of the street and walked off. There was an odd, tight look about his expression. A thin smile twisted at his lips. His eyes were hard and cold as he walked past Fly's Photographic Studio and on. And then he stopped short. He stared briefly, and walked on.

Jack Baldwin was standing by the alley corner on Fourth Street between Fremont and Allen streets. His hands seemed to rest lazily on his hips but were dangerously close to his guns. He was facing a tall, dark man dressed in the semi-dandified clothes of a gambler and as Newman approached them he heard Baldwin say, "I still think you're the son who framed me in the saloon last night!"

"Look, Baldwin," said Harry-Joe, the ill-famed dealer who was slippery enough to frame his own mother, men said. "I don't deal in the Oriental Saloon, I work in the Bird Cage for Newman. You been so damned drunk since Chalmers knocked you down and paid you off that you don't know where you been or who robbed you!"

Baldwin spat, thickly. His eyes wavered a little and his mouth opened as though to speak. He stared down the alley for a moment, then brought his tired eyes back to Harry-Joe's face. He seemed completely unaware of Newman's presence in back of him. "Well, well, it's a hell of a note that a man can't find an honest game any more."

Newman made a faint signal and Harry-Joe nodded. The gambler then said, "Where do you get all this jack you been throwing around, Baldwin? Chalmers' pay ain't carrying you on forever."

"That's my business," was the angry, pugnacious retort from Baldwin. "And don't keep talking about that big-talking son, Chalmers. Someday I'm going to cut him down to size."

Newman laughed and called attention to his presence there. "A lot of people have said that, Baldwin, and Chalmers is still here. Didn't you see the fight in the street just now? Somebody tried to kill him in that fight. And missed. It's a damned poor ambusher who can't kill a man who's not even looking at him." Newman grinned thinly and his eyes shifted to Harry-Joe's lean dark face. He watched a dull flush come over the gambler's face and laughed shortly. "Oh well, there'll be another time. Chalmers can't live forever."

Baldwin scratched his head and grumbled under his breath. His mind went back, gropingly, to what the argument had started from. "Well, somebody robbed me. Framed the deal and robbed me. I'm almost out of drinking money." He rubbed his two-day beard and swore. "Got to find some more, somehow."

Newman laughed sourly. "There's always the Bisbee stage to hold up, or the payroll at Charleston, or something like that. A man could rustle a few cattle, too. Hell, it seems half the county is doing that now—why don't you get in on it too?"

"You go to hell," said Baldwin, and started away.

Harry-Joe started to speak but Newman rammed an elbow into his ribs and motioned to him to leave. Then Newman walked up beside Baldwin and said quietly, "I was trying you out, Jack. Now listen to me. Sober up. I'll give you a bottle to go to your room with, and you can taper off without trouble. When you're sober, go to Johnny Behan, the sheriff. He's looking for good gunmen as deputies. I'll put in a word for you—if you'll sober up, now!"

Baldwin looked at Newman in utter amazement. "Me, sober up?" he asked. "You damned fool!" And Jack Baldwin walked on with a half swagger and half stagger. But an hour later he was at the bar in the Bird Cage Theater asking for the bottle Newman had promised him to sober up on. He got it. His face became almost wolfish as he held the bottle and stared at Newman.

"Now, Newman," demanded Jack Baldwin, holding the bottle. "What do I have to do to earn this bottle and that job—kill Chalmers?"

"No, you crazy fool!" Newman laughed at him. "You've got to promise to let Chalmers alone. He's my brother-in-law now. Let him alone, I tell you. Sober up and try to be a decent man for a change. We can use them in this town and country. Promise?"

"Well, well." Baldwin reeled slightly as he stared from the bottle to Newman and back again. "All right, I'll go this far with you—I won't *start* a fight with Chalmers."

"That'll do," said Newman, and laughed. "Now, go sober up. I'll see Johnny Behan and get that job for you."

It was two days later when Jean and Sam Chalmers started for the big ranch house in the bright and shining Brewster buggy. It had been Jean's idea, sending a man to the ranch for the team and the buggy, while they stayed at Nellie Cashman's in the very room where they had had their serious quarrel the night after their wedding. But there had been no quarreling this time. Only happiness.

Chalmers' arm was still bandaged, but not causing him much trouble, as they walked down the stairs, said good-by to the smiling and lovely Nellie, and went out into the brilliant sunshine to the buggy. The team was restive in the grip of the tired-looking hostler. He said, "Good morning, folks. Or maybe it ain't such a good morning, Chalmers. Here's Jack Baldwin, wearing a star and coming straight at you, man!"

Chalmers dropped his carpetbag and stood, flipping open his coat so he could reach quickly for his gun. He had heard plenty of talk and been warned several times about Baldwin, and now he waited quietly, with a soft word to Jean.

"Steady, darling. I can handle him."

Jack Baldwin came up and stopped. He moistened his lips, paused, then spoke rapidly. "I'm sober," he said. "I'm not backing down on what I said about you, Chalmers. But I'm sober and I'm wearing a star. I'm with the Behan crowd now, the sheriff's crowd. You took sides with Earp. Or so people say. It's the wrong side. Maybe we'll meet, someday soon. I hope so and I think so. And now, good morning to you both."

Close to her husband's side now, Jean watched Baldwin raise his hat and walk on without looking back. She turned then and looked at Sam Chalmers. "Will it never end?" she asked slowly. "Never?"

"As far as I'm concerned, it's ended. If they let me alone I'll never draw gun again except to protect myself. Baldwin is wrong. I haven't taken sides with the Earps. They can fight their own battles with the sheriff's ring, and kill or get killed. I have nothing to do with it. I know which side I think is right. And I'm sure which side is working with the rustlers and outlaws. But as long as they let me alone I won't draw a gun."

Chalmers was looking at the hostler now. "You heard me say that, Bill. Tell 'em about it, will you?"

"Sure, sure, Sam. I'll tell 'em all." The hostler caught the gold piece Chalmers flipped him and held the bits of the restive team as Chalmers and his wife got into the buggy. He waited for Chalmers to gather the reins in his right hand and then stepped aside. He watched the buggy make the turn into Tough Nut Street and start down toward the Charleston road. He nodded. "The man meant it all right. Just shows what a pretty wife can do to a feller." He shook his head sadly. "Hell, if a man can't get drunk, put on a red shirt, and then go out and kill somebody, what's left in life, anyhow?"

"I wouldn't ask it if you hadn't spoken about it first." Jean leaned against Chalmers and touched his right hand lightly. "But it's a promise? You'll stop all this fighting and killing? You'll keep out of it, no matter what happens?"

"Unless they raid my cattle. Then——"

"Then," she broke in quickly, "you'll let the law take care of it!"

"All right, if the law can. I'll promise that." He felt her stiffen a little and guessed instantly what was coming. He waited almost sadly.

And it came. "That's it. It's just like you, Sam. I've come back to you without asking a promise. I love you. I'm going to be a good wife to you. And you won't promise me that one thing. You'll qualify it so you can break your word and do as you like!"

He sat for a moment thinking swiftly. They were going to stop at the Wiswold ranch for all her belongings. And he had the feeling that she would jump out of the buggy there and not come back to him. That his marriage was over after two days together, unless he gave her her way. He sighed.

"I promise," he said slowly. "I promise to keep out of it all, and if my cattle are raided or my men killed, I'll let the law take care of it."

"Sam, Sam darling." She was close to him and her pretty face uplifted to his. "I'll make it up to you!"

He smiled down, hiding his bleak thoughts. He knew it was a promise he could not keep. But he had made it and he would try. Let the law take care of it? he thought coldly. How could he tell her that to a big majority of the people in the newly formed Cochise County the sheriff's office was either working with the outlaw crowd or totally blind? Tell her that her brother-in-law was with them also? Chalmers knew that, but he could not prove it—yet.

Chalmers wondered what would happen when he could prove it. Wondered also what moves Newman would make when he heard of Chalmers' promise. Hell, it was like asking the rustlers to raid his stock! Telling them he would not follow them and kill or hang the whole thieving, murderous crew. Let the law handle it. Johnny Behan. He spat. Maybe he was wrong about Johnny Behan. Maybe someday the truth would come out. He hoped so but he doubted it.

They drove on to the big ranch house after getting Jean's belongings and there happy days turned into happier weeks. Spring came in a burst of life and color, summer, fall, with cattle fattening on the grama grass. Chalmers took Jean on a trip to Mexico for cattle buying. He bought five thousand head from Ramon Elias and was royally entertained at the big hacienda. They came home ahead of the cattle and found Wayne, now his foreman, had driven two thousand head of beef stuff north to Benson and the S. P. cattle cars waiting there.

Wayne came back with his men and rounded up five hundred head to be driven to the San Carlos reservation. The cattle left with the men and the men came back and the money stacked up in the bank at El Paso. Bisbee was booming now under the consolidation of the Douglas-Phelps, Dodge interests and the Copper Queen. Chalmers banked some money there and more in Tombstone. But he kept his El Paso connections, for he never knew when he might need a big loan for further expansion.

Strangely, as he often thought, his men and his cattle were let well alone. Losses were so small, if any, that they passed almost unnoticed. Wayne thought they had a few losses, probably to roaming Indians or prospectors who killed a calf or yearling for beef. It was not worth thinking about on a spread like the still expanding Chalmers outfit. And often, staring about, hearing the mad things that happened in Cochise County, Chalmers wondered. Thought almost sourly: They'll hit me yet. It can't last.

Then he would hold Jean close to him, smiling down at her and thinking he would enjoy it while he might. For somehow he knew that his hot-tempered, high-strung, and nervous wife would react instantly to any hint, even, that he was breaking his word to her. And for fear of being forced into something, Chalmers kept as far away from Tombstone and the troubles that were rising higher and higher there and in Cochise County as he possibly could. Yet he knew it could not last. He was too strong a character, too well known for them to let him alone.

And he was right, for not long after the New Year's holidays and drinking parties had subsided, George Parsons and John Clum, two of the outstanding citizens in Tombstone, came riding up to Chalmers' big ranch house to see him.

Jean was smiling yet white-lipped as she greeted the two well-known men from Tombstone, for she seemed to guess at once what it meant. Yet she said nothing, only smiled and walked away after the greetings were over. She stopped at the big door and looked back at them, standing solemnly in their dusty riding clothes and waiting, most obviously, for her to leave the room. Only then did she speak. "You will stay for supper and spend the night, of course." Then she shut the door behind her.

John Clum was a man whose courage and character showed in his face, and Parsons was a fit running mate for him. Clum had spent many years in the West, partly as an Indian agent, and more as editor and co-owner of the famous newspaper, the Tombstone *Epitaph*. He was a direct and forthright man, and came straight to the point.

"Chalmers, all hell is popping open. We've got the vigilantes organized as the Citizens' Safety Committee, and we need you!"

Chalmers almost groaned. But he covered it under the simple remark, "Go on, John," for he needed time to think.

Clum talked for a time and Parsons added more. Much of it Chalmers already knew from actually seeing it happen, hearing of it through word-of-mouth witnesses, or reading it in the *Epitaph*. But there were new things on the make now, and the causes were new also to Chalmers. Clum and Parsons cleared it up for him.

"It's Doc Holliday," said Clum angrily. "He's given the political ring the very lever they want, it seems. He and some of his pals robbed the Benson stage the other day. Or so everybody is saying and there seems to be some proof of it. Why in

105

hell Wyatt Earp has kept him around is more than I can see. It simply shows how a good man can get fooled."

"Doc saved his life one time and you know how Wyatt is. That makes him a friend for life, regardless of what he does. And Doc is a first-rate fighting man, and comes in mighty handy," said Chalmers.

"But a man in Earp's position can't have that kind of friends with things as they are now!" Parsons spoke sharply. "We're trying to clean up the outlaw element, and that is part of Earp's job. He can't monkey around with men who robbed stages. And have you heard what happened to Morgan Earp?"

"You mean Virgil's shooting, don't you?"

"No, I mean Morgan. He was ambushed and murdered last night while playing pool in Campbell and Hatch's poolroom. Shot twice, he only lived forty minutes."

"The murdering hounds," was Chalmers' comment in a grim voice. "Ambushing is no game for a white man!"

"And look where it leaves us and Wyatt Earp. Virgil wounded and left with a shattered arm that will cripple him for life. Morgan dead. The other Earp boys except Wyatt are not good fighting men. Earp has plenty of friends, including all our Citizens' Committee. But has he, have we, enough to whip that gang of outlaws when even the sheriff's office doesn't work very hard against them? Look, Chalmers." John Clum's voice was pleading and, at the same time, demanding. "We need you—now!"

Chalmers sat quiet, still. Parsons started to speak, but Clum motioned him to silence. Outside they all heard a young Mexican woman singing a soft, low song of love and fighting, the sort of folk song that the Mexicans sing so well. Love and death, two things that are so far apart yet so often intertwined. So they sat and listened while Sam Chalmers made up his mind. He got up once and walked the floor twice, stopped at a small window, and stared out.

Some of his men were breaking horses in the distant pole corral. A vaquero was breaking a beautiful horse to single-foot, for Jean. Jean, his wife. Love and death. Wyatt Earp, his brother murdered, now standing alone, they said, against the crowd. A man against a wolf pack. But Wyatt had friends, gunmen could be sworn in as peace officers. A new town marshal appointed, a stronger man than the one who had taken the disabled Virgil Earp's place. Chief of police, they called him now.

"It's not my job yet," said Chalmers flatly. "They're letting me alone, and that's all I ask. And I promised my wife I would keep out of it. There's two sides to this thing, somehow. I'm on the side of law and order, peace and quiet. But, gentlemen, my hands are tied. I promised my wife not to get mixed into the troubles and the politics of Cochise County. And that ends it. It's a promise I won't break."

Parsons and Clum stared at him for a long moment, and then Clum put it into words. "Coming from any man but you, that would be open to suspicion. But we know you too well, Sam Chalmers. You've got us stopped. But," and he grinned thinly, "how long do you expect them to leave you alone?"

Chalmers shrugged and did not answer. Parsons said slowly, "I'm putting one more thought in your head, Chalmers, without trying to explain what I've seen, and what others have seen too. Jack Baldwin, your old foreman, is a deputy sheriff now as you know. He's friendly with a lot of men he should be killing, or arresting, instead of gambling and drinking with —and Newman is one of them."

Chalmers still did not speak and Parsons took a long chance then. He went on evenly.

"Clytie Collins, Newman's wife, is doing her turn every night now at the Bird Cage. And every night, when her turn comes, Jack Baldwin is in the front right-hand box. Think that over."

Dull color flooded Chalmers' face. He took a quick step toward Parsons and then stopped. He spoke slowly, his voice a little high in pitch.

"You're a guest in my house, Parsons. But even as a guest, don't ever say that again about my wife's sister."

Parsons bowed stiltedly and said, "Sorry, I thought you ought to know." He looked away from Chalmers to Clum and wondered if Clum was thinking the same things he was thinking over. Jack Baldwin, a sworn enemy, playing up to Newman's wife and Jean's sister? How, he thought, could a smart man be that blind?

17

SAM CHALMERS and Jean were in Tombstone the day Wyatt Earp, Doc Holliday, and four others left the town for good. It was a grim sight. Something reminded Chalmers very strongly of his first meeting with Earp. Only this time, instead of being with them, he stood on the street corner and watched them leave. And his thoughts were hard as the granite reefs of the mountains, as bitter as water from the Amargosa springs. And for the first time in his life, perhaps the only time, Sam Chalmers felt real anger with Jean, his wife.

Crowds lined the streets of Tombstone that day. Some sick with rage, some mocking and ready to laugh, yet not daring. For Wyatt Earp had changed since his arrival in the town. He had been a calm, cool, forceful man without a nerve in his tall body, it seemed. But the ambushing of his two brothers had changed him. Virgil, crippled for life, had taken Morgan's body west, to Colton in California where the family lived. Only Warren of his brothers stood by him now. It seemed to Earp that the world had turned on him. And he wanted to kill. Wanted more than anything else in the world to kill the men who had murdered Morgan without giving him a chance. And he knew their names. He was a vengeance-ridden man now and it showed in his face as he rode down the street.

Warren Earp, Doc Holliday, Turkey Creek Johnson, Texas Jack Vermillion, and Sherman McMasters were the men who rode with him, and the men who suddenly lined up beside him as Sheriff Behan and a deputy stepped out to stop Wyatt Earp from leaving.

"I've got a warrant for you, Wyatt, you too, Doc, for the murder of Frank Stilwell in Tucson. I'll have to serve them. Get down and give me your guns."

Wyatt Earp stared at the sheriff for a moment and probably Johnny Behan was never any closer to sudden death. But thoughts surged up in the mind of Wyatt Earp. He and Doc Holliday had killed Frank Stilwell, but it was a long ways from murder, he believed. For Stilwell had been one of the men who had plotted the death of Morgan Earp. And there were others left—alive. Wyatt Earp wanted those others dead. And he was coldly, ragingly, determined to get them and kill them if he had to chase them to the very gates of Hades itself. A fight with Johnny Behan now might end that pursuit and Wyatt knew it.

"I'll not surrender to you, Johnny, for I know what it means. You'll disarm me and make me fair game for a murderous attack such as got Virgil and Morgan. No, to hell with you and your warrant. I'll surrender to Sheriff Bob Paul of Pima County, and no one else. Get out of my way, Johnny."

"This is a Pima County warrant," said Behan officiously. "I intend to serve it."

108

"Serve it and be damned to you, Johnny," answered Earp coldly, "but get the hell out of my way *now!*"

For a moment Sheriff Behan hesitated, and then stepped back. Wyatt Earp spoke sharply. "Come on, boys, but don't hurry. Anybody that wants to try to stop us is going to have plenty of time to try it!"

Slowly, steadily, unhurrying, the men rode down Allen Street to where it ended in a curling road that angled and twisted like a snake down a long hill. To their right as they went was Boot Hill, where new graves were dug almost daily. They disappeared, and not one man made a move to follow them.

"There," said a flat voice behind Chalmers, "there goes the last chance for real law and order in this town. At least until we have that election. Maybe then we can throw out Behan and get a real sheriff in here."

"Maybe," said another voice coldly, "and then maybe not. Behan has lots of friends in this county."

Chalmers turned slowly. The other voice, hard and mocking, not only was familiar but carried a plain threat in it. Chalmers turned and smiled. Straight into Curly Bill's mean eyes. He smiled for a brief moment and then his lips thinned a little as he said, "Bill, with Wyatt on the loose and looking for certain men, I wouldn't bet a 'dobe dollar that you'll live long enough to vote at our first election as a separate county!"

Curly Bill smiled and ran his tongue around his lips. He seemed easy and relaxed, like a man debating some small matter in his mind. Then he said quietly, "I'm still here, and we've run Wyatt Earp out of Tombstone!"

Chalmers laughed in his face, took Jean by the arm, and walked slowly toward the hotel. They were in town to buy supplies, and had come in the topped buggy with its flashing, bright yellow wheels. Chico Gonzalez, Harley, and Brett had come in the big wagon. Now the three Chalmers riders fell in behind their boss man and his wife and walked along slowly. Chalmers stopped at the door and said, "Are you going in? I think I'll take a walk."

"No. I'm not going in. I'm going with you wherever you go, Sam. I know what it means when you get that look on your face and want to take a walk. Sam, you made me a promise. The day you break it, I leave you. And if I leave you, it will be for good and all." She took his arm and said, "Now where do you want to walk?"

Chalmers smiled and walked back to Allen Street. He

109

walked slowly, looking at the many faces, some hard and cruel, others mean and rough, many pleasant and kindly. And it was in his mind that mankind can be fooled. Fooled and puzzled and misled. Sometimes forever.

And Sam Chalmers, smiling, sometimes bowing and raising his high white sombrero to greetings, wondered bleakly: "Have I been misled by my love for this girl on my arm?"

In front of the Bird Cage Theater, Jack Baldwin was just helping Clytie out of Newman's buggy. Newman stood in the doorway with an oddly puzzled look on his face. He stared down the fifty yards to the corner of Fifth and Allen streets where Chalmers was walking toward him. He saw him. Saw the three men strolling behind the ranchman.

He spoke, crisply. "Jack Baldwin. Get away from here. Chalmers is coming with his wife and three men."

Baldwin stiffened, then relaxed quickly. "All right," he said. He turned and strode up the street to the corner, crossed and started down the north side of Allen Street. At the corner of Fifth as he stopped by the doorway of the Oriental Saloon, Curly Bill and John Ringo came out of the saloon.

"Jack, Johnny Behan is looking for you. He's gathering a posse to ride after Wyatt Earp and his gang." Curly Bill laughed sharply. "There's quite a few of us going along too."

Jack Baldwin grinned at the two outlaws who were going to ride with a sheriff's posse after a rival peace officer, and walked on toward the sheriff's office.

Curly Bill's words carried across the street to them now as he raised his voice. "Hey, Newman, want to ride on the posse that's going out after Wyatt Earp?"

Newman said sharply, "No," and turned his back on the men across the street. He smiled suddenly, his eyes fixed on Chalmers as he said, "Aren't you lucky that you don't have to fight anymore, Sam? Did you know people were asking how it was that your cattle and Henry Wiswold's never were bothered by the rustlers?"

Chalmers took a quick step forward. It jerked his arm free from Jean's grasp. His voice thickened a little as he answered slowly, "I think we both know the answer to that one, Newman."

Chalmers heard a sharply indrawn breath that was like a gasp and turned his eyes quickly. It was not Jean, it was Clytie who had gasped. Newman's wife, and she was staring almost in fright at him, Chalmers. He thought instantly, Jack Baldwin has talked. And then he saw the slow smile rise and spread

110

across Clytie's face. She said evenly, "Why can't we all have dinner together tonight?"

Keeping his eyes fixed on Clytie's face, Chalmers answered slowly, "There's no reason in the world why we can't have dinner together—tonight." He put an odd emphasis on the last word and saw an instant reaction in her face. And then she smiled quickly, shortly.

It was about a month later that Wyatt Earp led his men up to the big door of the Chalmers ranch house. They were a tired, hard-bitten-looking crowd of gunmen, but there was a certain elation in their faces. Earp spoke, his voice flat and hard. "Can we bunk here tonight, Sam? We haven't been in a bed since we left Tombstone."

"Of course. Sleep here and eat with us. Supper is in two hours."

"But not in the house with you and Mrs. Chalmers." Earp spoke gently as he saw Jean coming out of the door. "Howdy, Mrs. Chalmers. We're pretty dirty, and I thought we'd better eat with the men."

"But you can clean up, can't you?" She smiled.

"I—I think we better eat with the men, ma'am." Earp spoke stiffly and did not take his eyes from Jean's pretty face. "You'll forgive me, please?"

"Of course," she said, and walked back into the house.

Earp jerked his head in a small signal as he turned toward the big barns and horse corrals at the foot of the long hill that crowded the San Pedro River to the west. Chalmers followed, and as they got out of ear range of the house windows, Earp said flatly, "Johnny Behan is after us with a posse of about twenty men. He swears he's going to run us down this time and serve that Pima County warrant on me. You know what it means, and you know what that damned posse is like when I tell you that the Citizens' Committee sent word that Bob Paul refused to ride with it. And he's the sheriff of Pima County!"

Chalmers swore. He looked once toward the house and his lips set. He was out of it because of a word given to Jean. Out of it. Could his being in the thing change it any? he wondered. He knew that for the time being at least law and order had ridden out of Tombstone with Wyatt Earp. And it was a cold thought that came to him; if Behan's posse caught Earp and his men, only death could end the deal.

He said slowly, "What have you been doing lately?"

Earp laughed. "We rode into a mess at some springs a couple

111

of days after we left. Iron Springs." He waved his hand to the north. "I got Curly Bill." He nodded briefly. "We went to the Dragoons and I got a couple of others that were mixed in Morgan's murder. There's a few more I want to get, and then I'm riding out of the county. I may or may not be back. If Bob Paul wants me to stand trial for killing Frank Stilwell, I will."

They put up their horses and then walked back to the bunkhouse. It was an hour before sundown and the air had a clear, crisp look, showing the distant hills and the Mule Mountains, with the long canyon leading up to the pass that overlooked the new copper camp at Bisbee. And as they paused briefly in the bunkhouse door, the light showed a compact group of horsemen riding toward the ranch and coming toward them at a long trot.

"It's Behan and the posse." Earp spoke grimly. "By the time we saddle and get going, they'll be here." He tightened his fists, loosened them, said almost sadly, "Sam, I'm damned sorry it has to happen here at your home. I know the promise you gave your wife——"

"Get in the bunkhouse, all of you," ordered Chalmers. "Let me handle this. Don't fight unless you have to. And if you fight, I'm with you."

He looked about. He made a half turn and looked toward the house. Jean was no place in sight, but Chico Gonzalez was flirting with a girl who leaned out of the kitchen window. "Chico. *Aquí, andale.*"

Chico came on the run, and listened alertly to his orders: "Go tell the men to gather around. Tell them they have seen nothing, or no one. I'll do the rest of the talking."

In five minutes, and before the posse had reached the river bottoms a mile away, Chalmers had a dozen men loafing about the bunkhouse walls, outside. Wayne was hunkered down near the door whittling a stick. Nelson, Galloway, and Horton were crouched in the door of the bunkhouse, throwing cold hands of poker and betting idly. A vaquero came out with a bucket of water in which were four coils of rawhide, soaking wet. He started to fashion the first knot of a new riata, and slowly began to work on it. A dead cigarette dangled from his mouth. Harley, Brett, and two other vaqueros were discussing the merits of saddle horses, and trying to decide if color made any difference in stamina. They agreed that it did but could not prove it.

Chalmers whistled a tuneless thing and walked toward the

112

kitchen door. Five men loafed there, quiet and at ease. But every man in sight had either one or two pistols belted around his waist. And then the posse, with Sheriff Behan and Jack Baldwin at its head, came over the crest of the small hill where the ranch house stood, and stopped.

"I'm looking for Wyatt Earp and his men," said Behan sharply. "Have you seen him?"

Chalmers stood and stared at the sheriff. And he did not answer. Behan flushed.

"Chalmers," he snapped. "I'm a sheriff with a posse, in the performance of my duty. I call on you to answer me. Have you seen Wyatt Earp and his men?"

"So that's a sheriff's posse, is it?" Chalmers snorted in derision. "Hell, Behan, you've got a gall riding after Earp with a gang like that. I bet there's warrants out for half that crowd you call a posse!"

Behan began to storm. "Chalmers, answer my question or I'll make you. Have you seen Wyatt Earp?"

"What do you want him for?"

"I have a warrant for his arrest, for murdering Frank Stilwell. And I intend to serve it!"

"The same warrant you mentioned about a month ago, on Allen Street. Why didn't you serve it then?"

"Nothing to do with this now!" Behan yelled angrily, his voice rising in an oath. "Chalmers, I don't want trouble here with you and your men. I know you promised your wife to keep out of things, and I respect that promise. But I demand that you answer me. Have you seen Wyatt Earp today?"

"A demand backed up by a posse that is half outlaws," snapped Chalmers. "To hell with you and any bunch of so-called lawmen like those fellows. If I had seen Wyatt today I wouldn't tell you. Now get off my ranch, Behan. Ride. Or you'll have the trouble you say you don't want with me!"

"Why, Sam." Jean's voice came from the kitchen window. "You know——"

He whirled on her, his voice rising in a cold command. "I know what I promised to you. Get back in that house!"

His voice was so hard and sharp that it seemed to brush her straight backward and out of sight. And seeing her disappear, Chalmers turned again to Behan. "Get going, Behan. Ride or fight."

Behan looked at the circle of Chalmers cowboys, all quiet, easy, waiting. He looked at the bunkhouse windows where he had almost certainly seen movement. The movement of waiting men inside there. Armed men. And he fought down his anger.

Slowly Johnny Behan relaxed. His lips were drawn in a thin line, and he spoke in a thick, angry voice. "I know where you stand now, Chalmers. It confirms what Newman and Jack Baldwin have told me. I know where you stand, and I'll remember it."

"Boss," came a hard voice from the doorway where three of Jack Baldwin's old riding mates stood. "Damn a man who turned on his old boss and his own outfit. Turning is bad enough, but talking is worse. Can I kill him, boss?"

"No shooting," ordered Chalmers flatly. "Behan, are you leaving?"

Behan did not answer. He turned his horse and rode away with his posse after him. Jack Baldwin turned and looked back once. He thumbed his nose and rode on. At the derisive gesture, Galloway got to his feet with a leap. "I'll kill that son if it's the last thing I do!"

"No, you won't, I'll handle Jack Baldwin in my own way. Remember that, all of you."

As Chalmers turned to go into the house, Earp's grim face showed in the window. He spoke harshly. "Sam, why didn't you tell Johnny Behan that there was an election coming? Tell him he was appointed by that crooked bunch of politicians, but the people were going to have a chance to put in a decent man next time? To elect you!"

"You're dreaming," snapped Chalmers. "I won't run."

"Ever hear the story of the boy that was drafted in the Civil War? He said, 'They can draft me but they can't make me fight.' And the sergeant said, 'Well, we can put you where the fighting is, and let you use your own judgment then!'" Wyatt grinned. "They're going to elect you sheriff, Sam, and let you use your own judgment!"

"Where did you get that fool notion, Wyatt?"

"From the Citizens' Committee, direct." And Wyatt Earp pulled his head back into the bunkhouse.

Chalmers turned and walked toward the kitchen. Jean met him at the door and her face was white as she said, "I heard that, Sam. If you break your promise to me it's the end."

For a moment he fought the desire to ask if Newman had had anything to do with her words, and then he thought: Oh, what's the use?

114

18

NEWS in the open country is carried in strange ways and with sometimes uncanny speed. A word dropped here, a wink, an odd gesture; men taking several unrelated things and details and coming up with a conclusion that is right, or wrong, as the case may be. The moving on of the Earps and the things they did before leaving swept the Sulphur Springs Valley and the San Pedro country on wings. A death here, a meeting there, some frightened Mexicans running out of oak trees near a spring, Sheriff Behan and his three successive posses, all failing to get Wyatt and his friends. Colonel Hooker turned the posse away gruffly from the wide and usually hospitable doors of his great Sierra Bonita ranch. And then Wyatt Earp, his brother, and the four friends rode across the line into New Mexico, and the fighting lawman's story in Arizona was written.

But the Tombstone country had more to talk about, to fill the place. Would or would not Sam Chalmers take over the job? Would he run against Johnny Behan in the first election the newly formed Cochise County was to hold? And, running, would he win? And what would happen then? There were many answers to the questions, but nothing to back up the answers and prove them truths. Nothing but the flat and stubborn statement repeated whenever anyone asked Sam Chalmers if he was going to run. "No."

The outlaw-rancher crowd, however, made it plain and stated it often: they could make him run—away. Like Earp did, they said. And they laughed when they said it. John Ringo, Buckskin Frank Leslie, with their crew, and many more, Mexicans and whites and Indians. The lost men, the men who bragged and got drunk and cursed anyone who interfered with what they chose to call "their rights." They'd make Sam Chalmers run, they said over their whisky; make him follow Wyatt Earp, so they would!

The Bisbee stage was robbed four times in three weeks, the Benson stage almost as often. Men were shot in the streets of Charleston and Tombstone for little or nothing. A man who carried money and either showed it or looked as if he had it needed a guard at all times. People were murdered in their

115

own homes, on the trails, the roads, and Cochise County ran up the bloody toll until the territorial governor took it up with Washington and the President of the United States was asked to take action. Martial law was the word that was passed around the underground, take it easy for a while until they forget.

It came to Sam Chalmers in dribbles and drops and brought some sick moments to him. He found he had to stare often at Jean, her plump and pretty face and figure, the hair that haunted him always, the color of a palomino's mane. He would watch her brush it and think that life came in a sparkle with her there. He would waken at night and hear her soft breathing beside him, a faint mutter if he stirred, and in the cold before dawn he would feel her instinctively move closer to him for warmth and protection. And he knew that if he lost her he lost life and something more, a something never to be recovered.

And then in a cold raw dawn, or a bright and warm one, he would stand outside the great house smoking his first cigarette. Peace, content; the rattle of pots in the kitchen where the Mexican women got breakfast for them all. Some children playing, goats, chickens, cattle and horses in the distance, a small Inca dove cooing its odd little notes, a desert phoebe diving and ducking from the eaves after bugs, pulling up near him and whistling softly, "Fee-bee, fee-bee," and flying away again.

That was life in its sum. But he had it only because he was strong and powerful, man enough and rich enough to have hired gunmen about to protect those good things of life for him and for Jean. And there were a lot of people in Cochise County who did not have his strength and his gunmen. There was no zest in living with that grim thought in his mind. He would stare grimly at the shaded window and think: She's in there dressing, and she made me promise not to mix into this rotten deal.

And then she would come out, smiling at him, and tell him breakfast was ready. They would walk in, arm in arm, and she would pour his coffee and send back the eggs if they were not cooked the way he liked and she would fuss and pet him. And he would think: Men are suckers for a woman and her ways, and God, how we love it!

Then Jean would ask him what he was smiling at, or why he was mumbling, and he would laugh and pass it off with a joke. But away from her, his thoughts turned again to grim things. And he would shift again: Jean was worth it, or was she? Was anything worth what you paid for it?

They drove toward the Wiswold ranch one cool day, together in the bright-wheeled buggy. Jean seemed happier than he had seen her in a long time, and joked with him all the way. They swept through the last bunch of cottonwoods and came out where the Wiswold ranch house squatted. Five Mexican woodchoppers were there with thirty burros heavy with fine oak firewood cut in the Huachucas across the valley. They greeted Chalmers with broad smiles and promised him a load of thirty burros of wood within a week.

Henry Wiswold finished his dickering with the woodcutters and showed them where to stack the wood. Mrs. Wiswold came out and caught Jean in her arms, and they talked idly of the weather, cattle, and what they had been doing since their last visit. And a quick thought came into Chalmers' mind. He had not stepped down from the buggy when Jean did. Now he gathered the reins in his firm hands and said, "I'll drive on to Charleston. Be back in an hour. A man I want to see."

"No, you won't!" Jean ran at the buggy before he could start the horses. "Stop, Sam! You can't go without me. I'm going to watch you every minute until the election is over. I simply don't trust you!"

Quick anger rose in him and he stared at her. "Jean," he started to say, but he stopped. His eyes shifted. Newman was standing in the doorway, and Clytie, his wife, was coming out to greet them. Chalmers spoke flatly. "All right, Jean. I'll put up the team."

As he turned it toward the barns he looked back. Newman was watching him and laughing softly.

When Chalmers came into the big living room of the ranch house Newman smiled at him and winked. "We've been hearing all about it, Sam. You sure sound henpecked! It's funny how a woman can take a man and twist him around her little finger, isn't it?" And the big man chuckled. "Take Clytie, now, I don't dare call my soul my own." Then he laughed, heartily.

Jean spoke flatly. "We've made a deal and I intend to keep Sam to his promise. I'm not going to let him get away, where Clum, Parsons, and all those other men on the Citizens' Committee can work on him!"

"Sam, they sure know how to handle us, don't they?" Newman asked, making it a statement. He eyed Chalmers' clothes, a finely tailored gray suit, polished halfboots, white shirt, the snow-white sombrero of finest clear nutria. And he nodded.

"You've changed a lot, Sam. Burned the old work clothes and the straw sombrero? Hell, man, that straw sombrero was a part of you. You'll never be the same again. Funny what a woman can do to a man."

Chalmers read him as though the big man had put it into words: Changed to the point of being harmless now. The clothes, the white sombrero, the polished boots. Soft, easy-living, that was what Newman read, knowing it took something from a man. A woman can soften any man, if she is the right woman. Chalmers nodded, sat quietly, and let the talk flow about him, smiling but saying little.

Jean was chattering and birdlike, and often coming back to her command over Sam Chalmers. She was talking for her family, letting them see how she twirled that big strong man, the dangerous Sam Chalmers, right around her fingers. And by the mere threat of words, too. And, thought Sam Chalmers, they can do it if you love them.

Newman suddenly broke in, and it was as though he had come to a sharp, needed decision. "Look here, I almost forgot. We want you all to come to Tombstone tonight. I've reserved a box at the theater, rooms at the Grand Hotel for you. It's going to be a big night, with a new show. We've got a troupe of Mexican dancers from El Paso, and Clytie has learned some new songs. Hits, they'll be, smash hits!"

Chalmers said slowly, "I don't think——" And then Jean broke in.

"Of course we'll go. We'll be delighted to go, and we must hear Clytie sing those new songs." And she smiled at Newman, not at Chalmers.

Chalmers thought slowly, forcing a little smile to cover the quick play of emotion on his face: She's feeling her power now. It gives me a chance to get mad and break my word. But I won't. It's not worth it.

They had dry champagne with the dinner, and another bottle of sweet champagne with dessert. Newman was a fine host, but somehow a mocking one when he looked at Chalmers. They left the private dining room in the theater and went up to their box, with Clytie Collins, as she was billed, leaving them to put on her make-up for her turn. The Mexican dancers whirled and twisted on the stage and one girl, exotic, passionate, and beautiful, swirled and tossed her flying skirts as though in a mad tumult of emotions. The house rocked with applause, waiters ran around with glasses and bottles, and as the Mexicans finished their encore Jack Baldwin walked into the box across from the Newman party.

Sam Chalmers saw him enter and sit down, and his expression did not change. He looked about. People were standing at the back of the house, crowding up into the balcony, pushing their heads in the big door from the saloon in front. All waiting to hear Clytie Collins and her new songs. A crowd such as the theater had not seen in a long time. Townsmen, miners, ranchers, store people. Chalmers had a cold thought that it might mean something. And then he waited.

Clytie sang, and sang beautifully. Old songs and new. The house rocked as the crowd cheered and applauded and shouted for more. She sang three new songs, two encores, and then bowed her way off the stage as the curtain dropped. Chalmers looked over and saw that Jack Baldwin had left his seat and disappeared. He puzzled over that for a moment, and then turned to speak to Jean. His eyes caught a vacant chair; Newman had left.

"I think I'll get a drink," said Chalmers, and rose. But Jean caught his arm.

"Call a waiter," she said. "I'd like something too. That big dinner made me thirsty."

He stood almost helplessly for a moment. Something was calling him and he did not know what it was. The sounds of the shifting audience dulled a little and now Chalmers heard something. A dull sound, repeated, that made him jerk his arm away from Jean and break out of the box on the run. Unerringly, like a hound on the scent, he headed for Clytie Collin's dressing room.

Clytie Collins' dressing room was at the right, with a big white star painted on the door. As Newman crossed the stage toward it after the curtain had dropped on Clytie's turn, he glanced once at a stagehand. The man nodded briefly. Newman then looked over toward the rear door that opened into the alley. Sime Canby and Faro Johnson, two of his gunmen, stood there. They looked at him and each face was expressionless. Newman then unbuttoned his long black frock coat, shifted his holstered gun a little forward, and let the unbuttoned coat swing back over it. Then he walked into the dressing room without knocking.

Jack Baldwin stood near the rear window, Clytie sat at her dressing table wiping off the thick layer of cold cream she had smeared on to remove the grease paint. In the mirror she smiled at her husband and went on wiping off the cream and grease paint.

"Hello, Newman," said Jack Baldwin, smiling. "Clytie sure stood them in the aisles tonight! I never heard anything like it. Man, you must be proud of her!"

Newman laughed lightly and nodded. Finding Baldwin there was nothing unusual, in fact Newman had encouraged their growing friendship, for very good reasons of his own. Then, slowly, like the dropping of the final curtain on the stage when the show is over, the smile ran down and faded from Newman's handsome face.

Newman noted that Jack Baldwin had on a business suit, cut tight and snug, with the coat buttoned up to show his fine chest and shoulders. And the gun bulge was plain on his right thigh—but covered by the bottom of the coat. Newman spoke flatly.

"Baldwin, how long do you think you fooled me?"

Newman grinned thinly as he saw the quick shock, the sudden change of expression. He gave Baldwin long enough to drop his hand, but not long enough to get his coat out of the way. Then Newman drew and fired twice. Baldwin jerked, stepped backward, and tried to speak. His hand went to his chest, and his knees broke under him. He curled down, half crouched against the wall, and his eyes turned up slowly.

Newman looked briefly. Baldwin was dead. He turned and backed against the door, then suddenly stepped toward his wife. She made a strangled, muted sound, and then words came. "Don't kill—me."

His right hand held the gun and his left slashed out at the low-cut dress. He caught it at the top and jerked swiftly, once. There was a tearing sound and her right breast was exposed. He stepped back, smiling coldly.

"Cover yourself, my dear," he said evenly. "I can hear people running this way. Cover yourself and make your choice. Either someone shot him from the window, or I came in to find him—er—bothering you. Make your choice, but quickly!"

"You—you framed this. You want to get something on me. You've tired of me. You want that Mexican dancer——"

"Make your choice. Now."

Newman turned and threw the door open. Stagehands were crowding up to the door. Chalmers fought his way through them and stopped in the doorway. He saw Baldwin's body against the wall, and his face turned white.

Newman spoke once. "Clytie."

"My—husband—killed him," said Clytie Collins. She stared at Newman in what seemed to be agony, and she spoke again. "He—Jack went crazy. He tore my dress." She moved her hand, closed the torn place, and then fainted.

Somebody called from the stage, "What's happened? What's happened?"

Newman walked past Chalmers and went on through the stagehands and grips. "Roll up that curtain," he ordered. The curtain hissed its way to the top and stopped with a thud. And then Newman walked out onto the stage with his gun still in his hand.

"Quiet, everybody," he ordered. He waited for the crowd to calm down, and then he spoke again, sharply, sternly. "I'm sorry this happened, for he was a good friend of mine. I guess Jack Baldwin had too much to drink. I walked in, and my wife called for me to help—I shot him. I did what any husband would do. I shot him. I'll not run away the way the Earps and Doc Holliday did. I'm here if you all want me to stand trial. I don't believe there's a man in the world who wouldn't do what I did in the same circumstances. So I'm not afraid to stand trial for killing a drunken scoundrel who was molesting my wife."

Newman stepped back. "That's all. Lower the curtain."

"The hell it's all!" Chalmers strode forward now, and his voice was hard and sharp, a little high-pitched as it always was when he was thoroughly aroused. "Don't drop that curtain, I've got something to say."

He waited a brief moment, and then spoke. "Jack Baldwin was my friend. That fight we had was faked. I wanted him to get in with certain people and learn what he could. And he did. It cost him his life. Jack was my friend. Mrs. Newman is my wife's sister. I've nothing more to say about that, now."

He let the whispers run through the house and die. Then he spoke again, raising his voice now. "You all know I refused to let my name be put up for sheriff at the coming election. I promised my wife I would let the law take care of the things that are happening in this county. That I'd keep out of it. But Jack Baldwin was my friend and I'm responsible for his death. I don't question Mrs. Newman's words. I don't question Newman's shooting Jack. I just say his death changes things. It leaves me with some unfinished business. I don't like that. I'm going to finish the business by running for sheriff. I'm going to ask all decent, self-respecting folks to vote for me. And I'm going to be elected. I know that because in the end right wins.

It may take a beating for a while, get some pretty tough blows, but in the end it wins."

He paused, grinned thinly at Newman, and then went on to the crowd. "So I'm going to be the next sheriff of Cochise County. I'm going to make a speech then. It's not going to be a long speech like this one. It's going to be the shortest acceptance speech on record. It isn't going to be aimed at anybody except a certain few men I know. Nobody else has to listen to that speech, short as it is. Just five words. Aimed at the outlaws. Those five words are, GET OUT OR GET KILLED."

For a moment there was silence. A mutter came, then a roar. Chalmers held up his hand for silence and waited three long minutes before he could calm the shouts of friends and foes.

"Now here's the rest of my campaign promise. I've got to make this Bloody County so safe a baby can play in the streets with a bagful of diamonds, and not lose one. I'm going to do it by deputizing all of my thirty-one cow hands and vaqueros—at my expense. They're good boys, good cow hands, and mighty fine fighting men! And best of all, they won't cost you voters a cent. I'm going to pay their wages, good wages, to help me keep my word to the outlaws. And I'm putting it on record for them to think about—GET OUT OR GET KILLED!"

19

ANOTHER roar of applause went up from the theater audience as Sam Chalmers finished his speech. He stood there for a moment, listening and staring straight ahead. He did not look up at the box where Jean and her parents still sat. It was not that he was afraid to look, it was simply that he was not thinking of her. He was thinking of Jack Baldwin, dead.

A man had to play his cards and handle them as best he could. A man had to take orders or give them, and had in turn to pay the penalties of his work. A man lived or died, thought Chalmers, and sometimes it was very hard to be the one who lived. Especially if you had to give the orders that caused the deaths.

So Sam Chalmers stood and listened to the shouts and the handclapping, and thoughts kept moving in his mind. At last he turned and walked toward the wings and heard the slow hiss of the curtain coming down. He thoughts came jerkily back to the moment and he knew what that curtain's dropping could mean. For he saw Newman standing about ten feet from him. Against the wall were five stagehands, staring bleakly at him. In front of them stood the gunman Sime Canby, while a few steps to Newman's left stood Harry-Joe and his brother Faro Johnson, Gamblers, dealers, killers; they were from Missouri, men said, and of the breed called in the West "Black Missourians." Part Indian, part white, and all mean. Dour, lean, tall.

Chalmers knew that the time had come to make no mistakes, in judgment or actions, not even small ones. From here on every move he made had to be the right move or it was all over. One mistake, and he would be dead. The outlaw element would control things, and no one could say where or how it would end. Or when the strong man needed to control them would arrive. If he played it wrong.

A quick guess and a quicker decision were made instantly, and Chalmers strode on. He ignored Sime Canby, he ignored Newman. If his guess was right, Faro Johnson or his brother Harry-Joe was the man who had tried to murder him at the O.K. corral fight. And Chalmers knew Newman well enough to believe he would give the murderer another chance. This, he thought, probably was the chance. So if he handled it properly he could win against them all. For that reason, in a snap decision made in a scant single stride, Chalmers walked straight at Harry-Joe and Faro Johnson. They stood firm. They were between him and the stage door into the long corridor between the theater wall and the ground-floor seats.

Chalmers did not hurry and he did not slow down. He strode forward, his head lowered slightly into his shoulders, his hands swinging loosely, and his eyes hard and alert. He kept them fixed squarely between the two dark and lean faces, and did not shift them. He walked on, straight at them and toward the door.

As he neared them, his eyes fixed and hard, Chalmers half raised his hands and spread the fingers. He was like a man pushing his way through heavy curtains as he pushed those hands out ahead of him. He closed them firmly on Faro's right arm, Harry-Joe's left. He was not rough, nor too gentle, as he did it. He simply put pressure on those arms, shoved the two men aside, and walked on to the stage door. He did not look back.

If he had he would have seen Harry-Joe's draw. A look of wild rage spread over the faces of the two brothers. They had

123

been bluffed and they knew it. Harry-Joe got his gun out first, and then Faro's came out. Chalmers was in the doorway, throwing open the door and walking on, still without looking back. And it took more than human courage to do it. But he had that strange courage that is given to certain leaders, that strange deep-grown belief that he could not be killed. And as Chalmers went through the doorway he heard one word.

Newman said the word. It was a sharp command: "No!"

Even then Chalmers did not look back. He shut the door behind him and went on to the short stairs up to the boxes. At the foot of the stairs he stopped. Jean was coming down them alone, her face set and angry.

At the foot of the stairs, in a heavy silence, she took his right arm. Chalmers spoke gently, but his words were heard over the entire room. "I think you had better take my left arm, dear. You see, my gun is on the right side. I may need it."

White, wordless, she obeyed him. Bowing to someone, he neither knew nor cared who, for it was only a gesture, Chalmers smiled and walked out the door into the street.

Neither spoke as they walked down to the Grand Hotel and up to their room. Chalmers shut the door and stepped to the window to draw the shades. The glass exploded almost in his face, but he was already dropping down as it did. For he had caught, briefly, the figure of a man across the street and looking up.

Jean cried out. Chalmers spun sideways, rose, and jerked down the shade from the protection of the wall. Then he edged to the other window and made the same moves. He turned and looked at Jean and said simply, "I'm sorry, but it's started."

"What else did you expect?" Her voice was cool and distant. She half turned her back as she saw him hold out his arms. "You threw the challenge at them, and they've accepted it."

He stepped to her side even as she turned her back on him. He caught her right hand in his and made no effort to turn her around to face him. He began to talk, evenly and quietly.

"You've got to understand this before you leave me," and his very graveness made it plain he did not expect her to weaken and remain with him. "No one person, no one thing in this world is as big as the whole. Someone has to fight and suffer, that all may profit. So some suffer and some profit in the good things of the world. Some men are strong and some men are weak, yet their strength is not something to praise and the other men's weaknesses are not something to condemn. It is their lot, that is all. Weakness and strength are in all of us, for while we may be weak in some things we can be strong in others. And I think it is right that way, or it would not *be* that way. If we all were strong in the same things the world would suffer for it. If we all were weak in the same things mankind would degenerate. History proves that, and proves that the real danger lies not in the possession of strength but in the misuse of it. The bad man, the outlaw, uses his strength for evil things and succeeds until the good man comes to stop him. And the good man is always stronger, in the end. That's my creed, Jean; that's what I live by. I think I'm strong enough to whip the outlaws and I'm going to do it."

He was smiling a little, but at the back of her head. He went on evenly. "I'm going to do it as the sheriff of Cochise County. Not Sam Chalmers, but sheriff. The law, duly elected and qualified and under oath to keep the law and to enforce it. So I won't be breaking my word to you, Jean. I said I'd let the law do the job, and I'll be the law!"

She jerked her hand away and turned on him. "A trick. A cheap trick such as you played on Bigelow Newman, back there in Texas to get your start here. All you think of is power, money, having your own way. You will never change. You will always think you are right, and you will always outthink the other person as you have me, and Clytie's husband."

"Newman told his version of it. Will you listen to mine?"

"No!" she snapped at him. She was badly hurt and hardly aware of how angry she was. He knew that, and accepted it, as she went on. "A cheap, contemptible thing. You pride yourself on your strength, on being right—yet you stand where you are now because you played a cheap and contemptible trick on those poor Texas ranchers. A trick to cheat them out of their money. You gave them hardly five cents on the dollar for those notes, and Bigelow Newman was going to pay them back that fall!"

Chalmers opened his mouth and then shut it. He knew, and bitterly, that she was so aroused nothing would penetrate her anger. It was no use, he thought swiftly, to tell her what Newman had actually done about those notes—killed the one man who had dared to try to collect them. Nor was he, now, going to tell her what he himself had learned about Newman, and what Jack Baldwin had managed to tell him on one brief meeting in the night outside the ranch house. Nor that he, Sam Chalmers, of his own accord, had paid off the ranchers in full when his own money began to roll in. Those things were either gestures for the public to learn and admire, or something a man did for the good of his soul. And if you spoke of it, it was a gesture alone.

So Sam Chalmers simply stepped back and dropped his arms to his sides. "So you are leaving me now?"

"No." And then she hurried on, as though afraid she would weaken. "I'm leaving the day you are elected sheriff. And— oh, Sam, I hope you lose!"

He caught her in his arms suddenly. "I'll win. I'll win and I'll do my job. I won't hope that you will weaken, my dear, for I'm afraid that we're two strong-willed people who can lick almost anyone but ourselves. So I won't hope that you will weaken and change your mind. I know you won't. I'll just hope that someday you will understand, and forgive me for doing my own job in the best way I know how."

And when he kissed her she was sobbing.

Sam Chalmers was elected sheriff of Cochise County and Jean left him the very day the news came to them. She was white-lipped, eyes hot, and she would not kiss him good-by as she rode away, leaving most of her clothes packed and ready for a wagon to take after her to the Wiswold ranch. Sam Chalmers watched her disappear over a roll of land and he tried to tell himself: Someday she will ride back over that hill to me, and I'll be here waiting for her. The thought brought little cheer to him.

On the day Chalmers took the oath of office he had with him a hard-looking bunch of men: Harley, Brett, Jones, Nelson, Galloway, Webster, Chico, Arsenio, Jayme, Wayne, the fighting Texan, and four of his men. The others had been left at the ranch to guard it and the cattle and horses. For Chalmers had a feeling the outlaws might strike first.

He was duly sworn in, and then he turned and swore in the men he had brought with him. That done, he strode down the steps and swung into the saddle and his star-wearing men mounted behind him.

Across the street by the O.K. corral where the bitter Earp-Clanton feud had been settled so swiftly, Chalmers saw Newman backed by Canby and the two Johnsons. Chalmers rode into the middle of the street and pulled up his horse. He sat there for a moment, facing Newman and the three gunmen, and then he raised his left hand to his hat. He took off the hat and waved it at Newman. "See it, Newman? It's my old straw sombrero. The one you remember I wore when I got that bunch of cattle from you. And you thought I'd burned it. You

126

fool. I'm wearing this hat from here on! Here on until the finish is over and the last shot fired."

Newman did not laugh, did not change expression.

Chalmers swept the crowd with quick-shifting eyes and then spoke, almost angrily. "Hell, I'd hoped some of the outlaws on my list would be here so's I could order them out right now. But they're not. *Bueno,* I'm riding with my deputies. I'm going to the ranch first to swear in all my men as deputy sheriffs of Cochise County. And then we go out hunting for the outlaws that Cochise County can do without. I've got their names, I know where to find them, and I've got the message for them, GET OUT OR GET KILLED!"

He heard the wild cheer that rose from many throats. He waved the old straw sombrero to them, clapped it back on his head, and called out, "Come on, boys!" And so Sam Chalmers rode down Fremont Street and out of town.

20

So THE grim fighting orders went out and were passed along in the mesquite thickets, the springs hidden in the canyons, the rustlers' camps, and the old hide-outs of the outlaws. From the Huachucas to the Chiricahuas, from Iron Springs to Galeyville, from Benson to Bisbee, and back up past Sulphur Springs to Willcox. From ranch to ranch and man to man it spread, Get out or get killed, until it reached far beyond the county limits.

For some, the words and the memories of Sam Chalmers' cold black eyes staring at them were enough. For others, not enough. They would fight, they said. They said it over bottles of beer or whisky, in dives and dumps and down alleys where a decent man dare not go. Tombstone rang with it; Fairbanks, Contention, Charleston, and all the other places where the word to get out or get killed had gone, all heard that some were not leaving. They waited and they wondered.

And they were due to learn soon.

Three times in the next eight days Chalmers and his men rode into Tombstone and along the streets, but not with prisoners to be tried at the expense of taxpayers' money. They rode down the streets and straight to Boot Hill, with shovels to bury the dead.

127

On that eighth day when Chalmers and his men made the third ride to Boot Hill, Bigelow Newman stared down Allen Street after them. He stood at the corner just outside his Bird Cage Theater, and no one could have guessed his thoughts. He turned slowly in a quarter circle and stared briefly at the hills to the south where the raw lines of mine dumps and shaft headings showed. Men moved like small insects, walking, scurrying, driving mule teams and horse outfits. Steam rose in clouds and sometimes a whistle blew in short, angry blasts. He rolled his head slightly and then shrugged.

He kept turning in brief, quarter circles as though a condemned man taking his last look at the world which had been good to him. The Mule Mountains, the Dragoons, the rolling ridges and sharp gullies and mesquite flats, the great basin of the San Pedro, the Whetstones, the pass to Nogales, the Huachucas, and the wide break to the south where the land changed subtly and the Mexican range country began. Newman saw it all and grinned. And his expression hardened. He was not leaving it. He had not been told to get out or get killed, but he knew that was coming. And he was not going to get out or get killed, either one. He was staying, alive.

Newman never had been under the illusion that he was fooling Chalmers and never wanted it otherwise. From the beginning it had been a battle between them and both men had known it. Newman had sent Curly Bill and his men out to get Chalmers and the cattle there in the Sulphur Springs Valley in the beginning. He had also told the outlaw leader to let the Wiswolds alone. It had been a bad break for them when Curly Bill had found Chalmers in the company of the Wiswolds and had had to let them alone. Things might have been different, thought Newman; but it was not too late to change them now.

He walked back to the door of the theater, went in through the bar, and called to Sime Canby to come with him. They walked upstairs and in Newman's small office, with the door shut, Newman gave his orders. It took him a little while, for he had to name different men he wanted told, but it could be summed up briefly: No more backing up. Make the stand in Charleston. Fight it out there.

And at just about that moment Sam Chalmers was leading his men away from Boot Hill. He rode down the ragged slope into Walnut Canyon and rode up it for about three miles, following its twists and turns. He led the men up a branch canyon for a short time, then up a slope onto a long, winding bare

128

ridge that headed more or less east toward the pass into Sulphur Springs Valley, and on.

They rode steadily on, leaving the ridge, and crossed rolling, grassy land where a few cattle grazed and raised curious eyes to watch the small army go past. To the north the Dragoons were a ragged line that dropped and rose again in a rough, rocky ridge. To the south more rolls of land led the eye to the canyons they had ridden going into the San Pedro Valley for the first time, and the Mule Mountains were a colorful background for the grassy grazing lands. About nine miles out of Tombstone itself they came to a pyramidlike hill and from there on the land changed gently into the rich bottoms of the Sulphur Springs Valley.

Here they met a cowboy who told them of the death of John Ringo: shoeless, empty bottles about him, and a bullet blasting out his brains. His own gun beside him. Doubt even then was in their minds that Ringo had killed himself, and doubt will always exist.

"That's one less," said Chalmers, and rode on at the head of the group.

They gave the grim warning at two ranches in the valley, and rode on south, rounding the Mules and going into Bisbee from the flat, southern land at the mouth of the canyon. Four men there got the warning. They camped in a tight group that night up the canyon near water, and had sentries out. They rode on at dawn, crossed the divide, and dropped down the sharp canyon into their own range lands.

The ranch was as usual, calm and peaceful, and for two days they rested. Then Chalmers sent them out for a swift ride straight north to the streets of Charleston. They were a nerveless, cold bunch of men, utterly without visible emotion. Flat-sounding voices spoke when needed, but no joking, no singing, no ribald stories broke through the taut lips in their freshly shaven faces. They had cleaned up at the ranch, they would be bearded and dirty again when they got back. It was a grim, merciless, completely unemotional business. It was the law, justice, in action. Led by a man who solemnly believed he was right and saw little sense in wasting time in the courts where juries could be hung by one man.

"Get out or get killed," he laid it down for them in the streets of Charleston, with his men in a wide line behind him. He looked them all over and he spread it a little wider for them to hear. "Some of you here are decent folks, some of you play ball with the outlaw crowd because you are afraid not to, or because it is easier that way. Stop it, now. The law is here. I'm coming back with my posse in exactly seven days. I want to know then who is on the side of the law. I'll know from this: decent people will leave their guns at home. The outlaws will wear them. So, there it is. We'll be back in seven days to kill anyone who wears a gun."

They went on through the hills and picked up Walnut Canyon and made the same ride into Sulphur Springs Valley, Bisbee, and home. And they did not have to fire a single shot in the entire trip. A few who wanted to argue felt their minds change swiftly after staring into Sam Chalmers' snapping black eyes for a time. They felt, perhaps without having brains enough to analyze it, that they were not looking into the eyes of a man. They were seeing the law, utterly implacable, completely impartial, and without a trace of mercy for the man who overstayed the warning, get out or get killed.

So, on the seventh dawn after the warning had been passed at Charleston, Sam Chalmers led his men out of the ranch lands and north. They were fresh, rode fresh horses; they were heavily armed and had a big supply of ammunition for those arms. And they meant business.

Five miles south of Charleston, Chalmers stopped them. He gave brief orders to Harley and Brett. They were to cross the river and get on the Tombstone side. They were to prevent anyone from going into Charleston from their side. And they were to shoot at and kill anyone who rode toward them wearing a gun. Harley and Brett left and disappeared into a cottonwood thicket.

Chalmers led his remaining men, twenty-nine in number, through a thicket of willows on a feeder stream, and then north about two or three miles from the river, but following its general course. When about opposite the town of Charleston, he stopped them and they all had a smoke or a chew, followed by an almost casual glance around, and then all eyes fixed on Chalmers. He looked at them proudly. They knew their jobs and there was not a doubt in any mind there, not even a small one. They were the law in action.

Chalmers nodded briefly, almost jerkily. "Thirty feet apart, rifles and pistols ready, and keep moving forward in a line. Kill any man who has a gun or a rifle. If they try to hole up in a building, don't pass that building until they are dead. Don't hurry, ride at a walk. But if a general fight breaks out—and it probably will—you boys know what to do. Just take care of

130

yourselves as best you can, and kill any man who carries a weapon."

Chalmers then picked up his reins and rode toward Charleston. His men spread out at thirty-foot intervals and moved with him. They rode down into a shallow gully and came out of it, passed more mesquite, and then came into the clearing where the first buildings of Charleston rose in a ragged, scattering line. Two children cried out at sight of them and ran into an adobe hut. A man straightened up from chopping wood, grinned, and raised the ax. He sank its blade deep into a log and then straightened again. His hands rested on his hips and those hips did not support a gun belt. He watched them ride on and he shook his head.

In some of the buildings, homes, and stores there was unusual activity, in others only silence, with a few curious, sometimes frightened or worried faces staring out at the thin line of riders moved on so slowly, so direly.

Had they galloped, trotted even, had they seemed worried, or intense, it would have been different. But they moved so slowly, so steadily on. Their faces had such a set, emotionless look to them. Their hands seemed nerveless and steady as they rode with reins dropped over saddle horns, rifles and carbines held at the ready. Only the horses' plodding hoofs, only the quick-shifting and keen eyes told the story. It was the law, moving in.

Chalmers was in the center of the line and riding on a slight slant toward the rear of the big general store. Trinidad Chavez and Pete Laskey saw him coming and their lips thinned slightly at the sight. Chavez said, "Well?" and Pete Laskey shook his head. "I don't want any part of it," he answered grimly.

Laskey turned then and looked at two women standing near the front of the store. "I'd get back," he warned them. "It's Chalmers and his men. There's a bunch of armed men holed up in the two saloons across from us. I'd get back if I was you women." He watched them turn slowly to look at him and he spoke again, his eyes shifting to a window close to him. "Chalmers is just passing here now, you'd better hurry, Mrs. Chalmers."

Jean saw the grim-jawed face go by at the window level, under the wide brim of the old, now somewhat battered straw sombrero. She cried out, sharply, "Sam!" And again, "Sam!" But he did not turn toward her.

Chalmers had seen the glint of metal at a window in the saloon where he had first confronted Curly Bill and John

131

Ringo. Both men now were dead, but there was metal gleaming at the window. And metal meant a run or rifle.

A voice rose at the far end of the line of horsemen. It was Jeepers Jones, passing the word a man had called to him. "They've holed up in the two saloons, Sam. The town's mostly backing us!"

Chalmers called, "Close in a little," and as he said that he shifted suddenly in his saddle. The gleam of the metal in the saloon window had disappeared. He thought it meant a shot and he was right. It whistled past him as he shifted, and now he spurred his horse sideways and slanted his rifle barrel toward the saloon. He shot three times. Twice dust kicked near the window corner and the third time there was no dust. A man's hand appeared suddenly from inside the window. It clutched at the frame, slowly relaxed, and disappeared. Chalmers rode on. A dozen shots rattled out now. He swung his horse and emptied his rifle in a slow, even fire at the window. He shoved it in the boot almost lazily and drew both pistols, and rode on.

They closed in slowly under fire. Some dismounted and took shelter behind walls and corners. Two others found cottonwood trees that gave them good protection. Chalmers' horse was killed before he fired a shot from his pistols and he flatened there in the dust behind its body. The whole scene seemed languid, lazy, except for the sharp roar of shots, the screams of someone, the splashing sound of glass shot out of a window.

Distantly, in a break in the firing, they heard the dull hammer of horses crossing the bridge on a gallop. Then the drumming of the horses died in a burst of shooting. Chalmers rose slightly and fired an even roll at ducking figures he saw in a doorway. There was a rattle of shots back and he heard them thud into the horse's body. He heard a man cry out, somebody scream. He heard a voice shout, "Rush them, boys!" And did not realize it was he himself who gave the order. He reloaded.

As though in obedience to another's command, Sam Chalmers got up and started for the saloon door on the run, shooting as he went. No frenzied, yelling rush. Just a steady drive forward of men who wore stars on their vests and shirts and wore them proudly. Grim, deadly justice. Then Chalmers stood in a smoky, powder-smelling room and looked at bodies on the floor. He walked to the door and stared out into the street.

For the first time he realized now that Jean and her mother stood on the porch steps, staring at him. He looked steadily at

132

his wife and saw her turn away. He thought bleakly that she probably was crying with relief at seeing him alive and was too proud to show it after leaving him. He walked back into the saloon and stared at some of the men there. Galloway and Nelson had come in the back door, Jones and Wayne were in a window.

"Anybody seen Newman?" he asked.

"No. We got two of his gunmen in this bunch though, Faro Johnson and his brother," Wayne answered him.

"All right. We'll go up to Tombstone now," said Chalmers. "We'll give Bigelow Newman his warning. And from there on I'll take care of him, personally."

Chalmers clipped his lips down hard over the last word and could not help looking out the door. Newman was Jean's brother-in-law. Was the son-in-law of the older woman, Jean's mother. And he had to kill Newman. He watched the two women get their horses and ride away toward the Wiswold ranch. Yes, he had to kill Newman.

"Sam," came a soft-voiced order from one of his men, "look down that way," and Brindle Nelson jerked his thumb toward the south.

Chalmers looked. He saw Jean and her mother stop their horses to speak to some people in a buggy. The people in the buggy were Newman and his wife and even from where he was, three hundred yards away, Chalmers could see or sense the tension in the man.

He stared at the group for a time as they talked, and saw Jean making jerky little gestures as she pointed back toward Chalmers and his men. He knew what she was saying, telling of the swift and bitter fight, and its ending. The finish of the organized outlaw element in the town.

Chalmers watched, his dark eyes fixed, his expression somehow without meaning. He saw Newman nod, and slowly start to swing the team around. He was going back with the Wiswolds to their ranch, Chalmers knew. Going to avoid the showdown now. It was in Chalmers' mind that would be the simplest thing to do, to let Newman end the moment by driving off. Protected by his wife and her family, and sure that Chalmers would make no move in front of them. Sure that Chalmers would sacrifice his ends to keep from completely alienating his wife, forever.

Jaw setting angrily, black eyes snapping, Chalmers named four men and said sharply, "Come with me. Jeepers, I'm riding your horse, get your saddle on something else." He walked toward the horses. Galloway, Horton, Nelson, and Wayne followed him. They mounted and rode after the Wiswolds and Bigelow Newman.

21

JEAN was looking back as Chalmers and his four men started after them, and she cried out jerkily, "They—they're—coming."

Newman said quietly, "Calm down, don't be alarmed," and somehow wondered at his own coolness. He pulled up his team and turned them to face back toward Charleston, then sat quietly and waited. He glanced once at his wife and saw she would not meet his stare. His lips thinned a little, and that was all. He thought coolly, She hates me, but for the moment she is going to save my life. And so he sat, waiting.

Chalmers came up on the trot, his old straw sombrero shoved on the back of his head. His four men rode behind him and pulled up when he did. They said nothing, just watched Newman and waited. Chalmers did not move his hard stare from Newman's face. He did not look at his wife, at her mother, or at Newman's wife. He eased in the saddle and said sharply, "Newman, I've brought it down to you."

He waited a moment, and Newman did not speak. Chalmers then went on, evenly. "It's your turn now. Get out or get killed. You've got seven days to wind things up and let the theater owner get another manager. Seven days." Chalmers pulled out his watch and snapped open the hunting case, looked at the face, snapped the case shut with a click. "We'll call it noon, seven days from now. I'll be in Tombstone and if you're still there I, personally, am going to kill you. Good morning."

When Newman did not speak, simply sat and smiled mockingly at him, Chalmers spun his horse and started to ride off. He heard a quick cry from Jean, "Stop, you can't do this!" And when he did not answer she rode after him.

Jean forced her horse between those of his men and drew up beside him, her face white and angry. "You're not going to do this. You can't murder my sister's husband and wreck her life just for a whim, a notion! You aren't divine, omnipotent, a god on horseback. You're a man, like anybody else on this earth.

134

Why should you be so conceited, arrogant, highhanded? You can't ride through this world killing people!"

"I took on a job, Jean. I'm at the end of the job. You may not believe me, but Bigelow Newman must go. He has his choice. And the end rests with him, not with me."

Chalmers had not raised his voice, and his words seemed so completely without emotion that it was hard to realize he spoke of killing a man, of the death that ends all things on earth. Jean stared at him, white-faced, numbed mentally by what she saw so clearly in the expression, the mind back of it, of this man. Her husband. She drew back slowly, pulling her horse away from him as though she feared even the contact with him or his horse. Her hands clenched and loosened twice. Then she spoke.

"I'll find a way to stop this," she said. "I've got seven days to stop you from killing my sister's husband. I'll think up a way!"

Chalmers said, "Jean," and then he stopped. He knew beyond doubt or question that the thing was out of his hands. Newman would either leave the valley or get killed by him. What came after that was something else again.

Chalmers sat his horse, turned slightly in the saddle, and watched Jean ride back to join her family. He saw Newman turn his team, and the whole group start off toward the Wiswold ranch. Then Chalmers led his men back to Charleston to rejoin the others.

Wayne, the fighting Texan, rode beside Brindle Nelson on the way back to the ranch. He was a lean and tired-looking man, strangely deceptive for a gunman. Too tired, it would seem, to make hurried moves. But Nelson had seen him in action and knew him for what he was. Wayne shook his head slightly as he stared at Chalmers' flat back and easy seat in the saddle.

"This Newman buzzard, now," said Wayne. "He's hell on wheels or any other way he wants to go. Killer, that's him. Now take me, I'm a fighting man. I make my money that way and have since I was fifteen. But if I had it on my mind that I was going to give Newman his walking papers, I'd be thinking about it. I wouldn't be thinking about my ranch and my cattle and giving orders about how we spend the next week or so. It ain't human."

Brindle Nelson dug around in his brain and came up with something beyond him, something that was hard for him to express. But he had the idea and somehow he made it plain.

135

"Sam Chalmers ain't a fighting man, and you are. That's the difference. He's cleaning things up so's we can live in peace, and when that's done, he wants to live in peace, feeling he's earned it. While you, a fighting man, just clean up and move on. He don't like to kill folks, he does it because he has to. You like the game. You like the gamble part of it. Will you get that son, or will he get you? Are you faster? Or if he's faster, how can you trick it to overcome that handicap? It's a game. You play it as such and you like it. Chalmers don't. He never gives a thought to the other man killing him, because he's so damned sure he's going to earn that peace he's fighting for. And the other man knows Chalmers is sure he can't be killed. It wins for Sam Chalmers before the fight starts. He's going to kill Newman, regardless of how Newman tricks it to win."

Chalmers turned in the saddle and was smiling a little. He pointed, calling out, "There's some of our feeder stuff now, Wayne. It's fattening. That's the wild outlaw stuff you brought in from the Elias rancho, remember? And look at it now. Try to count those ribs, try to hang your damned hat on those hip-bones, will you?"

Chalmers was riding the stirrups so he could see over some mesquite to another meadowlike patch beyond where a big bull stood guard over about twenty cows.

Nelson winked at Wayne and said, "See what I mean, fella?" and Wayne nodded absently.

But it still puzzled him. The man wasn't human, he felt. You just didn't lose a wife and go out to kill her brother-in-law without showing it somehow.

But Sam Chalmers did. The work on the great ranch went on day after day until late afternoon of the sixth day from the time the warning had been given. He gave some final orders about the horse herd to Chico, more orders to the boys, and then told Harley and Brett to get horses ready, they were to ride with him that evening after supper.

They left in a dull gray light and without any special fare-wells. It was just another job for a man with a star on his vest. They reached Tombstone at midnight, put up their horses at the O.K. corral, and went to the rooms Chalmers hired by the month now, so often was he in town. And they went right to sleep.

They got up at eight o'clock and had breakfast in a small eating place on the side street near the courthouse. They walked over to the courthouse and people spoke pleasantly enough, but with odd expressions on their faces. Everybody knew the word had been passed. John Clum and Parsons were waiting in the sheriff's office and followed Chalmers, at his nod, into the inner room.

They said, together, and half anxiously, "Well, Sam?" and looked relieved when he grinned at them.

Clum spoke flatly. "You've got to look out for a trick of some kind. He's a deadly fighter, they say, and he's still got Sime Canby around someplace. It looks certain now that Newman planned half the hell that happened around here, in the way of robberies, stage holdups, and ore-train raiding. But unless somebody in the crowd is willing to testify to that——"

Chalmers broke in pleasantly, "Hell, John, why go over that angle now? In just"—he snapped open the hunting case of his watch, looked at the face, snapped shut the case again—"two hours and thirty-nine minutes Bigelow Newman is going to be dead."

Clum and Parsons sighed. They all went over some papers that had come in about the determination to call for martial law. Clum had been over to talk to the commanding officer at Fort Huachuca, and felt certain that it was coming at any time now.

"Don't worry about it," said Chalmers, throwing himself back in his chair. "Look over these reward dodgers and tell me if any of these men have been seen around here. You fellows in the Citizens' Committee get around more than I do now."

"But martial law——" Parsons started to say.

"When Newman dies, organized robbery and murder will stop in Cochise County," said Chalmers flatly. "Then martial law can be here, or not, it won't make any difference."

They went over more papers, talked of other plans, and at eleven-thirty Chalmers got up. He put on his old straw sombrero, tested his guns in the holsters by drawing them slightly and letting them drop back. Then he drew them again and studied the loads in each cylinder, despite the fact they had not been out of the holsters at his sides since he had reloaded that morning. He took off his outer coat and said, "I'm going out now. Harley, you and Brett walk up the sidewalks. I'm going to walk along the middle of the street toward the Newman house. If you see Sime Canby, and he has a gun on, kill him. That goes for anybody else who wears a gun and makes a false move. From here on there's not going to be any trouble in Tombstone."

They went out into the street and found a hundred people

137

standing about. Children ran, and some women backed off, frightened now that they realized the shooting would begin at any moment. Some men whispered, somebody cheered and was told sharply to shut up. A voice rose from the outer edge of the crowd.

"Chalmers," it called. "Newman is at his house. Down Fifth Street and——"

"I know where it is," said Chalmers.

He walked to the corner of Fifth and let Brett walk across to the far side where the high, two-story walls of Schieffelin Hall rose. Harley stayed on the lower side and Chalmers went into the center of the street. He turned left then and walked along Fifth. Behind him was a gathering crowd that moved gingerly along, not wanting to miss anything and yet not daring to get too close for fear of getting killed in the coming fight.

They walked past three tent shacks, two of brick and frame, and then neared an adobe-walled house. Far out across the flats were the Dragoon Mountains with the Sheep's Head so plain in the great rocks. But Chalmers was not looking at it. He was eying the front door and two windows at the adobe house. Now he saw movement and he walked on, not changing his speed at all.

It was Newman with Clytie Collins close to his side. She was saying something to him, pleadingly, and hanging onto his arm. He shook her off and laughed. At the top step, before coming down, he called out, "She wants me to go, Chalmers. She's that sure I'm going to kill you. She wants me to leave and not kill her sister's husband."

"Don't worry about that, Mrs. Newman," said Chalmers thinly. But he didn't look at her. He was watching Newman.

Somebody in the background yelled wildly and a gun spoke flatly, twice, its shots echoing against a wall. "He got Sime Canby," a voice shouted. But Chalmers did not look around. He still watched Newman. It was even now, unless the man had someone else hidden around.

Chalmers' eyes were hard, sparkling fixed, and intent. He saw Newman striding forward and knew instantly what the big man's next moves would be and his keen mind went leaping forward as though he could see the whole picture. There was a mesquite, gnarled and heavy, about five feet to the left of Newman, and just two more steps would bring him opposite it.

In Chalmers' mind the thing registered. He's going to draw and jump at the same time. I'll throw the first shot halfway

138

between the tree and him, and the second at the far side of the trunk, level with his heart. That tree trunk isn't wide enough to protect his body.

Newman said, "Chalmers," and then he jumped sideways. His hand dropped and he fired once, fired again as he seemed to blend with the tree.

Chalmers too had moved sideways, one step. He drew and fired with almost the same move, and fired again. Both shots went almost exactly where he had planned.

A curiously long, lingering sound went through the crowd, a wordless thing. Just the low sighing of more than a hundred people. The sound came as a long-held breath sifts out of taut lungs. Chalmers heard it dimly. He was watching the right hand that held the gun. It held there at the side of the tree trunk for what seemed a very long time. He thought almost angrily: I missed his heart.

He saw a hatbrim move out a little and his gun came down slowly for a shot. He saw the hand with the pistol move, but it was downward, that move. And he kept his own pistol lowering slowly. Newman's hand relaxed suddenly and the pistol dropped, the hand followed it. Newman's hat, face, shoulders, then body came surging into view. He fell, limp, flat, and motionless.

Chalmers had a cold thought then: It's all over. I've killed Jean's brother-in-law and I'll never have a chance to get her back. Never. He looked up and saw Clytie standing in the doorway staring at her dead husband, and for a moment it made him half sick. Especially when she looked up and stared straight into his, Sam Chalmers' eyes for a moment. And then Clytie came out the door and started walking down toward Chalmers, passing her dead husband. She was like a woman in a trance as she walked forward, her hands clenched at her sides.

She stopped near Chalmers and raised her voice a little above the normal speaking tone as she said, "This is something I want you all to hear, now. If ever a man deserved death, it was my husband. Had he been killed a few years ago, most of the trouble in Tombstone would not have happened."

She stopped, swallowed, and then went on steadily, "Sam, will you take me to my mother now?"

22

At the wide front door of the Wiswold ranch house Sam Chalmers raised his old straw sombrero and said with almost haunting emotion, "Tell Jean I'm sorry."

"I'll tell her the truth," said Clytie stiffly. "It was your duty and you did it."

"Somehow I don't think that will make any difference," said Chalmers. "She's a stiff-backed woman with strong ideas. I guess that's why I love her. I don't think it's going to help to tell her anything. It's just something we've got to lick, between us."

He rode on with Harley and Brett, looking back at times, hoping he would hear the pound of a galloping horse behind him. A horse could bring Jean back to him. But he did not hear that galloping horse nor did he see any sign of her riding after him. And he thought that Clytie's story had not changed things in any way. It remained something that they had to settle between themselves. For them alone. Happiness depended on that settlement, and they were two stubborn, determined people who would not give in. He knew it and he could not change it, he thought.

And then at the front door of the ranch house as he rode up he saw Jean. He almost yelled with joy, but what he saw in her expression froze him for a moment. He stepped down slowly and stood looking at her, waiting. She spoke in a steady, cold voice.

"Sam, I came down last night to tell you that if you would call this thing off, let Newman leave of his own accord and so save my sister's happiness, I would come back to you. But you couldn't wait. You had to go in town ahead of time. And you've killed him. Killed my sister's husband. Sam, Sam, if you had only waited."

"It would not have changed things," he said quietly. "It had to happen and it did." He puzzled for a moment and then felt there was little sense in telling her about Clytie. It would be stronger coming from her sister, and mean more. He felt a curious belief rising that she was going to ride away and never come back. She was that stubborn and so was he. He knew that if she rode off now he would not go after her. She was going to

140

have to come to him. It was her fault, she had started this matter and laid down the terms. There was nothing he could or would do about it. He stared into her eyes and read somehow the same thoughts, and he sighed. It was hell but it was there to be faced.

"Jean, I love you. I will always love you. I'm going to live here where we were happy together, and I'm going to hope that someday I'll see you ride over that hill out there, coming back to me. And I'll wait for that day, my dear."

"You won't even say you're sorry you killed him!"

"He had to die. I just happened to be the man there to kill him."

"I—I——" She suddenly wheeled and half ran around the corner of the big adobe ranch house. The house that was going to be so big, so lonely now. Her voice rose. "Jayme, Fermin! Where is my horse?"

The men left him, wordless and shaking their heads. Chalmers stood beside his horse, his face set and brooding in expression. His hands clasped, white-knuckled, over the saddle horn. His eyes were fixed, waiting for something. In a moment they focused on it. Jean, riding away from the ranch house. He heard a Mexican woman in the kitchen cry out in that age-old wail of sorrow, "Aiy-ai-aiy."

Chalmers watched her go. She rode down the slope toward the first bottoms of the feeder creek, rose on the long rise of the low hill beyond. She disappeared without looking back. Chalmers made a muted sound, his eyes on the blankness of that ridge to the north of him. He thought of what he had told her: "Someday I'll see you ride over that hill, coming back to me." And he knew he was lying to himself when he said it. She would not come back. She was as stiff, as stubborn, as he was and she would not give an inch.

"But she's got to." He spoke to himself, yet aloud in a low, tired voice. "I can't give in any more than she can. It just isn't in our natures to weaken and change. Maybe that's why we love each other, love this hard country that makes a man fight to win it and keep his place in it. You've got to be tough and hard and you just can't weaken. That's why Jean and I belong in it. But it's going to be a hell of a place to live without her."

He drew a deep breath. It was curious, but the crest of the hill seemed to be getting closer to him. It still was a bare hill, though, and no sign of Jean riding back to him. But—it kept getting closer. He thought bewilderedly: Hell, I've mounted and the horse is trotting; it started by itself and it's trotting

141

now. But he was wrong. Wrong on two counts. He had unconsciously started the horse forward and the horse wasn't trotting, it was galloping now.

He rode fast now, thinking that if he hurried he would see her a quarter mile away, going through the big north meadow. See her just as soon as he crested the ridge. He could stop there and watch her ride away. See her perhaps for the last time.

At the crest of the hill he pulled up sharply and his hands dropped to his side. She was not riding through the big north meadow. She was not beyond the meadow, either. She was pulling up her horse right there on the hill beside his and she was holding out her arms to him, just as he was reaching toward her.

Neither spoke. They did not have to speak to know. In a few moments the horses turned of their own accord and walked down the hill toward the ranch buildings. Chalmers had Jean's right hand tight in his left. It was warm and a little moist from the charging emotions. He swallowed and said, "That north meadow looks ready, I'll put some feeder stuff on it this week."

Jean said, "Yes, Sam," and she squeezed his hand. And then they looked deep into each other's eyes, smiling and content.

Brand
of a
Man

For Henry and Matt Kentta

A GRIN softened Owen Delaney's brown eyes. He was a man in his middle twenties, unshaved and travel-stained, his dust-caked hat pushed back to expose a shock of rebel black hair. His nose had obviously been fist-broken recently and well, but the flaw, now that he was smiling, gave a pixie quality to what otherwise might have been somber features. His shoulders were noticeably broad, but except for the gun belt and holstered six-shooter around his middle, there was little to call attention to his waist, for he ran directly to legs, and when he moved it was with the mincing step of a horseman who is startled to find solid earth beneath his boots. Picking up the saddle he had carried too long, he started toward the corral, expecting the boy to notice him, but the boy was too occupied with his own trouble.

The lad—no more than ten, Delaney judged him—had led a saddled horse from behind the apparently abandoned barn, and now the boy was engaged in an animated conversation with the animal and he was punctuating his conversation with words his father undoubtedly hadn't taught him intentionally. Owen stopped by the corral fence and stood there a full minute, listening to the running tirade, then, a growing uneasiness at his eavesdropping claiming him, he cleared his throat loudly and said, "When you get that big ranch you're figuring on buying, you suppose you might have a job for a right good bronc buster?"

The boy spun in his tracks. The sudden movement startled the horse and the animal shied. For a moment the boy and the man stared at each other, a smiling, unshaved stranger with a gun, and a wide-eyed kid, unmasked by surprise until his face was as easy to read as gathering weather. The boy was hurt and bewildered, too young to understand the adult world around him, too old to cry openly about it. His surprise turned with a blazing suddenness into a desire to strike out at anything adult around him, and Owen Delaney was the nearest target.

"You got no business snooping around here!" the boy shouted, and whatever pent-up emotion was in him broke loose all at once. He came running toward the fence full

5

tilt, ducked through the rails and threw himself at Delaney, a kicking, clawing, curse-spitting bundle of fury.

Owen backed off from the startling attack, and in an instinctive move of self-preservation he grabbed the boy by the front of his bib overalls, twisted his hand, and lifted the youngster free of the ground. For a second Owen was holding a writhing bundle of arms and legs, then the flailing fists and kicking feet slowed their motions, like a clock motor running down, as the boy's sense of helplessness grew. Still Owen held him, but now the grin was back in Owen's eyes. "Whoa, now," Owen said. "Whoa, easy. You and me are gonna get ourselves wore out on each other before we meet!"

"You ain't got no damn business———" the boy started.

"And quit that cussin'," Owen said. "I might be a preacher, for all you know." He put the boy down, watching him carefully, but the boy's anger was already running out. "That's better," Owen said.

"You ain't got no business snoopin' around," the boy said, still trying to hold onto his defiance.

"That could be, likely enough," Owen said. "But it didn't look to me like anybody was living here and the drinking water in that pump looked mighty cool and inviting. You wouldn't deny a thirsty man a drink, now would you?"

The boy's anger was on the verge of reviving. "You one of Mead Weber's riders?"

"If I am," said Owen, "I ain't on the payroll. I never been in Oregon before in my life. I was just passing through, saw this ranch here and thought maybe I might get a job."

The boy was doubtful. He looked around carefully and said, "Where's your horse, then?"

"Lost him in a poker game two days back," said Owen. "And let that be a lesson to you."

The boy was almost convinced he had made a mistake and embarrassment started to claim him. He started backing off, his eyes on Owen, but he was soon stopped by the fence at his back. His eyes darted wildly, like the eyes of a trapped animal, then he half turned, stared at his horse, and said, "I ain't never seen a saddle just like yours before."

The discomfort of the boy was so acute Owen could feel it. He touched the heavy, double-rig saddle with the toe of his boot and said, "No? That extra cinch comes in handy if you got a big he-cow on the end of your line."

6

The boy risked a glance at the extra cinch and Owen said, "See a lot of saddles like this up in Wyoming now'days."

The boy eagerly grasped the escape of the turn in conversation. "Gee!" he said. "You all the way from Wyoming?"

"I been there," Owen said.

A startling thought apparently claimed the boy's mind completely and exploded into words. "You a cattle buyer?"

"Afraid not," Owen said.

"Oh," the boy said. His disappointment was apparent, but he tried to hide it. "I knew you wasn't," he said. "There ain't no cattle buyers coming."

It was an echo of adult disappointment, Owen knew, and now he took another look around the abandoned ranch, nestled here in the crook of the arm of a larger valley. Through a notch in the hills he could see distance, a valley well watered and deep with grass, and beyond its green wealth the towering Blue Mountains jealously horded the last of winter snow in the folds of timbered slopes. A day behind him, rock-crested and lava-strewn hills carried scatterings of sage and juniper eastward toward the broken volcanic wastes of Idaho, and beyond that, like a memory he chose to forget, was Wyoming. He looked at the boy and asked, "Was this your folks' place?"

"Until today, it was," the boy said. "We sold out." His chin was up and there was defiance in his features, a young boy imitating an older man, his father, probably. . . . "It ain't no good here in Oregon," the boy said. "Everybody's got cows and there ain't no place to sell cows——" His voice had risen into a defensive treble. "We're going back to Missouri. My Mom's folks live back there and it's gonna be real good——" Tears were uncomfortably near.

Owen nodded. "I been to Missouri," he said. "Mighty pretty. I guess about the most fun I ever had in Missouri was catching catfish as long as your leg." He gave the boy a quick glance and found interest. "You see how it is," said Owen, "you get yourself a pole and a hook and a bobber. Got to have a bobber so when those big liver-lip cats get to gummin' at your bait——"

"But they got horses in Missouri, ain't they?" the boy said.

"What?"

"Horses. Pa says we don't need horses. Pa says I got to

7

sell my horse." The boy was back through the fence, and now he had the reins of the saddled horse and his free hand was clutching the horse's nose, as if in that way he could hold the animal.

Owen Delaney felt a wash of memory. He thrust his hand through the fence and said, "My name's Owen Delaney. What's yours?"

The boy took the hand seriously, shook once, and said, "I'm Bud Patterson," then, quickly, "but they do have horses in Missouri, don't they?"

"Mules," Owen said.

"Mules?"

"Mules."

The boy was visibly shaken. "I still don't see why I got to sell Blaze," he said, standing close to the handsome sorrel. "I raised him up and trained him myself."

"I reckon your Pa knows what's best," Owen said.

"But I don't want to sell him!" the boy said, finding sufficient logic in the fact. "Not to Casco Weber, anyway. Casco don't know how to handle a horse——" He looked at Owen, a sudden hope in his eyes. "If I do have to sell him," he said, "do you want to buy him? I could tell you how to take care of him and all——"

Owen felt the inadequate weight of his last silver dollar pressing against his leg. He avoided the boy's eyes and said, "I consider that a compliment, Bud, you offering to sell me a fine horse like that, but I guess I can't swing it right now." He realized suddenly this was one of the few times in his life he had seriously regretted being broke.

"But if you was going to buy him," Bud Patterson insisted. "How much would you give me for him?"

Owen looked at the boy, knowing his hurt and his need. He tipped his head and gave the horse an expert appraisal. "Pretty fine horse," he said. "Mind if I look him over close?" The boy was eager to show off the animal and Owen climbed through the fence. He circled the horse twice, ran his hand down the muscled legs. His lips pursed, one eye squinted shut, he asked the boy, "Can he roll all the way over when he rubs the sweat out of his hide?"

"Every time!" the boy said.

"Well, there you have it," said Owen, spreading his hands as if the old wives' tale settled it for sure. "He's a hundred-dollar horse."

"They only offered Pa twenty dollars!" the boy said.

Owen simulated disgust and said, "Anybody that would

8

offer twenty dollars for that horse is an out-and-out horse thief."

"I know it!" the boy shouted. "That's what I told Pa! Casco Weber is nothing but a horse thief! Will you tell Pa? Huh, Owen?"

The second mention of Casco Weber's name gave an uncomfortably personal slant to Owen's purely figurative statement and he hastened to mend his fence. "Of course, now, you got to remember that sometimes it ain't what something is worth; it's what you can get. Like you say, there's no market for cattle and times get hard and there's somebody got a little money when he can take advantage——" He was getting himself in deeper and he knew it. Abruptly he said, "This town of Ten Mile I been hearing about. How far is it?"

"Just over the hill. About two miles. Will you tell Pa?"

"I got to get to gettin'," Owen said.

"That's where I'm going," Bud Patterson said. "Ten Mile. I'm supposed to meet my pa and ma there. Casco Weber is supposed to pick up Blaze, but I don't know if I'm gonna let him. Not for no twenty dollars. Damn ole horse thief."

"Good talking to you, Bud," Owen said, picking up his saddle. "Maybe I'll see you in Missouri someday. When you get one of them big catfish on your hook, you think of me." *Catfish,* he added to himself. *All mouth and no brains.*

But Bud Patterson had found an understanding friend, and he had no intention of losing him. Owen had started to walk away, the saddle on his shoulder, when the boy called his name. Owen stopped but didn't look back. "Yeah?"

"That saddle's pretty heavy, ain't it?"

"I've packed lighter."

"It's a long two miles to town. You got to cross the crick."

"Oh?"

"Blaze will pack double."

Owen hesitated. Inside his run-over boots his feet had a bright red feeling. *The devil with it,* he thought. *If God had been so set on a man walking He would have give him more legs.* He turned back and, grinning, he said, "Doggone it, Bud Patterson, that's neighborly of you."

He watched while the boy swung expertly into the saddle and brought the horse through the gate of the corral. Owen tossed his saddle on the fence. He accepted the

9

stirrup the boy freed for him, lifted himself up, then picked the saddle from the fence. The horse shied at the clumsy load, but Bud handled him fine.

They rode down the lane, and the boy seemed to have forgotten his troubles. "Tell me about Wyoming," he said. "What's it like there?"

From his vantage point on the back of the horse Owen had a good look at the abandoned ranch. The front door of the house stood open, sagging a bit, as if too tired to support its own weight. The curtainless windows stared disconsolately out at the hard-packed yard. The roofed-over haystacks, chewed out at the bases until they resembled big yellow mushrooms, indicated winter feeding of stock, but there were no cattle in sight. "Wyoming?" Owen Delaney said. "Like a lot of other places, Bud. Mighty big country for some and small as a closet for others."

"How come you left there?" the boy asked.

"There's a fellow down in the John Day country owed me a drink for three years," Owen said. "I figured if I didn't get there pretty soon he'd like as not drink it himself."

"We heard tell there was big cattle ranches in Wyoming," Bud said. "Pa and some of the others they thought maybe there'd be some cattle buyers coming here, but I guess it's just talk."

Talk, Owen thought. *Talk and dreams . . .*

Owen tilted his face to the sun—a gypsy sun, headed north for the summer. The vagabond creek in the valley sought a roundabout path toward the Snake River. Early this morning a flock of great, honking geese had taunted Owen from his blankets.

The horse shied suddenly, and at the side of the road a laggard, earth-bound squirrel sat bolt upright on a rock and spit high-pitched, chattering accusations at the double-burdened horse as it passed. He'd spend the summer here, that squirrel, then the fall and the winter, and around the seasons again, raising a family, living his small orbit of existence, finally dying. A small animal, willing to challenge something a hundred times its own size for the privilege of sitting on a rock . . . Owen came back to the present.

Everyone had a dream, he supposed. Gold in the hills, wheat in the valley, cattle buyers on the way, ready to make a man rich . . . He glanced back at the deserted ranch, and there was a momentary wash of memory on

10

his face, a memory with sadness and hurt and bitterness. He shook his head and shrugged and erased the picture from his mind. A ranch had failed. A dream had ended. But it was none of Owen Delaney's affair.

The boy said, "That's just what Casco Weber is. A horse thief. You'll tell him so, won't you, Owen?"

BEYOND the hill and across the creek the town of Ten Mile, too, had been built on a dream. Gold, with its attendant activities, had boomed the mushroom camp into a substantial little city of brick buildings and false fronts. Two churches once vied for lost souls who roared in and out of fifteen saloons, and a mark of social distinction was a man's position in the volunteer fire department. Men talked of the future of Ten Mile, the metropolis of eastern Oregon, and women dreamed, while the few cattle ranchers in the lush valley found a ready-made market for their beef in the ever-increasing hordes of miners, freighters, businessmen, and all the flotsam and jetsam of the frontier. In the mid sixties it was a bright dream that couldn't die. Now, less than twenty years later, it was dead.

The placers petered out, and the miners left. Freight lines stopped running to Ten Mile, and in time even the Star Route mail ceased coming here. One by one business establishments closed and now only three remained open. Mead Weber's General Merchandise store, Mead Weber's Golden Eagle Saloon, and, squeezed between the two, narrow and thin, as if gasping for existence, a bank with the still-imposing name of Miners' and Cattlemen's Exchange. Ten Mile sat in the sun, like an old man dreaming of his past, and the creek that gave the town its name carried the golden memories through the valley and the canyons and lost them beyond in the river.

In a well-furnished apartment above the bank in the now-dead town of Ten Mile a man and a woman who had been married thirty years found difficulty in facing each other. The man's name was Harold Osgood. He owned the bank, but at the moment he was beginning to fear he didn't own his soul. He was positive his wife, Mattie, knew his fear.

He was an unimpressive man, average in height, average in build, a man who had become a financial success and had trouble believing it. His wife, a woman of fifty,

11

stood a head taller than he, in spite of the low heels she always wore, and whenever possible she sat down in his presence. She knew people around town said she was big enough to go bear hunting with a buggy whip, and she knew the description was apt, but as long as Harold didn't say so, Mattie didn't care.

She was moving around the room now, engaged in her eternal dusting, a fascinatingly plain woman with large hands and feet and a love for her husband that was so acutely real it was painful to her. Without looking at Harold she said, "Isn't there something you can do about it?"

"What do you expect me to do?" Harold asked. His face was thin, drawn with the grabbing pain of an ulcer that bothered him with increasing frequency. "Jake Patterson wants to sell his ranch, Mead Weber wants to buy it. Isn't that simple enough? Why do you have to make it sound more important than it is?"

"Because it is more important, Harold," she said.

Harold tugged the lapels of his coat tightly into place. "I think you're overlooking the fact that my first obligation is to Zoe Middleton," he said. "And at this point, whatever is good for Mead Weber is good for Zoe." He was pleased with his own simple analysis and he jerked his head, like a chicken taking a drink of water.

Mattie rehearsed the words in her mind before speaking. "The Pattersons are such old friends," she said. "I just thought you might be able to work something out——"

"Nothing I can do," Harold said.

"Why, Harold?" Mattie asked. She wanted a direct answer now. She wanted him to come right out and say he couldn't do anything because he was afraid of Mead Weber. If he would only say it, maybe she could help him. . . .

Harold Osgood gripped the lapels of his coat, as if trying to hang onto himself. "Mattie," he said, "I believe I know how to run my business."

You do, she thought, *but you don't know how to run yourself.* She looked at her husband, loving him, knowing there was nothing more she could say. She had given him his chance to discuss it with her and he had refused the chance. Her voice was tired. "You do what you think is right, Harold," she said.

He started to leave the apartment to go to his appointment downstairs. He stood there by the door, and Mattie

12

could feel his thoughts, his reluctance to go against his own ideals, his fear to refuse. He turned suddenly and came back to her and kissed her. "I love you, Mattie," he said. "You're a wonderful wife." He darted through the door and was gone and she heard his rapid footsteps descending the stairs.

She closed the door behind him and for a long moment she stood there. She looked at her huge hands and down at her feet and tears came to her eyes. *He really means that*, she said to herself. *He's such a good man. Why can't he stand up for himself?* She picked up the turkey-feather duster and started dusting the books.

Downstairs Harold Osgood opened the door of the bank as he had every morning since the gold rush of the sixties. He stood briefly looking at the town, proud of the part he had played in its establishment, even more proud of the part he had played in holding it together. He looked at Mead Weber's General Merchandise store, remembering when it had belonged to Al Zelinski, and he looked at Mead Weber's Golden Eagle Saloon, remembering when he had loaned Til Calegari the money for the original fixtures. Suddenly Harold Osgood was tired, and it was the tiredness of shame. He went to his desk at the back of the room, knowing he wouldn't have long to wait.

He removed his coat and hung it carefully, then took a green eyeshade from the wrought-iron costumer and put it precisely in place on his half-bald, bullet-shaped head. The sharp morning sun, seeping through the bank window, filtered through the eyeshade and threw a green shadow across the banker's birdlike features, giving them a sickly, chartreuse cast. He heard the door open and without looking up he said, "Come in, Mead."

The man who walked briskly across the room said, "You don't sound very chipper, Harold."

"Because I don't like it, Mead," Harold said, pushing out a chair. "I don't like a bit of it. These people are old friends. This isn't the way we first discussed it at all."

Mead Weber sat down, a ruggedly handsome man of thirty with curly blond hair, a blocky chin, and blue eyes that never quite smiled. "Money is the only friend a man has, Harold," Mead Weber said, "and we're going to make plenty of that." He tilted back in his chair, took a penknife from his pocket, and started carefully cleaning his nails. Glancing up, he said, "You agreed to it, Harold. You're the one financed buying the cattle. I'm just doing the job."

"But it's the way you're going about it——" Harold Osgood's face was starting to perspire. He hated that about himself. The only outlet he had for anger was a perspiring face. "Mead," he said, "you've got this business built just like a pyramid——"

"Sitting on its point, teetering back and forth, ready to be pushed over any minute," Mead Weber finished. "I know. You've told me before."

"I've told you before and I've told you the truth," the birdlike little man said. "If I could just get it through your head——"

A bellowing roar of laughter from the saloon next door blasted through the walls of the bank. The laughter seemed to strike Harold Osgood like a fist. He sat frozen, and any confidence that was in him drained out like sand from a broken bag.

Mead Weber looked up, the grin on his face full. "Sounds like my big brother is having a good time," he said.

"All night," Harold Osgood said. He took a handkerchief from his pocket and dabbed his forehead. "All night long it was like that. My wife didn't get a wink of sleep."

"She's big enough to stand it," Mead Weber said.

A flush stained Harold Osgood's cheeks, but he ignored the reference to his wife's size. He looked across the desk to where Mead Weber still cleaned his nails with the knife. "Mead, is there anything you aren't telling me?"

"Nothing important," Mead said.

"Then why did Casco have to come to town?"

Mead shrugged his ample shoulders. "Thirsty, I guess," he said.

"Mead, if you're planning anything you aren't telling me about——"

Mead Weber snapped the knife shut. He took his feet from the desk and leaned forward. "If I am, Harold," he said, "what will you do about it?"

Harold felt like a bird plucked of all its feathers, knowing he was naked, knowing he had no place to hide. "Mead," he said, "why do we have to be underhanded about it? Why can't we just admit we know there are cattle buyers scouting the country? That's all I ask, Mead. If we could do it that way, I'd back you all the way, you know that."

14

"Are you crazy?" Mead asked. "In the last month I've bought up close to a thousand head of cows, and I bought them at ten to twenty dollars a head. If those ranchers between here and Pendleton were sure of a market, the price on those same cows would jump to sixty dollars a head. You're a businessman. You shouldn't have any trouble seeing that."

"But we've still got to hold them, Mead. We've got to have grass. Those cows won't eat rocks."

"Funny," Mead said. "That's just what Casco said." He looked steadily at the fidgeting little banker. "You know what Casco thinks? He thinks we ought to just move that herd into this valley without asking anybody."

Harold Osgood got to his feet. His tongue stuck to the roof of his mouth and he had to try twice before words would form. "No, Mead," he said. "I told you. I'd never stand for that."

Mead shrugged. "Then what are we arguing about? There's been no trouble, has there? Patterson and the others have wanted to sell out. We're offering them a fair price."

"We're stealing their places," Osgood said. "You know it."

"Would you rather see Zoe and me lose a thousand head of cattle?" Mead asked.

Harold Osgood felt sick to his stomach. He was trapped, and he knew it. He wasn't exactly sure how it had come about, but it had, and now he was into it over his head, afraid to back out, afraid to go ahead. All he knew for sure was that within the last two months cowboys with money in their pockets—money supplied by Harold Osgood—had appeared at isolated ranches in places as far as a hundred miles from here. They always had the same story. They could use ten or twenty head, if the price were right. They were small purchases, not enough to excite suspicion, but now those small dribbles of cattle had been gathered into a herd of a thousand beasts, and the herd was headed for Ten Mile Valley. It was as if Harold Osgood had created a monster that was moving in to devour him, and his only salvation was to sell out men who bragged openly of Harold Osgood's honesty.

"Let's hurry it up, Harold," Mead Weber said. "The Pattersons are next door at the store, waiting." Mead picked up a handwritten list, a sort of inventory he had made up of the few possessions the Pattersons had thrown

15

in with the sale of the ranch. Harold's hands were shaking as he took the list, but a practice born of long habit made him glance through it.

Halfway through the list his eyes stopped. He snatched off his green eyeshade and immediately popped it back on again. "The boy's horse?" he said. "What on earth do you want with the boy's horse?"

"I told Casco I'd buy it for him," Mead said. "Twenty dollars. It's a good horse."

"No," Harold Osgood said. That had always been a difficult word for him to pronounce, and he said it again, trying to give it authority. "It's ridiculous," he said. "You've got more horses now than you know what to do with."

"Casco wants him," Mead said.

"I don't care what Casco wants——"

"Harold, I don't think you mean that," Mead said.

Again the anger ran out of Harold Osgood. No, he didn't mean it, and he knew he didn't, just as surely as he knew he was going to do anything Mead Weber told him to do. It was a difficult thing, admitting fear, even to himself. He couldn't admit it to his wife, Mattie, but that is what it was. Deep, physical fear that soured the marrow of his bones. The booming laughter came from the saloon next door, and Harold Osgood remembered a night, during the mining boom, when he had heard that laughter and he had seen a drunken miner with a broken back, threshing hideously in the dust of the street while Casco Weber stood over him and laughed. . . . "It seems such a senseless thing," Harold said.

"Casco's in a good humor," Mead said. "Let's keep him that way."

The sickness was back in Harold's stomach, threatening to gag him. He got up and went to the safe, put the inventory inside, and took out a handful of bills. "Will you try to make this do, Mead?" he said, handing the money across.

Mead Weber counted the money, then took off a twenty-dollar bill and stuffed it in his pocket. "That one's mine," he said, getting to his feet. "I already paid for the horse out of my own pocket."

"Out of my pocket," said Harold.

Mead laughed and slapped the little man on the back. "You're a card, Harold," he said. "You really are."

Mead was halfway to the door when Harold mustered up the courage to ask the question. He gripped the edge of

16

the desk for support, took a deep breath, and said, "Have you and Zoe set the date?"

Mead stopped. A hint of color flushed the back of his neck and Harold wondered if he had gone too far. But Mead didn't turn around. "Not yet," he said. "Maybe today."

He walked outside, and for a moment he stood on the sidewalk in front of the bank, angered by what he considered Harold Osgood's prying into his private affairs, angered actually because he hadn't been able to give a positive answer to Harold's question.

Standing here, no more than twelve feet from the door of the saloon, Mead could hear the racket inside plainly, the slam of a hamlike fist on the bar, a bellow of laughter, the familiar voice of his brother proclaiming to the world that he was a he-wolf, out to howl. The drunken bellowing of his brother angered him, too. *The devil with him,* Mead thought. *Let him drink himself stupid. He'll either stay out of trouble or get into it, and I don't much care which.*

The Patterson wagon, loaded high with household goods, was drawn up in front of Mead Weber's General Merchandise and now Mead's attention turned that way and to the business at hand. Two men were talking to Patterson—Frank Levering and Scott Granger, Patterson's two neighbors, and, hearing Jake Patterson's thin, reedy voice bragging about selling out, Mead thought with a grim humor, *if I let Jake talk long enough he'll talk the other two into selling.*

Mead started toward the store and a girl came out, arm and arm with Martha Patterson, and immediately Mead's anger left him and he felt a warm pleasure. He had known Zoe Middleton ever since the two of them had been kids together. He had thought she was beautiful then; he knew she was now, and the fact that she was wearing his engagement ring never ceased to amaze him. It was like an accomplishment—bigger than the two signs in town that bore his name—almost as big as his plan to take over the valley. A sudden howl of laughter from the saloon intruded on his pleasure, and he saw Zoe look that way and saw the annoyance she felt. In that moment Mead Weber knew he hated his brother.

Jake Patterson had seen Mead, and his voice lifted in his own brand of humor. "Yes-sir-ee-bob, Frank," Jake said to Levering. "I advise you to give Mead a yank before he gets off the hook. I hope he don't find out that mowing machine I sold him is short a Pitman rod before I get out of town——" Patterson was a little boy whistling in the dark, a man choked on the gall of failure. There was a stiff pride in the man, and he had to joke now to keep that pride under control. He was a man who had fought for what little he had, faced with the sudden realization there was nothing left for which to fight. "Dern kid," he said to his wife. "He should ought to been here by now." To Mead he said, "I let you take me jest a leetle on the boy's horse. Done it a purpose. Didn't want to be too hard on you."

"Give and take, Jake," Mead said. He could afford to be magnanimous. He had just purchased Patterson's ranch for one tenth of what it was worth and he had purchased it without putting up one cent of his own. He stopped directly behind Zoe Middleton, leaned forward, and with his lips close to her ear said for her alone, "It's been a long day, Zoe. I thought you'd be in earlier."

She turned and gave him that quick, fleeting smile that always made him unsure of himself. He was conscious of the deep blue of her eyes, the golden wash of her hair, the loveliness of her figure, but he was conscious also of the fierce determination and stubbornness of which he knew this girl was capable. There was a pride in her that went back a long ways, and sometimes Mead Weber wondered if there wasn't a close connection between love and the breaking down of another's pride. . . . "I hate to see them go, Mead," she said.

"You hate change, Zoe," he said. "Trouble is, things go right on changing anyway." To Patterson he said, "Everything checked out fine, Jake." To go along with Jake's private joke, he added, "Except for that darned mowing machine." He turned to Frank Levering and Scott Granger, family men with ten kids between them, and he said, "By golly, I'll tell you, a man has to watch the gold in his teeth."

"Hear any more talk about them Wyoming cattle buyers, Mead?" Frank Levering asked. He was an older man, his hair white, his face seamed, his mouth drawn down at one corner from years of supporting a crooked-stem pipe.

"Yes, talk," Mead said. He shrugged. "A man hears plenty of that."

"Where there's smoke there's fire," Zoe Middleton said. "I'm still in the cattle business, thanks to Harold, and I'm not going to sell out regardless of what kind of offer Mead Weber makes me." She made a quick face at Mead.

18

"Ain't likely Mead would make me the same offer he'd make you, Zoe," Frank Levering said. His eyes twinkled like sun-touched frost on a roof top.

"Trouble with Zoe," Scott Granger said, "she'd rather starve to death in Oregon than be a millionaire someplace else."

"I'm afraid you're right, Scott," Zoe said. Her voice held affection for an old friend. "Dad did a pretty good job of making a rancher out of me, it would seem."

"Had to promise her we'd live in her end of the valley before she'd even let me take that ring out of the box," Mead said. He took the money from his pocket and said, "Well, Jake, I guess I can't put off parting with it any longer——"

"Yonder comes Bud," Martha Patterson said. She shaded her eyes. "Land sakes, that youngster! Who's it with him?"

THE MOMENT Bud Patterson saw his parents the excitement that had been building in him burst. He slammed his heels into his horse's ribs and the spirited sorrel jumped forward. Caught off guard, Owen Delaney had to grab for the cantle with one hand. The heavy saddle he was packing banged against the horse's side and the animal shied violently. By the time Bud brought the horse under control they were practically on top of Jake Patterson's wagon and they couldn't have been more the center of attention if they had built a bonfire in the street.

Martha Patterson was calling for Bud to be careful; Jake was berating the lad as a darned fool. The boy, apparently, was hearing none of it. To Owen it seemed the lad was yelling at the top of his voice, and his yelling was directly concerned with Owen.

"Owen says it wouldn't cost nothing to feed Blaze, Pa. Owen says there's plenty of grass between here and Missouri, if you know how to go. Pa, I don't have to sell him, do I? Owen says——"

Owen looked down into the blank faces and saw one dozen eyes, all centered on him, and out of those dozen eyes he saw one pair of deep blue and he became acutely conscious of his unshaved cheeks and his battered appearance. He leaned down and gently dropped his saddle, then swung off the horse. He was greeted by silence, and for a moment he stood there, half grinning, then noting the

19

strong family resemblance and, putting two and two together, he said to the older of the two women, "You're Mrs. Patterson, I take it?" His grin was full, the pixie grin, aided by the mildly askew nose. "Quite a boy you got here," he said.

"I don't believe . . . ?" said Mrs. Patterson.

"Delaney, ma'am," said Owen, taking off his hat. "Owen Delaney. Got caught without a horse and Bud here was kind enough to give me a ride into town." He spoke to Mrs. Patterson but he saw the girl. The blue eyes were on him. Her hair was golden, her face oval, but not too full, the cheekbones high, the chin firm and determined. Her skin, too, was golden, as if she worshiped the sun, and her lips were full and soft. "I don't usually walk," he said, and he said it directly to her.

The best-dressed man in the crowd was between Owen and the girl, a man of thirty, Owen judged, well built, handsome, successful. He had an open smile, a friendly man, and yet there was something cold behind those eyes, something Owen didn't like, and he didn't like the way the handsome man looked at him but saw only the gun on his hip and the saddle at his feet. "Down on your luck, cowboy?" the handsome man asked.

"Never all the way," Owen said. He hadn't meant for it to sound exactly that way, but it came out as a challenge.

"Go on over to the saloon there and get yourself a drink and something to eat," the handsome man said. "Just tell the bartender Mead Weber said it was all right."

There was no longer a grin on Owen Delaney's face. He could feel the girl's blue eyes and he was conscious of the boy. He looked at Mead Weber and said, "I work for what I get, friend. I pay for what I eat and drink."

"No offense meant," Mead Weber said. "I was just trying to be friendly."

"Why?" Owen said.

He didn't wait for an answer. He reached down and picked up his saddle and as he did, Bud Patterson snatched at Owen's sleeve and held it. "Wait a minute, Owen," the boy said. "Tell Pa what you told me about Wyoming." The boy was selling his new friend to anyone who would listen. "Owen's a bronc buster," he said. "He come all the way from Wyoming and he drove a herd of cows up from Texas and he fought Indians—— Pa, Owen says there's a lot of great big ranches in Wyoming and they surely do need cows——"

The old man with the white hair and the frosty eyes

and the crooked-stem pipe showed a sudden interest. The man beside him with the stamp of cattleman in every line of his face lifted his head suddenly. Mead Weber, it seemed to Owen, was immediately on the defensive, and now there was a harshness in his face Owen hadn't noticed before. *Push this man and he'll fight with any weapon he can get his hands on,* Owen thought.

It was Jake Patterson who turned the boy's eager statement to idle, childish prattle. "Yeah, we know all about them big ranches in Wyoming needin' cows," he said. "Long as them longhorn Texas jack rabbits hold out and there's fellers like you to drive 'em I reckon them Wyoming ranches won't worry." He turned to his son. "Bud, you yank your saddle off that sorrel——"

"Wait a minute," the girl with the blue eyes said. "Did you just come from Wyoming, Mr. Delaney?"

"Roundabout," said Owen.

Her question was blunt. "What did you do for a living there?"

He gave her a slow appraisal. She had a shadow of a dimple in her left cheek. "Threw rocks at the moon, mostly," he said. "What do you do for a living here?"

The sudden noise from the nearby saloon stopped her answer, and he had a feeling it was just as well.

The double doors of the saloon were banged outward, as if by a great blast of air, and now a man stood there, his back to the people in the street, his hands grasping either side of the doorframe, his shoulders filling the opening. The man was laughing, his shoulders shaking with the deep-down satisfaction of his mirth, and his voice came out with his laughter, a barrel-chest voice, raw with whiskey. "All my life," the big man said, "when my daddy was stealin' cows from old man Middleton, I used to tell myself someday I'd buy my own saloon and drink it dry. Now I own a saloon and my baby brother is gonna marry old man Middleton's filly daughter." The laughter burst forth again, obscene, drunken, and loud. "Can you beat that, Henry?" the big man asked of the unseen bartender. "I ask you, can you beat it?" He took a step back through the door and his voice was a threat. "Answer me, damn you," he shouted, "or I'll come back in there and use your head for a bung starter."

The answer was apparently forthcoming and satisfactory, for now the big man turned and walked out on the porch. For a moment he stood there, lurching, his head shaking as he focused his eyes on the crowd.

Everyone except Mead Weber, Owen, and the boy had turned away from the big man on the saloon porch. Owen glanced at the Pattersons, the two ranchers, and the girl. There was anger in the face of Jake Patterson, a quiet but helpless distaste in the two ranchers. The girl was as disgusted as anything else, he thought. Mead Weber's face was flushed.

"Hey, Jake Patterson!" the big man yelled. "You old hayshaker, you. About time you got here. You, boy! Bring me my horse. I'm gonna teach that horse to drink whiskey."

Bud Patterson seemed frozen to the ground. He had his arm around the neck of the horse. His eyes were wide, unblinking, and then he turned to the only help he knew. "Pa," he said, "I don't have to sell him, do I?" Owen saw every word strike deep into Jake Patterson's vitals.

"We talked it out, Son," Jake said. "A deal's a deal. Ain't that what I always taught you, Son?"

Owen could feel the boy's emotions as clearly as if they were his own. This was the moment of truth for young Bud Patterson. Everything that had been boiling inside him—all the adult world he couldn't understand—was facing him in this second. The world of childhood was tumbling around his ears and the black void of adulthood was like an abyss in front of him and Casco Weber was standing there, ready to push him over the brink. . . . The boy's emotions broke with a sob and tears flooded down his cheeks. "You can't have him!" he yelled at Casco. "You can't have him! I don't care if a deal is a deal. I don't care about nothing! Owen Delaney says nobody but a stinking, dirty horse thief would offer twenty dollars for Blaze. Owen Delaney says that's what you are, Casco Weber, a dirty, rotten stinking horse thief!" The voice broke off in muffled sobs as the boy buried his face against the neck of the horse.

There was dead silence. Casco Weber stepped down off the porch of the saloon. He walked slowly toward the group of people, and there was no lurch in his step. He stopped, his feet spread, a half smile on his battered features. "And just who in the devil is this Owen Delaney?" he asked. His voice now had a surprising softness.

Owen looked at the sobbing boy. He saw the tortured face of Jake Patterson, the face of a father naked in failure in the eyes of his son. Mrs. Patterson held a handkerchief to her face. And he saw something else—felt it—and that was a fear, a tangible thing that was in the air, seeping from all these people, from Mead Weber himself, and he knew, as certainly as if someone had told him, that everyone here, with the exception of the girl, was afraid of Casco Weber. It wasn't a new fear, nor a fear of the moment, but an old thing that went back in time, and not an imagined fear, but a fear with reason behind it. He knew this was so, and at the same time he knew that he himself was not afraid.

The big man's question hung in the air, waiting for an answer, and Owen gave it. "I guess *I'd* have to be Owen Delaney, wouldn't I?" he said.

Casco looked at the battered clothes, the run-down appearance of the man in front of him. They were about the same height, but where Owen was as lean as a piece of rawhide Casco was heavy. His stomach bulged over his gun belt, pushing his underwear through the gaps of his shirt. His arms were as thick through as a man's leg. His face looked as if it had been slammed against the ground too many times, but when he grinned there was something almost friendly about him, like a huge, ugly pup baring its teeth, then wrinkling its nose, turning a snarl into a deceiving smile. He smiled now, made a half circle around Owen, nodded his head once and said, "Yeah, I guess you'd be Owen Delaney, all right." The smile died. "What's this to you, Owen Delaney?"

"Casco, forget it!" Mead Weber ordered. "This is just a grub-line rider, fresh in from Wyoming."

That last bit of information seemed to Owen to have been tacked on as a signal of some sort. It was there in the emphasis, the pacing of the words. But if it was a signal, Casco either missed it or chose to ignore it. He reached out suddenly. The heel of his hand caught Owen in the hollow of his shoulder, spinning him half around. "I asked you a question, drifter," Casco said. "What's this to you?"

There was no further word from Mead. One of the ranchers—Patterson, Owen thought—was breathing deeply, a rasping, asthmatic sound. "The boy's a friend of mine," Owen said.

The grin was back on Casco's face. He kept moving, circling, his head moving up and down as he eyed Owen from the toes of his brush-scratched and lava-cut boots to the tip of his high-crown hat. "You pick the wrong friends, Delaney," Casco said. He pretended to have noticed Owen's saddle for the first time, but immediately Owen knew this was the real object of the big man's attention. Owen side-stepped, but it was too late. Casco caught his toe under the fork of the saddle. With a mighty kick he lifted the rig from the ground. It traveled only a few inches, but it was sufficient to catch Owen on the shins and the weight of it knocked him off balance. "Now pick that thing up and get out of here," Casco said.

For the briefest second Owen saw the girl. Zoe Middleton's eyes were bright—hopeful, Owen thought. Owen caught his balance and now every semblance of his grin was gone. He stood there, feeling a deep-down rage he had supposed he had long ago learned to control. The skin on his face was tight and hot. His mouth was dry, and his voice sounded to him as if it were coming from outside his own body, saying words he had heard someplace a long time ago, a long ways away. . . . "Nobody tells me where to go or when," the voice said. "I'll leave when I'm ready and not before."

"You're ready," Casco Weber said. "Right now." He turned and started to walk away.

"Wait a minute," Owen said. He moved forward. His right hand reached out and gripped Casco's shoulder, ready to spin him around. It was the move Casco had expected and wanted. His big arm jerked back like a piston and his elbow caught Owen savagely just below the ribs. It was quick and brutal and savage. It drove the air from Owen's lungs and sent him sprawling.

He lay there in the dust of the street, gasping, half sick to his stomach. His ears were ringing and the voices sounded far away. "All right, Casco," Mead Weber said. "Forget it, will you?"

"You let me handle this, baby brother," Casco Weber said. "There's some things you do good and some I do better. You put your name on these signs around town and make love to the ladies. You do that fine. Me, now, I'm gonna put this double-rig saddle on bronco boy there and ride him out of town. That kind of work, I like fine."

FOR A moment the world spun and blurred in front of Owen Delaney's eyes. He gasped, his breath caught, his vision cleared, and he saw Casco Weber, as big as a mountain, coming toward him, a man so supremely sure of himself he did not know the meaning of caution. It was this alone that gave Owen an advantage. The big man bent down, his hands reaching, and in that second Owen

24

doubled his legs and kicked out and up. His boots struck Casco in the stomach, straightening him, and Owen flipped to his feet.

He didn't stop there. The momentum of his lunge threw him forward in a half run. He had his right fist doubled, his arm close to his side, and now the arm shot out and his fist landed squarely in the center of Casco's mouth.

Casco stepped back, shaking his head, and drops of blood flew from his mangled lips. He was surprised, but only for a second. His big head settled into his shoulders until his neck was no longer visible and there was a low, rumbling sound in his throat. He came in then, a big man, depending on brute strength, and Owen was waiting. Owen side-stepped the rush and clubbed Casco on the butt of the jaw.

Again, briefly, Owen saw the girl. Her own fists were doubled, her lips were drawn tight, and suddenly she shouted, "Get him, Delaney!"

Owen spun in his tracks. Again Casco was coming in with that bull-like rush, his arms wide. There was no time to side-step this one. Owen ducked. His shoulder caught Casco in the chest, and as it did, Owen straightened. The force of Casco's rush was his own undoing. Owen's shoulder acted as a fulcrum, and the big man was lifted from his feet. Owen's arms caught Casco around the legs. He wrenched, and Casco landed flat on his back. "Get him now!" Zoe Middleton shouted. "Get him while he's down!"

Still half stunned from the blow in the pit of the stomach, Owen took the time to catch his breath. He stood there, his feet spread, his hair in his eyes, gasping for breath. Casco got to one knee. He paused there, then threw himself to his feet, and this time his weight knocked Owen flat.

They rolled in the dirt of the street, striking against the legs of the onlookers, banging the wheels of the Patterson wagon. It was savage, raw, primitive, and the gouging thumbs of Casco Weber sought Owen's eyes, his throat. He had to break loose, Owen knew. On his feet he felt he could handle himself. In the bearlike embrace of this man, no man would have a chance. . . . He drove his knee wickedly into Casco's groin, heard the big man's grunt of pain, and he threw himself free and lurched to his feet. He was standing directly alongside Mead Weber and he heard Mead's voice, close to his ear, "Casco! I said it was enough!"

"It will be enough when I finish it," Owen said. He was panting for breath.

"Let it go, Mead," Zoe Middleton said. "Casco's had it coming for a long time. Delaney's taking care of himself all right."

He risked a look at her then, and there was a bright excitement in her eyes, as if she herself were in the fight. She met his gaze squarely and honestly, giving him her approval and her backing, and then the moment was gone and again Casco was on his feet, lunging in.

Owen hadn't been wrong in his estimation of the big man. Down on the ground, in a rough and tumble, Casco was a killer. On his feet he was as clumsy as an ox. Owen's strategy became plain. He must hit the man—cut him to ribbons—wear him down—and at the same time he must keep on his own two feet and out of the way of those grasping arms. He felt the jar of the blow up to his elbow as he smashed Casco's face. *Not too hard,* he told himself. *Keep on your feet.* . . .

Time and again he thought he couldn't make it. Even a glancing blow from Casco's fist was enough to shake a man to the bottom of his boots. A solid blow was like an explosion inside Owen's head. But it was a fight for survival, Owen knew, and his one thought was to wear the man down to where he could handle him. His mouth was full of blood and there was a roaring in his ears and when he hit he felt as if he were striking a pillow, and the apparent ineffectiveness of his blows set up a driving rage in him that gave him the strength to walk into Casco's clumsy, clubbing fists. At times he thought he heard the girl calling encouragement, always to him, never to Casco. He thought he heard it. Or was it only because he wanted to hear it?

He kept hitting, hitting, hitting, and then suddenly he knew he was no longer taking as much punishment. Suddenly he knew he had won. He had taken everything Casco could give him and he was still on his feet, still fighting. . . .

The certain knowledge was as if someone had dashed a bucket of cold water into his face and now he saw Casco clearly, a gasping, bleeding face, a head that rolled from side to side, a pair of eyes that were startled, bewildered, almost afraid. . . . Owen Delaney drove his fist into that blurred face. He followed through, hitting again and again, and then he was against a wall, unable to go further, and he realized he had Casco pinned against the wheel of Jake Patterson's wagon.

The Patterson team was rearing and plunging. The wheel twisted, and Casco lurched to one side. Owen reached out with his left hand and grasped at Casco's shirt. It tore free of the big man's body and now Owen felt soft flesh, the flesh of a man's throat. He threw his weight into his arm, jerking Casco close, and he hit him with his right fist, driving him back against the wagon again. Again he reached for him, but this time Casco twisted away, and as he did, Owen saw his opening. His right fist came up from his knee. It landed, and Casco staggered away, then fell, full length and flat on his face.

He wasn't out. He lay there in the dirt, then lifted his weight on his hands, and he was sprawled, belly down, like a giant lizard sunning himself on a log, his body pumping up and down with the labor of his breathing. He seemed finished, but he wasn't. One arm collapsed, but it was not from exhaustion. As his left shoulder hit the ground, Casco rolled completely over and his right hand whipped down toward his holstered gun.

Zoe Middleton's screamed warning was still in the air when Owen jumped. He saw the gun clear the holster, saw it start to move out from Casco's side, and then he landed, his boot smashing solidly against Casco's forearm. The gun hand opened and the gun was there in the dirt. There was a wildness in Owen Delaney. He kicked the gun, then followed and kicked it again, as if it were a living thing, and again he kicked it, into the middle of the street.

Owen was half aware of the man running up the street toward him, a small, old man with a gun in his hand, a badge on his calfskin vest. Owen felt the gun jammed against the small of his back, then the old lawman stepped back, and his gun was swinging, impartially covering both Owen and Casco. "All right," the old man said. "That's all of it. I'll handle this." He had a voice of authority, a small, bristly man of sixty-five. His skin was like parchment, and he looked as if the land had long ago drained all the juices from his body. "What's it about?" he asked.

Owen was gasping for breath. His shoulders were working up and down. He looked at the deputy sheriff and knew the deputy could handle himself. He didn't want trouble, but he couldn't help himself now. There, for a moment, when he had seen the gun in Casco's hand, Owen Delaney had known he could kill, and the knowledge that he could sickened him, but now he knew it and he had to

27

admit it. He saw Mead Weber moving in; he knew the deputy was holding a gun on him, but now he had to say it, get it out in the open. He shoved Mead Weber roughly, nearly knocking him off his feet, and he looked down at Casco. His voice was desperate, almost pleading. "Don't ever try to jerk that gun on me again, friend," Owen Delaney said, "because the next time I won't tromp you, I'll kill you."

There was a long silence, and as Owen stood there the sickness left him and he looked at his shirt, torn beyond repair. He could feel his face now, a throbbing mass of flesh, and his nose felt as big as a melon and he knew it was broken again. There was almost humor in the knowledge of it as overwrought nerves sought to settle themselves. He shook his head, clearing his vision, and now he saw the deputy clearly. The old man was staring at him, understanding him too well, and Mead Weber, too, was watching, again seeing only that gun on Owen's hip. *Say it,* Owen thought. *I'm a killer.* He was afraid to look at the girl, and suddenly there was no fight in him at all. "What did you want me to do?" he asked. His voice was harsh. "He came at me, didn't he?"

"He had it coming," Mead Weber said. "There's no hard feelings on my part."

Owen didn't answer. He started to walk away, but the deputy stopped him, his voice thin and dry. "I got a law on the books about drifters riding in here starting trouble," he said.

"Yeah," Owen said. "I figured you would have."

"Mr. Delaney didn't start it, Jim." It was the girl. Her voice was calm and even. Owen turned then and looked at her and she met his gaze squarely, as a man would meet another man's gaze. She was a woman, beautiful and soft and feminine, but at the same time she was brittle and hard and unyielding. . . .

"I don't care who started it, Zoe," Jim Torrance, the deputy, said. "I just mean to see it don't keep going."

Casco Weber was on his feet. Looking at him standing there, Owen was surprised at the amount of damage his fists had done, aware of how he himself must look. That startled, bewildered look was still in Casco's eyes, and now there was no anger in Owen at all. He managed a grin and offered his hand. "All right?" he asked.

Casco was holding his right arm out from his side. It was wickedly bruised, but it wasn't broken. For a second he seemed ready to return Owen's offered handshake, then

28

he shook his head. When he spoke it was almost as if he was speaking to himself. "No, Delaney," he said. "It's not all right." He drew the back of his left hand across his mouth and looked at the blood, seemingly having a hard time realizing it was his own blood, then he started to chuckle, but the sound wasn't genuine. It had a weird note of hysteria in it. "You know something, Delaney?" he said. "All my life I been thinking what I'd do if any man ever whipped me. I made up my mind I'd shake his hand. That's how I figured I'd feel."

"I was lucky," said Owen. "I'm offering to shake hands."

"I figured I'd feel that way," Casco said. "But I don't. I was up all night. I was all drunked up." The detached tone left his voice and now he was speaking directly to Owen. "I don't want to shake hands, Delaney," he said. "We'll go it again. And the next time it will be different. The next time I'm gonna ram your left leg down your throat and I'll stand there and make you chew it off, right up to the kneecap."

With a sudden movement Casco elbowed both Delaney and his brother Mead out of the way. He ignored Jim Torrance, the deputy. He glared momentarily at Zoe Middleton and said, "I don't like nobody pullin' against me," and then he stalked up the street the short distance to the saloon. Again Casco paused, his back to the knot of people in the street. A visible shudder ran through his big shoulders, then he slammed his fist against the saloon door and went inside.

Owen looked at the girl, and there was a growing feeling in him that he should apologize. "Sorry," he said.

"Don't be," she said. "If you throw rocks at the moon as well as you fight you ought to knock it down someday." She turned away, giving him no chance to pursue a conversation.

"You better come along with me, Delaney," the deputy said.

"If you say so," Delaney said. He picked up his double-rig Wyoming saddle and stood there, waiting for the deputy to make the first move. The deputy seemed reluctant, and, watching him, Owen thought, *He was a big man, once, but now he's taken this job because it is all he can get and the best he can expect is to get a chance to put a drunk or a vagrant in jail.* He saw the slight limp, the old tiredness in the man, and the tiredness was in the lawman's voice when he said to Mead Weber, "You see to it

29

your brother gets out of town and gets sobered up. I've had enough of it."

"All right, Jim," Mead said.

Owen fell into step alongside the deputy and they moved down the street together, a man of sixty-five and a man of twenty-five, and somehow they were alike, both old for their years, both living with their pasts. Without looking at him the deputy said, "A man don't get far, drifting from place to place."

"I got to Oregon," Owen said.

"And found trouble," Jim Torrance said. "Where to from here?"

"Got a friend in John Day," Owen said. "He owes me a drink."

"You sure that's all of it?"

"That's all of it."

"It better be," Jim Torrance said. "They don't like trouble in John Day."

"I'm not after trouble," Delaney said.

"But you don't run away from it if it looks you up?"

"Casco Weber?" Owen shrugged, and a grin tugged at his swollen features and found his eyes. "I didn't have a chance to run, Sheriff."

"Maybe not," Torrance said.

Delaney's eyes were roving the street, seeing the boarded-up windows, the deserted buildings, lingering on the two boldest signs in town. "MEAD WEBER GENERAL MERCHANDISE"; "MEAD WEBER GOLDEN EAGLE SALOON." "Big boy, this Mead Weber," Owen said. "He's got his sign on a lot of things."

"You mean something by that?"

"The girl," Owen said. "He looks at her like he owns her. She's got a ring, so maybe he does."

"You can forget the girl," Jim Torrance said.

"Why, Sheriff?" Owen asked. "Has Mead Weber got his sign on you too?"

Jim Torrance stopped there in the middle of the street. He turned and faced Owen squarely. "Nobody's got a sign on me, Delaney," he said. "And don't push me. I was going to give you a place to sleep tonight and let you go in the morning. Don't invite yourself to a longer stay."

"Fair enough," Delaney said, but he didn't forget the girl. He turned and looked back, and he saw her standing there by the Patterson wagon. She was watching him, and for a second their glances met across the distance between them. "What's her name?" Owen asked.

30

"Mrs. Mead Weber, as far as you're concerned," Jim Torrance said. "I told you to forget it."

A JEALOUSY born of deep-seated uncertainty touched Mead Weber as he looked at Zoe Middleton. She was watching Delaney, and there was unmasked admiration in her eyes for the man who had finally whipped Casco Weber. The old, driving desire to be rid of his troublesome brother had never been stronger in Mead than it was at this moment.

"Doggone it, Mead," Jake Patterson said. "I'm sorry that had to happen. The darned kid——"

Immediately Mead Weber was back to the business at hand, a business that had possessed him like a mania ever since Harold Osgood had suggested the probability of a cattle boom in this country. He meant to own every ranch in this valley, but equally important to him was the necessity of keeping the respect of Zoe Middleton. He glanced at her again and she was watching him as if ready to judge his every word. . . . "Forget it, Jake," Mead said. "You know how Casco is when he gets an idea in his head. He doesn't need the boy's horse any more than he needs a third ear."

Bud Patterson, still trembling with the excitement of the fight, overheard, and there was a guarded hope in his eyes. Jake said, "You already give me the twenty dollars——"

Again Mead felt Zoe's eyes on him. The whole business about the horse had been stupid, Mead knew. It had been typical of Casco, and again he felt that surge of anger toward his brother. "You keep the twenty, Jake," Mead said. "For old-times sake. And lots of luck to you."

"Now, Mead, a deal's a deal," Jake protested, but even as he protested he was cramming the money back into his pocket. The boy stood there, staring at Mead Weber, unable to believe what he had just heard, and then he saw Zoe smiling at him and saw her nod. He had always been able to trust Zoe. He looked at Mead, wanting to thank him, not knowing how, and then with a whoop he was into the saddle. He dug his heels into the sorrel's flanks, wheeled the animal, and headed down the street at a full run, needing the feel of wind and freedom on his face.

Delaney and the deputy sheriff were two blocks down the street. The boy headed the horse straight toward them and they had to split and dodge out of the way. The boy's

31

voice was a ringing triumph. "Owen! I get to keep Blaze!"

"Good!" Delaney shouted, and Mead heard his laugh. He saw Zoe smiling, still watching Delaney, and Mead felt an almost overpowering urge to remind her that it was he, Mead, who had given the boy his horse, not Delaney. Zoe turned toward him then and now the smile was for him alone and everything was all right. . . . She put her hand on his arm.

"That was an awfully nice thing to do, Mead," Zoe said.

The surge of need for her approval he felt was frightening in its intensity. He captured her hand on his arm with his own hand, wishing he could hold that hand forever. "It's like I've been telling you," he said. "I'm a real nice fellow."

She wrinkled her nose at him. "If you don't quit it, you'll convince me."

"Is this a good time to ask you when you're going to let me put that other ring on your finger?"

"It's a good time," she said, "but you've got business to attend to."

She turned and walked away and Mead felt an old familiar weakness in his knees. She was always so close and yet so far away and the constant fear in him was that one of these times she would walk away like this and refuse to come back. *I'd kill a man who tried to take you from me,* he thought, and he realized his heart was pounding against his ribs, his breath nearly choking him. He forced a calmness he didn't feel and said, "We squared up, are we, Jake?"

"All square, Mead," Patterson said, shaking hands. It was final. Patterson felt it and all pretense left him. He looked old and beaten. "If I was your age and had some money to back me up like you do, I wouldn't sell out, Mead. I'd tough it out, some way or another. I put my whole life in that place."

"I gave you all it was worth, Jake," Mead said, an edge of anger in his voice.

For a moment Patterson stared at Mead. "No, Mead," he said. There was a new toughness in his voice. "You give me all I could get. There ain't enough money in the world to pay me what it's worth." He walked away.

Levering and Granger, Patterson's two neighbors, had moved over onto the sidewalk, not wanting to intrude on the business talk. Seeing Patterson start his team, Levering raised his chin and called, "You folks stay on out to my place tonight, then. Thelma's expecting you."

The wagon moved slowly down the street and, watching it, Mead felt a surge of triumph. Two more ranches to go, and then he and Zoe would be married and he would own it all. He didn't even consider Harold Osgood's part in it. Since the death of her father, Osgood had handled all of Zoe's affairs. He'd do whatever was best for Zoe. He thought of his brother and a scowl he couldn't hide crossed his features. Casco was a different matter. He felt surely that it was Casco who was standing in Zoe's way of setting a wedding date. It wouldn't be easy for a girl like Zoe to accept Casco as a brother-in-law. . . . He remembered his promise to Jim Torrance and started toward the saloon, but Frank Levering called to him.

"Me and Scott here been talking," Levering said, taking the constant, heavy pipe from his mouth.

"That so, Frank?" Mead said. Again his heart was pounding, but it was for a different reason. He felt like an angler watching a two-pound trout approaching his bait. Levering and Granger were weakening, Mead knew. He'd get the money from Osgood some way, Mead knew. He'd get it if he had to beat it out of the little banker. . . . "Maybe I'm wrong," Mead said. "I'm taking a mighty long gamble, lining up so much range with the cattle market the way it is."

"I don't reckon it's a gamble if a man can last it out long enough," Levering said. He had a slow, matter-of-fact way of speaking. "This country will come back someday. Can't help it. I figure they'll find a way to mine what ain't been took out yet, far as that goes. If they don't, it's still the best cow country in Oregon." The older man sighed. "You're young enough to wait for it, Mead. I ain't."

"Well, the deal I offered you still holds," Mead said. "Whether I'm right or wrong."

"I'll talk it out with my wife," Levering said. "I ain't one for movin', myself, but those six girls of mine ought to be into a school."

"I guess you're right at that, Frank," Mead said.

Again Mead started toward the saloon, and this time it was Zoe Middleton who stopped him. She came out of the store and, seeing Mead, walked directly to him and offered her arm. Smiling up at him, she said, "Going anyplace in particular?"

"Only where you want to go," he said.

"I have to talk to Harold and Mattie a minute," she said. "It can wait." She gave his arm a small squeeze. "We used to walk together a lot, Mead."

"We'd have the rest of our life to walk together if you'd say the word," he said.

They strolled up the street, past the saloon, the row of deserted buildings. . . . "It makes me sad, seeing this," she said. "Dad was so proud of this town." They passed a tall, abandoned building with the insignia of a fraternal order carved in the gable. "Remember the dances we used to go to here?" she asked.

"It's where I met you," he said. "How can I forget it?"

"You lie like a heathen," she said. "I was eight years old when I met you."

"Eight years old," he said. "All pink and white, the daughter of the wealthiest cattleman in the valley. My dad and my brother and I forget how many rag-tail cousins were camped up the river a mile and Jim Torrance suspected us of stealing chickens." He grinned. "He was right, too." He shook his head. "No, Zoe, I still say it was at that dance I first met you. I had a job in Zelinski's store. Now I own it."

"That means a lot to you, doesn't it, Mead?"

"I doubt you could understand how much, Zoe."

They walked to the end of the street and turned down toward the creek and for a while they skipped stones across the smooth waters of the ford. In time he took her in his arms and kissed her and she pushed away from him, gently. "Is anything wrong?" he asked.

"I don't know, Mead," she said. "I really don't." She turned then and made him meet her eyes. "Mead, did you have to buy out the Pattersons?"

"What's the matter?" he asked, turning it into a joke. "Afraid I'll run out of money before we're married?"

She didn't take it as a joke. "I don't know, Mead," she said. "Where is it all leading to? The store—the saloon. . . . This is the second ranch you've taken over in the past month." There was a deep seriousness in her blue eyes. "It's as if you couldn't stop, now that you've started. To make the store and the saloon pay, you need more customers, and yet you keep crowding people out of the valley."

There was a faint trace of careful anger at the corners of Mead's mouth. "Isn't 'crowding' a harsh word?" he asked.

"Perhaps it is," she said, "but it's what it amounts to. These people are desperate, Mead. It's been six years now since the mines closed down. Six years without a market for their cattle."

"It's been no different for me," he said. "Nor for you, for that matter."

"That isn't really so, Mead," she said. "Harold has handled things well for me. I haven't really wanted. As for you, if there's a ten-dollar bill within five hundred miles of here, somehow you manage to know about it and get it."

"Is there anything wrong with that?" He was no longer trying to control his temper.

"No, there isn't," she said. "As a matter of fact, I admire you for your ability and so do a lot of other people. But not all of us are cut from the same cloth, Mead. You wave a little money under the noses of these people and they panic." She looked at him directly, accusingly. "You bought Patterson out today for one tenth of what his place is worth and you know it."

"How do you think your dad got as much land as he did?" he said. "Isn't that plain business?"

"Perhaps it is," Zoe said. "But Harold tells me you've made the same sort of offer to Levering and Granger. Harold says they're considering it."

The knowledge that Harold Osgood had discussed business with Zoe angered Mead beyond control. He took her arm, not meaning to be rough, unable to help himself. "Listen to me," he said, pulling her close. "I've come a long way in this world. I've fought hard for everything I have. I've got no sympathy for anyone who can't take advantage of the opportunities offered him."

"I know that, Mead," she said, pulling away from his grip. She smiled. "Here we are again," she said. "Right on the edge of a quarrel."

"Zoe, if I could only understand you," he said.

"Don't try so hard," she said. "Shall we go back?"

He didn't want to, but it seemed best, and now when he tried to take her arm she folded her arms across her breasts and walked beside him and there was an unspoken uneasiness between them. "Think it will rain?" he then asked. It was a private joke between them, a way of ending a quarrel.

She didn't give the usual answer. Instead she said, "That drifter—what was his name? Delaney? Do you suppose he'd know anything about all these Wyoming rumors?"

He felt a quick, unreasonable anger toward Owen Delaney and said, "He doesn't look to me as if he'd know much about anything."

"He knows how to fight," she said.

"That's pretty important to you, isn't it?" he said.

"I like a man who stands up for his rights, if that's what you mean. I think any woman does."

"Have I ever backed down from mine?"

"Mead," she said, "why do you always have to turn every statement into a personal affront?"

"I didn't know I did."

They were nearly back to the saloon now and Zoe stopped, looking briefly at the town that was capable of supporting so many people and yet supported so few. In a moment she put her hand on Mead's arm. "A favor, Mead?" she asked.

"Anything, you know that."

"Don't keep tempting Levering and Granger. Let them hang onto their hopes, the same as I have. Let's take the time to find out definitely about all these rumors. Maybe this Owen Delaney knows something."

"Suppose he does?" Mead asked. He could feel his pulse throbbing in his temples. "Suppose there actually are cattle buyers heading for Oregon?" He looked at her steadily. "Would there be anything wrong in you and me owning all the valley?"

She looked at him a long time, knowing him so well, knowing him so little, a growing realization in her voice as she said, "You'd like that, wouldn't you, Mead?"

"That's right, I'd like it," he said.

"You still feel you have to prove yourself, don't you?"

"Do I?"

"You always have, Mead," she said. "You've always had to have just a little more than anyone else."

"And I've had it."

"Don't start stepping on people, Mead," she said. Her voice was soft. "The rest of the people in this valley have a right to live too. Most of them have been here longer than you have." She looked at him. "Ambition isn't a pretty thing if it gets out of hand, Mead. Don't start pushing people around."

"Aren't you getting me mixed up with my brother?" he asked.

"I don't know, Mead," she said. "If I knew the answer to that I'd know the answer about that other ring you've offered me." She turned abruptly and walked away from him, and again he stood there, determined but unsure, then he went directly to the Golden Eagle Saloon, his entire anger directed toward his brother.

Except for the bartender Casco was alone in the place.

He sat at a table near the back of the room, an unopened bottle in front of him. He was rubbing his right arm where Owen Delaney's boot heel had broken the skin and mashed the flesh, and as Mead entered he looked up, his big, broken face ugly and twisted. Seeing him, Mead felt a moment of despair. He glanced around the saloon, big enough to accommodate a hundred men. He remembered when ten bartenders had worked furiously at the bar. There was one, now, and he was seldom busy. The saloon, like the rest of Mead's holdings, was only a symbol of success. He went directly to the table where Casco was sitting and said, "Well, you succeeded in making a fool of yourself again."

"I'm gonna kill me a drifter, Mead," Casco said. "I made up my mind to do it."

"You're going to do what *I* tell you," Mead said. "You can start with getting back out to that cow camp where you belong."

"You giving me orders?" Casco asked. He didn't wait for an answer. "Because if you are, I'm telling you to go to hell." He reached across the table and gripped Mead's arm, twisting it slightly. "Don't let your name on these signs here in town go to your head," he said. "We're still partners, fifty-fifty, all the way, and don't you forget it."

"Did I say we weren't?" Mead said.

"You didn't say it, but you act it," Casco said. "I'm your brother, and don't you forget that, either."

I wish I could, Mead thought, but aloud he said, "You're the one falling down on the job, not me. I found a market for our beef, didn't I?"

"No," Casco said. "Harold Osgood found it. You talked him into keeping quiet about it and that's all you done, and while you done that I been out on that range for a month, sleeping on the ground, eating beans, rounding up that beef. I been doing the dirty work while you been laying around." He waved his hand. "All right, that's all right. But now I got a thousand cows headed this way and they're gonna have to have grass. It was your job to get that grass. What have you done about it?"

Casco had thrust his face close and his breath reeked with twenty-four hours of steady drinking. Mead half turned, the distaste plain in his features. "I just bought out Patterson, didn't I? I've already got the McCaskill place."

"Two cockleburr spreads," Casco said. "How about Levering and Granger? How about Zoe Middleton?"

"I'll handle Zoe," Mead said.

37

There was a lewdness in the sudden slack of Casco's mouth. "Yeah," he said, "I'll bet you will. I wouldn't mind that myself. And while you're having that kind of fun I'm out there chasing cows eighteen hours a day and you're struttin' around playing Mr. Big. You like it that way, don't you?" His voice had risen. "Well, I don't. You better start remembering who you are and how you got there." He stabbed his thumb against his chest. "It was *me* seen to it you got to go to school. It was *me* stole cows to buy you books and clothes to wear. I had to whip our pappy every morning for a month to get him to let you go to school so as there would be one Weber who could read and write and handle a deal like I said to handle it!" Casco was breathing heavily. "Don't you forget none of that, baby brother."

"I'm not apt to," Mead said. "You changed my diapers, too."

"Yeah, I changed your diapers." He made a scribbling motion on the table and his voice was strident. "Maybe I can't even sign my own name, but I know a good deal when I see one. We got one here, and I ain't gonna see you mess it up just because you want to pussyfoot around and be the big mucky-muck gentleman. Another week and everybody in Oregon will know there's Wyoming cattle buyers headed this way. I've been picking up cows for ten dollars a head, see? Good cows. You let this news get out——"

"The news isn't out yet, is it?" Mead said. His own voice had risen.

"Ain't it, now?" Casco said. "Zoe Middleton was talking about it a month ago."

"She was guessing, like everybody else," Mead said. "She tried to talk Patterson out of selling, but he sold, didn't he?"

Casco settled back in his chair. "You get this, Mead," he said. "I been nursin' that herd along, three, four miles a day. We're gettin' into lava country and there ain't grass enough to move that slow. We're gettin' close to here, and you can't hide a thousand cows in your pocket. I had a job to do and so did you. I done mine. Now it's time to do yours. I'm gonna start pushin' those cows hard, and when I get 'em here, I'm gonna push 'em across the river and right into that valley and if some of your fancy friends get hurt, that's gonna be too bad for them. You got that straight?"

"I'll have the grass," Mead said.

38

"You better," Casco said. He stood up. For a moment he looked down at his younger brother, a wash of affection in his eyes. With something close to tenderness he laid his hand on Mead's shoulder, then snatched it away. "Don't try to be two things, Mead," Casco said. "You got to make up your mind what it is you want, the girl or the valley."

"I've made up my mind," Mead said. "I want both. I mean to have both."

"That's fine, Mead," Casco said. "I hope you get 'em. But if it comes to a choice, you're gonna get the valley. I'll see to that."

He reached out and took the unopened bottle from the table, thrust it in the front of his trousers, gave Mead one parting glance, and strode out of the saloon. The bartender said, "You want a drink, Mr. Weber?"

"Yeah, Henry," Mead said. "I guess I do."

Henry was small. He wore a neatly trimmed mustache and he had a dignity about him befitting a better place. Putting a bottle in front of Mead, he said, "You ought to talk Casco into leaving that drifter alone, Mr. Weber."

"What?"

"Casco's made up his mind he's going after that drifter with a gun." Henry poured the drink, his dark eyes giving Mead's face a brief search. "I've been around a lot, Mr. Weber," Henry said. "A man sees a lot in this business. He gets so he can judge things."

"What are you getting at, Henry?"

"This Owen Delaney," Henry said. "He's a killer, Mr. Weber. It stands out all over him. Jim Torrance saw it too."

"Jim locked him up, didn't he?"

"He can't keep him forever," Henry said. "When he lets Delaney out, you better see to it Delaney keeps moving. If you don't, Casco's going to choose him. You can take my word for it, Mr. Weber. Casco won't have half the chance against Delaney with a gun he had with his fists, and he didn't have much show there."

Mead tossed off his drink. He noticed the palm of his hand was sweating. "Thanks, Henry," he said. He went outside and the glare of the sun blinded him, and for a moment it seemed the street was teeming with people and every store in town was doing a thriving business. The valley, the girl, and the town, too, Mead Weber thought. He could have it all. . . .

His heart was pounding against his ribs and he felt giddy and lightheaded. He glanced briefly at the bank and

39

saw Harold Osgood's hatchet face at the window, saw Harold withdraw quickly, as if Mead's glance were a slap. He moved on and now he knew Mattie Osgood was standing in the window of the apartment, looking down at him. Mead didn't risk a look, but he knew she was there. . . .

The devil with the Osgoods, Mead thought. *It's Casco I have to worry about. He could spoil every bit of it with his blundering. . . .*

The bartender's words were ringing in Mead's ears as he moved down the street, still feeling Mattie Osgood's eyes on his back. *Casco won't have half a chance against Owen Delaney with a gun. . . .*

Mead Weber made up his mind. He turned and walked rapidly toward the sheriff's office at the far end of the street.

In the apartment above the bank Mattie Osgood let the curtain at the window drop back into place. She had seen every move in the fight between Owen Delaney and Casco Weber. She had no idea who Owen might be. At this moment she didn't care. She only hoped that Harold had seen that fight.

AS JAILERS went, Jim Torrance was not a bad host. He readily permitted Owen's saddle a place on the uneven pine floor of his combination office and jail, pointed out a pump and zinc-lined trough where Owen could wash his face, then went one step further and brewed a pot of coffee. He was lonesome, and had been for too many years. He was still a deputy sheriff; he still drew a monthly warrant from the county. But he was living on the friendship of his superior and he knew it. He was assigned to the Ten Mile area where he wasn't needed, a man on a pension.

Jim Torrance sat at his desk, his feet propped up, his hat pulled down to shade his eyes. From the street it looked as if he was asleep, but he wasn't. Only once did he make a direct comment. Owen had taken off his shirt and, with a bar of yellow soap, was scrubbing his torso. With no apparent change in position Jim Torrance said, "That bullet hole in your shoulder looks fairly fresh."

Owen stopped, a towel covering the lower half of his face. His eyes moved to his left shoulder, to the puckered, bluish-white flesh, circled with red. "Fairly," Owen said. He went on with drying himself.

"Like as not it will pester you when you get older," the sheriff said.

Owen caught the old man staring at him intently and he sensed a double meaning in the remark. *You're right, old man,* Owen thought. *A bullet can pester you. Whether you fire it or get hit with it. . . .* He glanced at himself in a piece of mirror that hung above the sink. He had taken a bad beating and his face wasn't a pretty thing to see.

"Mind if I shave?" Owen asked.

"It's your face," Torrence said. "What's left of it."

"The razor's in my saddlebag," Owen said.

"You got legs."

A faint grin twinkled in Owen's eyes. "Ain't you afraid I might have a gun in there, too?"

"If you do have, I'll stop you before you can use it," the sheriff said.

Owen chuckled. "You old devil, I believe you would."

He shaved, wincing as the razor scraped around the raw places on his face, finding it necessary to leave a semblance of a mustache because of the swollen tenderness of his upper lip. When he had quite finished, he took a clean shirt from his bedroll and put it on. Jim Torrance poured two cups of coffee and signaled Owen to help himself.

"You want me in one of those cells?" Owen asked.

The sheriff shook his head. "You ain't going no place until I tell you," he said. "Have your coffee."

The coffee was better than average. Owen sipped it slowly, enjoying all of it, and he saw Torrance reach into a pigeonhole of his desk and take out a printed sheet, a standard form for booking prisoners. The deputy smoothed the paper with his hand, picked up a stub of pencil, then tossed the pencil aside.

"I'll fill it out for you, if you want," Owen said.

Torrance shook his head. "Never put much store by a thing like that," he said. "I could ask you all the questions, you could give all the wrong answers."

For a long moment Owen looked at the lawman, then he shook his head. "You've got it wrong, Sheriff," he said. "I've got nothing to lie about."

The sheriff's sun-faded eyes flicked briefly across Owen's face. "In that case," he said, "there's no sense putting you on record, is there?" He shoved the paper aside. "There is one question nagging me."

"What?"

41

"What happened to your horse?"

Owen grinned. "A freighter back down the line held four of the biggest aces I ever saw in my life."

"It happens," Jim Torrance said. "More coffee?"

"Every time, if I can't get whiskey."

"Guns, cards, whiskey, and women," Jim Torrance said. "You've tried them all, I guess."

"Never all at the same time," said Owen.

There was a hint of humor in Jim Torrance's eyes, and then his attention was attracted by a shadow that fell across his desk, and he looked up to see Mead Weber coming by the window. Torrance started to get up to open the door, then decided against it, and when Mead came into the office, Torrance still had his feet on the desk. He gave Mead a questioning glance, but didn't ask his business.

"I got Casco out of town," Mead said.

"As well if you kept him out," Torrance said. He removed his feet from the desk. "That what you wanted to tell me, Mead?"

"It was Delaney, here, I was concerned about," Mead said. "That was a devil of a welcome we gave him."

"He handled it," Torrance said.

"I feel responsible, Delaney," Mead said. "I'd like to make it up to you if I could." There was an open honesty about Mead when he wanted to show it. "If you could use a few days' work," he said, "I can use a hand. I got some colts I want to start gentling out." He looked at Torrance. "Of course, if it's all right with you, Jim."

"I was gonna turn him loose anyway," Torrance said. He met Owen's gaze directly, but there was nothing to read in the old man's eyes. "You want a job, Delaney?"

"I whip one brother and get offered a job by the other," Owen said. He grinned, so that it could easily have been a joke. "I'm not getting mixed up in a family squabble, am I?"

"You decide," Jim Torrance said. "You can take the job or stay here. I don't care which."

"If you're worried about Casco, forget it," Mead said. "I've got him working a little dab of cows I run up north of here. He won't be around."

"I'm not worried about him," Owen said.

"You want the job, then?" Mead asked. "Seems the least I can do."

Owen shrugged. "I was looking for a job when I came here," he said. "One's as good as another."

"It's a deal, then," Mead said. "A couple of my boys are over at the stable loading up some grain to take out to the ranch. You can ride out with them. Jim," he said to the deputy, "take him over and introduce him to Pete and Webster."

Owen thought he detected a faint hint of color in Torrance's cheeks. "Delaney won't run away," he said, "or if he does, I don't see it matters much. He can introduce himself to Pete and Webster." He reached up and took Owen's well-worn gun belt from the peg where he had hung it. Shoving it across the desk, he said, "You better wrap that thing up in your bedroll. There's no snakes around here I know of."

"Thanks, Sheriff," Owen said. He wrapped the belt around the holstered gun and put the bundle in his saddle-bag. Picking up the saddle, he grinned at Mead Weber. "Any particular place you want me to start, boss?"

Mead grinned back. "The boys plan on being out at the ranch in time for dinner," he said. "You might start there."

"That's the best thing I am at," Owen said. He nudged open the door with his shoulder, shared his grin with the deputy, and said, "Next time I meet up with you I hope it won't be official."

"Keep out of trouble and it won't be," Jim Torrance said.

Outside Owen paused briefly, looking for the livery sign, then, finding it, he angled across the street. From the window of the sheriff's office Mead watched him, and without turning said, "What do you think of him, Jim?"

"He's running," Jim Torrance said. "I ain't figured out yet if it's away from somebody or toward somebody." He lifted his head slowly and looked at Mead Weber. "Why'd you hire him, Mead?"

"I promised Zoe I'd give him a job," Mead said, and the second he said it he wondered why in the devil he had used that particular lie.

The two men at the stable had seen Owen's fight with Casco, and although they were not openly friendly, there was a certain respect in them as they shook hands briefly and acknowledged Owen's introduction of himself. "All loaded," the one called Webster said. "You can toss your riggin' up on top and make yourself comfortable. Ain't far."

The flat-bed wagon was loaded heavily with sacked grain. Neither Pete nor Webster offered to hand up his

43

saddle, so Owen tossed it up, then climbed up after it. Mead's two men were taking their place on the wagon seat and they didn't bother to look back to see if Owen was settled before Webster yelled at the team and started the heavy wagon rolling. It bounced and jostled across the ruts in front of the livery door, then straightened out and headed directly up the main street of town. The sun was beating down, the smell of sacked grain pleasant, and Owen wiggled himself between two bags as best he could, crossed one leg over the other, pulled his hat down over his eyes, and prepared to make himself comfortable.

The wagon had gone no more than a block, he supposed, when he heard Pete say, "Mornin', Miss Middleton," then Webster, "Mornin', Miss Zoe."

He didn't hear the answer, but by now he knew the identity of Zoe Middleton. He thought of his freshly shaved face and his clean shirt and he was suddenly like a small boy rattling a stick on a picket fence in front of a new girl's house. He wanted to be seen. He lifted the hat from his face and half sat up. He had chosen exactly the right moment.

She had stepped aside to let the wagon by, and she was right there by the rear wheel, no more than six feet away. It was the best look he had had at her, and he was sorry the wagon was moving. What he had at first considered a rather masculine quality was not that at all. It was just a firmness of flesh, an honest directness in her eyes, a way she had of drawing her hair back rather severely, a solidness of bone structure in her face. She was looking directly at him, her lips slightly parted, the quizzical hint of a frown puckering between her eyes.

His grin was as wide as a corral gate, as full of pleasure as a tomcat in a milking barn. "To answer your question, Zoe Middleton," he said, "I work for a living, as you can see."

With that he stretched back on the full sacks of grain, put the hat back over his face, and looked for all the world as if he had been sleeping there forever and planned to continue sleeping there from now on. He heard her laughing, a throaty, honest sound that somehow had a trace of devilment and humor in it. It was a pleasant sound, but it brought back a memory, and a lot of the pleasure of it was gone.

With an ability learned from long hours in the saddle and the necessity of catching sleep where and how he could, he dozed off immediately, and it seemed only a moment before the lurching wagon stopped and a gate screeched against rusty hinges. Sitting up, Owen saw that the wagon had climbed a knoll, and the town of Ten Mile was less than a mile below him.

Even this small rise above the valley gave him an un-interrupted view, and he took it all in, cataloguing it in his mind by force of old habit. The valley was wide and long, with the creek that gave the town its name hugging this, the east side, of the valley. He could see the arm of the valley where he had first met Bud Patterson, but he couldn't see the Patterson ranch buildings themselves.

The land on the east side of the creek was arid, scattered with lava and sage, rolling into the same barren hills he had crossed on his way in from the ford on the Snake River, but the valley itself, across the creek, was lush and green, all the way to the towering Blue Mountains beyond. He wondered briefly why Mead Weber had chosen this apparently less desirable side of the valley for his range, then put the thought aside. A man took the cards that were dealt him, he supposed.

Beyond the town, toward the north, he could make out the distinct outline of two ranch headquarters—small out-fits, it looked from here—and he noted, too, that the entire valley was unfenced. He wondered where Zoe Middleton lived, and he put that thought aside, too, and concentrated on the road that looped across the valley and up a small ridge to disappear out of sight. That was the road he would be taking, as soon as he had worked long enough to earn a horse. . . . The wagon went through the gate, stopped while Webster closed the gate and climbed back up, then moved on a comparatively short distance and stopped in front of a barn. Immediately Owen was aware of a dozen pair of eyes watching him.

The men stood grouped around the wagon, tall ones, short ones, fat ones, skinny ones. They were bearded and rough-looking, as if they had been out on the range for a long time, and as far as Owen could see there wasn't a one of them who didn't wear a gun. There was no show of friendliness in any of them—only curiosity—and as they watched, Owen reached into his saddlebag, took out his gun belt, and, standing there on the sacked grain, deliber-ately strapped it on.

Webster had climbed down from the wagon and walked around in back. Without looking at Owen he jerked a thumb in his general direction and said, "Name of De-laney. Mead hired him."

One man stood slightly apart from the others, a man with a dished-in face and a piece of bone missing from his jaw. The crippled jaw made him talk out of the side of his mouth. "What happened to him?" he asked. "Get hung up in a bob-wire fence?"

"Tangled with Casco," Webster said.

The man with the broken face grinned—the first show of friendliness. "Most of us have, one time or another," he said.

"This one whipped him," Webster said.

There was a quick exchange of glances among the crew but no comment, and Webster said, "Come on down, Delaney. I'll show you where to wash up."

As Owen followed Webster across the yard, he heard one of the younger men say, "You reckon he really did whip Casco?"

"Not permanent, he didn't," the man with the mutilated jaw said.

The ranch was well laid out, the main house well kept and substantial, the barns and outbuildings large, freshly whitewashed. The bunkhouse could accommodate twenty men, Owen judged, and there was a separate cookshack, a thing he hadn't seen since a big, absentee-owned ranch he had worked on back in Wyoming. Either Mead Weber was well off or he liked to look as if he was. . . .

Owen washed the wagon dust from his face and hands at a soap-slick bench near the cookshack, then in turn pumped water for Webster. He was drying his face on the roller towel when a short, stubby Chinese with a white apron came out of the cookshack and banged a wagon bolt against a triangle with as much energy as if the crew had been six miles away.

The table was long and well supplied. The man with the battered jaw moved aside and made way for Owen, but there was little or no conversation at the table. A platter of steak made the rounds, wound up empty, was snatched by the ever-present Chinese and replenished. The sourdough biscuits were as light as a maiden's touch, the gravy, made with canned cream, seasoned to a hungry man's dream. Owen ate ravenously, topping his meal with two cups of coffee and a wedge of the best dried-apple pie he had ever tasted.

"If I could find a woman who could cook like that . . ." Owen said.

"I offered to marry Wong, there," the man with the

46

mashed face said. "He ain't said yes, but he ain't said no, either."

"You keep talking, Mister Kline," the Chinese said. "By and by I get a cleaver. Then I talk."

Kline chuckled softly and nudged Owen with his elbow. They shared a cigarette together, Owen and the man with the broken face, and when Kline had finished his smoke he ground the butt out on the heel of his boot. Looking at Owen, he said, "I don't know what your ruckus was, Delaney, but I'll give you a tip for what it's worth. You might as well let Casco whip you and get it over with. He will, sooner or later. Once he whips you, he'll help you up and be your friend. He paid all the doctor bills on this face of mine." The man rubbed his hand along the sagging jaw that was minus a bone. "Mead gives the orders," he said. "Casco gets the work done. Remember that, keep your mouth shut, do your job, and you'll eat like you just did three times a day. It ain't half bad."

He turned and walked directly away. Owen shrugged, then went over and started helping Webster unload the wagon of sacked grain.

FRANK LEVERING and Scott Granger stayed on in town after Patterson left, but they purposely avoided talking with Zoe Middleton. They had a decision to make between them, and they had reached the point in that decision where they didn't want anyone convincing them they were wrong. They knew Zoe Middleton would protest their selling their land regardless of how they argued. That was Zoe's way. To her, land was holy.

They were not related by blood, but the two ranchers had become as close as brothers over the years, drawn together by good times and bad and their mutual, religious background. They came from strong Pennsylvania Quaker stock, and although neither man had been inside a church for years, the old training clung to them, and the violence they had seen between Casco Weber and Owen Delaney had shaken them deeply.

Scott Granger was a thin, reedy man who spoke with a nasal twang, and in time, sitting there on a bench in front of an abandoned building, he said what was on his mind. "Jake's doing the right thing, Frank," the rancher said. "Even if there was a cattle market to open up it wouldn't do us much good. I ain't even run a tally on my range in three years. We'd have to hire a crew, stage a roundup . . . How many head you figure you and me and Zoe got between us?"

"Five hundred, maybe," Levering said. "No more. Most of them would be up in the hills back of Zoe's place, this time of year. Patterson's strays would be up there too. Have to cut *them* out for Mead——"

"Like you say, our kids ought to be into a school——"

"I figured maybe I'd see what Osgood thought," Levering said. He twitched his shoulders and tugged at the heavy pipe he smoked, and there was a touch of wry humor in his faded blue eyes. "Come down to it," he said, "it's up to Harold to decide. I ain't made a payment on my note in five years."

The men stood up. Granger kicked at a loose board in the sidewalk. "Zoe ain't gonna like it," he said.

"Zoe ain't got a wife and six kids," Levering said. "And I ain't got a banker handling my affairs for me."

They walked the short distance toward the bank, quiet men who had a faith in God and a faith in the goodness of man; practical men who knew when they had reached the end of their rope. It was near noon and the sun beat straight down on the dusty street and there was little shade except under the roofed-over porches.

Harold Osgood had drawn the blinds at the bank and he looked lost and alone there behind his desk in the semi-dark room. He looked up when Levering and Granger came in, and he hoped the driving excitement that had gripped him wasn't too obvious.

Harold had watched that fight between Casco and Owen Delaney, and now, two hours later, he was still a part of it, and he was physically and mentally exhausted. He had stood there at the window of the bank, his startled, round eyes peering from behind a half-drawn shade, and it was as if he himself had struck and received every blow. His knees had been so weak he had thought at times he would collapse; his breathing was like the rattle of dry parchment in the empty room. Time and again the little man had dreamed of standing there in the street, beating Casco Weber to a pulp, and now it had happened, right before his eyes, and it was as if he had awakened suddenly to find he wasn't dreaming at all. The fight was over, and Harold Osgood, projecting himself, had won, and now he was beaten and tired, but he had never felt so good in his life. At this moment he was fully convinced he had come to the end of his dealings with Mead Weber. . . . He scampered around his desk like an eager squirrel and greeted Levering and Granger warmly. "I'll get some light in here," he said, and he hurried to lift the shade on the front window. As he did, some of the sureness left him. Mead Weber was coming down the street from the direction of the sheriff's office, heading toward the bank.

"Well, boys?" Harold said, taking his place behind his desk.

"I come to give you my check in full," Frank Levering said. "If I had it." It was an old joke he always made.

"What would I do with it?" Harold said. He was a fine banker—a financial genius, in his way, and yet, after thirty years in the banking business it always embarrassed him to realize that people owed him money. He took off his ever-present eyeshade, mopped his bald head with the flat of his hand, and put the eyeshade back on. "Terrible thing," he said. "That fight." He was so full of it he had to say something.

"No man ever settled anything with a fight," Levering said. "No man ever will." The conviction of his old religious training was in his voice, a sense of indignation made him add, "Not that Casco didn't have it coming to him." His tongue clicked against his teeth. "Beats me how Mead puts up with him."

"What would you do?" Granger asked. "It's his own brother."

"Blood plays strange tricks," Levering said. He shook his head, the mystery of it beyond him, and in a manner so typical of him came directly to the point of this visit. "Me and Scott wanted to talk to you about our places, Harold. Mead made us an offer."

The room was swimming before Harold's eyes. Again he was out there in the street, his fists tearing at Casco's face. He was a big man, strong and sure, his own man, every inch of the way. He tried to control his shallow breathing and he looked at Levering and Granger, knowing what he should do, knowing what he had to do. . . . *Just hang on, boys,* was all Harold Osgood had to say. *I've carried you this far; I'll carry you a little further. I've got every reason to believe a cattle market is a lot closer than you think.* . . . That was it. That would do it. That was all he would have to say, and he would be free of Mead Weber's domination and the valley would prosper for everyone, not just for one man, and Harold Osgood would have that deep-seated satisfaction of knowing that he had had a big part in it. . . .

He hid his hands beneath the desk and he controlled his voice in a way he had learned through long practice. "I'll tell you what I think, boys," he said, and then he stopped. The door of the bank opened and Mead Weber stepped in.

Mead stood there, a big man with a friendly face, spoiled by eyes that seemed to see inside Harold Osgood. "Am I interrupting anything?" Mead asked. If he was, he didn't care about it. He came on across the room, pushed open the swinging half gate and stood there by the desk, smiling down at Harold, his mouth smiling, his eyes searching and probing. . . .

Harold Osgood felt the perspiration start at the back of his neck. It seeped from his pores and ran in a small rivulet down the crease of his back. "No, Mead, nothing," Harold said. "The boys and I were just talking about things in general. . . ." A moment before he had been a man of decision and the feeling had been a heady tonic, singing through his veins. Now again his physical self was a birdlike person lost in a maze of financial minutiae, dominated completely by Mead Weber. And Harold Osgood was rapidly coming to hate that physical self, for he knew with a certain honesty he had that the physical self was being motivated entirely by fear. He knew Mead Weber well, and he knew that Mead Weber, pressed far enough, was as dangerous as his brother Casco. Mead would kill a man who got in his way, and Harold Osgood knew that as certainly as he knew his own fear. . . . "Just things in general, Mead," he said, and he hated the sound of his own voice.

"Just mentioned the offer you made us, Mead," Levering said, his sentence punctuated with long, deliberate drags at his unlit pipe. "Like I told you, I wanted to think on it."

"Can't blame you for that, Frank," Mead said.

"Zoe, now," Levering said, sucking on the pipe, his shaggy brows lifting with each intake of breath, "she figures to wait it out. Sooner or later, the cattle market's bound to come back, she figures."

"I wouldn't deny that," Mead said. "I figure it the same way or I wouldn't be taking a chance on buying up all this land." He shrugged. "When? That's the question."

Levering took a match from his pocket. For a moment he studied the head of it, then snapped it expertly into flame with his thumbnail. He held it briefly and stared intently at Harold Osgood. "It's what I wanted to talk to

50

you about, Harold. You handle Zoe's affairs for her. You ain't advised her to sell out. How long *you* think it will be, Harold?"

Harold Osgood started scurrying through the papers on his desk like a frightened squirrel looking for nuts that weren't there. He could feel Mead's eyes on him, boring into him, and it was as if Mead were putting words into his mouth. "It's a little different with Zoe," Harold said. "Her dad did well, you know that. There's still a little money in the account. . . ." He was running out of words and he was getting sick to his stomach and the ulcer was starting to gnaw and grab, like a hot-fingered hand kneading at his vitals. . . . He looked at Mead and Mead was smiling that half-masked, triumphant smile that made a man feel so helpless. . . .

"I think Harold figures I'll look out for Zoe," Mead said. "Isn't that it, Harold?"

"It's such a personal responsibility," Harold said. "Zoe's dad was my closest friend."

"I'll put it to you plain, Harold," Levering said, "and I'd as soon Mead heard it." The pipe was going now and a perfect circle of smoke lifted above Levering's head. He looked like what he was—a man so scrupulously honest he wouldn't even lie about the weather. "I put a lot of years in this valley," he said. "So has Scott, here. Far as school for our kids goes, Zoe said she'd teach 'em some." He looked up quickly. "If it's a gamble worth taking, I'd like to take it along with Zoe and Mead. But it comes down to the fact I got to have help to do it." He took the pipe from his mouth and now there was embarrassment in his voice, the embarrassment of a proud man asking for money. "You been more than fair, Harold," he said. "You've carried all of us further than we had a right to expect. You want to back us for another six months?"

Yes, Harold wanted to say. *It won't take six months. Another six weeks will do it. Maybe even less.* The words were there, ready to be said, but they wouldn't come out. It was the same as when he had taken Owen Delaney's place in the street and smashed his fist against Casco's face. It was true and real, and yet it wasn't true at all. He looked at Mead Weber and Mead's expression hadn't changed a bit. "I wish I could, Frank," Harold Osgood said. "I truly wish I could, but I just don't see how I can. . . ."

Frank Levering sighed. He laid the palm of his big hand on the desk and he looked old and tired. "I didn't expect you could, Harold," he said, "but I had to ask. My wife will want to know if I asked you." He stood up and Scott Granger stood up too, taking his lead from Levering, following faithfully. "We'll just have to take range count of the cows we've got left, Mead," he said to Weber. "I'll want to talk it out with my wife." He stood there, closing and unclosing his right hand as if he had just suddenly discovered it as something foreign to his anatomy, something useless with which he didn't know what to do. . . . "My kids won't like moving," he said. He shrugged. "You and Mead work out the agreement, Harold. I'll be in tomorrow and we'll look it over."

Harold Osgood couldn't answer. His throat was constricted, his mouth dry, and his stomach pained fearfully. He didn't realize for certain that Levering and Granger had left. He only knew that he hated himself more surely in this moment than he had ever hated himself in his life, and now Mead was there across the desk, looking at Harold, smiling that half-smile, and it wasn't the face of Mead at all, it was the face of Casco, and it needed to be smashed and torn. . . . "I'm not going through with it, Mead," Harold heard himself say. "I went along with you because I thought it was best for Zoe, but it's not right for anybody if it destroys what men have worked for all their lives." He realized then that he was shouting. "Those men have their rights and I have mine! I'm going to back them up if it takes every last dime I have left and you or no other man is big enough to stop me!"

He was on his feet, his heart pumping in a terrifying manner, his breath torturing his lungs. He saw Mead Weber stand up, but Harold wasn't afraid, and then Mead's hand reached across the desk and gripped the two lapels of Harold's coat. The big hand squeezed and the fabric of the coat pulled tight, binding Harold's arms. He was jerked hard against the desk, and now his face was close to Mead's face and Mead's voice was saying, "You'll what, Harold?"

A moment of terror gripped Harold and he fought it as savagely as he dreamed of fighting Casco. "You heard me!" he said.

"Yeah," Mead said. "I heard you." He released his grip and Harold stepped back, but before he could get out of the way Mead's hand lashed out. His open palm caught Osgood across the mouth and sent the little banker sprawling. Harold hit the floor and rolled and he lay there, shaking in every nerve of his body, the fearful taste of blood in his mouth, his eyes rolled back as he stared up at Mead Weber, towering over him. "You didn't mean it, did you, Harold?" Mead asked.

Harold couldn't answer. He wanted to answer, but he couldn't, and there were sounds coming from his throat and he realized with a horrible terror that he was crying, sobbing like a baby. . . .

"I'll kill you, Harold," Mead Weber said. "Just remember that. You cross me up once and I'll kick the brains out of your head."

He was gone, Harold knew, but still he lay there on the floor, trembling, unable to move, not through any physical hurt but from shame and humiliation. Helplessly he beat his fist against the floor, again and again. . . .

Upstairs, in the apartment above the bank, Mattie stood at the window that gave her a view of the town. She saw Levering and Granger come to the bank and she knew what they wanted. She saw them leave, and she knew they had lost. Later she saw Mead Weber leave the bank, and a hurt she couldn't conceal gripped her.

Harold's footsteps were on the stair and she went to the table and rearranged the crackers and milk and canned peaches she had fixed for his lunch every day for thirty years. She heard him pause outside the door and knew he was taking a deep breath, getting hold of himself, and then he came in. She saw his split lip, the faint smear of blood on his chin, and she wanted to go to him and take him in her arms and hold him, as she would have held a child. . . . She said, "I saw Frank and Scott. Did they want an extension on their loan?"

"What do you think they wanted?" he said. There was a sharpness in his voice—an unusual thing with her—but she didn't mind. She understood how it would be. She didn't press the conversation.

She turned and looked at her husband and all the goodness she knew was in him flooded through her and the thought of the days when he had courted her, a shy, funny little man, but so honest and sure of his love for her and she had wanted him to love her, so very desperately. . . .

She stood behind his chair, not touching him, wanting to so much, and she said, "We've had a lot of good times together, Harold."

He stopped eating momentarily, holding a spoonful of peaches halfway to his mouth. "We'll have more," he said.

"But they're never the same, are they?"

She felt him drawing away from her. "What do you mean by that?"

"Just thinking," she said. "Remembering when you started the bank here . . ."

"Precious little money then."

"Something more important, perhaps."

"I wonder."

"No, you don't, Harold," she said. "You know it was." She smoothed the sparse hair on the back of his head with the palm of her hand, disliking her hand because it was large and strong. "Remember what you told me? Being a banker is a public trust. Like a doctor, you used to say." Her breath caught. "Even like a preacher."

"Haven't I done all right?"

"Of course."

"Mattie, what is it you want of me?"

She heard that familiar tremble in his voice, the sound of anger, and she knew so well that it was anger with himself. He had always run his business as he believed, and they had become wealthy. But what good was the money unless he used it to keep faith with himself? That is what she wanted to ask him and yet she couldn't bring herself to ask it.

"I was thinking of Levering and Granger," she said. "Of Jake Patterson, too. I was thinking of how perhaps we ought to help them if we could."

"Well, we can't," he said. "Times change and conditions change. Can't you see that? I'm doing what has to be done. No more, no less."

You're not, Harold, she thought. *You're not at all. You're letting Mead Weber dictate every move. . . .* She knew she couldn't speak further about it. Her voice would betray her. She couldn't accuse her own husband of being a coward. "More milk, Harold?" she asked.

"For heaven's sake!" he shouted. "Will you quit nagging at me?" He got to his feet and slammed his napkin against the table and went out the door, banging it closed behind him. She heard his footsteps on the stairs, angry at first, then faltering, stopping, and there was a long silence as he tried to make himself come back and apologize, and then the footsteps went on down the stairs, slow and heavy for such a little man. . . .

Mattie Osgood stood at the window and cried inside. She saw Mead Weber swing into his saddle and head out of town, toward his ranch.

54

You're killing my husband, the voice inside Mattie Osgood cried out after him. *You're killing the only thing I ever had to love.*

THE DAY was hot, and the early afternoon sun drove its rays into Owen Delaney's bare skin as he helped unload the sacks of grain from the wagon. He had removed his shirt and the muscles rippled under the fair skin of his shoulders. The bullet wound twinged like an uncomfortable memory.

He had talked briefly with Kline, the man with the ruined jaw, and now Owen realized that what he had taken as reticence in the crew was another thing entirely. With the exception of Kline and Webster every man on this crew was practically as new to the job as was Owen himself. They were strangers to each other, some of them drifters, like himself, some of them men who were working for the first time in months, a few were men from the town with families to support. Everyone seemed at loose ends, with no foreman to direct them, and even if there had been, there didn't seem to be much work to do. It reminded Owen of a roundup crew hired ahead of time to guard against a labor shortage.

He was lifting the last sack from the wagon when he became aware of Mead Weber riding down the lane toward the ranch headquarters. Heaving the sack onto the pile, Owen turned and gave Mead his attention. Weber made a striking impression on the back of the big chestnut he rode and Owen caught himself thinking of Zoe Middleton, and he was surprised that he remembered her so distinctly. He rolled a cigarette, and he was standing there shirtless, the cigarette unlighted, when Mead Weber reined up alongside him. He knew Mead was staring at that bullet wound in his shoulder, but he made no move to hide it. *Let him think what he wants,* Owen decided.

Mead swung down, a graceful-moving man, and as he turned the sun touched his profile, outlining it sharply, and Owen was surprised at the amount of resemblance between Mead and Casco. Together they seemed as different as nature could have possibly made them, but now, just for a brief interval, Owen saw that same thick upper lip, the same slash to the mouth—a mouth that had a certain innocence about it when it smiled, but a mouth that could be cruel and hard. Mead turned, and the im-

55

pression was gone. "Making out all right, Delaney?" he asked.

"Frog hair fine," Owen said.

"They feed you?"

"They set it out. I fed myself."

Mead chuckled. "I didn't have much chance to talk to you there in town," he said. "Come over to my office and I'll get you on the books so you can start drawing pay." He had turned his horse over to Kline, and he said, "Rub him down good and give him some oats." Mead's voice had lifted so the other men could hear. There was something close to childishness in Mead's enjoyment of giving orders.

Owen gave Kline a sidelong glance and caught Kline's wink. The wink twisted the man's broken face. "Yes, sir, Mr. Weber," Kline said. He led the horse away, and if Mead had any idea Kline was making fun of him he didn't show it.

"Come along, Delaney," Mead said.

Owen had a perverse urge to add his own "Yes, sir, Mr. Weber," but he let it go. He followed Weber across the hard-packed yard toward the substantial house, possessed with the feeling he was watching a man playing at ranching, yet certain of the fact that Mead was not a man who could be pushed around easily. Again he caught himself thinking of Zoe Middleton, and to himself he thought, *He'll dress you pretty, girl, because he'll want to show you off, but he'll have to have four or five other women on the side, just to prove to himself he can get them. . . .* He felt a quick resentment toward Mead Weber.

The "office" was in reality a bedroom off the back porch, but Mead had fixed it up with a battered roll-top desk and a swivel chair. There was a calendar on the wall, put out by a farm-implement firm, and a rack for rifles. The rack held three carbines, the fourth space empty, and Owen wondered if it was Casco's gun that was missing.

"Sit down, sit down," Mead said, waving Owen toward a chair. "No need to stand on formalities."

Owen stared at the man. *Is this jigger real?* he asked himself. He took the chair, catching it with his toe, pulling it over, and he sat down. Deliberately, then, he put one battered boot on the desk and piled the other on top of it. He shoved back his hat, but he didn't take it off. He was aware of Mead's annoyed glance, and it pleased him to know he had caused it.

"Cigar?" Mead asked, offering a humidor.

"Sure," Owen said. He took the cigar, sniffed it,

shrugged, as if to say it would have to do until he could get something better, bit the end from it, and spit the tobacco on the floor. "Got a match?" he asked Mead.

For a moment Mead seemed caught off guard, then he produced a match, struck it under the desk, and supplied the light. Owen drew deeply and expelled the smoke through his nostrils. Mead watched, as if fascinated by the performance, then he walked to the window, peered out, and without looking at Owen said, "From Wyoming, eh?"

"I didn't say so for sure," Owen said.

"But you are."

"All right, I am."

Mead paced swiftly, once across the window, once back, then, turning, he said, "You might as well get it right, Delaney. If you work in this country, you work for me."

"And if I don't want to work?" Delaney said.

"You'd have to talk that out with Jim Torrance."

"I'd as soon not," Delaney said.

Mead turned slowly. His eyes appraised Delaney, from his boots on the desk to the top of his hat, and then they drifted down to the gun on Delaney's hip. "Tell me, Delaney," he said. "What *did* you do in Wyoming?"

"It's a big country," Delaney said. "There's lots of things to do."

"But you don't plan on going back to do them, is that it?"

"I'm headed the other way," Delaney said. "I got a friend over in John Day. He owes me a drink. Soon as I get me a horse, I'll go have the drink."

"No intention of staying here?"

"None."

"Suppose I offer you a good proposition?"

Delaney knocked the ash from his cigar. "How good?"

"Foreman?"

"Maybe," Delaney said. "Why me?"

"You look like you could handle it."

Delaney glanced at the desk and said, "That bottle there for looks or is there something in it?"

Mead picked up a decanter, took a glass from the top of the desk, and poured a drink. "This is English glass," he said, indicating the decanter. "It rings when you thump it." He clicked his fingernail against it to demonstrate. "Worth a lot of money. I bought it from a woman in town. Big people, they were, but they went under when the mines closed."

"And you didn't."

57

"That's right, Delaney. I didn't."

"It's not bad whiskey," Owen said.

"It's the best."

"We were talking about a job."

Mead Weber sat down. He was suddenly confidential, as if it were all a joke. "No use pretending with you, Delaney."

"It's not English glass?"

"You must have come through Kelton."

"Stayed there a day or so."

"And Boise City?"

"She was blond," Owen said. "And friendly. Is there another drink in that English glass bottle?"

There was another drink and Mead hastened to pour it. "There's been a lot of talk," he said. "About cattle buyers from Wyoming, headed this way. You think there's anything to it?"

"I haven't any cattle to sell."

"I think there's something to it."

"It could be."

Mead was fidgeting in his chair. "We got a peculiar situation here," he said. "A few small outfits, hanging on by the skin of their teeth."

"Like Patterson?"

"Like Patterson."

"So?"

"I've made quite a mark for myself in this country, Delaney," Mead Weber said. "I own the store in town, the saloon——"

"I saw the signs."

"I figure I could maybe do people around here a favor," Mead said. "Not that I'm not looking out for myself. I am. But what good is a cattle ranch if there isn't any market for cattle?"

"You said there would be."

"Might be, Delaney. I said there *might* be."

"There will be. Boise City is flooded with cattle buyers. They'll head this way."

"Nobody here knows it for sure," Mead said.

"And you'd as soon I wouldn't tell them?"

"I'm a businessman, Delaney. I didn't get where I am by telling everything I know."

"All right," Delaney said. "Make me an offer."

"I did."

"Foreman?"

"That's right."

58

"You think your brother would like that?"

"Would you care?" This time Mead poured the drink of his own accord.

"You'd have to have cattle," Owen said. "You'd have to have grass to hold them on. You don't make up a trail herd overnight."

"I've got cattle, Delaney," Mead said. "A thousand head."

"The grass?"

"There's a valley across that river."

"So there is," Delaney said. "And there's people in it." He lifted the decanter. "Join me?"

"A pleasure," Mead said. He took the drink and held it, his eyes on Delaney. "To the future," he said.

"It's bound to get here," Owen said.

"I mean to have a big piece of it."

"I figured as much."

Mead chuckled softly. "Nothing surprises you, does it, Delaney?"

"Nope."

"I like that in a man."

"The job," Owen said. "What does it pay?"

"A percentage, maybe, for the right man," Mead said. "I'll be truthful with you. I haven't got a cent. It's a gamble, but you strike me as a gambling man."

"It's possible," Owen said. "I lost a horse that way."

"I'll have a pretty big operation here, Delaney," Mead said. "I want men around me who can see things my way."

"Can't blame you for that."

"Well?" Mead said. "How about it? You interested?"

Owen took his feet from the desk. He leaned forward and carefully ground out the cigar in an ash tray. "Afraid not, Weber," he said.

The flat refusal seemed to catch Mead off balance. For a moment he was flustered, then he regained his composure and said, "You mind telling me why?"

"Because you're buying into trouble, Weber," Delaney said. "There's always one who doesn't want to sell and refuses to be moved."

The friendliness was gone from Mead's eyes. That thick upper lip was tight against his teeth and there was nothing innocent about his mouth. "I didn't figure you for one that would back down from a little trouble," he said.

"Maybe I don't," Owen said. "But I don't look it up, either." He grinned. "And I don't take sides, Weber. You can take over the whole valley, for all of me. You probably will, and you'll get rich doing it."

"You could cut in on a piece of it, Delaney."

Owen stood up. For a long time he looked down at Mead, almost as if he were laughing at him, and he shook his head slowly. "I wouldn't cut in on a piece of it, Mead," he said. "When the time was right I'd be found in a gully with a bullet in my back." He laughed softly. "You're not trying to hire a foreman, Mead. You've got a dozen out there could handle the job. You're trying to hire somebody who can handle your big brother for you. I whipped him once. You figure maybe I can do it again. Those signs in town have just got your name on them, not your brother's. I figure you don't like the idea of sharing anything, even with him." He tugged his hat into place. "No deal, Weber," he said. "Your brother is your problem, not mine. I don't hire on to tromp any man's snakes."

There was no softness in Mead Weber now. He was a man who found it hard to take no for an answer. He stood up slowly, a touch of color in his cheeks, his lips tightly drawn. "That's a dirty accusation to make, Delaney," he said.

"It's a dirty world we live in, Weber," Owen said. "You just showed me a piece of it." He started to walk away and a motion of Weber's arrested his attention. Mead's right hand had moved back, just touching the skirt of his coat, and as the coat moved, a holstered gun was exposed.

For a moment the two men looked at each other, and then Mead said, "How do you know I'll let you walk out that door, Delaney?"

A smile lifted the corner of Delaney's mouth, but it failed to find his eyes. He met Mead's gaze squarely and said, "How do you know you could stop me, friend?"

The silence hung between them, charged and tense, and then Owen turned his back and walked through the door. He paused, waiting, then moved on, walking slowly, his hands away from his sides.

The crew had found some chore to occupy their time. The yard was empty. The screened-in cookshack was straight ahead of him, and the Chinese cook was nowhere in sight. Owen walked straight to the cookshack, as if he had been planning to go there all along. He opened the door and went inside. A big slice of dried-apple pie was there on the cook's table.

Through the screen Owen could see Mead Weber, standing in the doorway of the office. There was a growing uncertainty in Weber as he watched Delaney's movements, but Mead's coat was still pushed back, his hand was still on the butt of his gun.

A crawling uneasiness ran down Delaney's spine as he picked up the piece of pie. He stepped back outside and stood there, leaning against the wall of the cookshack, his eyes on Mead Weber. Weber still had his hand on his gun.

Deliberately, then, Owen Delaney started to eat the pie. He chewed it slowly, relishing every bite of it, his eyes never leaving Mead Weber's face. Weber's hand was still on the gun, but even from this distance, Owen was sure he could see the perspiration on the ranch owner's forehead, and in time Weber's hand moved away and he tugged his coat into place.

Owen wiped his mouth with the back of his left hand. His saddle was there near the cookshack, where he had left it, and he picked it up. Slinging it across his shoulder, he headed down the lane, back toward town. There was a vacant feeling between his shoulder blades, and his shirt was sweaty and sticking to his back.

A FEW miles north of town Casco Weber, a bottle in his hand, rode with all the uncomplicated serenity of a man drinking himself sober. He was an ignorant man, by most standards, but surely not by his own. He saw a problem, he looked at it, decided how to whip it, and then went ahead without any complication of moral or aesthetic values. He thoroughly liked being the man he was and had no intention of changing.

Casco took a drink from his bottle, swallowed noisily and was conscious of the sting of the whiskey against his split lips. Delaney had whipped him; that Casco admitted with complete candor, but the thoroughness with which Delaney had whipped him was another thing. There for a few seconds, just before he had gone down for the last time, Casco had been completely and clearly aware of the fact that Delaney could not only whip him this one time but Delaney could whip him again and again, any time he took the notion. Casco pressed the cork in the bottle with the heel of his hand. There was nothing at all complicated about his decision. He just wouldn't meet Delaney with fists again. The next time he met Delaney, he would kill him.

If Casco ever worried at all, it was about Mead, for he

considered his younger brother his sole and full responsibility. He had long ago attached himself to Mead in
much the same manner as a man picking the runt of a
litter of pups for his own personal pet.

It had been quite a tribe, the Webers—the old man, six
cousins, an intermingled, intermarried bunch of hard-
drinking, hard-fighting backwoodsmen from the hills of
Tennessee, as happy a lot as ever cut a throat or ate another man's beef. They came to Oregon because Oregon
was new and Tennessee wasn't any longer, and for no
other reason, and they brought their ways with them.
Casco remembered the old days well. He was proud of
his family. Mead wasn't, and that was the main point of
difference between them. They didn't argue about it, for
to Casco there was no point of argument, but he did sometimes wonder just who in hell Mead thought he was.

The trail he rode was rocky, lifting straight into the
barren Magpie range, and as he rode he made close note
of the forage along the way. He'd be bringing a thousand
cattle through this pass in a day or so, and he wanted to
know just how fast he would have to push them.

At the top of a long slope he reined up and looked back,
and there below him was a splendid panorama of the entire Ten Mile country. The abandoned mines were bright
slashes of scar tissue on the virgin slopes of the Blues, and
between those mountains and this eastern waste lay the
valley, green and lush, the sparkle of a network of creeks
lacing down to the main stream, the low ridge that cut
the valley into two parts plainly visible, the snake track of
the John Day road wandering across the humpbacks.

An abutment of lava outcropping blocked his view of
the Weber ranch headquarters, but he was conscious of
its position, here on the east side, and again he was thinking of Mead. A mine superintendent had built that ranch
house, an Eastern man with no conception of range value,
but he had built the house big and well and when it was
abandoned, Mead had wanted it, simply because it was
the most imposing house in this part of the country.

But it was the valley itself that presently had value and
purpose, and Casco gave his attention to that. At the far
south end, in its separate arm, the Patterson place was a
postage-stamp clutter of buildings, and in his practical
way Casco saw it as good horse pasture. Farther north
were the ranches of Frank Levering and Scott Granger,
close to each other, like the men themselves, set in the
shelter of the low ridge that ran the entire north-south

distance of the valley. Beyond that ridge, well watered, expansive, running back into mountain canyon pastures, was the Middleton ranch, the home ranch buildings hidden in a grove of cottonwoods, the rolling grassland extending like an invitation. Good holding ground, Casco thought to himself. He knew it would work out fine.

He reined his horse and rode on, across the ridge and down the slope, toward the sparsely grassed valleys where the trail herd was making up. Water was scarce here, and Casco worried about it, as the herd increased in size. He wanted to get those cattle on over into Ten Mile Valley. The fact that people owned that valley and might not want to relinquish it had entered Casco's mind but it had certainly never concerned him. Levering and Granger were a couple of hayshakers, not even worth considering. As for Zoe Middleton, Mead was going to marry her, so it would all be in the fanily anyway.

Casco thought about that. To him one woman was pretty much like another, necessary to a man's appetite and little else. If Mead figured he had to have Zoe Middleton, that was Mead's affair, but Zoe Middleton's grass was much more important to Casco. Casco shook his head. If Mead was so set on marrying Zoe, why in the devil didn't he go ahead and marry her? Casco found the bottle and took a drink. Sometimes he just couldn't figure Mead at all.

It wouldn't have surprised Casco to know that Zoe Middleton, too, sometimes worried about Mead, for he wouldn't have given the question that much consideration, but it would have surprised Zoe to know she had anything in common with Casco.

She finished her weekly shopping at the store and signed the credit slip that would be turned over to Harold Osgood for payment. She would have liked very much to handle her own affairs, but her father had been a strong-willed man and now, nearly a year after his death, he was still making his edicts felt.

As she walked toward the bank she thought fondly of her father, knowing she was a great deal like him, but she sometimes wondered if the stubbornness that was so much a part of her wasn't really only a rebellious urge to prove to herself that she could stand alone.

She stopped for a moment to talk with Harold, but Harold seemed highly occupied with his own affairs. She tugged his eyeshade down over the bridge of his nose, kissed the top of his bald head, and said, "You're getting to be a grouchy old banker."

"And you're getting to be a mighty fresh young lady," Harold said. "Go on upstairs and tell Mattie I said to teach you some manners."

He watched her go up the stairs, a solidly built girl in the full flower of her maturity, and a wave of affection for her nearly choked him with its intensity. He and Mattie had never had children of their own, and they had lavished their reserved affection on Zoe. The proudest day of his life, Harold guessed, was the day Grant Middleton, Zoe's dad, had stood here by this very desk and said, "If anything was to happen to me, Harold, I'd want you to take care of Zoe's affairs. You fix up the papers so it will be that way." He was a rough man, Grant Middleton, a man without apparent emotions. He had stood there, glaring at Harold from under shaggy brows, and he said, "You're a pigheaded, penny-pinching skinflint, Osgood, and you got too much sentiment in you to let you amount to much, but you're the most honest man I ever knew." He turned then and stalked away, then stopped, and without looking back he had said, his voice quiet and soft, "Don't let them push you around, Harold. You're bigger than most men, if you'll just believe it."

Harold missed Grant Middleton like sin. . . .

The shaft of light struck him as the door of the bank opened and he looked up and, standing there in the doorway was a man, a man like Grant Middleton, tall and broad of shoulder, a man who stood in the bright light of the doorway with feet slightly spread, a holstered gun on his hip, and he packed a saddle in his left hand, holding it by the horn, the double cinches trailing on the floor. It was a moment before Harold recognized him, and then he knew, and Owen Delaney was like a symbol of everything Harold Osgood wanted to be, a fighting man who had beaten Casco Weber into the dirt of the street. That magnificent control Harold had learned to exercise came to his rescue again. "Can I help you, Mr. Delaney?" he said.

"Maybe," Delaney said. "I'm looking for a job. I thought you might know of something."

A swift thought passed through Harold's mind and was gone. He hadn't realized he would be capable of even thinking of hiring a man because of his fighting qualities; he knew he would never actually do it. "Things have been pretty slow in this country," Harold said. "Mead Weber

64

is about the only one——" It seemed to Harold that Delaney was looking through him, seeing his thoughts, those almost sleepy, hooded eyes reading his mind. . . . "I don't know of a thing," Harold said.

"All right," Owen said. "I thought you might."

He turned to leave, and now Harold didn't want him to go. He got to his feet and, fumbling for words, said, "Wait a minute, Delaney—— If a few dollars——" He coughed, strangled on his own embarrassment. "That is—well," he blurted, "if you could use a meal, my wife——"

Owen looked at the banker, momentarily angry, then the touch of hurt pride passed and a grin found his eyes. "That's all right," he said. He reached into his pocket and took out his last silver dollar. Looking at Harold, he said, "Tell you what I will do, though, banker." He flipped the coin. "I'll match dollars with you if you want."

Harold showed no indication of being interested in the idea. Owen left the bank, and as he did he nearly collided with the two men coming in. They were well dressed, but they had ridden a long way, and they had two loaded pack horses tied at the hitch rail alongside their saddlers. Owen gave the two men a swift appraisal, then noted the brand on the horses, recognizing it immediately as the brand of one of the big syndicates in Wyoming. At the same moment he saw Jake Patterson lash a lathered horse across the river ford and into town, and he knew at once that something was wrong.

Shortly after leaving his wife and young Bud at the Levering ranch, Jake Patterson borrowed a horse and went for a ride. He hadn't told his wife, but he had to be alone. Failure was a big thing, and a man had to get used to it by himself. . . .

He hadn't really meant to do it, but he rode directly back to his own ranch, a desire in him to see it once more, and it was while he was there that the two men from Wyoming stopped to ask directions and have a drink at his abandoned pump. They were cattle buyers, they told him, and there were more on the way. Did Patterson have any cattle to sell? they wanted to know.

For a long time Jake Patterson had stood there, letting the full impact of what had happened to him possess him. He had sold out—thrown away a lifetime of work. And if he had only waited, less than one day more . . . It was then he first realized the enormity of his own decision and, demanding something on which to blame that decision, he fixed on the idea that it had all been deliberately planned against him. Mead Weber must have known these cattle buyers were coming. . . .

A helpless rage started building in Jake Patterson. He mounted and headed for town, lashing the horse he had borrowed from Levering's wife into a white lather. He thought first of going to Jim Torrance to demand protection from the law, for until now there had never been any thought of violence in Patterson's life. But no law had been broken. He had been cheated—swindled—robbed, and no formal law could do anything about it. Jake knew that, and the knowledge that it was so only served to gall him further. Now it was a failure of society piled on his own failure, and as he dismounted and tied his horse he still had no real knowledge of what he would do.

Wildly he tried to place the blame. Mead Weber was first, because Mead now owned his ranch; but Harold Osgood, too, for Harold had let him sell; and he blamed Zoe Middleton, for although Zoe had tried to talk him out of selling, she hadn't talked enough. It was a blind, crazy rage, born of too many long winters and too much summer sweat and a thousand blasted hopes, a blind rage of confusion that could make a momentary killer of a man who had been peaceful all his life.

At that moment Mead Weber, coming back in from the ranch, turned his horse in at the far end of the street. Through his red blur of anger Jake Patterson saw Mead, and now there was no longer any doubt in Jake's mind. He turned in at the general merchandise store.

There were no customers in the store and the clerk was out in back. Jake Patterson walked behind the counter in the hardware section. He took the first gun he came to—a double-barreled, twelve-gauge shotgun—and, breaking open a box, he took out two fresh shells.

He was walking toward the door, shoving the shells into the gun, when the clerk came back into the store and saw him. The clerk called to him, but Jake didn't turn. He walked through the door and out onto the porch, pausing only long enough to snap the gun shut and cock both hammers.

In Mattie's apartment Zoe finished a cup of tea Mattie had made for her, put down her cup, and said, "Mattie, what's it like to be in love?"

"Good heavens, child," Mattie said. "Don't you know?"

Zoe turned quickly, and there was a touch of anger in her voice. "No, Mattie," she said, "I don't know."

Mattie carefully rearranged the empty teacups. "You're engaged to Mead," she said.

"And he's the only man I've ever gone with."

And he's the wrong one, Mattie wanted to say, but she couldn't bring herself to say it. This wasn't her daughter, and even if it were, Zoe was a grown woman with a right to make up her own mind. "You'll know in time," Mattie said. "There's no hurry."

"There is a hurry, Mattie," Zoe said. "I'm lonesome. I don't like trying to run a ranch by myself. I'm getting a little older every day. Mattie, I want to get married," she said. "Is there anything wrong with that?"

"Of course not," Mattie said

"But I want the ranch, too," Zoe said.

"It's a good ranch," Mattie said. "It meant a lot to your father and I know what it means to you. What could be wrong with keeping it?"

"It's simple, then, isn't it?" Zoe said. "I marry Mead and I keep the ranch."

Mattie felt a moment of panic. She was never sure of Zoe. Had this been Zoe's way of asking for Mattie's approval of her marriage to Mead? Mattie picked up her knitting and her needles clicked alarmingly. "Ask your heart, Zoe," she said.

Zoe looked at the big, plain woman, knowing her so well, and there was a certain handsomeness in Mattie's features, the handsomeness of goodness and honesty and love. On impulse Zoe crossed the room and kissed Mattie solidly on the cheek. "I have asked my heart, Mattie," she said. "I still want to know what it's like to be in love."

Mattie thought of Harold. "You'll know," she said.

"Then I'm not in love," Zoe said, "because I don't know."

She went over to the window, and she could look down onto the street in front of the bank. She saw the two saddied horses and the two pack animals tied there, and she wondered about them, and she saw Owen Delaney come out of the bank.

She let her attention stay on Owen. He was taller than she had first supposed. He looks like a man who might have fun throwing rocks at the moon at that, she thought, and she knew that that was exactly the sort of thing that had been missing from her life for too long a time. . . . She saw Mead Weber riding down the street and felt a small sense of guilt. After all, she was still wearing Mead's ring. . . .

That was when she saw Jake Patterson come out of the store, packing the shotgun. She didn't know how she knew, but she knew. She turned quickly and she felt the skin on her face drawing taut.

"Mattie!" Her voice was soft. "There's going to be trouble."

OWEN WATCHED Mead dismount, there in front of the bank, then immediately became aware of Jake Patterson coming up the sidewalk, the shotgun held across his chest. Watching, Owen saw the smile on Mead's face, false, but wide. "Well, Jake," he heard Mead say. "Out spending your money already, I see." Mead chuckled. "Guess I can't complain, so long as you spend it in my store." Now Mead was looking at the two saddlers and the two pack horses, and Owen saw the growing excitement in the man. Mead finished tying his horse and strode toward the bank.

"I want to talk to you, Mead," Jake Patterson said.

Mead stopped, more annoyed than alarmed. The smile turned to a scowl. "I'm sort of in a hurry, Jake."

"You're always in a hurry, Mead," Jake Patterson said. "You were in a big hurry to steal my ranch."

Mead was facing Patterson fully now, the scowl turning to a flush of anger. "Our business is over with, Patterson," he said.

"No, Mead," Jake said. He moved the gun, and now the barrel was pointing down and the two cocked hammers were visible.

Some of the color left Weber's face. He took one step forward and the shotgun came up, and now there was no longer any doubt. Patterson's face was a drawn, tight mask, the face of a man who had worked hard all his life at being a failure and now, suddenly, couldn't take any more. "You crazy, Jake?" Mead said. He was breathing heavily, his nostrils flared, and he stood there with his feet spread, his arms half lifted from his side, as if ready to reach out for the shotgun but afraid to try it.

"I want what's mine, Mead," Jake Patterson said. "You knew there were cattle buyers coming. You knew my ranch would be worth something. You stole it from me, and now I'm taking it back."

There was a bluster in Mead Weber's voice. "I don't

even know what the devil you're talking about," he said. "Now put that gun down before I get Jim Torrance to lock you up."

"So Torrance is in on it too, is he?" Jake said. "You and Osgood and Zoe and Torrance." He laughed, a high, wild sound. "You had it worked out good, didn't you?" The man's finger trembled against the twin triggers of the shotgun, and now there was a sudden scurry of sound inside the bank, the hurry of footsteps, and through the open doorway Owen saw Zoe and Mattie. The two Wyoming cattle buyers were coming up toward the door, and Harold, his face a sickly white, was moving up, his feet carrying him forward while his fear held him back.

"Jake!" Zoe called.

Jake's chin lifted slightly. "You too, Zoe," he said. "You had it all worked out fine."

Owen's eyes had been frozen on that cocked shotgun, but now he saw Zoe move forward. She walked slowly, her face expressionless, and she was moving up alongside Mead, directly toward Jake Patterson. She put out her right hand, palm up. "Give me the gun, Jake," she said. "Whatever it is, we'll talk about it. We're old friends, Jake, all of us——"

For an interval too brief to measure there was doubt in Jake Patterson's eyes. Watching for it, Owen saw it, and in that interval he threw himself forward, not striking with his hands, but with his hands out, like a man in an open-armed dive, and the full weight of his body struck Patterson in the side, knocking him off the porch and into the street, and Owen was on top of him. The shotgun exploded, and through the welter of dust and powder smoke Owen saw the horses rear and plunge, and Mead's mount break loose. He heard a woman's scream of fear or pain, and the roaring doubt of not knowing which it was was in him as he drove his fist into Patterson's stomach and felt the smaller, older man go lax.

Owen got to his feet and the shotgun was there in the dust of the street. There was a blind rage in Owen as he picked up the gun. He grasped it by the barrel and, turning his entire weight, he smashed the butt of the gun against the heavy porch post. The butt shattered and the shock of the blow ran up the barrel and stung Owen's hands and he swung the weapon again, smashing the lock, ruining the breech. He heard Zoe's voice, close, and he knew she was shouting. "It's all right!" she said.

He turned, the anger running out of him, and she was

standing there, her face close to his, a white face, her eyes wide, as if she were afraid, not of what had nearly happened, but of what was happening to him. There was perspiration streaming into his eyes. He had lost his hat, and his hair was over his forehead. He looked at the broken weapon in his hands and it was as if he were seeing it for the first time, then he dropped it quickly. There was anger in his voice. "Are you crazy?" he shouted at her. "You might have been killed!" Behind Zoe he saw Mattie Osgood.

He became conscious of the activity in the street. Jim Torrance, his bullet-wounded leg hindering him, was running up the street, and Henry, the bartender, was in front of the Golden Eagle, standing there, a glass in one hand, a towel in the other, his hands arrested in the exact position they had been in when he heard the blast of the shotgun.

Jake Patterson, the wind knocked out of him, had gotten to his hands and knees. He started to get up, gave a convulsive gasp, and started to curse. "I'll kill you, Mead Weber!" he said. "I promise you, I'll kill you!"

Owen saw the white lines on either side of Mead's mouth and again he thought of the surprising resemblance between Mead and Casco, and now Mead was moving forward, his mouth tight and ugly. He reached down and gripped Patterson by the coat collar and jerked him to his feet with his left hand, and his right fist smashed Patterson in the face. "Mead!" Zoe shouted, but Mead's arm was drawn back again and again he hit Patterson and Patterson sagged away from it but Mead's grip on his coat collar held him up.

Jim Torrance, panting, out of breath, threw himself between Mead and the struggling Patterson, and Mead's fist caught Torrance a glancing blow and sent him sprawling backwards. The deputy's bad leg gave way and Torrance sat down in the dust of the street and Owen saw the expression on the old man's face, a man who had little left in his life but his dignity and now his dignity was gone. . . . Owen stepped in. His hand was open. He raised his arm and chopped the edge of his hand solidly against Mead Weber's forearm.

The blow broke Weber's grip on Patterson's coat collar and Patterson staggered back, both hands clutching his face. Blood trickled between his fingers.

There was a dead silence as Owen and Mead faced each other. "I hate a yellowbelly coward, Weber," Owen said.

"I hate a land thief more. You're both of them." He turned and picked up his saddle. He could feel Zoe's eyes on him. He knew she had heard what he had said to Mead. It was all right. He had wanted her to hear.

He started to move away and he heard one of the Wyoming cattle buyers say, "I don't know. We don't want to get mixed up in any local squabble. . . ."

"You can forget it happened," Mead Weber said. "It's a personal thing, that's all. Osgood here can tell you."

Owen glanced back. The little banker looked as if someone had kicked him in the pit of the stomach. He still wore his eyeshade and his face had a sickly green cast. The banker's wife was standing by him, an imposing woman with hurt eyes. Owen saw the banker nod, heard his thin voice. "It's as Mr. Weber says . . ." Owen walked on, and he was nearly to the sheriff's office before he realized Jim Torrance had fallen into step alongside him.

"They say you took the gun away from Jake," Jim Torrance said. His voice sounded far away.

"You would have done the same," Owen said.

"If I could have."

Owen felt a stab of pain for the old man beside him. He wished he could help him, but he couldn't.

"You should have let Jake kill him," the deputy said.

"You know better," Owen said. "Right or wrong, a dead man stays dead. The man who killed him pays for it, one way or another."

There was a long silence and then Jim Torrance had to know. "The law after you, Delaney?" he asked.

Owen thought about it. "Not the kind of law you're talking about, Jim," he said.

"What, then?"

"There's an outfit in Wyoming," Delaney said. "They call themselves Regulators. They've got a black list for people they don't like. I'm on it."

"They got a reason for not liking you?"

"They think so."

"So you *are* running from trouble," Torrance said.

"That's right," Delaney said. "I'm running from trouble."

"You think it will work?"

"It has," Owen said. "I'm not in Wyoming, am I? It's as simple as that."

"Is it, Owen?"

The old hurt and anger was strong in him now, and he thought of a woman and a ranch and a gallows tree and a rigged judge and jury. . . . What the devil was expected of a man, anyway? "I like it this way," he said.

They had reached the sheriff's office and the old man stopped. Owen wanted to move along. He thought of the road that led across the valley, up by the Levering and Granger places, on over the ridge, and, though he didn't know this, by the Middleton ranch. He wanted to be away from this place, and yet he lingered, and the red sun, low in the west now, threw a blood-red shadow on the town like a portent of evil. . . .

"This town will grow now," Jim Torrance said.

"That what you want?"

"I got no cows to sell," Torrance said. "This town was a peaceful place for a man like me to sit back and die comfortable. Set like we are at the edge of the hills here, every trail herd that leaves Oregon will like as not make up right in this part of the country." His sigh had a trace of old memory. "It'll be rough for a while."

"You'll handle it."

Jim Torrance shook his head. "No," he said. "I won't. But you could."

"Me?"

"It'll go wild for a while," Torrance said. "Then people will start getting nervous about it. People like Levering and Granger. It always happens. When it happens, there's a job for a man with a gun." He looked squarely at Owen. "It might pay well."

"Did it pay you well, Jim?" Owen asked.

The old man shifted his weight on his bullet-riddled leg. He was old and tired, his day of glory done. He was near the end of the line and he knew it. "It's a question I ask myself, Owen," he said. "I haven't found the answer."

"A man has to find his own answers, I guess, Jim," Owen said.

"So you'll drift."

"That seems to be my answer," Owen said. He lifted the saddle and moved on down the street and turned at the corner onto the John Day road. Jim Torrance watched, a deep-down sadness in him, then he limped back up the street, toward the bank.

Mead had brushed the dirt from his clothes and was as much in control of himself as if nothing had happened. Torrance heard him invite the two cattle buyers next door to the Golden Eagle for a drink, then, turning to Torrance, Mead said, "Did you lock Patterson and Delaney up?"

"No," Torrance said.

72

"Why not?"

"Because I didn't want to," Torrance said. He saw the antagonism in Mead's eyes, then Mead and the two cattle buyers were heading for the saloon.

Harold and Mattie Osgood, along with Zoe Middleton, were still standing in front of the bank, and as Torrance approached them he heard Zoe ask, "In heaven's name, why, Harold? If you even suspected things might open up soon it was your place to keep Jake from selling out."

"I didn't know," Harold said. "I could only guess. I wanted to protect you and Mead——"

For a moment Zoe stared at Harold, and the anger that had claimed her was gone. She couldn't believe Harold capable of any planned wrong. "We'll have to talk this out, all of us," she said. "I want Jake in on it, too. Would out at my place be best?"

"Zoe," Harold said, "it's only two cattle buyers."

"The gold rush started with one nugget," Zoe said. The emotional upset of the fight was passing and her natural enthusiasm was starting to claim her. "How long since we've had a roundup? We'll have to hire a crew, break out some horses——" She looked at Torrance. "Didn't that Delaney claim to be a bronc buster?"

"I doubt he'll take a job," Torrance said.

"She's old enough to ask him herself," Mattie Osgood said. "Let her."

Zoe turned, a quick surprise in her eyes. Harold was staring at Mattie, a shocked look on his face. There seemed to be a constant communication of thoughts between this man and his wife. Zoe had sensed it before, and she sensed it strongly now. She didn't know what either of them was thinking, but she was sure they knew. When she met Mattie's gaze it was as if Mattie were urging her, telling her to hurry. . . . "He took the John Day road," Mattie said. "You'll pass him on your way home. Why don't you ask him if he wants a job?"

Harold ran his tongue across his lips. His voice was almost a whisper. "Mattie," he said, "why Delaney?"

"He's a man, isn't he?" Mattie said. "Help will be scarce."

"I'll ask him if I see him," Zoe said.

She left them and walked down the street toward the store where she had left her buckboard and team. She knew that Levering and Granger would be out to see her as soon as they learned of Patterson's fight. As she hurried along there was an odd excitement in her that had nothing to do with cattle buyers.

She took her team and buckboard from the lean-to shed without help. She slapped the lines and the team broke into a startled trot as she turned into the dust of the John Day road. Ahead of her she saw Delaney, and the red sun threw his shadow, long and black, and it reached out toward her. As he walked the gun on his hip swayed, and the gun butt, too, was there in the shadow that lay in the dust of the road.

THERE WAS a gentle rise to the road here as it lifted up the slope of the low ridge that ran through the valley and the sound of the approaching buckboard rattled in the evening stillness. Owen put down the saddle and stood there at the side of the road. He had known for some time that Zoe Middleton was driving the buckboard.

He thought she would pass him by. She was sitting straight in the seat, a tall girl with a studied reserve, then she reined up and without looking at him said, "As long as you're going my way, you might as well ride."

"It beats walking any time," he said. "I'm obliged." He tossed the saddle into the back of the buckboard and, hesitating, said, "You want me to drive?"

"It doesn't matter," she said. She handed the lines down to him and moved over, and he climbed to the seat. The soft springs gave under his weight, and she gripped the side of the seat and held herself from sliding down toward him. He made a soft, kissing sound to the team and dropped the lines against their backs.

The buckboard moved up the road and he risked a look at her. She was looking straight ahead, her chin tilted slightly, giving her face a tense look. They drove in silence.

The road steepened and switched back upon itself, always lifting, and then they were to the top and the horses' flanks were heaving slightly, their nostrils flared. Owen reined up, giving the team a breather, and he looked out across the other half of the valley, a new valley, between the Blue Mountains and the hogback ridge.

The buckboard looked tall in the setting sun, and the man and the woman, outlined against the evening sky, were small creatures in a vast land, but they were creatures of power, capable of changing a land, and Zoe felt the magic of it, just as she had so many times before, pausing

74

in this exact spot. In this moment she was alone in the world, and the bitter hurt that had driven Patterson to his moment of folly was clear to her, for she, too, in his place, would have done the same, she knew. She thought of Mead, the doubt that had been growing in her suddenly full flame, and she knew that she didn't love him.

The confusion of the day pressed in on her, and she looked at the valley and at the evening sky, and it was offering her a freedom, a chance to breathe and think. . . . There was nothing planned about her movements. Her hands loosened her hair and spread it, spilling it across her shoulders, and the sun picked up chestnut glints and the evening breeze, lifting sweet and warm from the valley, bathed her face with a liquid intimacy. She closed her eyes and threw back her head, then drew back her shoulders, and she laced her hands behind her neck and inhaled deeply, as if in this way she could ignore reality and absorb only the security and peace the valley had always given her. . . .

She heard Owen's long, drawn-out whistle of appreciation.

She was immediately conscious of the tightness of her blouse, strained against the full contours of her body. Her eyes flew open and she snapped upright in the seat, a quick anger claiming her.

He wasn't even looking at her.

He was looking at the valley—her valley—and there was something in his expression that startled her at first and then put her at ease. She turned to follow his gaze, wanting to see this familiar scene with his eyes, knowing, somehow, that he saw there the same things she saw and believed. . . .

Sunset spilled its paint through a notch of the hills, brushing the long, verdant valley, and the green of the grass mixed, visibly, it seemed, with the golden light of the sun until an exquisite purple was there on the palette of the valley floor. For a moment all was suspended in time and space, and then the mauve shadows moved toward the sun, up the slopes, reaching, like a woman's arms, avoiding the troubled darkness of the timbered canyons, and briefly there was a wedding of the bright, ambitious blaze of day and the soft caress of night, and then, like the echo of a triumphant blare of bugles, it was gone, and the soft peace of evening was on the land.

He spoke so softly it was part of the moment. "Sometimes," he said, "it seems like the world ought to be made up of sunsets. No yesterday, no tomorrow, just a now that lasts forever."

She looked at him and the shadows hid the bruise marks of Casco's fists and the violence she had seen in him was gone with the sunlight and he was a man alone, a man with memories, and those memories, she knew, had a sadness and a longing in them. The expression faded from his face, and, as if he was ashamed of his moment of sentiment, he said, "Not a bad-looking valley."

The moment between them was gone. "It's my range," she said. "All the way back to the mountains. The home place is down there in that grove of poplars. I was born there."

He looked at her and said, "Means a lot to you, owning land, doesn't it?"

"You would have to have had a place like this to know," she said.

She caught the anger in his eyes and she was sorry, knowing she had put it there, but before she could speak it was gone. Immediately then he was a man without ties and without purpose. He lifted the lines and shrugged. "So you'll marry Mead Weber. You'll be a big cattle queen and everybody will live happily ever after." He clucked to the team and the buckboard moved down the slope. "It's too bad," he said, eying her appraisingly. "You could do better."

Her shoulders became rigid and her mouth set. "When I want your opinions," she said, "I'll ask for them."

"No need to," he said, shrugging. "I give 'em out as they come to me."

They drove on in silence, and the long, lean twilight settled across the valley, giving its softness to the rutted road, adding its special magic to the sharp outlines of the towering mountains, and ahead of them the Middleton ranch headquarters stood strong and magnificent, and then, as they approached it, the illusion started to fade. The Middleton ranch, like the town of Ten Mile, had known better days.

The man who had established this ranch had been a man whose roots went deep, Owen knew, and, looking at Zoe, he knew the father had passed his love of the land along to his daughter. She had changed, and now she was a woman come home, and she looked as if the mere fact of being here gave her a new confidence, an ability to face trouble. There was a new positiveness in her voice as she directed him to stop the team by the yard gate. She had a real pride in this place, and she wanted him to be aware of that pride.

He pulled the team to a stop and wrapped the lines around the brake, and as he did he noticed the ample pole corrals, the barn, big enough for a winter supply of hay, a bunkhouse for twenty men. But the bunkhouse was empty and had been for some time, for weeds grew through the cracks of the porch. There were only three horses in the corral.

There was surprisingly little to show that anyone lived here at all, Owen noted, and what few things there were, he knew, were Zoe's touches. A handful of hollyhocks swayed near the front door of the substantial house, budding now, ready for summer bloom. A woman will plant flowers, he thought, even if she knows she's going to move the next day. . . . There were flimsy curtains at the windows that faced the barnyard; the window that looked across the valley was undraped and large.

But it was in the more practical things where the neglect showed itself most strongly. Great patches of shakes were missing from the barn roof, lifted by the winds of more than one winter. The corral fences sagged. The windmill was operating, but it needed grease badly, and it howled and complained and splashed a pitiful driblet of water into a large wooden tank. The ranch, from a distance, had seemed rich—even elegant. Now it seemed empty and alone, a monument to a past.

"You live here alone, do you?" Owen asked.

"I'm capable of taking care of myself," she said.

He smiled inwardly at the typically feminine answer. He got out of the buckboard and stood there in the semi-darkness, his arms lifted toward her. "Give you a hand?"

Her response was one of old habit, he knew. She was capable of fighting a losing battle with a ranch, and yet she was used to respect, and she accepted his arms readily. She was light and soft and there was a perfume about her that pleased him, a lurking fragrance to her hair as it brushed his face. There had been women in Owen's life, but it had been a long time since he had held a lady this way—and there was a distinction. He found himself prolonging the pleasure, holding her free of the ground, and her eyes were on a level with his eyes. . . . He held her until they were both conscious of each other, and he felt the warmth of her body against his. He put her down. "I'll put your team away before I leave," he said.

77

She had started to walk away and now she stopped, and without looking at him she said, "Have you eaten?"

"Not since the last time," he said.

"I'll fix something," she said, then added quickly, "I have to cook anyway." She went on toward the house, walking too fast, he thought, and he waited until she had gone inside. He saw the flare of a lamp, and the yellow light spilled through the lightly curtained window and lay on the shadows of the yard, a warm shaft of security in the gathering darkness. Old memories were strong in him as he unhitched and led the team to the windmill tank to drink.

Afterward he took the team to the barn and unharnessed. There was a musty, unused smell to the barn, and only the pleasant warmth of the fresh-sweating horses was of the present. There were a dozen saddles here, hanging neatly on pegs, but they were covered with dust, the leather stiff from lack of use. He found a pitchfork and started to pitch some hay into the manger, but the handle broke under the first load. Using his hands, he half filled the manger from the meager supply, then decided to rub down the horses. He found an old gunny sack, tore it, and was using that to wipe the straggly remains of winter coat from the horses when he became aware of the sound of approaching rigs.

He went outside the barn and stood there, and, his eyes now accustomed to the darkness, he could see them coming down the lane, outlined against the light patch of sky.

There was a surrey, followed by a two-wheel cart, and a boy on horseback. He recognized the rider immediately as young Bud Patterson, and as the procession approached, he knew it was Zoe's neighbors. Frank Levering drove the surrey, and Jake Patterson was at his side. Martha Patterson was in the back seat with a woman Owen took to be Mrs. Levering, and that would be Mr. and Mrs. Scott Granger in the cart.

The boy saw Owen almost at once. He shouted Owen's name, then spurred the horse forward with his heels. Jerking the animal to a sliding stop, he yelled, "Hey, Owen! I didn't know you was here! Owen, there's a whole bunch of cattle buyers from Wyoming in town and we ain't gonna move to Missouri!"

"Shut up, Bud," Patterson snapped. The rigs had drawn up, and Patterson was leaning out, looking at Owen. That deep anger was still plain in Patterson, and it had made itself felt in the others. They were grim-faced, determined.

"You want to say what you're doing here, Delaney?" Jake Patterson asked.

"Rubbing down a couple of horses," Owen said. "Why?"

"How we know you ain't spyin' for Mead Weber?" Jake snapped. "You was working for him. You was quick enough to jump me."

"You leave it, Jake," Frank Levering said. "I'm the one to do the talking here. It's what we agreed on."

In the house Zoe heard the approaching rigs, followed by the exchange of voices. She knew who the visitors were, for she had been expecting them, and a great tiredness seized her.

As long back as she could remember, Patterson, Granger, and Levering had been coming here in moments of decision. Sometimes it was with trouble and sometimes it was with a flush of success, but always, in any special moment, they came to the big ranch across the ridge, for her father had always been here, like a tower of strength and wisdom, a role for which he was fitted. And now, without knowing it would be this way, she had assumed the role, for she had held to the ranch, and the ranch, with its acres of meadow hay and its back pastures in the mountains, was the key to the valley. Those were her neighbors and friends out there, and through old habit they had come here to make their decision, as they had done for years. She knew how it would be. A surrey, a two-wheel cart, young Bud on his horse. She took off her apron and went outside and she tried to simulate surprise.

There was an awkwardness she hadn't felt before in all of them, and it was only then that she realized her true position. These were her friends, people with whom she shared open range, but she was engaged to Mead Weber, and, with the purchase of the Patterson place, Mead had moved into that range.

"There's two more cattle buyers come to town after you left, Zoe," Levering said. "Torrance told me. They got a crew of drovers with them."

She felt helpless and terribly alone. She wanted to say something but she didn't know what she was expected to say. In that moment she felt her inadequacy as a woman, and she turned to Owen, not knowing why she did, knowing only she did not want to be alone. The lamplight from the open door was full on his face and she saw the bruise marks from Casco's fists, but she saw something else. There was an understanding of her need there, and, as if

79

he belonged here, he said, "We were fixing to have supper. Won't you step down and join us?"

It was as unexpected a thing as he could possibly have said—a thing he had no right to say—and yet it was the right thing, and she felt a wave of gratefulness. The women started talking all at once, and Zoe wondered how many other women beside herself had found refuge behind a cookstove. Her hands busy with familiar tasks, she would have time to think. The women would help with the supper, and the old easiness between all of them would return, and the men would settle their minds. Never make a decision on an empty stomach, her father used to say.

"You folks go on," Owen said. "Bud and me will take care of your horses."

"Now, Zoe, we don't want to put you to no bother," Thelma Levering said.

"I brought a pot of beans I had on the stove," Betty Granger said. She was a fluttery woman, and she laughed. "It ain't much, but like Scott says, it beats nothing."

Familiar phrases, coming out of the past, heard over and over in this very place, and now these people were old friends and there was nothing to worry about. She saw Owen leading Levering's team toward the water trough, and Bud Patterson was walking alongside him, matching his step, imitating his stride. She remembered her father saying, if young boys and dogs like a man, there's good in him. She found herself shushing the protests of the women. "Now it's no trouble at all . . ." And they were going up the familiar path to the front porch and the women had pots of food, carefully covered with flour-sack dish towels.

IN A matter of moments the women were busy in the kitchen and the men had seated themselves in the living room, in almost preappointed places, it seemed to Zoe. She excused herself and went to her bedroom, where she changed to a crisp, gingham house dress. The dress was yellow, with a feel of summer about it, and the square-cut neckline and tight waist were flattering to her figure. She paused to put a silver clasp on her hair, pulling it in at the nape of her neck, letting it fall loosely on her shoulders. She glanced at herself in the mirror and was not displeased with her reflection.

The three ranch wives all had a habit of prefacing their remarks with a reference to their husbands. It was a habit that had always annoyed Zoe, but tonight it didn't. Tonight she was almost envious of their right to use the expression. There was a tension and worry in all of them, as there was in Zoe, but they covered it well and they had someone with whom to share it, each of them, someone to carry the load. Through the open doorway she could hear the voices of the men, a low, rumbling sound, and at times she heard Jake Patterson's voice rise in anger, and then she could hear Levering's positive voice and Jake's complaint would die.

The meal was on the big oak table before Owen and Bud came back in. Owen had washed, and the black glisten of water was on his hair. That unruly cowlick could as well have been a wave, she thought, and then she became conscious of the silence in the room and she knew the men were reluctant to speak in front of Owen. She saw no reason why that should be so. She gave Owen a smile, and it was for him alone. "Oh, Owen," she said. "You sit here." It was her home and he was her guest.

Owen took the appointed chair and young Bud, forgetting all manners, shouted, "I get to sit by Owen!" and he shoved himself into the tangle of chairs. Scott Granger had just pulled out a chair. Granger half turned, and Bud collided with him, then stepped back, and as he did, his swinging hand caught the butt of Owen's six-shooter, just as Owen started to sit down. The angle of the holster and Bud's swinging hand met at exactly the right time and the gun flipped neatly from the holster and thudded to the floor.

There was a dead silence as all eyes were on Owen, and Zoe saw the color climb Owen's throat and reach his face. Bud, more embarrassed than anyone, reached for the gun, and Owen stooped quickly and picked it up. He held it briefly and said, "I always keep the hammer on an empty chamber." The gun was clumsy in his hand, then, with the ease of old habit, he flipped the gun expertly back into the holster.

Bud's eyes were round. "Gee," he said. "Could you teach me to do that, Owen?"

"Sit down and eat, Bud," Jake Patterson said.

Owen reached for the meat platter, intending to pass it. His outstretched hand froze as he sensed the silence and saw Frank Levering bow his head. Again Zoe saw the color in Owen's cheeks before she bowed her own head, and as Levering rumbled through his lengthy prayer she thought of Owen. He was miserable, she knew, but some-

81

day the memory of this moment would be funny and he would look back on it with someone and laugh. She remembered how many times her own father and mother had started a conversation with, "Remember the time . . . ?" And then they had gone on to talk of some incident no more significant than this, and in those moments they had shared a personal intimacy. She wondered if those moments weren't a great part of love, and she tried to imagine herself sharing such moments with Mead Weber and she couldn't.

The prayer finished, Frank Levering took his place as spokesman. "We figured we ought to decide on what we'd best do," he said. "Of course, it could be we're getting ourselves excited over nothing. Three or four cattle buyers don't mean the whole country is gonna boom. Take the mining boom, now. We all thought that would last forever, but it didn't. Could be these are the only buyers we'll see."

"I doubt that," Delaney said. "From what I've seen in Wyoming and Montana both, I'd say there's a market for every cow Oregon can raise." He glanced around the table. "They ought to be willing to pay just about what you folks ask."

The reticence to take Owen into the conversation was gone, for here was a man who had information to share. "Big outfits up there, is there, Delaney?" Levering asked.

"Hard to believe how big," Owen said. "Matter of fact, a man would have to see it to believe it." He was the center of attention, and he talked easily. "It's a big country to begin with," he said, "and after the Government signed that treaty with the Sioux and Cheyenne the land was just laying there, ready to be moved onto. Lot of pretty fast dealing went on," he said.

"I seen a paper a few months back offering to sell a man stock in some land and cattle company back there," Granger said. "I never was one to gamble like that, though."

"A lot of people are," Owen said. "I've seen Englishmen in red coats with a pack of pot hounds following them around and there was one ranch I worked on where the cowhands had to *parlez-vous* French before they could understand the boss." He laughed. "Trouble is, a lot of those really big syndicates have got plenty cattle showing on their books but none on their grass. Lot of those ranch managers worry more about a meeting of the stockholders than they do about their range count. Catch a manager when his stockholders are about to come out and take a look at their investment you might be able to sell him a lot of cows fast at about any price you wanted to ask."

Both Levering and Granger were chuckling, but there was no levity in Jake Patterson. They were including him in the conversation, but the fact remained that he had sold out. Jake said, "We've heard this talk before, all of us. But how about them Texas cattle? We heard there was a solid line of Texas cows between the Gulf and the Canada border."

"Ever see a Texas longhorn, Jake?" Owen asked. "Four legs and six feet of horns held together by ticks. Gets cold in Wyoming, too. These shorthorns here in Oregon ought to stand up to the winters all right. Texas cows don't."

"And besides," said Zoe, "who would want to eat Texas beef when they could be eating good Oregon beef?" She speared a second steak onto Owen's plate. "There, Owen Delaney," she said, "did you ever taste beef like that in Texas?"

"Never," he said, "but I never had a cook like you in Texas, either."

Their glances met, and she started to blush. The complete stupidity of such a childish thing as blushing angered her, and the more she thought about it, the more she blushed, and the less able she was to take her eyes from his. And then, as if it were contagious, the color was climbing into his cheeks. . . . He took a gulp of hot coffee and nearly strangled on it and Zoe hurried to the kitchen and worked furiously at doing something that didn't need doing.

The meal was over, and again the tension was there between them, for the real issue hadn't yet been discussed. There was a wide archway between the dining room and the kitchen and, helping clean up the dishes, Zoe could still hear and be a part of the men's conversation. She heard Patterson's voice, high with anger, say, "I told you, and I still say it! I'm moving back onto my place. Mead knew this was coming up when he bought me out!"

Levering's voice was patient, the voice of a peacemaker with a religious background that made him abhor trouble. "I won't deny Mead knew what he was doing, Jake," he said, "but you can't hang a man for being smart at business. You can cuss him," he said, glancing at Zoe, "but you can't hang him."

"It's still crooked," Patterson said, and now his wife was trying to warn him with her eyes, glancing first at him, then at Zoe, trying to remind her husband that Zoe and Mead were engaged.

"No, it ain't crooked," Levering said. "It's just short-sighted on our part." He banged the bowl of his pipe into the palm of his hand. "Just today," he said, glancing at his wife, "me and Scott here told Mead we was ready to sell out to him too. The thing now is to tell Mead we decided against it."

"I'm talking about me," Patterson said. "What does that do for me?"

"Zoe, honey, we ain't blaming Mead," Thelma Levering said.

Delaney had kept out of it. Now he said, "From what I've seen of it, it's big country. Looks to me like there ought to be room for all of you."

"There ought to be," Frank Levering said, "but is there? This is all open range. Us four here always run that range together. If Mead moves cows in on Patterson's grass there ain't nothing to stop those same cows from eating my grass." He ducked his head, as if hating to say it, then said, "When he moves in here on your half of the valley, Zoe, it's gonna leave me and Granger sittin' like an island, completely surrounded by Weber's cows."

It was a statement, but it was a direct question, too, and Zoe didn't have an answer she could give. She looked at Owen and he was watching her closely. He shrugged. "You two could fence off your grass, I guess," he said.

"It's what we talked on, Zoe—Scott and me," Levering said. "We wondered how you and Mead would feel about it."

She wished they would quit considering her and Mead as one, and yet they had every right to consider them as such. It was no secret that she and Mead were engaged and she had given no indication that there was any doubt in her mind about the success of that engagement. "Why not?" she said. "If it comes to that. I'm sure Harold would advance the money to both of you."

"I ain't sure he would, Zoe," Levering said. "It must be Osgood advancing Mead the money to buy up this grass, ain't it?"

She realized then how deeply she was enmeshed in this and now they weren't old friends here to discuss this with her. They were here because they were afraid of her, for in their eyes Zoe Middleton, Mead Weber, and Harold Osgood were aligned against them. Zoe had sufficient land to surround them. Mead was businessman enough to do it. And Harold, managing Zoe's affairs, had the money to back it up. She was quickly angry. "How can you believe that Harold wouldn't do what was best for all of us?" she said. "If it weren't for Harold we would all have gone under long ago."

"It comes to a different thing, Zoe," Levering said. "It could be like Delaney here says there'll be a lot of cattle moving out of Oregon. A man could have a mighty big range here and be in the cattle business and like as not get rich." He hesitated. "Or a man could have small places, like me and Granger, and get in on the edges of it and still do all right."

"In what way?" Zoe asked.

"Hay, for one thing," Levering said. "Me and Scott both got some of the best meadow hay in this part of the country. Horses, for another. Them trail outfits will need horses." He looked steadily at Zoe. "Too many cattle running through our places would ruin what hay we could have this summer," he said. "If Mead moves too many cows onto Patterson's grass . . ."

"Then back me up and keep him from it!" Patterson said. He slammed his fist against the table. "I'm sick of all this mealymouthin'! Harold Osgood and Mead Weber figure to take over this whole valley. I know it and you know it, and the quicker we face up to it and tell Mead and Harold we won't stand for it, the quicker we'll be done with it!" The rancher's face was florid, his nostrils flaring in and out, his chest heaving.

Young Bud was on his feet. "We're gonna gun-fight 'em, ain't we, Pop? Owen, you gonna help us gun-fight 'em?"

Owen's voice was low. "Didn't you have enough of trying a gun today, Patterson?"

The anger was raw in Patterson's voice. "Maybe it's gonna be the other way," he said. "Maybe you're gonna turn that gun of yours against me. That it, Delaney?"

Owen stood up slowly. There was a white patch of anger at either corner of his mouth. "I piled you today, Patterson, to keep you from killing a couple of women," he said. "At that range, a double barrel shotgun wouldn't have gotten just Mead Weber."

Bud was looking from his dad to Owen and back again, not understanding, and Martha Patterson started to cry.

"It's this kind of thing we can't have," Frank Levering said. "It don't lead to nothing, this kind of arguing." He was standing now and he put his hand on Zoe's arm, a gesture of old friendship and trust. "We don't want trouble, Zoe," he said, "me or Scott either one. We don't hold to trouble. We figure you and Mead and Harold won't want

85

none either. We want to talk it out with you and settle in a way that's right." His shoulders sagged. "I guess that's all there is to say to it, Zoe." He looked at Jake. "Jake?"

"Do it your way," Patterson said. "I'll do it mine. With or without you. I'm moving back onto my place. I'll offer Mead his money back, and if he won't take it, I'll shove it down his throat. Martha, you and Bud come on out of here."

The women squeezed Zoe's hand and whispered their good-bys and they walked softly, as if any untoward sound might set off trouble. Taciturn, small-voiced Scott Granger hadn't said a dozen words all evening. He ducked his head in a good-night gesture, then hurried toward his cart.

Owen watched them, then started across the yard toward where he had left his saddle. Zoe's voice stopped him. "It's too late to start walking tonight," she said. "You can sleep in the barn, if you want."

"Thanks," he said.

He had taken a few more steps when she said, "Would you like another cup of coffee?"

He turned and looked at her and she was standing in the open doorway, the light from the lamp behind her spilling around her. He said, "Yes, that would be all right." He walked back, his hat in his hand, and he sat down at the oak table, taking the chair he had used before.

She busied herself, stirring up the fire, and he watched her, enjoying the pleasure of being here, feeling the nearness of a woman. She took the coffeepot from the stove and poured a cup for him and one for herself. "I was thinking," she said, still pouring the coffee. "I'll be hiring some help." She looked up then. "Do you plan to stay around here?"

"No," he said.

She sat down and for a while she cradled the heavy coffee mug in her hands. The silence grew long and he said, "Why did you call me back? Are you curious or are you lonesome?"

She saw no need for pretense and she said, "Both, I guess."

"It's a bad combination for a pretty woman," he said.

She let the compliment go, if it was a compliment, and, looking at him, she said, "All right, I'm curious. What are you running from, Owen Delaney?"

"Am I running?"

"I offered you a job. You turned it down."

"I don't like what your job could lead to," he said. "I don't like trouble."

"You stopped Jake Patterson today," she said. "You whipped Casco Weber."

"The first was a case of taking a gun away from a fool," he said. "The second was a case of trouble looking me up." He looked at her a long time. "Why worry about it, Zoe?" he asked. "You're on the right side of the fence. Go ahead and marry him. A woman could do worse. He'll make a lot of money—buy you pretty clothes. You and pretty clothes were made for each other."

"Suppose I don't want to marry him?"

"Don't you?"

"I said suppose."

He smiled at her, and it was as if they were old friends. "How did you happen to get engaged to him, Zoe?"

There was a trace of anger in her voice. "If I said I was in love with him would that be reason enough?"

"It would be one reason," he said. "Another might be you were lonesome. Like now. Or maybe you were a girl, trying to carry on a man's work, and you were scared."

"You have a lot of answers, don't you?"

"I'm practical," he said. "That's all."

"It would be practical to go to work," she said.

"Not here." He was looking directly at her and she sensed a double meaning in his answer and again she felt the color at her throat.

"So you'll drift," she said.

"That's right. I'll drift."

"Has that been the entire pattern of your life?"

"I tried standing still once," he said. "It didn't work out."

He stood up and he put on his hat, and when he left she was still sitting there, staring into her now cold coffee. He felt the wash of the night air on his face, a cool air, laced with ribbons of warmth. He went to the barn and in the dark he took his bedroll and laid it out in the hay. He stretched out in his blankets, but he didn't sleep. Far into the night he lay there, his hands laced behind his head, and as he stared up at the dark rafters of the barn the night was full of a thousand memories.

"I'VE BEEN wanting to talk to you about it, Mattie," Harold Osgood said. He was pacing up and down in the apartment above the bank, his supper on the table uneaten. He was sick, but none of the many pills or tonics he kept in reserve would cure this sickness and he knew it. He stopped and looked at his wife, big and placid and trusting, a woman without a worry, so far as Harold knew. "Business isn't a simple thing," Harold said. "It's hard for a woman to understand these things."

I only want to understand you, Harold, she thought. She said, "Should I warm you some milk?"

"No. No," he said. He waved her away. "I want to lay it out. Just talk about it. You don't need to say anything. Sometimes it clears things up for me to talk them out." He sat down heavily, as if he had run out of words and strength both, and she wanted to go to him and tell him it didn't matter how these things had come about. What did matter was what he would do next.

"It was just good business, Mattie," he said, and now he was asking her to understand. "Al Zelinski was closing the store. The town needed a store, Mattie, and Mead was willing to take it over. I made him a proposition. A sort of partnership, you might say. There's no need to go into it . . ."

No need at all, Mattie thought, *except that that was the beginning and once Mead got hold of you he wouldn't let go and you couldn't break the grip. . . .* "I wish you would eat something, Harold," she said.

"I should never have let him have the saloon," Harold said. "Perhaps someone else could have taken it and done better with it." He looked up. "That's what I've always wanted, Mattie, you know that. I've wanted to help as many people as I could."

Mattie picked up her knitting. "And then the McCaskill place?" she said.

He was immediately defensive. "It was on the east side of the river," he said, "next to Mead's holdings. If anyone was to take it over at all, Mead was the logical one." Harold stood up. "No," he said. "I don't regret that in the least."

You didn't know, did you, Harold? she thought. *You're good and trusting and kind and you didn't know that one piece of land would never be enough for Mead.* She had to know. "Harold, did you know these cattle buyers were coming?"

She hated the misery she had put in his eyes, but by his voice she knew he was telling the truth. "I knew, but I didn't know when. I wrote to a land and cattle company

88

in Wyoming. I told them of the cattle we had here. Mattie, it was my duty to do that, don't you see? It was my obligation to try to bring business here. I've held this town together. Without me there wouldn't be any town. I wanted to see it come back, Mattie."

"Did you think Mead could do it alone?"

"It wasn't for Mead alone. It was for Zoe. I'm first responsible for her, Mattie. I wasn't happy about it when she told me she was going to marry Mead, but I couldn't stop it, could I?"

Then perhaps I have failed as much as you have, she thought. *It was my place to talk to Zoe and tell her she was making a mistake.* She said, "No, Harold, you couldn't stop it."

"I thought whatever was good for Mead was good for Zoe."

It was that simple and, knowing him so well, Mattie knew there had been no motive beyond that for Harold's apparent duplicity. At least there hadn't at first, but now there was, and, looking at her husband, she knew what it was and it hurt her deeply to know, but she didn't know what she could do about it. It had gone too far, and one day Mead Weber had the upper hand and Harold wanted to back out but he was afraid. Her husband was a coward. Mattie knew it, and it killed her to know it, but the fact remained. She said, "You should never have let Jake Patterson sell out this morning, Harold."

His anger toward her was quick and she knew he had not closed out Patterson of his own free will.

"I couldn't stop Patterson from selling out," he said. "He had made up his mind to it."

"And now he knows he was wrong," Mattie said. "Have you thought what you'd do about it?"

"Why should I do anything?" Harold said. He was starting to perspire and the perspiration ran down the seams of his cheeks. "Am I responsible for every poor business deal that's made in this country?"

"You used to feel you were, Harold."

"The Patterson place is sold," he said.

She was careful now. "Has Mead bought up the mortgage from you?"

The anger in him was gone. He sat down in the chair again and he clasped his hands between his knees and as he sat there he looked broken and old, a small, thin-boned man with little hair and tired eyes, an ugly little man. He looked up. "Mattie, what must I do?"

"The right thing," she said. "As you always have."

"The right thing is to give Patterson's place back to him."

The hope in her was strong and her love for her husband was an overwhelming thing that seemed to fill the room and stifle her with its intensity. "Then you must do that, Harold," she said.

"Mattie, I can't," he said.

"Why?"

"Mead and Casco have a thousand cattle headed into the valley. They intend to run them in on the Patterson place."

"But if you tell them they can't have the Patterson place . . . ?"

He sat there, staring at his hands. "Mead threatened to kill me if I did, Mattie," he said. He looked up, saying it honestly and truthfully. "He threatened to kill me, Mattie," he said, "and I'm afraid."

Mattie Osgood stared into space. She could feel the fear in her husband and it was real and tangible, like a thick odor in the room, and it was justified. A sickening thought came to Mattie Osgood as she put her big hand on the back of her husband's head. *Can you possibly kill him beyond this, Mead Weber?* she asked herself.

There was no moon that night. The Magpie range stood stark and cold in the full starlight, the rocky crests blue black in the predawn darkness. The light in Mead Weber's office was a yellow stab of intrusion in the quiet of the ranch yard. Mead made himself another pot of coffee and waited.

Early this evening he had sent Kline, the man with the mutilated jaw, out to get Casco, and since then Mead had waited, just as he was doing now. Alone in the night, Mead's thoughts had run free and clear, and now the excitement in him was live and real. The cattle buyers were in town. Mead's gamble had paid off.

He had had a few moments of worry there with Patterson, not because of Patterson himself, but because of the reaction of the cattle buyers. But, as if he had taken it over for this very purpose, Mead's Golden Eagle Saloon paid off. After a few drinks it had been easy enough to convince the buyers that the Patterson affair was of no importance. The thing now was to see that nothing further came of it.

And that was where Mead needed Casco, and the knowledge that he did need Casco built a resentment in him. By

himself Mead wasn't a whole man, and a whole man was
what he had to be. He had done well, but he had had to
use Harold Osgood and now he was going to have to use
Casco, and he wanted, more than anything else, to be rid
of both of them.

There was a deep affection in Casco for his younger
brother, Mead knew, and Mead had taken advantage of
that affection. He sometimes thought of Casco as a savage
dog, held on a leash, a threat, ready to be turned loose
at the proper moment. It was good for a man to have such
a dog, but the worry was that such a dog, unleashed, might
turn on the master that had chained him. Sooner or later,
Mead knew, that would happen with Casco, for in the future Mead envisioned he would be a man of means, but,
above all, a man of prestige. Casco had no part in that future.

It was near daylight when Mead heard the approaching
horses. He went to the office door and stood there, and he
saw the hulking form of Casco, thickened by a sheepskin-
lined coat, loom out of the darkness, followed closely by
the slighter shape of Kline. Mead felt a moment of revul-
sion toward Kline and his mangled face. He felt a moment
of respect for his brother's brute power. Kline took the
horses and went on toward the barn, and Casco came
tramping heavily toward the house. He shoved Mead aside
and stood there in the office, blinking against the light like
a great owl shaken from daylight sleep. "What the devil
took you so long?" Mead asked.

"Listen, Mead," Casco said, "I been up two days and
nights. I been drunk. If you had something to say to me,
why didn't you say it when I was in town?"

"Because it hadn't come up then."

Casco blinked against the light. His face was swollen
from whiskey, patched purple with the bruises of Delaney's
fists. He hadn't shaved, nor had he washed, and lint from
his brief stay in his blankets clung to his stubble beard. He
rubbed the back of his hand across his jaw and said,
"What's the matter, Mead? You got trouble?"

"No, not trouble, really," Mead said. "I just wanted your
advice."

Casco laughed. "That's good," he said, "but I don't believe it. You never come to me for advice in your life. You
holler for me when you got something you can't handle."

It was the truth and Mead knew it, and he resented the
truth of it. "All right," Mead said. "The town's full of cattle buyers."

The news seemed more than Casco could handle all at once. He stared at his brother, and Mead felt he could almost hear the big man's brains working. "By God, that calls for a drink," Casco said finally. "You got a drink?"

Mead moved the English glass decanter toward the edge of the desk. Casco picked it up. It looked like a piece of pottery in Casco's clumsy hand. He thumbed out the glass stopper, letting it fall to the desk, and he drank directly from the decanter. He expelled his breath with an ugly sound and flopped down in a chair. "One thing that school I put you through done for you," he said. "You know good whiskey." He looked up. "You sold the cows? When do I move 'em in?"

"Now just don't get too fast," Mead said.

"You mean we got to hold 'em a while and you ain't got the grass. That it?"

"That's not it."

"What, then?"

"Jake Patterson is getting ideas," Mead said. "He thinks I ought to give him his ranch back."

Casco chuckled. "Let him think."

"He came after me with a shotgun today."

"That little woodpecker?" Casco laughed soundly. "What'd you do about it, Mead?"

"Took the gun away from him. Told him a deal was a deal."

"I'd a took a half hitch around his neck with the gun barrel and cinched down on it," Casco said. He took another drink and shook his head as if he still couldn't believe it. "That hayshakin' little woodpecker." He was suddenly serious. "Wait a minute—— You didn't call me back in here because you can't handle Jake Patterson, did you?"

There was a flush of anger in Mead's cheeks. "I told you. There's cattle buyers in town. We're ready to move and I wanted your advice."

"Say what's on your mind, Mead," Casco said. His voice was unexpectedly quiet. "I don't mind doin' your dirty work for you. I always have done it. But don't start givin' me all that high mucky-muck book talk like you do in front of Zoe Middleton."

"What the devil is that supposed to mean?"

"If you don't know, I'll tell you," Casco said. He took a long drink and set the decanter down too hard. "I know you real good, Mead," Casco said. "You got to have everybody like you. You got to have your name on a sign. Now tell me what you want. I got a thousand hungry cows

92

movin' this way. I can have maybe two hundred of 'em in here tomorrow, if you get word out for the boys to push 'em in fast. You want me to push 'em in here so them buyers can see 'em, you say so. You want me to get the grass to put 'em on, you say that, too, but you say it plain out in my kind of talk."

"Maybe we should move some in," Mead said. "I can send Webster out to tell the boys to move in as many as you think." He glanced up, then away. "Maybe you ought to take a couple of the boys and go on over to the Patterson place and just stay there." He tried to minimize it. "I don't figure Patterson will really try to move back, but it wouldn't look good if he did. Those cattle buyers don't want to get tangled up in any range trouble——"

"And it might give Levering and Granger ideas," Casco said.

Mead poured Casco a drink. "If you and a couple of the boys move in Patterson's cabin and just stay there, that ought to discourage Patterson from trying anything."

"Suppose it don't discourage him, Mead?"

"It will."

There was a mixture of anger and affection in Casco's muddy eyes. "You don't believe that, Mead," he said, "or you wouldn't of sent for me."

Mead's anger was sudden and bright. His voice was loud. "How in the devil do I know what will happen?" he said. "I can't be every place at once. I'm just telling you what I think we ought to do, that's all. We're partners, aren't we?"

"Yeah," Casco said. "We're partners. All the way." He stood up, and now that they were together, the lamplight flaring upward on their faces, there was a sharp resemblance between them. "Don't worry," Casco said. "I'll do your dirty work for you, just like I've always done. But this time you're in it with me. All the way. If there's trouble, you're gonna be in on that trouble, and if Zoe Middleton gets in the way she's gonna be in your way as much as mine."

"Now wait a minute——" Mead said.

"You wait a minute," Casco said. "If you hadn't been trying to make time with that girl you could have had this whole valley a month ago. You could of moved in and took it over, like I told you to do. You done it your way, Mead, now we're gonna do it my way, but you're gonna be right there with me. You ain't gonna throw it all on me just so you can look good with that girl." He snatched the de-

93

canter from the desk and tilted it to his lips. It was empty. With a sudden savageness he smashed the decanter against the edge of the desk, breaking it into a thousand pieces. "You wanted my advice? All right, I'll give it to you. If I'd a wanted a girl as bad as you do I'd a gone over to Boise City and bought me one for the right price. You're payin' too damn much for this one."

Mead's fist lashed out and caught Casco solidly on the side of the head. "You dirty——" He lunged forward, his fist ready, but Casco reached out and pushed him back.

Casco was grinning. He hadn't even felt the blow. His big hand gripped the front of Mead's handsome shirt. The hand twisted in the fabric, then lifted, and Mead had to raise to his toes. "There's two things you don't never want to do with me, Mead," Casco said. His voice was soft. "You don't never want to try to whip me and you don't never want to think I'm as stupid as you think I am." He released his grip and shoved Mead back into a chair. "We'll take care of Patterson, all right," he said. "We'll get out there right now. You dress warm, baby brother. It's kinda nippy this morning."

Outside the sky was blood red. The hidden sun threw a single shaft of light through the broken clouds. It flashed briefly on the windows of the town below, then moved across the valley, and finally there was a stain of red on the snow patches in the mountains that stood behind the Middleton home place.

The ray of sun found Harold Osgood sitting by the window in the upstairs apartment. He hadn't been to bed. He and Mattie had talked all night. "It's what I'll do, then," Harold said. "I'll give Jake Patterson another thousand dollars for his place." He looked up. "We might as well go now, Mattie. Jake is staying over at the Levering place." He looked as if he needed more assurance. "It's the thing to do, Mattie."

It wasn't the thing to do, Mattie knew. It was a compromise—an offer of charity to salve a man's feelings. It wasn't what she wanted Harold to do at all. She wanted him to stand up to Mead Weber and be a man. She wanted him to give Patterson's place back to him. She looked at Harold, loving him with a deep-down hurt, knowing she wanted these things of him because she loved him so much. But she wanted him safe, too. . . .

The sunray crossed the valley and ended a sleepless

night for Frank Levering. He hated trouble, and he had to see to it that trouble didn't start. It was his belief. He dressed and went outside and started across the pasture to where the Pattersons had camped in a grove of trees.

Jake Patterson was gone. He had taken his wife and his son with him.

Jake Patterson had moved back home.

THE Blue Mountains earned their name that morning, the shadows deep on their slopes, the new sun brilliant against the snow patches on their peaks. Standing by the barn, looking up at them, Owen Delaney felt a new perspective toward this land and this place, a new understanding for Zoe's love of it. The mysterious mist lay in patches on the meadows. There was a bite in the air, but the tumbled clouds were not threatening, and by noon they would be piled in sculptured beauty above the barren ranges to the east.

As early as it was, he knew that Zoe was up, for thin smoke trailed from the kitchen stove. He watched it a moment, then went back to his war sack and took out soap and a razor. He went to the windmill tank and scrubbed himself, then shaved, using the water of the tank as a mirror. He was standing there, stripped to the waist, testing the effectiveness of his shave with the palm of his hand when she called, "What are you doing? Admiring yourself?"

"And not half bad, either," he called back. "Good morning."

"Breakfast is ready when you are," she said. "It's formal, so put on your shirt."

She disappeared into the house and he waited a minute, letting the memory of her linger in his mind, then he put on his shirt, put away his gear, and went across the yard and into the now-familiar dining room. The smell of fresh coffee and the light warmth of the stove gave a softness to the overlarge room. She came to the door of the kitchen, a spatula in her hand, and she said, "How do you like your eggs?"

"Cooked," he said.

"You'll get hot cakes," she said.

Their conversation was easy and unstrained, as if they had known each other a long time, and although the small smudges under her remarkably blue eyes told him she hadn't slept well, there didn't seem to be any worry about her and no mention was made of last night's meeting.

The close intimacy of breakfast remained between them, and he wondered, as he had before, why it was so proper to take a girl to supper. It had always seemed to him that all guards were down at the breakfast table. Pretense was a companion of candlelight and wine and darkness. He looked up and said, "If there's any chores you want done . . ."

"If you want to be on your way . . ."

"That buckskin out there in the corral," he said. "If you wanted to sell him . . ." He found himself embarrassed. "Maybe I could trade you some work for him."

"I offered you a job last night," she said. "You turned it down."

"I didn't know my feet would hurt this morning," he said.

She laughed. "I was going to round up a few horses," she said. "You can help me do that, if you wish."

"Glad to," he said.

He got up to leave and she said, "It won't take up too much of your valuable time, will it?" There wasn't any sarcasm in the question. She was teasing.

"I'll see it don't," he said.

She was dressed for riding when she joined him out by the corral, a man's shirt, a divided skirt, a soft felt hat. She looked capable and sure of herself, and the *V* of the shirt exposed the golden tan of her throat. "Take the buckskin, if you want," she said. "I ride the black. There are saddles in the barn."

"I'll use my own," he said. "I'm used to it."

"These horses are all broken out with single-cinch saddles," she said. "That flank cinch on your saddle is apt to make that buckskin a little nervous."

"I'll watch him," he said. "If I aim to own him he'll have to get used to my kind of riggin'. Anyway," he added, "I figure a man has to learn to ride his own saddle."

"More philosophy?" she asked.

"Maybe. Hadn't thought of it."

He caught up her horse first, then the buckskin, and when he offered to saddle up for her she imitated his manner and said, "I figure a woman has to learn to saddle her own horse."

He chuckled softly. "Your deal," he said.

The buckskin didn't like the unfamiliar cinch and he made his dislike known. Owen handled him expertly while Zoe called encouragement and by the time he had the horse calmed down and they were on their way they were both laughing, retelling old stories of bucking horses and thrown men, and the stories seemed new in the telling.

The morning was made for riding, the day rapidly warming, the broken clouds throwing magnificent patches of moving shadows across the mountains and the floor of the valley. Spring flowers lingered in sheltered places, and only the hint of summer brown touched the grass in scattered spots where the soil was shallow. The valley was lush, and vagrant breezes searched through the grass, moving it in rippling waves, catching it at times in sharp crosscurrents. He was aware of the fragrance of the land and the nearness of the woman and in this moment it seemed to him that he could, again, stand still. But the world was not all made of morning, any more than it was made of sunsets, and in time a man must face himself in the darkness. A man could drink, he supposed. Or he could gamble. Or he could move along, away from himself. He had tried all three. The moving served him best.

They rode to the top of the ridge, the only dividing line between Zoe's land and the ranches in the other half of the valley, and now he noticed that the Middleton range lay in a long crescent, one point touching Ten Mile Creek to the north, the other point circling down to meet the arm of the valley where he had first met Bud Patterson. The road he had taken was plain from here. He thought of the statement Levering had made last night. . . . *When you and Mead are married, Granger's place and mine will be like an island, completely surrounded by Weber cows.* It was geographically so. A movement below caught his attention. He stood in his stirrups and said, "There's a buggy coming, yonder."

She shaded her eyes and looked in the direction he indicated. The sun caught the wheels of the buggy and flashed as if spokes were mirrors. "Harold Osgood," she said. "Those bright red wheels on that buggy are Harold's only concession to vanity." The humor left her voice. "I wonder why he's going over to the Patterson place?"

He knew that all of yesterday's worry was with her again, and he was sorry it had to be. Here, for these few moments, he had forgotten himself, and it had been like a great load lifted from his shoulders. "You want to ride down there?" he asked.

She nodded her agreement, and they started down the slope, the only sound now the whisper of the horses' hoofs in the deep grass. The jar of the rifle shot was twice as startling because of the quiet.

The buckskin shied, and as Owen fought him under control there was another rifle shot, and then a third. The Osgood buggy was out of sight, beyond the small shoulder of the hill, as was the Patterson ranch house itself, but now the shouting of men rose clearly. He looked at Zoe and her lips were tight, the color gone from her cheeks. Without speaking to him she spurred her horse and headed down the slope at a run. The buckskin wanted to follow, but he held it in, and now there was a sound of pistol shots. "Come back!" he called, then he sank his spurs deep and followed.

He hit the road to town at the bottom of the slope and by now Zoe was out of sight around the bend. He spurred on, and the view of the little ranch burst out on him. There were a number of people in the yard, and he saw Zoe first, standing with Harold Osgood and Mattie, and beyond them, a drawn gun in his hand, was Casco Weber. He saw Kline and one other. "All right, Patterson!" Casco shouted. "Come out of there, now, sensible like." Owen saw Patterson's wagon. It was turned on its side and the household goods were scattered around the yard. "We got you surrounded, Patterson!" Casco shouted. "Come on out!"

Zoe started to run toward the house and now Owen was out of his saddle, running after her. He caught her, and the force of his rush nearly knocked her down. Holding her with all his strength, he said, "Haven't you ever seen a gun before?"

She struggled against him, but he held her, and now the door of the house inched open and Patterson stood there. He looked small and sick, and he held his rifle out in front of him, grasping it by the stock and the barrel. "Just toss it down, hayshaker," Casco said. "Toss it down real easy and come on out. I want to talk to you."

Patterson dropped the gun and stepped out. The minute he did, Casco holstered his gun and moved forward. He caught Patterson with both hands and slammed him back against the cabin wall. The breath spurted from Patterson's lungs and Casco jerked him close and slammed him back again. Zoe had broken away from Owen. She ran forward, throwing herself at Casco, beating his shoulders with her fists. "Stop it!" she screamed. "Stop it, you hear me?"

Casco made a quick, half turn. His elbow caught Zoe in the ribs. It knocked her down. "Keep out of this, girl," Casco said. "I'm talking to the hayshaker." He pushed his hand into Patterson's face and shoved the rancher's head back against the wall.

Owen was watching Zoe, there on the ground. He felt the roaring in his ears and it was another time, another woman. He had no feeling of movement, no conception of time or place. He knew only that his fingers were locked in the tendons of Casco's shoulder, that he was jerking the man back. He saw Patterson slide down the wall and he knew Patterson's wife and young Bud were there and he caught a glimpse of Harold Osgood and he knew he had never in his life seen such fear. Over it all he heard the hysterical laughter of Kline. Kline was still on his horse, his boneless jaw sagging, and he laughed with his mouth wide open.

Owen jerked Casco around and hit him. Casco stepped back, ready to fight, then he stopped. He looked at Kline and the other man on horseback and he saw them reaching for guns.

Casco Weber raised his hand. To Kline and the other he said, "Stay out of it, boys. Let me handle this. Delaney, here, is a friend of mine."

Only then were things sharply in focus and Owen was standing back, a distance of six feet separating him from Casco. Casco was grinning, just as he had grinned in town, a confident grin. "Hello, Delaney boy," he said.

"Just leave it alone, Casco," Delaney said. "You've had your fun, now leave it alone."

Casco made no move to rush in, as he had there in town. This was a different Casco, a more deadly man. He stood there, his hands slightly out from his sides. "You got in something ain't none of your business, Delaney," he said. "You got a bad habit of doin' that."

"Leave it, Casco," Delaney said. "Just leave it where it is."

Casco laughed softly. "You're messin' in here tryin' to help out a lawbreaker, you know that, Delaney?" Casco said. "This Patterson, here. He sold out to my brother and then he turned around and moved in on my brother's place."

There was perspiration on Owen's face. He felt the salt taste of it at the corners of his mouth. His eyes were fixed on Casco's eyes, and he could read Casco's intent. Casco didn't want to fight with his fists. Casco wanted to use a gun. He heard Zoe sob, once, and he heard the quick laugh of Kline.

Somewhere, as if from a long distance, he heard Harold Osgood's reedy voice pleading, "Stop it, somebody! Can't somebody stop it?"

"You're pretty good with your fists, Delaney," Casco said. He was still smiling. "You good with that gun, Delaney?"

"Casco, I got no fight with you!"

Casco's lips were suddenly tight against his teeth. "Draw it, Delaney!" he said.

He saw Casco's move, slow and clumsy. He waited, knowing there was no hope, and Casco's gun was clear of its holster before Owen drew and fired. The black, stinging cloud of powder smoke was a veil in front of his eyes, the smell of it was like a hot branding iron in his nostrils. A quick curse broke across Delaney's lips, and he ran forward, almost as if he wished to hold Casco from falling. . . .

The big man spun in his tracks. He tried to catch his balance and couldn't. He fell, heavily, half on his side, half on his back, twisted that way, as if the bullet had shattered his spine. His eyes were wide, terror-stricken, and then the terror was gone and his lips twitched and he found that old grin. A tiny froth of blood came across his lips. "You're a damn good man, Delaney," he said, and he slumped back and the nauseating sickness of knowing he had killed again gripped Delaney's stomach and then turned to a blind rage.

Patterson was running toward him. "You killed him!" Patterson shouted. "Let's get some guns and get the rest of them!"

Owen's gun barrel lashed out and caught Patterson alongside the head. Patterson staggered back, his hand flying to his temple. He faltered, half out on his feet. "That's right, Patterson," Delaney said. He knew he was shouting and he couldn't help it. "I killed him. Does that make all of you happy? That's a dead man, laying there on the ground. Take a good, long look at him. When you start getting sick looking at him, he'll still be dead."

"He tried to run me out——" Patterson said.

"Is this your place?" Owen said. "You sold it, didn't you? You risk the life of your wife and your kid for something that isn't even yours and you want me to cheer? You're a fool, Patterson." He looked at Casco and said, "If I could bring him back to life I would, and this time I'd help him move you out."

He felt the hand on his arm and he half turned and it

was Zoe. She was looking up at him, pleading. "Owen, you don't know what you're saying——"

He became aware of two more riders, coming up from behind the house, and he knew one of them was Mead Weber. He saw Mead throw himself from the saddle and come running forward, saw him kneel there beside his dead brother. Mead looked up. "You dirty, gun-slinging swine," he said. "I'll see you swing for this."

The anger and sickness in Owen was crystallized now. He reached down and gripped Mead by the coat collar and jerked him to his feet. "Don't waste your play-acting on me, Weber," Owen said. "Yesterday you tried to hire me to kill him."

"You're a liar, Delaney!" Mead said.

Owen didn't bother to hit him. He just jerked him close and held him helpless. "Don't you ever call me that, Weber," he said. "Not ever." He released his grip and shoved and Mead stumbled backward. Owen walked away, not wanting any of them to see the violence that still stayed with him.

Behind him he heard Zoe say, "I want to talk to you, Mead."

"About what? About murder?"

"I'm asking you what you plan to do."

"I've got a thousand cows to worry about," Mead said. "This is my place. I bought it and paid for it. I mean to use it."

"And Levering's place too?" she asked. "And then Granger's and eventually mine?"

"Zoe, listen to me," he said. "Do you think that's my way?" He looked around the ruined yard, the scatter of household utensils, the dead man on the ground. "Do you think I wanted this?" he asked. "Why do you think I'm here? I was trying to stop Casco."

Owen half turned. "Now you're the liar, Weber," he said. "As far as I'm concerned, I killed the wrong man."

He swung into his saddle and he saw Zoe standing there in front of Mead, her chin up, her head back. He saw her tug at the ring on her finger. "Don't try to hide behind Casco again, Mead," he heard her say. "You've done it all your life. Don't try it now. He's dead." He saw her take the ring from her finger and throw it at Mead's feet.

There was something close to panic in Mead. "Zoe, please," he said. He started toward her, his arms extended. Her look stopped him. "Zoe, I *bought* this place," he said.

"There's some things you can't buy, Mead," she said.

"I'm one of them. My land's another." She turned and walked away and she didn't stop when Mattie Osgood called her name. She came directly to Delaney and said, "I'm still offering you that job. Do you want it?"

The anger had left him. He shook his head. "I left my gear at your place," he said. "I'll pick it up. I'll take this horse, too. I figure I earned him. Gun wages come high."

OWEN was tying his bedroll behind his saddle when Zoe and the Osgoods arrived at the ranch. Zoe was riding in the buggy, her saddler leading behind. She looked in Owen's direction, but she didn't speak, and when they got out of the buggy at the house Owen saw Mattie and Zoe help Harold out of the buggy, saw them lead him inside. He gave a final tug to the knot in the saddle strings, then led the saddled horse over to the house. The door was open, and he could see Zoe standing there. Harold was in a chair and Mattie had put a wet cloth on his forehead. Zoe turned and saw Owen. "I thought you were leaving," she said.

"I am," he said, "but I want a bill of sale on this horse. It's got your brand on it. I don't want to be picked up for horse stealing."

"So you're running out." Her voice was bitter.

"That's right."

"And what am I to do?"

"That's your affair," he said. He didn't look at her.

"No advice?" she said. There was deep sarcasm in her voice. "You're always so free with your advice."

"Yes," he said, "I have some advice. I gave it to you. Get married and wear pretty clothes."

"You saw me give him his ring back."

"Then sell out. You'll get a good price."

Harold sat up in the chair. "Zoe, that's what I've been saying. I'm responsible for you, Zoe. I promise you I can get you a good price——"

"Shut up, Harold," Mattie Osgood said.

The little man turned toward his wife, startled. "Mattie!"

"The big ones are taking over, Zoe," Owen said. "That's how it is in Wyoming. That's how it will be here. You join them or you sell out to them. That's how it is. I've been on both sides of it."

"Have you?" she said. "Then why didn't you take one side or the other? You took neither one. You ran."

He fought the rising anger. "Look," he said. "I'm not out to change the world. I'm just trying to live in it."

"If everyone thought the way you do," she said, "the world wouldn't be worth living in."

"You listen to me, Zoe," he said, "and you believe me. There's no piece of land on earth worth getting killed for."

"You really believe that, don't you?" Zoe said. "Pack up and run. Drift on over the next hill. What have you got to stand still for? You wouldn't know what it meant to fight for something you believe in. The minute the going gets rough, pack up and move along. That's the kind of a man you are, and that's the kind of a man you always will be." Her hands were on her hips and her scorn for him was thick in her voice. "Tell me, Owen Delaney," she said, "what have you ever fought for in your life?"

The moment she asked it she was sorry. She saw the change in him, a deep-down, lasting hurt, and she heard it in his voice when he said, "I fought for a piece of ground once, Zoe Middleton. Just like you're thinking of doing. I stood up and fought for it and four people died because of it."

She would have stopped him then if she could. She could feel the torture inside him, see it in his face. There was a deep-seated hatred in his eyes that frightened her and she knew, even while he spoke, that she had been wrong about him. He wasn't just a saddle tramp. He was a branded man, running from himself because to stand still meant facing a pain that wouldn't die. . . .

"I fought for my land," he said. "I fought for a woman's right to security. We believed that, the two of us. We had to fight for our rights, we said. A man can only be pushed so far and then he has to stand still. She believed that, and so did I."

She knew, then. She closed her eyes and the torment in this man was like a dizziness around her. "Your wife, Owen Delaney?" she asked.

"That's right," he said. "My wife. She stood beside me with a gun, because that's the way we believed it had to be. She stood there and they shot her down and she died in my arms——" His emotions broke, and his voice was a roaring wave against her ears. "I killed three men because of it. I tracked them down and I killed them, one by one, but she was still dead. Can you see what that means, Zoe Middleton? She was dead, and all the killing in the world isn't going to change that." There was perspiration on his face and she saw his shoulders heaving, as if he were crying inside. "I've been a hell of a long time trying to figure out if my pride and a piece of ground was worth it," he said.

He turned and went down the porch steps and he stood there by the horse, his face pressed against the skirt of the saddle. She walked slowly down the steps and over to him and she put her hand on his arm. "I'm sorry, Owen," she said.

"Don't be," he said. "Just don't make the same mistake.".

He started to mount, but she took his arm and held him. "Owen," she said, "don't live with a lie."

"Is it a lie to be dead?"

"You did what was right, Owen," she said. "You must believe that. You had to make a stand, regardless of the cost. We all do, some time or another in one way or another. It's the price of living decently, Owen. You must know that." She felt the pulse in her throat. "She was proud of you, Owen," she said. "I'm a woman and I know. I would have stood by you, and I would have been proud, just as she was." On impulse she stood on tiptoe and her lips brushed his cheek. For a moment she thought he would take her in his arms, and she wished it were so. . . .

He swung into the saddle. "Just live your life," he said. "That's all that counts."

"Do you think it would be a life for me, giving up all this?" she asked. "Do you think it would have been a life for her if you had sold out and run?"

"I don't know, Zoe," he said. "I only know she would have been alive."

He reined the horse around and rode out toward the gate in the lane. He was slumped in the saddle, as if there were a great tiredness in him, and he didn't see the rider come out from behind the barn. He didn't look up until he heard the voice say, "Hold up."

He looked up then and Jim Torrance, the deputy sheriff, was sitting there in his saddle, an old man with a badge on his vest and a gun in his hand. "You going someplace, Delaney?" the old man asked.

"I was," Owen said.

"You changed your mind," Jim Torrance said. "Get back in the house. You killed a man today. I'll be wanting to hear about it."

They sat in the living room, Jim Torrance, Owen Delaney, Zoe Middleton, and the two Osgoods. A single fly droned drearily, and Harold Osgood's round eyes followed

104

it. In time the deputy sighed and said, "All right, tell me about it."

"There's not much to tell," Owen said. "I tried to talk him out of it. He went for his gun. I got there first."

"You're pretty good at that, ain't you, Delaney?" Jim Torrance said. "From what I hear, you've done it before."

"You got some private information, Sheriff?" Owen asked.

"Those cattle buyers in town," Torrance said. "They've heard of you. They tell me you tracked down three men and killed them. You're black-listed by every outfit in Wyoming." He looked up slowly. "You want to deny any of it?"

"No," Owen said. "I won't deny it."

"But Jim, there's more to it," Zoe said. "There's Owen's side. They tried to run him off his land, Jim. They killed his wife."

"That don't give him a right to make his own law, Zoe," Torrance said. "All I got to go on is he come into my town and he gets in trouble with Casco. He's packing a brand as a killer, and now Casco's dead. I got to know a lot more about it."

"He's told you all there is to tell," Zoe said. "It was self-defense. Isn't my word good enough for you?"

"You, Harold," the deputy said. "You saw it?"

Harold nodded. He acted as if his throat was constricted, as if he was having trouble speaking. "I saw it," he said. "It's as Zoe said." He looked up quickly and with a pitiful attempt at control of his voice said, "I would have done the same thing in Delaney's place, Jim. Delaney didn't have a chance to do anything else. I'd swear that in court, Jim."

"I figured as much," Torrance said. He got to his feet and it was an effort for him to do it. "Mead ordered me to come out here," he said. "He told me to bring you back, Delaney, dead or alive."

"You going to take me, Jim?"

"I'm not even going to try," Torrance said. "I guess I'm not used to taking orders." He rubbed his hand across his face. "I don't deny Casco needed killing," he said, "but there ain't gonna be more of it. Patterson sold his place and Mead bought it. If Mead wants to move cows in there, that's his right, and if anybody tries to stop him, I reckon then I'll have to side Mead."

"Jim!" Zoe said. "You can't believe that's all it is! This side of the river is open range, Jim, you know that."

"Honey, I don't make the laws," Jim Torrance said. "I

just try to enforce what law there is. And I can't teach manners to a cow. Only chance you got is to fence off what you don't want grazed off." He held up a hand to Zoe's beginning protest. "I talked to Levering and Granger about it and I talked to Mead. There ain't a one of the three want trouble, Zoe, and I don't like to see you spoil the idea. Mead's willing and ready to meet with all of you and work something out. I advise you to do it, Zoe."

Harold Osgood was on his feet. There was a surging hope in the little banker. It was in his eyes, in his every movement. "It's the thing to do, Zoe," he said. "It's just what I told you, coming in from Patterson's. I was only trying to do what would be best for you, Zoe. I promised your father I'd do that. We'll work out something. I know we will. I'll get everybody together. We'll meet at the bank, first thing in the morning——"

Zoe looked at Mattie and Mattie was watching her husband. There was nothing to read in the big woman's face. She sat there silently, watching her husband. . . .

"There's nothing to gain by having trouble over it," Jim Torrance said.

"No," Osgood said. "No, of course not. Levering and Granger. They're both solid men. We'll work it out fine, Zoe."

"I'll stop by and tell Levering and Granger if you want, Harold," Jim Torrance said.

"Good, good," Harold said. "You do that, Jim. Ten o'clock tomorrow morning at my bank."

"How about Jake Patterson?" Mattie asked. Her voice demanded an answer.

Harold's head sank a little lower on his shoulders. He didn't have his eyeshade on, but he reached for it and went through the motions of putting it back in place. "Yes," he said. "Jake Patterson."

"He should be there, Harold," Zoe said.

"Yes, by all means," Harold said. "He should be there."

"I'll see to it," Jim Torrance said. He took a watch from his pocket, glanced at it, then through the window at the sun, checking one time against the other. The day was nearly done. "I better be on my way," he said. He stood there in the door a moment and, speaking to no one in particular, he said, "Decide it for yourself, Delaney. I figure it would be best if you moved along."

They heard Torrance ride off, and in a moment Mattie signaled Harold it was time to go. Zoe and Owen went outside with them, and just before she got in the buggy,

106

Mattie turned swiftly and kissed Zoe on the cheek. It was the first time she had ever made that gesture.

They drove off, Harold and Mattie, Harold so small and precise, Mattie hulking and plain and somehow almost pretty in her plainness, and Zoe and Owen watched them go. They stood side by side, and they became aware of the sunset, softly flooding the valley.

"It's best, Zoe," Owen said.

"No," Zoe said, "it isn't best. It will lead to a compromise of some kind, that's all. Mead won't be satisfied until he has the entire valley."

"Not then, either, Zoe."

Her arm brushed Owen's arm, and she stood that way, close to him, needing the nearness of someone, needing to talk. "It's funny," she said. "I've known Mead so long. I've always known what he's like, really, but I wouldn't let myself believe it. There was always Casco to blame. Casco was a typical Weber and Mead wasn't, so whatever happened, I let myself blame Casco." She looked up and Owen was looking down at her, his eyes understanding. "That was a compromise too, wasn't it, Owen?" she said. "I was lonely and I wanted to be in love with someone, so I made myself believe I was in love with Mead."

He looked away, into the gathering shadows. "You could still compromise that way, Zoe," he said.

"Do you believe that, Owen?"

Her eyes were soft as he looked down at her. She was looking up at him, her lips slightly parted. And in that moment Owen Delaney knew that love was not a flower that bloomed once and died. Love was a deep well that could replenish itself and the press of his own loneliness was an overwhelming force. . . . She met his embrace gladly, her lips moist and warm and eager. . . .

The red-wheeled buggy toiled up the hill and Mattie Osgood looked back once. She saw Zoe and Owen, standing together, and then she turned and looked at the road ahead. Harold had been talking steadily, but she had only half heard. "I'll give Patterson the extra thousand dollars, the way I planned," Harold said. "That'll be the thing to do."

It's not the thing to do, Mattie thought, *but perhaps it has to be. There is a weakness in all of us, and weakness has a price. The only strength about us is our love for each other.* . . . "And the others, Harold?" she asked. "Granger and Levering and Zoe?"

"You heard what Torrance said," Harold said. "Mead's willing to work out something."

There are no parts to love. It is all, or it is nothing. "You'll have to back them up, Harold," Mattie said. "All the way."

"Certainly," Harold said. "You know I will."

But she didn't know he would, and she had to be sure. Mattie Osgood made her decision. "I mean this, Harold," she said. "You'll back them all the way, even if it means Mead Weber gets no part of the valley."

"Now wait, Mattie——"

She couldn't wait. It had to be said now, all at once, or it would never be said at all. "You have to do it, Harold," she said. She closed her eyes tightly. "If you don't back them up I'll have to leave you."

"Mattie! What are you saying?"

"I love the man I married, Harold. I love him more than my own life, and I've loved him for thirty years. If you back down now, Harold, you won't be the man I married and it's too late for me to accept another."

It was said, and she felt weak and tired, as if she had run too fast for too long a way. She wished she had learned how to cry.

Harold drove in silence. When he spoke finally his voice was soft. "I wouldn't want to live without you, Mattie," he said. His voice caught, and there was a startled sound in it, as if he had just discovered this for the first time. "Mattie," he said, "I don't think I could!"

THE MORNING broke gray and leaden, the peaks of the Blues obscured by scuds of rain-fat clouds. In the depths of the barren Magpie range a cowboy who had been in his saddle all night complained bitterly to Webster, the old man from Mead Weber's ranch. "You think these cows can go forever without grass and water?" he asked. "We didn't bed down until midnight. I met myself getting up. What the devil we trying to prove?"

"I follow orders, I don't give 'em," Webster said. "Mead said to keep these cows moving. We're moving 'em."

The herd was small—some two hundred and fifty head —the first of the gather of a thousand. The cursing crew pushed them out of the sage flats and up the slopes, on toward the Weber ranch headquarters. "Dangedest outfit I ever worked for," the cowboy said. "Spend a month nursin' these fat devils out of the hills then try to run the taller off of 'em in one night."

"Quit any time you want," Webster said.

"Quit, hell," the cowboy said. "I ain't drawed my pay."

"Then keep 'em movin'," Webster said. "Be glad it ain't Casco bossin' the outfit. Come noon we'll wet our whistles at the Golden Eagle. Cattle buyers in town, boys. Money in the bank."

The bellowing, dust-churning herd moved through the sage and juniper, eyes rolling, heads swinging, fat Oregon cattle, the first of the thousands that would stock the awaiting Wyoming ranges, and ten miles across the rise the town of Ten Mile stirred to new life.

South of the town, along the river, the smoke of four campfires rose straight, then bent against the low-hanging clouds. "Hey, boss!" a man with a Texas drawl called out. "This here the only town in Oregon?"

"Maybe not," the boss said, "but leastwise it ain't too crowded yet. Hear tell fifty miles east of here the price of cows jumped ten dollars a head the last two days." He scowled toward the other campfires. "Bad enough as it is," he said. "Looks like another outfit come in during the night. A man would think it was gold in Oregon instead of just cows."

"Ain't much of a town," another said. "Only one saloon. How long you figure we'll be around here, boss?"

"Long enough for 'em to get another saloon started, I reckon," the boss said. "I'm after three thousand cattle. You don't just go in the grocery store and buy 'em."

"Aim to hold the gather in that valley across the crick?"

"That's the deal I made with Mead Weber."

"Who's he?"

"Big man here. Owns the town."

"He don't own much. A one-saloon town."

The man was right. The town of Ten Mile wasn't much. A general merchandise store, a saloon, and a bank squeezed in between the two. An abandoned town with a memory of a roaring past. But already the possibility of its future was being felt.

There were only four cattle buyers camped on the river, each with a skeleton crew of picked trail hands, some thirty-two men in all. But those thirty-two men were

109

thirsty, and Henry, the bartender, had his hands full that night. Boots were worn out and supplies were low and fresh beef tasted fine after too much salt pork. . . . The clerk in Mead Weber's store tallied a day's receipts equal to an ordinary month's take, and, with Mead's approval, he hired a man to butcher a beef. One of Mead's wagons left before daybreak, headed for Boise City, some hundred and fifty miles distant. Freight lines ran to Boise City. The wagon would bring back flour and lard and bacon and beans.

And in the thin, narrow bank, squeezed between two buildings, Harold Osgood locked twenty thousand dollars in cash in his safe and receipted for letters of credit for twice that amount.

A Wyoming boy, born in Texas, put a nickel in the long-silent hurdy-gurdy in the Golden Eagle Saloon and found it still worked. The tinny bang of the machine rattled through the morning, and the abandoned buildings of the town listened to the racket with renewed hope and a silver dollar made a merry jingle on the long oak bar.

Frank Levering and Scott Granger were against sin in any form, Mead Weber used to say, but he noticed their smiles as they stepped aside to avoid a drunken cowboy who lurched out of the Golden Eagle and gave his ear-splitting yell to the morning sky of Oregon. "Powder River! Yee-haw!"

"You're pretty early for the meeting, boys," Mead Weber said.

"Enough noise here in town to keep a man up all night," Frank Levering said. There was a twinkle in his eye. "Reckon there'll be more coming, Mr. Weber?"

"Boys, we're going to be a cow town, whether we like it or not," Mead Weber said.

"I like it fine," Scott Granger said. "Enough here for everybody, I always say."

"You're right, Scott," Mead Weber said.

And there would be enough for everybody, Mead knew, but as he walked up the street he had no intention of letting everybody have it. He eyed the long-abandoned hotel and made a mental note to speak to Osgood about it. A hotel would be a gold mine, once Ten Mile became the center of the eastern Oregon cattle trade. He was already thinking of a freight line to run between here and Boise City. . . . Henry, the bartender, blinked his sleep-starved eyes. "I looked at that old roulette wheel, Mead," he said.

110

"It'll work all right. You get another man behind this bar I'll run the layout for you. . . ."

Enough for everybody. But why let everybody have it?

Mead Weber had never felt more confident. He had to remind himself that he was a man who had just lost his brother and as he looked at the two signs that bore his name he envisioned a dozen more. A fist fight broke out in the Golden Eagle between two men who had been drinking all night, and as Jim Torrance started toward the saloon Mead put a restraining hand on his arm. "Let it go, Jim," Mead said. "We want the word to get around that anything goes in Ten Mile." He glanced toward the John Day road. "Seen Zoe yet?"

"She'll be here," Jim Torrance said.

Yes, she'd be here, Mead thought. She'd be here and she'd stay here, and she'd share it all with him. He touched the ring in his fob pocket and had not the slightest doubt Zoe would take it back. She'll beg for it, he told himself.

Mead Weber never drank, but this morning he was as drunk as a loon on his own importance. He saw Kline coming down the street toward him, and the man's boneless jaw reminded him of Casco. "I put the board up, like you said, Mead," Kline said. He drew his sleeve across his crooked mouth. "I thought a lot of him, Mead. He didn't mean what he done to me. He was my friend, Mead." Kline moved swiftly away.

Wagon wheels ground against the stones of the river ford, and, looking that way, Mead saw the Pattersons. He was quickly annoyed but, knowing he couldn't avoid them, he waited, and when the wagon was near he said, "Jake, about yesterday——"

Jake Patterson didn't even turn his head. "Gonna be a meetin' at the bank, ain't there?" he said.

"Yes, but——"

"Talk it out there in front of witnesses," Jake said. He kept the wagon moving and never once looked back. Mead walked on down the street and he saw Thelma Levering and Betty Granger and knew that they, too, planned to attend the meeting. *Why in the devil do these hayshakers have to horn their whole family in on everything?* he wondered. He thought briefly of that word "hayshaker." It had been one of Casco's favorite expressions. *Why in the devil couldn't Casco have finished the job with Patterson?* he thought. He saw Levering's six daughters staring in a window.

Four riders came whooping into town from the camps

along the river. They slid their horses to a stop and tied up at the hitch rail in front of the Golden Eagle. "I'm Mead Weber," Mead said. "First drink is on me."

But even the flush of certain success and the feeling of importance he had worked so hard to achieve couldn't dispel the growing impatience in him as the morning dragged on without any sign of Zoe. The sun struggled hard to break through the overcast and never quite made it, and from time to time Mead glanced at his watch. He saw the Leverings and the Grangers up at the bank, their kids playing in front with young Bud, and he knew the Pattersons had already gone inside. He had talked briefly with Osgood this morning and knew that Harold, with his usual promptness, had been ready for an hour.

One worry bred another, and he thought of Osgood and wondered at the change he had sensed in the little man this morning. He couldn't put his finger on it, but there had been something different in Harold. Almost a sense of rebellion. Mead shrugged it aside. Harold had gotten his back up before. A threat to let Casco play with him was always more than enough to calm Harold. . . . Mead stopped suddenly, aware that for a moment he had forgotten Casco was dead. It was all right. He didn't need Casco to handle Harold Osgood.

His thoughts turned back to Zoe and he wondered what he would do if she didn't show up. Go to her? A few moments before he had been certain he could patch things up with her. Now he wasn't so sure. And suppose he couldn't? His breathing became shallow. *She's no different from any of the rest of them,* he found himself thinking. *If I can't deal with them on my own terms I'll move in on them, and if it comes to a choice between Zoe and the valley, I'll take the valley.*

A small line of perspiration formed on Mead's upper lip as he realised it was the exact decision Casco had told him to make.

He saw Jim Torrance again and asked, "You sure Zoe said she'd be here?"

"She said she'd be here," Torrance said.

"Well, where in the devil is she?"

THE BUCKBOARD had stopped at the top of the ridge above the crescent valley and Zoe Middleton looked back at the ranch her father had fought so hard to establish and hold. She felt a sense of betrayal as she anticipated the meeting there in town, for, regardless of what the meeting accomplished, it would be a compromise, and compromise had never been a part of her upbringing. She felt Owen's nearness and knew she loved him, and Owen, like the land, was a thing she wanted to keep and yet she couldn't know if she would be able to do that, either.

"You sure you want me with you?" he asked.

"I told you," she said. "I can't be alone any longer."

"We'd best go, then," he said.

They drove down the slope and through the near valley, past the Levering and Granger places, and when they came to the ford in the river she saw the crossing as a symbol of decision. She turned to him and saw the set of his face, knowing his inner turmoil so well, knowing too that she really did not possess him. . . . "Hold me, Owen," she whispered. "Just once more."

They crossed the river and came into the town, and as they did they looked past the town and toward the Magpies and there on the distant slope they saw a herd of cattle, coming over the ridge, as if arising from the earth itself, and they saw the herd start moving down the hill, toward the town and the valley. The hurdy-gurdy in the saloon started up again and a cowboy yelled, "Powder River!"

There was a bleakness in Owen's eyes that reached inside her and twisted her and she thought, *Can he ever really forget? Can I take her place?* She looked toward the bank and saw the Levering children, six of them, ranging in age from five to twelve, all girls, scrubbed and starched, their hair in braids, and she thought, *You should have been born boys.* Bud Patterson was there too, and the four Granger children. When Bud saw Owen there was a bewildered hurt in his eyes, and when Owen spoke to him, the boy turned his back.

The bank seemed dingy and small and insignificant, and Harold Osgood, his green eyeshade in place, was an inadequate little straw man caught in a cyclone. There were deep black circles under his eyes and the skin of his face looked doughy and soft, as if it had sweated too much. He had pulled a circle of chairs around his desk, and Frank Levering, a white-haired peacemaker, sat stiff and straight, like a judge at a trial. Mead Weber was there, and he stood up slowly when Zoe and Owen entered. On impulse Zoe took Owen's arm, and she saw the color rise

113

slowly in Mead's face. . . . "I won't sit in the same room with a murderer," Mead said.

"Owen stays or I leave with him," Zoe said. "You decide."

She was proud then, a woman standing beside her man, and her love for him was obvious and sure, a red flag of final rebellion waved in the face of Mead Weber. The corner of Mead's mouth started to twitch, like an affliction.

"He was out at Jake's place yesterday," Frank Levering said. "I reckon he ought to be in on it, Mead."

Mead Weber sat down slowly, but the rest of the faces had faded and he was seeing only Owen and Zoe. The line of perspiration on Mead's upper lip caught the light from the window and was sharply apparent.

"I want to be fair," Mead Weber heard himself say.

"It's all we ask, Mead," Frank Levering said.

Mead's struggle to bring his mind back to the thing that had brought him here was visible in his face. "I bought up a few cows," he said. "North of here, hundred miles or so. Anybody can make a mistake. I made one when I thought I'd have enough graze on my own place. I haven't got it. I bought the Patterson grass because I need graze for those cows. I intend to put them on that grass."

"You knew those cattle buyers were coming," Jake Patterson said. "You forced me out. You plan to do the same with Levering and Granger."

"That kind of talk won't get us no place, Jake," Levering said.

"Jake," Mead said, "I'll have to tell you the same thing you told me when I found that worn-out Pitman rod on that mowing machine you sold me. You should have looked before you leaped. Nobody forced you to sell out to me."

"I got the money here," Jake Patterson said. He reached into his pocket and took out the money Mead had paid him. He tossed it on the desk. "I'm giving it back, Mead. I'm calling the deal off."

Mattie Osgood looked up quickly. She was sitting by herself, back against the wall. She tried to meet Harold's eyes, but Harold wouldn't look at her. She had lain awake all night, knowing Harold was awake too, but she hadn't spoken to him. She looked at Harold and she waited and she saw Harold moisten his lips with his tongue. . . .

"Jake," Harold said finally, "you can't just back out

114

of the deal. There isn't a court in the world would back you up."

"I'm not talking about courts," Jake Patterson said. "I'm talking about a man's rights."

"Mead has rights too, Jake," Harold said.

Mattie saw the satisfaction in Mead's eyes, and then, for a fleeting second, Harold was looking at her. There was a plea for understanding in Harold's eyes. He stood up and he gripped the edge of the desk, as if needing that support. "I talked to Levering and Granger about it, Jake," Harold said. "They feel it's fair." He opened the top drawer of his desk and took out a packet of bills. "There's an extra thousand dollars here, Jake. It will bring the price of your place up."

"It's fair, Jake," Levering said.

There was a puzzled-frown crease between Mead Weber's eyes. It was the first he had known of this. Zoe started to get to her feet and Owen stopped her.

"You think that's fair to me, Scott?" Jake asked Granger. He was a man turning to a friend, an old friend and neighbor.

"More than fair, Jake," Granger said.

He turned all the way around and he was facing Zoe. She stood up, and this time she ignored Owen's restraining hand. She looked not at Jake but at Mead Weber. "If my father were alive, Jake, he'd take that money and stuff it down Mead Weber's throat," she said, and even as she said it she knew she was admitting her own inability to help Jake. She turned to Owen, asking him for help with her eyes. He didn't meet her gaze.

Jake Patterson knew he was whipped. He picked up the original money Mead had paid him for his place and he stuffed it in his pocket. Mattie Osgood's heart beat slowly and painfully. "It's the best we can do, Jake," Harold said.

Slowly Jake pushed the thousand-dollar bonus back across the desk toward Harold. "You keep your charity, Osgood," he said. "I'll keep my pride." He turned and walked slowly from the bank, and as he did his shadow was long behind him and it fell across Owen, sitting there, silently.

There was a sick embarrassment in that room, and Harold's breathing, like the rattle of dry parchment, was clearly audible. Frank Levering said, "There's still our places to think about, Mead. If you move your cows onto Patterson's place . . ."

Mead was confident now. "I thought if maybe I could work out a temporary lease with you," he said. He paused, seeing the interest in the eyes of Levering and Granger, and he picked up his advantage. "There's no fence between your places and the Patterson place," Mead said. "It would cost a lot to fence and it would take time. I can't keep my cows from drifting onto your grass. I'd be the last man on earth to say I could. If I can work out a grazing lease agreement with you—pay you for the grass my cows graze——"

Levering and Granger exchanged glances and Levering said, "I don't see why we can't, Mead."

The palms of Owen's hands were sweating. "There's no fence between their places and Zoe's place, either," he said. He saw the quick challenge in Mead's eyes, the interested stare of Levering and Granger, and there was something like hope in the eyes of Harold Osgood. He knew Zoe's hand was on his arm, and he felt her fingers tighten.

"I'll make the same deal with Zoe," Mead said.

The silence lay there, and in time Frank Levering nodded slowly. "It's the fair way, Zoe," he said. "It'll give us all some ready cash to work with. It'll give us time to fence, and if this cattle boom keeps up, like we figure it will, we'll take a new start at it next season——"

There was a hard knot in the pit of Owen's stomach. "Provided you can get Weber's cattle off your grass, once they're on there," he said. "Provided he don't overgraze it until it's not worth having back."

Mead Weber was on his feet. "You own grass, drifter?"

"He's speaking for me," Zoe Middleton said. She met Mead's angry gaze and faced him down. She had told him now, as plainly as if she had said it. She was gone from him and he wouldn't get her back. A drifter from nowhere had found her love and Mead had failed. A panic seized Mead, and he thought, *If Casco were here I'd have him handle Delaney,* and then the panic grew as he realized that Casco had tried to handle Delaney and Casco was dead. . . .

"I won't deal with a murderer," Mead shouted.

Owen Delaney stood up. "I don't want you to deal with me, Weber," he said. "But you can't stop me from saying what I think. I don't believe you'll ever pay Levering and Granger one cent for their graze. You'll force them out, and you'll keep right on moving onto Zoe's range. You don't care if the grass grows or not. All you want is a

116

holding ground where trail herds can make up, so your town will be full of cowboys every night. That's what you're after, Mead, and if your brother was alive, he'd be man enough to admit it."

Zoe was standing beside Owen, shoulder to shoulder with him. "What the devil right does Delaney have to have a say in this?" Mead demanded. His face was flushed and he was perspiring freely.

"He's speaking the truth," Zoe said. "Mead told me once he wouldn't be happy until he had all the valley and me with it. Now he has to face up to it, because he can't have either."

There was no longer any pretense in Mead Weber. His mouth was tight and ugly, his eyes hard. "And just what will you do to stop me, Zoe?" he asked.

"I'll shoot down the first cow bearing your brand that steps onto my grass," she said.

"I wouldn't do that, Zoe," Mead said.

"Yes," Zoe said, "you'd do it, and so would I. If you want to run cows on the Patterson grass, nobody can legally stop you and it doesn't seem anyone wants to. If Levering and Granger want to trust you, it's their funeral, not mine. But if one of your cows crosses my line, I've told you what I'll do."

A cold, dangerous calmness had come over Mead Weber. He looked at Levering and Granger, saw the acute worry in them, and he looked at Owen Delaney, hating this man more than he had ever hated anyone in his life, and yet afraid of him, for even Casco had failed to handle him. He knew then that he had to whip Delaney with something besides fists or guns. Again he saw the sick worry in Levering and Granger. One corner of Mead's mouth lifted in a half smile.

"How do you plan to do it, Zoe?" Mead asked. "With a hired gun?"

In that moment, Owen Delaney knew Mead Weber had won. Owen stood there, feeling naked and stripped, and he felt the eyes of Levering and Granger on him, accusing. He saw Harold Osgood get to his feet and he could feel the fear in Osgood reaching out and touching him. Dimly he heard Levering say, "Zoe, you got to be reasonable. Mead's trying to do what's right. . . ."

The confidence, the certain knowledge, was in Weber's voice. He had an advantage now, and he pushed it surely. "I'm through trying," he said. "You heard the threat,

117

didn't you? You expect me to turn tail and run? She's got a hired gun on her payroll—a man who's killed my brother and he's wanted in Wyoming for three other murders." Mead's voice was low. "What do you expect me to do, look down the barrel of a cocked gun and smile about it?" He turned on Zoe now, playing it for all it was worth. "If there's any trouble in this valley, it's square on your shoulders," he said, "and not on mine. You threaten me with a gun and I'll answer it with a gun. You make up your own mind!"

He snatched up his hat and started to leave, but now Levering and Granger were both on their feet, begging him to reconsider, and there was a gathering sickness in Owen as he saw the complete satisfaction in Mead's face. "Now wait a minute, Mead," Levering was pleading. "We don't want no trouble, you know that. We don't hold to guns."

"She's got one on her payroll, hasn't she?" Mead said.

Harold Osgood stood there, gripping the edge of the desk. His face was drawn and old and sick, and then he looked at his wife and a calmness seemed to come to him. His voice was slow, measured. He was forcing every word, but he was saying them. "It would be best if we fenced off right away," he said.

"That would take a lot of money, Harold," Levering said. "We ain't got it, you know that."

Mead was staring intently at Osgood, not knowing whether to believe what he was hearing, and then a slow understanding came into Mead's eyes. Harold was going along with him, helping convince them. He glanced at Mattie Osgood and, although her eyes were dry, Mead had a strange impression she was crying. . . .

"I'll put up the money," Harold said. "I'll buy the wire and the posts. There'll be help available while these trail hands wait for the herds to be made up. If we pay enough, we can get help, and if we have help enough we can fence in a hurry. I'll put up the money," he said. "You can still lease the grass, Mead," Harold said, "but it will be controlled grazing. Does your deal still stand?"

"Not with a cocked gun pointed at my head!" Mead said.

Owen looked at Osgood, unable to tell if the man meant what he said, and he saw Mead, knowing that Mead was trying to run a bluff, knowing for sure that bluff had to be called. "You can forget it, Weber," Owen said. "I wasn't figuring on staying."

118

Mattie Osgood had gotten to her feet, she was looking at Zoe, trying to tell Zoe something with her eyes. . . . "Owen!" Zoe's cry was sharp.

Owen wanted to answer, but he couldn't, and he walked out of the bank, into the dull grayness of the day. Levering's six girls were playing there on the sidewalk and Granger's kids were running around like so many squirrels. He knew that Zoe had followed him and he lengthened his stride, but she was running now and she overtook him and held to his arm and got in front of him, stopping him. "Owen, please!"

He took her roughly by the arms and held her, shaking her slightly. "Can't you see it's the only way?" he demanded. "Can't you see I'm the one excuse Weber has to start real trouble?"

"Don't you think he'll find another excuse?" she said. "Do you think a man like Mead Weber can't make his own excuses?"

"He doesn't need to, Zoe," Owen said. "He's won, and he knows it. Osgood will back down. Levering and Granger are already whipped. They don't know it yet, but they are. There won't be any shooting with them."

"Then there will with me," she said.

"You can't stand off a gun crew alone, Zoe," he said. "You know you can't, and if the time ever comes, you won't try."

"Then don't make me stand alone, Owen," she said.

The old agony of another time, another woman, was like a too loud echo in his ears. "I couldn't go through it again, Zoe," he said. "Can't you understand?"

"I can only understand that you're running," she said. "I can only understand that I'm asking you to stand and fight and I'm offering to stand with you. Please, Owen, don't make me get down on my knees and beg."

"You don't see it at all, Zoe," he said. "You don't see it because you don't know what it is to fight and kill and smell the stink of blood and death———"

"I'm willing to risk it with you, Owen. I'm willing, just as she was———"

"You think it's just you and me?" he said. "You think we're the only ones in the world?" He was still gripping her arms and he turned her roughly. "Look at those kids there," he said. "Think about Levering and Granger. They got wives, haven't they? Did you ever see a woman who had been shot in the back of the head with a forty-four? Well, I have. A woman with eyes and lips, just as real as

119

yours, and one minute they're smiling at you and the next minute there's just a hole full of blood where that smile was. . . ." He saw the stark whiteness in her face and knew he had been shouting; he saw the twisted pain on her lips and knew he had been digging his fingers into the flesh of her arm. He fought for control of his emotions. "Please, Zoe," he said, "can't you see what you're asking?"

She came into his arms and he held her, then, not daring to look at her, he said, "Go ahead and sell out, Zoe, and maybe someday, someplace——"

"You and I?"

"I'll hope for it, Zoe."

He saw the tears in her eyes and he knew that she, too, had made her decision. "There won't be any someday, Owen. Not for you and me. You're not free. You never will be."

"It's the price I'll pay for knowing you're alive, then," he said. "It's cheap."

She turned and ran back toward the bank and he heard her sob, a short, stabbing sound of pain.

She ran into the bank and they were all standing there, shaking hands, and she knew the deal had been made and she knew just as surely that it meant nothing. In her own loss and failure the weakness of Harold Osgood had never been clearer to her, and she saw him for what he was, a small, ineffective man, afraid of his own shadow. He'd back down, just as he had admitted to her he had backed down from Mead Weber before.

She ran up the stairs to the apartment, wanting to be alone. Mattie was there, waiting for her. Zoe threw herself into Mattie's arms and Mattie held her, as she would have held a little girl. "I know, darling," Mattie said. "I know. It's going to be all right. My Harold will see it's all right."

Zoe pushed herself away. She wanted to tell Mattie it wouldn't be all right—tell her she was wrong to believe in a man, tell her how deep and real the hurt of knowing you had misjudged a man could be. She didn't want Mattie ever to know the same hurt she was feeling. . . .

She started to say it, and then she couldn't. There was a smile of deep pride in Mattie's eyes. She was so sure. . . . And in this moment the big, plain woman was no longer ugly. She was as beautiful as Harold had always supposed her to be.

THE OTHERS had left the bank, and now Harold and Mead were alone. The sense of power that gripped Mead was dizzying in its intensity. In one magnificent moment any stigma of his past, real or imagined, was gone, just as sure as Casco, his constant reminder of that past, was gone. He owned it all, now, the town, the valley. And Zoe? It had been a passing fancy, he told himself. He could have any woman he wanted. He had stood up in front of them all and he had backed Owen Delaney down, and the fact that he had destroyed the last trace of any inadequacy he had ever felt. Casco had been unable to do it, but he, Mead, alone had succeeded where Casco had failed. He looked at Harold and felt a near affection for the little man. "We did it, Harold," Mead said.

"Yes," Harold said.

Mead had gone to the window and through the glass he could see the band of cattle, moving down the slope. "That's the first of 'em, Harold," he said. "Two or three days from now I'll have the whole herd in here. A thousand head. I'll push 'em across the river and we'll see what Levering and Granger can do about it."

"After we're through fencing," Harold said.

Mead laughed. "Sure," he said. "That was smart of you, Harold. It made up their minds quick."

The banker was still standing behind his desk. His shoulders were back, his chin up. "I meant it, Mead," he said.

Mead paused, not sure, then the grin came back. "Sure, Harold," he said. "Sure you did."

"You're going to live up to every word of your bargain, Mead," Harold said. "If you don't, I'll foreclose everything you have. I'll start with Patterson's place and I'll turn it back over to Jake."

"Harold," Mead said, "do you know who you're talking to?"

"Yes," Harold said. "I'm talking to a man who is going to keep his word."

Still Mead couldn't believe it. He started walking toward the desk, a puzzled frown in his eyes. "Harold," he said, "are you sick?"

"I never felt better," Harold said.

There was no longer any doubt in Mead's mind. The little man was serious. The grin came back into Mead's eyes. "You better start thinking straight, Harold," he said.

"I am," Harold said.

Mead reached across the desk. Harold made no move to get out of the way. Mead gripped the lapels of Harold's coat and he jerked Harold against the desk. "Start saying it again, Harold," Mead said. "Right from the beginning, slow and easy. And think about it."

There was a small quiver in Harold's voice and his face was a white death mask. Mead felt the banker's knees sag, and then Harold said, "You're through shoving me around, Mead, so don't try."

"Why you dirty——" The back of Mead's hand caught Harold across the mouth, splitting his lip. Harold's grip on the desk was all that kept him from falling.

He looked at Mead Weber and he smiled. "Go ahead, Mead," he said. "What will you accomplish?"

"I'll kill you," Mead said.

"I've thought of that," Harold said. "I made all the necessary papers last night. Levering and Granger would still get the money and you'd still get a foreclosure on everything you have."

Mead released his grip on Harold's coat. He brushed the back of his hand across his eyes, trying to clear his vision. "All right, Harold," he said. "It's a joke. Now let's sit down and talk this out."

"That's all there is to it," Harold said.

With a sharp curse Mead threw himself across the desk. His fist caught Harold in the mouth. Harold's grip on the desk broke, and he fell to the floor. As he fell, Mead came around the desk. Mead stood there, his feet spread, his fists doubled. "Now, damn you!" he shouted. "Are you going to listen to me?"

There was blood in Harold's mouth, but he had never said the word so distinctly. "No."

Harold saw the maniacal fury in Mead's eyes. He was afraid, deep down and sickeningly so, and yet at the same time there was a strength in him, as he kept remembering Zoe's father looking at him, saying, *"You're bigger than most men, if you'll just believe it."* It was so, and now Harold knew it was so. He thought of Mattie and how it would be to live without her, and he knew nothing could hurt him more than that. . . . Mead Weber's foot landed solidly in Harold's ribs. He felt himself picked up bodily, knew he was slammed against the wall. His mouth was full of blood and his eyes were swimming with it. He heard a strange, ridiculous sound and realized it was his own laughter, his

122

own voice. "No, Mead," he was saying. "No." He felt his eyes bulge under the pressure of Mead's hands on his throat, but there was no real pain. He didn't fight back. That would have been senseless. And he didn't know how.

The first crash of furniture echoed up the stairway and slammed against the apartment door. Mattie Osgood stood frozen, then she snatched open the drawer of a cabinet and her hand closed on a pistol that was there. She ran down the stairs, the pistol clutched in her hand, and behind her Zoe was following, calling her name. . . .

Next door at the saloon Owen Delaney laid his last dollar on the bar. It was enough for six drinks, with a dime left. He meant to have them all. He looked around the room. It was full of Wyoming men, all laughing, having a good time. He wished one of them would start a fight. He was aware of the quick stillness and he turned and he saw Zoe there in the doorway. "Owen!" she said. "Help!"

The railed enclosure around Osgood's desk had been smashed down. Two chairs had been broken and the desk itself had been knocked askew. Mattie stood there with the pistol in her hand, unable to use it for fear of hitting Harold. She could only call his name, over and over, and above her sobbing cry the panting breath of Mead Weber was the only sound in the room.

Weber was staggering from exhaustion. He wasn't hitting Harold any more. He was dragging him around, like a dog drags a rag. He had lost all sense of time and reason. He didn't see Owen Delaney's hurtling body. He felt himself slammed against the wall, and then he was being jerked around and a fist was driving him backward. He kept backing up, and the fist kept smashing him back, faster and faster. There was a crash of glass and Mead Weber knew he had been knocked through the bank window, and now he saw Owen standing over him, just the way he had seen Owen stand over Casco. . . .

"Get a gun, Weber," Delaney said, "because I'm going to kill you, as sure as I'm standing here."

Delaney was gone, and Mead Weber staggered to his feet. There was a crowd of people around, all staring at him, Levering and Granger and Patterson and a dozen more he didn't know. His clothes were ruined, his face bloody, his hair in his eyes, and he was standing there in the street of the town he considered his own and everyone was staring at him. He dragged air into his lungs with a torturing pain and gradually his senses cleared, and now he wanted to reach out and smash something—anything....

Mead shook his head, and his thinking became clear, and, had Casco been here, Casco would have been finally proud of his baby brother.... Move those cattle down. Now. Take over the grass and hold it. Owen Delaney is the only one in your way. Get rid of him.... He started down the street toward Jim Torrance's office and met the deputy halfway.

"Mead, what the devil?"

"Delaney," Mead said. "He's gone crazy. He's threatened to kill me on sight. Jim, you got to lock him up!"

Time, Mead thought as he watched Jim Torrance in his hobbling run toward the bank. *Just give me a little time.* ... He found his horse and swung into the saddle and headed out of town and up the slope. The cattle were clearly visible, no more than a half mile from town. *The cows first,* he thought, *then Delaney.*

He started thinking of the crew of men who worked for him. Kline, maybe, he decided. Kline had liked Casco and would welcome a chance to avenge Casco's death. There was that short Texan with the mark of trouble about him, and the two brothers who had drifted in one night and had welcomed the chance to keep away from well-traveled roads.... Pay them enough and they'd do it, Mead knew. Every man had his price.

Mead Weber gave his orders to move the cattle down into the town and across the river onto the Patterson grass. He sought out Kline, then, and the short Texan and the two brothers. Mead was a practical man. He knew he couldn't stand up to Owen alone with a gun. But he knew, too, that no one man could stand up to five guns and live.

THERE WAS no doctor in Ten Mile and it was up to Mattie and Zoe to do the best they could for Harold. The little man lay there behind the desk, his face battered beyond recognition. One arm was broken, and it twisted crazily, and the banker's breathing was a series of shallow gasps of pain. There were bright moments of consciousness, and at one time he looked at Zoe and his eyes smiled. "Patterson," he said. "He can have his place back. Posts and wire ... Big crew ..."

"Harold, please," Mattie said.

"I love you," Harold said.

"I love you, too, Harold," Mattie whispered.

Owen looked down at the broken body of the little man, knowing the stand he had made, knowing even better the fear that had been in Harold, remembering the shell of a man who had sat in Zoe's living room, a wet cloth on his head, a man sick beyond belief from the mere witnessing of violence. And now he had stood up to a man twice his size and taken everything that man could give him and still he wasn't whipped and Owen knew he never would be. . . . What had changed him? What could happen to a man to change him this much? He looked at Zoe, standing next to him. "Why?" he murmured. "In heaven's name, why?"

It was Mattie Osgood who answered. She stood up and she faced Owen squarely, and he saw open accusation in her eyes. "Because he's a man," she said. "Because he knew what he had to do." The eyes were suddenly soft. "Because we love each other, Owen," she said. "That's why."

Jim Torrance said, "You better come down to the office, Owen."

He welcomed the chance to talk to Jim Torrance, for Torrance was old and wise and he understood how it could be with a man. "You're right or you're wrong, I guess," Jim Torrance said. "There's no degrees to it."

"I'll have to kill him, Jim," Owen said. "You know it."

"As sheriff, I'll have to stop you from it," Jim Torrance said.

Levering and Granger came in, their faces drawn with worry. "Jim, we got to stop this," Levering said. "Mead's down at the saloon. He claims Delaney is gunning for him."

"Did you see Harold Osgood?" Jim Torrance asked.

"Yes, I know," Levering said. "But a killing, Jim . . . You're the only law we've got. You've got to stop it."

There was a tired anger in the eyes of Jim Torrance. He reached up and unpinned his badge and tossed it on the desk. "You be the law, Levering," he said. "I'm tired of it."

Down at the saloon the hurdy-gurdy was playing, its sound coming all the way to the sheriff's office, and now there was another sound, a drumming and a bellowing roar. It grew and the earth shook with it and the herd of cattle, pushed by the yelling cowboys, broke in a half stampede at the edge of town.

They swarmed down the narrow street, horns clashing, hocks clicking, and behind them the cowboys whooped and swung ropes and cursed and the dust swelled against the front of the abandoned buildings in choking eddies. . . .

"There's your law, boys," Jim Torrance said. "You made it, now figure out how to live with it. You asked for it by giving in to Mead Weber. You can't compromise with a man like Mead Weber by letting him take a piece of land. He'll take another and another, and finally it isn't enough to own everything. Finally he has to be the law, too." He shook his head. "He's never had his sign around my neck, boys. He didn't have it around Harold's." To Owen he said, "You got nothing to hold you, Delaney. Go on and leave. Levering and Granger won't stop you." He put on his hat and walked out, leaving the three of them alone.

"What will we do, Delaney?" Levering asked.

"I got no right to give advice," Owen said. "I lost that right. All I know is, it wasn't just a piece of land I fought for up in Wyoming. It's not just a piece of land Zoe's fighting for here."

He stood up, and while they watched him he drew his gun, ejected the shells, and reloaded. He spun the cylinder once, then shoved the gun in his holster. "It's private, boys," he said. "Don't blame yourselves for it."

He walked down the street, an old, familiar alertness in him, and he could see the river ford and now the cattle were in the stream, being hazed across. Down by the bank he saw Jim Torrance lounging against a post, looking off into nowhere. Jim had washed his hands of Ten Mile. . . .

There was a small catch of fear in Owen now and he walked along. There was no sense of hatred or revenge, but only of duty, a strong sense of knowing that some men would not stop running over the rights of others until they were dead. And some men had to do the killing. A man had to stand up for his rights if he were to be free, and a man had to be free to accept a woman's love. He thought of Mattie Osgood and the beauty he had seen in her eyes when she said, "Because we love each other, Owen. . . ."

He paused briefly at the door of the saloon. There was perspiration running down his back, a trembling fear inside him, there for an instant, as it always was, and then it was gone. He paused, his hand on the door, the footsteps behind him freezing his motion. From the tail of his eye he saw Levering and Granger. They both had rifles. "We're with you, Delaney," Frank Levering said. "Mead won't face you alone. His kind never do."

They entered together, Owen Delaney, Frank Levering, and Scott Granger, and the opening of the door seemed to pick up the noise of the place and push it against the back wall and hold it there. There were more than a dozen men in the saloon, but most of them were outsiders, wanting nothing of local trouble. Mead Weber stood at the bar. Kline was there with him, his hollow jaw sagging, and there were two men who looked alike and a short, dark man who wore a tied-down holster and a smile. "I told you, Weber," Owen Delaney said. "You've got a gun on now. You'll have to use it."

There was a doubt in Mead Weber's eyes as he saw Levering and Granger with the rifles. It was the last thing he had expected, and there was something frightening and final about it. He tried one last bluff. "I thought I told you to get rid of that gun slinger," he said to Levering.

"You told us a lot of things, Mead," Levering said.

"I'm staying, Weber," Delaney said. "Decide what you want to do about it."

The short, dark man with the smile was the only gunman in the bunch. He made his move identical with Mead, and Owen had to make a choice. In that thousandth part of a second Owen Delaney knew he was not a killer. His fight was with Mead and with no one else. He let the gunman have his chance at him. He picked Mead.

The roar of his own gun was deceiving, slamming through the room, and there was no way to tell how many shots had been fired. He knew only that through the smoke he could see Mead clutching the bar with one hand, and he saw the smoking gun in Mead's hand, so he knew Mead had fired a shot. The short, smiling gunman was on the floor, crawling on his hands and knees, as if searching for something, and then Owen saw old Jim Torrance, standing in the doorway, a smoking gun in his hand. . . . Kline and the others were ready, but Levering's soft voice said, "Don't try it, boys. He ain't worth it."

Levering and Granger hadn't fired a shot.

A crazy, half-sick relief swept over Owen. He turned to Jim Torrance and said, "I thought you retired, you old coot."

"Force of habit, I guess," Torrance said.

Owen slid his gun down the bar toward the deputy. "Put that tin back on your vest where it belongs," he said. "And

127

keep that gun of mine for a souvenir. I won't be needing it."

He went outside, not wanting anyone to know the dizziness that was in him, knowing that Jim Torrance knew. He saw Zoe running down the street toward him, calling his name. He held out his arms and she ran into them and he held her a long time. Across her shoulder he saw young Bud Patterson, and Bud's eyes were round and staring. . . . "Will you do me a favor, Bud?" Owen asked.

"I guess so, Owen," Bud Patterson said.

"Ride over to the Middleton place and see me sometime," he said. "I want to talk to you. About a lot of things."

"Sure, Owen. If you say so," Bud said.

A lot of things. . . . Of how a man couldn't run away from himself and of how love could die and still be born and of how a man like Harold Osgood could win a war without firing a shot. . . .

He felt Zoe's lips against his cheek, heard her whisper, "What now, Owen?"

"Let's go home, Zoe," he said.